Ricardo L. Nirenberg

CRY UNCLE

The Latino Press
1998

The Latino Press
First Edition, 1998
Copyright (c) 1998 by Ricardo L. Nirenberg
All rights reserved

Published by The Latino Press
Latin American Writers Institute
Eugenio María de Hostos Community College/CUNY
500 Grand Concourse, Bronx, NY 10451
Tel: (718) 518-4195. Fax: (718) 518-4240

The Latino Press is devoted to publishing the work of Latino writers living in the United States.

Library of Congress Cataloguing-in-Publication Data
Ricardo L. Nirenberg
Cry Uncle, 1st ed. / p. cm.
ISBN: 1-884912-09-5
1. Title. 2. Argentine Fiction-U.S. 3. Argentine Fiction-20th century.
4. Argentine Literature. 5. Latin American Literature

Cover design: Nancy Hofstadter
Painting: Guercino, *Amnon and Tamar*, National Gallery, Washington. D.C.
        (Distorted)
Layout: Giselle Reiter
Printed in the United States of America

to Isabel, my wife

"However hopeless it may seem, we have no other choice: we must go back to the beginning; it must all be done over; everything that is must be destroyed."
William Carlos Williams

"A mentsh zol leben shoin nor fun neigerikeit vegen."
("A man should go on living, if only out of curiosity.")
Yiddish proverb

1

First impressions stick, so Max will rather be introduced neither scratching his scalp or picking his nose facing a computer monitor, nor as in the photograph he envisions for the dust jacket of his first book (alert, glowing eyes, pleasantly ironic smile, hand under his chin). Neither too low nor too high, but hovering in between as he is now: unshaved, a bit dishevelled, sitting at the café-bar Chateaubriand before a Selzer bottle, a bottle of vermouth, and a plate with stale cheese.

Max peers at the couple sitting nearby, admires the waiter's nonchalant hauteur, watches the people walking up and down the street. The ineffable smell of Buenos Aires, at once acid and sweet! When a few years ago he took to writing poems, it was because he missed the smell and wanted to recall it. He composed between classes, after teaching Calculus and before Linear Algebra, but turning smells into words turned out to be harder than he expected, so after many flops, many sonnets *manqués*, today he is quite content with this: a smell at once acid and sweet. Here in Buenos Aires the air is humid, not subtle; brown waters converge from the jungles of Chaco and the Matto Grosso: you turn a street, and suddenly, in some secluded spot, the smell lurks, like a moist beast or a voluptuous mugger. Here, then, is Max Krocus, in the city where he was born half a century ago, where he sniffed and grew up, and where he has not been able to return for twenty years.

Max became a common criminal, wanted by the Argentine police, as part of the atrocious mess his father amassed during his lifetime and left after his passing. One way of putting it is that Onofrio Krocus was born fraudulently bankrupt; another, that he had the anti-Midas touch. By dint of eloquence alone, Don Onofrio had managed to recruit two partners to start a factory of vitreous enamels. One of them, Himmelblau, was acquainted with a colonel high up at City Hall who controlled the market for the city's blue and white street signs. But Max's father had already gone through a couple of stormy bankruptcies and sundry brushes with the law: to have any property under his name would have been risky. Max had just reached twenty-one, was legally of age; Don Onofrio had him sign a full power of attorney, and Max became forthwith the third, blind, partner in the firm, even though he only knew that white enamel is made with titanium or zirconium, whereas blue takes cobalt. The venture, at any rate, didn't prosper; not that street names are not changed often enough in Argentina, a country fabulously rich in military heroes, but Himmelblau's colonel was gone after the next military coup, and City Hall proved to be unreasonably stubborn in insisting that the enameled plaques should be free of cracks.

The factory folded after two years, leaving behind a

record of criminal liabilities and legal time bombs. Employer's contributions to the National Workers' Retirement Fund had never been made; a carboy of sulfuric acid had been labeled hydrogen peroxide and a worker had been badly burned; signatures had been forged, insufficient bribes had been paid. Don Onofrio Krocus was dead. So were Messrs. Weisskopf and Himmelblau, the other partners. Max was the sole person responsible and the only one alive liable for the imbroglio, and it is thanks to the Statute of Limitations — Time the universal healer, Time its own balm — that after twenty years he can be here, in Buenos Aires, nibbling tidbits at the café-bar Chateaubriand.

Having arrived yesterday by plane from New York, now Max wants to talk, touch, hug. His heart is full of being back, walking those streets where the soul seems to dissolve at dusk. He'd like to laugh, dance, cry; he'd like to amorously conspire, like the couple sitting nearby. Under and beyond that, larval, unacknowledged, the wish to do something exciting and forbidden. He wants to commit a *real* crime, his own burning by acid.

Eight P.M. Such balmy, overcharged and perfumed evenings are unknown in the North. Max calls, "Waiter, more olives!" He goes for shrivelled olives, mushy cheese cubes, strips of tripe and stale miniature breadsticks. Downtown, or at a ritzy Barrio Norte café, those would be fresh, firm, crisp, and perhaps mussels and tiny cheese croquettes would be thrown in; but Max prefers low-class joints and mushy, shrivelled things.

Lord Almighty. A woman's crossing the street *andante molto espressivo*, with the swing and the lilt that is the most fascinating feature of the local idiom. Who can resist that gait, the short skirt, the steep heels? He couldn't, no, he never

could, ever since that time when he was twelve and —
Pah! This is no time for reminiscing. "Waiter! How
much? Here, five thousand. Don't take anything away; I'll
be back."

Quick, out of here, forget the enigma of his ever-sticky
past, run across the street, catch up with her, ask, breathless-
ly, "Señorita, wouldn't you like to be my psychopomp?"
Makeup does a poor job of hiding the ravines on her
suety face. No hour-glass waist hers. Fortyish. Max repeats
his question slowly, quiveringly.

"What do you take me for?" she shrugs a contemptuous shoulder, knits her brow, puckers and twists her lips,
flutters her eyelashes.

"Señorita, don't be offended, please! I meant how
would you like to be the conductress of my soul through my
last journey, up, up and away, all the way up to seventh
heaven; how would you like to be my Challenger, my
Columbia, my Beatrice."

Not just citrus flowers and patchouli, but soups and
sauces too, sunny sea-shore days and summer nights: she
exhales a rich, deep, maternal perfume...

"You think you're smart, uh?" A few more steps,
soul-stabbing, a few more voluptuous swells under her
sweater; then, curtly, "Get lost." She adds under her breath,
"Dirty old man."

Max stops. He watches her walk away. The rounded,
full-orbed apparition crosses the street and disappears on the
crowded pavement. He turns around and walks back to the
Chateaubriand. "Waiter, more olives!"

Old, from her point of view, he may be, for age is rel-
ative. But dirty? Why? Even though he's fully fifty, why
can't he rub his nose against those round, soft shoulders,

10

then slowly, slyly, sink into the enchanted boscage of her armpits? What's dirty about a genuine wish to sniff? Unless she's being self-conscious: hasn't washed, ten layers of stale deodorant stowed under her arms. Oh well, anyway, he didn't have much hope of pulling it off. Had he succeeded, he would have brought her over to the Chateaubriand, offered her some Cinzano, cheese and olives. Talked about hyperinflation and TV soaps: what the hell does he know about soaps? Then, with luck, off they'd go, arm in arm — where to? Ha, think about it. To Mother's apartment?

Two weeks ago, at a Manhattan divorce court, Jennifer said, "Now you're free, Max, free to heed your true calling: wallowing in shit, crawling in the mud." How eloquent Jennifer became when she spoke of his baseness! "You pine-scented puritan, what do you know about life," Max replied. "Only this: what you need is not a wife; you should go back to your mother." She was right. But that shit word on her habitually clean lips hurt his feelings. Crawling in the mud... can a tree make beautiful flowers unless it is rooted in mud? Mud, for him, is Buenos Aires. But Father was even worse: he was a professional mud crawler. Max is just an amateur.

Max's first divorce, from Sharon, can be easily explained: divorces are major surgery, but routine. More common than hysterectomies and operations of the prostate, among individuals of a certain age. Sharon was Polish-American, had exquisite sensitivity for what she called "unfairness" and "rudeness" in other people, was making lots of money as an actuary, and turning more and more toward a radical feminism based on irrefutable statistics. She kept a tally of her orgasms and assigned him to the lowest quartile when he wouldn't perform. Like the two branches of an hyperbola, they started with nothing in common and drifted apart silently.

Jennifer, his second wife, was different: a physician from Maine, softer, ingratiatingly wise, her interests were similar to Max's; they played music together, she told him about her hospital cases, she knew some Spanish and listened to his sonnets: the marriage ought to have been a success. What drove her to distraction was his hopeless, relentless search — for what? Obviously, in fifty years, Max has had ample opportunity to inquire into what is it that he really wants. The ideal bosom? A woman as quiveringly caressing as the opening theme of Borodin's string quartet in D? The female immense, dead for millenia, still unborn, the woman to assuage and quench all others? No, he has almost reached the conclusion that mud is what he wants. Only in brown chaos such as is found in Buenos Aires, can Max find erotic excitement and a sense to life. Jennifer was too clean. She shaved her underarms.

The Sunday after the writ of divorce, when he called Mother on the phone (most letters from the U.S. are pilfered by Argentine postal workers), she said, "No, I don't want you to come, you have more important things to take care of, your courses to teach, your own life to patch together; no, don't come for me." Then, with a dying voice, she added, "Max, you can't imagine what I'm going through. It's hell."

Between Max and his mother there's a spiritual wire that wasn't severed with the umbilical cord, a link that defies all physical laws and has survived a twenty-year exile. Max doesn't think his mother is about to die, regardless of how much she whines. She goes out but rarely now, hardly walks, and often says, "I can bear it no longer." She suffers,

12

there's no doubt that she does: arrhythmia, arthritis, arthrosis, asthma, just for starters. At night, the sound of her breathing is not pleasant — a hiss, then the sucking in of air in a whoop and three short grunts, reminding Max of the annual draining of his boiler's expansion tank, before the cold weather starts in Upstate New York. When she stops gasping for air and falls asleep, she moans, struggling, it seems, not so much with her muscular, organic and articular pains as with regrets, anger and the might-have-beens that crowd her dreams. Onofrio's multiple love affairs, his double life (to her only posthumously revealed), keep him painfully alive in Mother's memory, resulting in a third and more enduring life, protected by her hatred. Bits of phrases and gestures, a shrug, a smile thirty years old, suddenly recalled, are cast in a perfidious, lacerating light. Onofrio's death, twenty years ago, was his last, his most unforgivable infidelity.

When Mrs. Krocus said with a dying voice, "Max, I'm suffering like hell," he packed his stuff and came in the next plane. He was alone, Jennifer had left him, classes were over, and the Statute of Limitations, setting him free at last from the unjust rigors of the law, allowed him to put an end to his exile. Mother suffers, but in spite of all, Max knows that she'll survive him. Of this he is absolutely certain. Her complaints remind him of the ecologists': the Earth is dying because of our depredations. Too much carbon dioxide and all that. Don't get him wrong: he doesn't doubt for a moment that the point is urgent and well taken. But we all know, don't we, that we'll die first, be buried and rotted to the bone, and our planet will keep going, rolling, hanging there, the flea-bitten bitch, the good ole minuscule speck — a little less ozone perhaps, a little more waste and global warmth, but we won't be denied a bit of ground in which to rot.

Max is not worried about his mother dying: she seems to him more lasting than the earth. His own death worries him more. Death, he suspects, is waiting for him in Buenos Aires. By what privilege was he, Max, able to escape the South American quagmire and build a new life in the Anglo-Saxon North, far from the brown chaos of home? A lonely, austere life, to be sure, beset by pragmatism and divorce; and not another home, but just a tent pitched on the desert of American academe; yet, by any objective criteria, it was a privilege to escape. Exile from Argentina was a blessing. Meanwhile, back home, the killings, the tortures, the underdevelopment, the misery, the hopelessness. Yes, thank God, exile was a privilege: undeserved, unjustified. And now, obscurely, he's got to pay for it. Somewhere in this acid-and-sweet-smelling city of Buenos Aires where he was born, lurking in some humid street corner or in some dark entrance hall, hiding in some hairy armpit, death, or perhaps happiness, which amounts to the same thing, must be ready to jump him, to bite him in the neck and suck him in.

2

Two kinds of trees contribute to the characteristic background smell of Buenos Aires: the bark and the spiked balls of the plane trees distill a subtle, fragrant acid, main ingredient in the smell of other cities too, like Rome or Paris; here, though, the *paraísos* or bead trees add their sweetly scented, tiny, violet flowers. Occasionally, from its strategic trellis behind a wall, a wisteria takes over and, throwing all modesty to the winds, the air drags us into drunken ecstasies. After he leaves the Chateaubriand and walks back toward his mother's apartment along the tree-lined streets, Max reflects: what sense would be left in those smells if Mother should die? What sense in those life-long-familiar sounds — street vendors, knife sharpeners, car horns, rubber rolling on the humid pavement? All soul-making sense impressions would, with her demise, become senseless. He realizes how deeply, how desperately he loves her. Suddenly, unexpectedly, the smell-borne miracle happens: Max recovers his childhood.

He is twelve, and the fruits of the *paraísos* are falling, getting crushed under the shoes of the passersby, covering the sidewalks with a putrescent mush. The street stinks comically, like a sweaty giantess in heat; which might explain why grown-up men, gentlemen in business suits, workers in undershirts, whenever they inadvertently slip, agitate their arms, recover the vertical, they curse, "*¡La gran puta!*" and without a smile go on their way. "The great whore": who can she be if not the mother of the whole thing, trees, sidewalks and buildings, the giantess in whose apertures we cohabit, the whore who is to blame, who is always the object of their curses? At dawn a flock of black-robed nuns with wicker baskets come out of the nearby convent to gather the bare pits; once back in their cells, they piously perforate them to thread rosaries.

Books held by a leather strap flung over his shoulder, young Max returns home from school by halts and stations. First stop the kiosk. On the tin sign for soap nailed above the window, the majestic form of a woman emerges out of a tub filled with foam, her well-turned leg pointing heavenward. He asks for the same brand of cigarettes Father smokes: strong black tobacco. On the inside wall, a decal for another brand of soap: the empress Popea's beauty secret was the milkbath. As soon as he gets home, he'll hide the cigarettes under his collection of soccer cards, because if Father finds them, he'll break Max's face, or his butt, which amounts to the same thing. What a lack of respect for one's elders, a cigarette in the hand of a twelve-year old! Yet, to keep his self - respect, a boy simply *has* to smoke.

Tonight he'll slip out of bed and to the terrace, where, under Canopus or whatever stars happen to be on duty, and while Father, Mother and Gloria innocently sleep, he'll light

16

up. Without forgetting to tap one end of the cigarette against a thumbnail first, as Father always does, although Max doesn't know why. Then he will pretend to be in some busy thoroughfare where he casually asks of a passerby: "Sir, could you give me a light, please?," and only then will he light his cigarette. He'll practice letting it hang nonchalantly from his lip, like the big boys standing at the street corner, over at Rivadavia, one foot against the wall, watching the broads go by; or like the tough guys in the movies, while firing a machine gun. He'll hold it close to his mouth, contorted in a smirk, and pretend he's discussing business or politics. Then, shifting the cigarette back to the base of his fingers, extending an arm forward in the perfect stillness of the night, he'll move a queen across an imaginary chessboard. Holding his hands up to eye level, reading the paper, gravely nodding his head (the news is weighty), he'll turn the page while scouring teeth and gums with his tongue (the cheese and chips that came with the apéritif are sticky), then take another puff. Holding the cigarette in one corner of his mouth with thumb and index finger, as if about to yank it off, he'll sputter through the other corner: "Now you listen, buddy..."

Suddenly switching to a quieter, more thoughtful mood, he'll flick off the ash and while he puffs he'll imagine that the bright end is another, more personal star. He'll imagine he is under a new sky, in a different country, where people speak English and smoke Chesterfields and Lucky Strikes, a land as perfect and glossy as U.S. cars, flying fortresses, record album covers and magazine ads: ah, some day he will take a bus all the way to the new international airport at Ezeiza and fly north! But right now the smoke rings are his proudest achievement: up they go, one after the other, like big O's vanishing in the dark. The night seems too ample to make sense by itself, without these rings, these halos, centered around him.

The door to the maid's room will be enveloped in darkness. Behind the door, Pancracia will be asleep. Or perhaps not: how could he know. Pancracia has been in the house forever. Perhaps she will be lying on her musty mattress, staring at the ceiling, smoking. Before going back to bed, before putting out the cigarette under the terrace tap and hurling the butt over the wall on to the neighbor's tiled roof, he'll inhale deeply, like Father, eyes closed, and keep the smoke inside him for as long as he can; then he'll release it through his nostrils down in two swift jets, dragon-like. The difference is, Father's mustache deflects the smoke. Ah, if only he had a bushy, tobacco-stained mustache! But no matter how hard he wishes for it (Max has read that you always get what you wish for, if you wish hard enough), no matter how hard he rubs, he can't find there even a shadow of down.

*

Second stop: one foot on the worn threshold and half the body inside, Max peeks. In the long, somber hallway the air is cool, and it brings, superimposed like harmonics in an organ tube, smells from behind twelve doors. He's peeking at a *conventillo*: twelve dingy apartments opening to a corridor. About half way inside, an enormous woman with colossal legs, blubber-armed, is scrubbing the floor. As she bends down to the bucket to wring the rag, her skirt is pulled up enough to let Max catch a glimpse of the gates to a titanic universe.

His main interest is in the sixth door, no different from

18

the others except that men flock to it like flies to a rotting corpse. Mechanics in their greasy overalls, the old baker in his floury jumper, clerks in three-piece suits: Max has kept watch and seen the aproned butcher go in, blood on blue, and the butcher's son, who is only fifteen but has quit school long ago; even the cripple who lives next door, his wheel-chair pushed by two nephews. And twice has Max watched the buxom whore come down the corridor, carrying herself like some antediluvian queen, and twice she crossed the threshold without a single glance at him. Exactly as if she had seen a mouse — but no, in that case she would have real-ly noticed. Ah, if Max only had a mustache!

His heart beats faster at the thought that for a third time that door may open, and out may come the whore, regally swaggering toward the street, right by him. What supernatural gift, what secret, or what gleaming sun inside does she hide that makes her walk so proud, so damn proud she doesn't deign to cast an eye on you, he wonders. But at that moment a whiff of boiling cabbage changes the direction of his thoughts; boiling cabbage and chlorine bleach rising out of the bucket of the giantess; also musty fleece and tufts and crushed bedbugs, a combination which he has dubbed "stink of mattress," because it was first smelled on Pancracia's mattress. And now, deeply inhaling the full draft of the corridor: isn't that a whiff of the whore's musky per-fume? The giantess drops her rag and eyes him up and down.

"What you doing here? What you looking at?" she says with a voice like the grating of tectonic plates.

Shaken up from his sniffing revery, Max recognizes the enormous woman: she's the whore's mother. "Why," he says defiantly, "this is a public place, isn't it?"

19

"Son of a whore," says the woman, and swab in hand, moves toward him. He doesn't wait, but slings the books over his shoulder and runs until he turns the corner. Ah, just let him grow up, just let the time come when he can shave (Max mutters in between breaths): then nobody will dare treat him like that; he will be free to come and go, smoking to his heart's content; free to go into that sixth apartment. And behind that door he'll find the clue to all the enigmas. What makes the whore walk so proudly. What makes Mother look the other way even more proudly (but with a different kind of pride: cold, contemptuous, unyielding) every time they pass her in the street. Yet once, when he was walking with Father and Mother, they came upon the whore, and there was a smile, hard to describe, on her heavily rouged lips. And why is that place, with its twelve doors and hundred smells, called a *conventillo*? Doesn't the word mean a small convent? Max is unable to imagine any connection between the imposing Gothic edifice where the nuns live, and the breezy hallway where the whore's mother swabs the floor. Language too has its mysteries.

*

The spiralled pole has stopped turning long ago, the milky globe envelops only a powdered host of dead insects, but the miniature tin basin still sways under the autumn breeze, and shines under the autumn sun. The barber is taking a fresh steaming towel out of the stove, while the customer lies prone, big red nose protruding like a giant strawberry on a frosted cake from the towel wrapped around his face. There's always a cigar balanced on the barber's wet underlip, a conical cigar. Max always hums Aida's

Triumphal March when he thinks of the barbershop; for that kind of cigar, pungent above all others, goes by the popular name of *toscano*, and one of Father's few records is of Verdi's piece conducted by Toscanini.

So when on a Saturday morning, if Max's hair is getting longish, Father slaps him on the shoulder: "C'mon, buccaneer, let's get shorn!," off they will go to the barber, Max humming the victorious strains of Radames. And once there, whether sitting on the barber chair getting his haircut, or on one of the rush chairs by the window, waiting while Father gets shaved, he listens to the men's banter, wondering at the marvelous depth of their experience. For they seem to remember every detail of every fight ever fought at the Luna Park, from fly- to heavyweight, and they can give you a thousand different reasons why Newell's Old Boys narrowly missed the National Soccer Cup six years ago. But what engages their passions most is their on-going discussion about trucks: the barber, faithful to his ancestral land, heaps praise on the Isotta-Fraschini, while Father raises the Scania-Vabis to the skies, and there never fails to be some other customer eager to put in a word for the Mack, or the Berliet. On occasion, from the barber chair, face fully lathered, Mr. Krocus will lecture to an untutored audience of three or four customers and a few more men who come there only for the talk, about more esoteric subjects.

"You have this particle here, see," he says raising a hand from under the white sheet and pinching with two fingers an evanescent point in space, "well, this same particle is also in Lobos, a hundred kilometers away. And I don't mean a minute later, mind you; I don't mean a second later or even the tiniest fraction of a second later: no, I mean at the same time."

21

"Come off it, Don Onofrio, that's impossible," someone objects.

"Impossible it may well seem," Mr. Krocus replies, "still, that's the way things are." And he gravely adds, "According to quantum mechanics!"

To twelve-year-old Max, this quantum mechanics has obviously to do with some kind of truck, much faster and much more powerful than even the Scania-Vabis; or with some kind of plane, of this he can't be positive. This much is clear: Father, who on Sunday mornings explains to him Infinitesimal Calculus, the experiment of Michelson and Morley and Einstein's Relativity, knows more about all kinds of things, earthly or celestial, than all the other men in the world.

The one with the strawberry nose is now all lathered up; the barber has finished honing his razor on the strap, and after a billowing puff of his *toscano* raises his blade to the customer's throat. Max suddenly realizes that it isn't easy to understand, how a man can trust another so absolutely as to put his neck so nonchalantly under a razor.

Max's last stop is the café. Nose pressed against the window pane, he looks inside. There are few customers: a square, bald man is sitting at a table, reading a newspaper and picking his nose; an old man is quietly and persistently stirring his coffee as if all his past life has been only in preparation for this act; the waiter is leaning against the counter, swatting at the flies with his napkin: behind him towers the espresso machine, a tin and brass fortification. Max knows this waiter: he's the one who said, when once Father took him to the café: "A chip off the old block, eh?" and patted his shoulder. Max likes that expression; he likes the waiter, the way he calls: "*un espress!*," hissing his s's, very much like steam released from the valves and pipes of the espresso machine. One Sunday Father took Max to the salon in the back of the café, to the billiard tables.

"Playing billiards," Father told him, "is more than an art: it is applied mechanics," and he showed Max a few caroms, some unlikely side-strokes and three-cushions. There was a sign on the wall:

SHOOTING MASSÉ IS ABSOLUTELY FORBIDDEN.

Max asked what shooting massé was, so Father gave a practical demonstration. Leaving his lit cigarette on the edge of the table and ranging the three balls on a straight line, Father held the cue vertically, and himself in a Praxitelean stance. For a long, long time (it seemed to Max) he eyed the cue and the cue-ball, for a long time he drove the cue up and down almost imperceptibly, taking aim, chewing on the ends of his mustache, until he hit the ball which went on, to Max's utter amazement, to hit, one after the other, the red and the other white ball. Later, in the street, he asked, "But Dad, doesn't the sign say it's absolutely forbidden to shoot like that, then how come...?"

Father dismissed the question with an airy gesture of the hand, "That sign's intended for the bunglers and scratchers, who might pierce the table with a massé shot, not for a pro like me."

Now Max wonders whether the bald man who's still picking his nose, and the old man who's still stirring his coffee, are bunglers and scratchers who are forbidden by law to shoot massé. He concludes that they are, very probably, since pros like Father have to be extremely rare.

Vergara, a kid who used to play marbles and

exchange soccer cards with Max, crosses the street towards him. He jovially nudges Max in the stomach. "Hey, macho," he says, "hey, macho, get a load of this," and pokes his hand, palm up, under Max's nose: a small photograph, a man showing off a long penis, erect like a Turkish minaret, while a woman lies next to him, dull-eyed, legs spread and waiting. Max stares at the man's penis. It seems even longer than Father's. Max saw an erect adult penis only once, when he opened the bathroom door and Don Onofrio was sitting on the toilet, holding the surprisingly large object in his hand.

As Max returns home, the house is unusually silent. Max finds Mother sitting in the living room, facing the radio set, which is turned off: her face is rigid and her eyes focused on infinity. For a long time he stands next to her, but she doesn't acknowledge his presence with the least sign of life. She's like a statue, an Egyptian sphinx. She seems glued to the chair. Finally Max touches her, pokes a finger in her cheek and turns it around: it's as if he had wound up and switched on a mechanical toy.

"They took him away!" she screams.

"Who?" Max wants to know.

"The police," Mother starts sobbing, "the police came and took your father away!"

That's all Max can elicit; she doesn't know why Father has been taken away. She just sobs. He, however, knows: Father has been arrested for shooting massé. Max sits by the window and reflects: should he tell Mother what he knows? But that rare adventure, going to the café and to the billiard room, is something between the two of them, father and son; Mother, of this Max is quite certain, has never been told. Telling her now would be cowardice on his part — even worse: a betrayal. What does a woman know of billiards,

24

caroms, cues and cue-balls? No, Father and he are in this together, and they will have to bear it together, grin and bear it in silence, like two men. With a sudden pang, Max imagines Father in jail, unshaven, hands grabbing iron bars. Mother and Max will visit him, of course, bring him beer and sandwichs, newspapers and magazines; Father will stick an arm through the bars, tousle up Max's hair and say, "So what's up, buccaneer?"

It won't be that bad, after all. Ah, but what if he is tortured! There's something called the electric prod: who hasn't heard of it? Who doesn't know for a fact that men who run afoul of the government or the police are prodded on their testicles? Max closes his eyes: he couldn't imagine such pain. Maybe Father has, God forbid, said something rash, badmouthed one of the Nation's generals, and been denounced. The waiter, the barber, the bald man in the café who burrows into his nose, who knows... And they also stick that prod up your anus, and turn the electricity on. Vergara, the same kid who half an hour ago was showing him the photo of the man with the long penis, once before showed him another photo of just a bed, no one on it; actually, it was only a bedframe, a metal bedframe of the link-spring type, plugged to an outlet. It's used in the jails, Vergara said, to torture guys and make them squeal; and he should know, since *his* father is a sergeant in the Federal Police. He also nudged Max in the stomach that time and asked: "How'd you like to fuck your sister on this bunk, uh?"

And Max answered with the phrase that was *de rigueur* in such cases: "Since I have neither sister nor lass/let us lie on the grass/and I will fuck your ass." What else could he have answered? Now he feels ashamed, remembering those stupid, perverse little rhymes, while Father at this very

25

moment may be subjected to the most atrocious electrical tortures; worst of all, a hole, a ridiculous, puckered hole seems to hover right before Max's eyes, purporting to be Vergara's anus: he can even smell it, which turns his stomach. To dispel the unpleasantness, he picks up from the coffee table an issue of the Selections from the Reader's Digest and leafs through it. The glossy paper, the pictures of so many smiling faces, those fluted, translucent jewels (but can they possibly be edible?) which go by the intriguingly hyphenated and capitalized name of Jell-O; those things soothe him. Suddenly, at the turn of a page, a lady in a golden sequined gown: with one hand she pulls back her long, lustrous hair, while the other rests on, or rather scarcely contains, the exuberant convexity of her hip. The gown is slit, leaving her thighs open to scrutiny, and in tacit complicity she winks an eye: "I love men who shave with Mennen!" Another incarnation of Popea, so fond of foam. Max rubs his hopelessly smooth cheeks: ah, life will be so much easier when he can shave, when he can start using Mennen! He looks through the window: maybe he'll catch a glimpse of the whore walking up the street, on such improbable heels, in such unlikely equilibrium, yet always avoiding the mush on which men slip. Instead, he sees a car stop in front of the house. It is a long, black Jaguar.

Resplendent in his English suit, polished Italian shoes and silk necktie, Uncle Chaim descends from his car and walks toward the house. He approaches decisively, jacket thrown upon his shoulders — like Napoleon's Marshal Ney, Chaim has no use for jacket sleeves. Max warns Mother. She immediately goes to the mirror and gives her hair a few pokes, while Max opens the door. Mrs. Krocus called her brother as soon as Onofrio was arrested, and although Uncle

Chaim visits only rarely, in these pressing circumstances he agreed to come.

Striding in briskly, Uncle taps Max on the head and throws the evening paper on the table, on top of the Selections from the Reader's Digest. Mother reads where her brother points, becomes paler than the paper, and lets it slip from her hands. Max picks it up: the police feature occupies half the page and starts with Father's name. The huge, initial capital O stares at him. Onofrio Krocus, age 39: it is a simple enough O, black, round, actually slightly oval, empty inside, but were it adorned with monsters intertwined, like those initial letters of the fairy tales he used to read but reads no more, were there real snakes issuing forth, it would be less awful, less repellent. He cannot read much further. He retains some words, half understood, here and there: "embezzlement," "fraudulent," "finally brought to justice," "the Villa Devoto jail," but his eyes are drawn, in fascination, to the start, to the big O and its terrible emptiness. Mother and Uncle Chaim are having a *tête-à-tête* on the love seat, discussing in a low voice. The barber too, at this very moment, must be unfolding the newspaper, calling to his customers, "look at this!" Almost choking on *toscano* smoke and saliva — Max can see the scene — all excited he calls, "hey, look at this!" And the kids at school! His heart sinks. The ones who are stronger will taunt him openly; the others will laugh behind his back. There will be whispers among the teachers, finger-pointing. He shudders thinking of Vergara's cruel jokes. Oh, if he could run away, but where? If he could hide during the day, every day, then at night sneak out to the terrace and smoke, all by himself, under the stars, every night. If he could only disappear. Stay with Pancracia in her room, on her musty mattress. Slip into that capital O, if it were a real hole and not just empty, murderous paper. Finally he resolves to lock himself in the bathroom, just sit and think. But Mother calls him.

"It has been decided that you will go to your Uncle's country house in Castelar: it's not too close, and not too far away. A few days, until things quiet down. Go get your toothbrush, your pajamas, and your school books."

For the last time, Max looks at the newspaper on the table. When he raises his eyes from the big O, he meets Uncle Chaim's eyes, bright, masterful.

Evening brings whiffs of smoke from distant fires, a promise of peace from distant woods. Lights are already on in shops and houses, and from the wires hung across the street, lamps glow with a pale, moist light, like fruits about to fall. The work day over, men are gathering at the café, the waiter weaves his way among the tables, holding his laden tray high above his head. The barber holds his razor over another lathered face, and by the door to the *conventillo*, the cripple in his wheelchair holds in his mind only one thought: the whore. A ray of the dying sun, reflected in the barber's tin basin and catching Max's eye, stings him painfully. Prisoners in their cells must long for the sunlight. Yet the garbage men parking their trucks, cops having finished their rounds and hanging from the handrails of overcrowded buses, cabbies heading home with off-duty signs on — free men don't seem to appreciate it. From Uncle Chaim's car all those people appear in a different perspective, as if seen from afar and from a higher plane — that of a prince casting an eye on the bustling populace from his royal carriage.

And what a carriage it is! Max has never smelled anything so intoxicating as the leather of those luxurious seats: rare, insidious perfumes are dissolved in them, golden gowns, bejewelled queens, rare furs. On the rich veneers of the dashboard the gauges are aglow; Uncle Chaim's gloved, seigneurial hands govern the steering wheel, on the hub a leopard rampant. His mustache black and well trimmed, no tobacco stains on it, and on his jacket not a speck of dandruff. He is like a prince astronaut! As if having guessed the boy's thoughts, Uncle Chaim pats him on the thigh and turns on the radio. A voice everyone knows, a song in English everyone is dancing to, everyone hums, words no one understands, charges the frame of night with promises and whispers. Soon they are in the open country.

3

She has been pouring maté for the last seventy years. As a girl she poured for her father and Chaim, then, as a wife, for Onofrio while he played solitaire, imagining harebrained business deals or crazy love affairs. She used to pour for Max too, while he sat at his desk twisting his hair, scanning Virgil or Euclid. And now she still pours, in spite of her arthritic hands. When, seeing her shaking, almost missing the gourd, Max objects, "Mother, let me do it," she indignantly replies, "Why, the day I'm not able to pour maté you might as well take me to a nursing home, or throw me in the gutter, to the rats."

Max understands. What's left of a woman who cannot pour maté? Somehow, believe it or not (and non-maté drinkers probably won't), the thing tastes better when prepared and poured by women. Jorge Luis Borges, in one of his best stories: "The woman shuttled in and out serving maté." Compare that with Eliot, typically Anglo-Saxon: "In the room the women come and go talking of Michelangelo."

The abyss between two cultures right there in a nutshell. Max likes putting things in nutshells.

The apartment is spare and spotless. A mahogany cabinet and a sideboard, both handsomely carved, relics from better days, from the old house in Flores. On the wall, the Zeide's clock, stopped at eleven. Four old chairs have molted their crumbling original leather for a flowery tapestry. A folding table, a TV set on a wheeled stand, and Mrs. Krocus's prize crystal chandelier. In her bedroom there is only her bed. Sometimes Max carries out a mock pompous search through recondite edges and forgotten corners, finally showing his mother the smudged tip of his forefinger. "Disgusting!" he grunts.

And even though she knows it's a hole-in-corner sham ceremony, a game they've been playing ever since he was a boy and she was still young and strong and an impeccable housekeeper, even so she flushes and flusters. "Oh my god, where? Aw, there. I cannot reach. I'll tell Norma to climb on the stool and wipe it off." Norma is her cleaning woman, who comes once a week, in the afternoon.

She offers him the gourd, the second pouring. The first, the bitterest, is for the server, according to maté etiquette. "Where did you go last night, Max?"

He shrugs and tells her to the Chateaubriand.

She understands. "Wouldn't it be easier for you to work right here? I won't say a word, I promise. I'll just pour maté for you until it comes through your ears." And as Max doesn't answer she pursues, "Unless, of course, you go to the café to meet women..."

"Women, Mother? At the Chateaubriand?"

"How should I know? How long has it been since I last set foot over there? I rarely go out nowadays, it's hard

31

enough for me to walk from my bed to the kitchen. But being such a handsome man... and now single, on top of everything... my God, women will..."

Mrs. Krocus gathers the fingertips of her right hand, meaning that women will crowd around Max. Sitting across the stool and the kettle from her, gladdened by the morning sunlight, he becomes aware of the richness of this language of gestures, that a loosening and a twitch, ever so slight, of those gathered fingertips would introduce new meanings having vaguely to do with anal sphincters, and that an up-and-down motion of her hand would raise questions such as, "How could they help it, those broads?" or, "Do you realize what a top prize you are?" But raising the same gathering of fingers to her mouth would mean something entirely different: women will devour Max.

"Mother, you seem to think that all the women around here have heard of my divorce."

"It wouldn't surprise me, those things travel fast," says Mrs. Krocus, handing her son the maté gourd. "You know I wouldn't flatter you, but in my whole life I have known only one man as handsome as you: your uncle Chaim."

"But everybody says I look like Father."

"Oh, no. Well, the nose, and perhaps the mouth... But Chaim was a thousand times more handsome than Onofrio. Proof is, Chaim had all the women he wanted, the choicest women in the country, while your father, poor loser that he was, had to make do with the likes of that slut... Nirma Yáñez."

"Malvina Cildáñez, Mother," says Max.

"Whatever," says Mrs. Krocus. "Also, Chaim always kept himself well, like you, into his fifties, when Onofrio had grown heavy, flabby and fat. You take after your uncle."

Max feels flattered. He can't admit to himself that he's glad to resemble Chaim, for that would constitute the highest treason. How useless it has been, his growing up. He still reacts with a jerk of the heart at any suggestion of Father being put down or unfavorably compared with Uncle Chaim. It makes him sick, yet what can he do? Mother has spent years alone, gazing at these walls, dusting her furniture, doing her post-mortem debunking of Onofrio and glorifying Chaim. Total failure Onofrio, glitteringly successful Chaim. He doesn't like Mother thinking, in typical Latin fashion, of her son's physical shape as part of his essence, though. She can't imagine the hours of strenuous exercise he puts in up in the U.S., the miles run and swum every week so as not to end up looking like Father, fat, double-chinned, Falstaffian.

"I'd like to take another look at the old photographs," says Max. "That one of Father and Uncle Chaim at the beach. Or the one where Father is surrounded by a bevy of women at an office party, like a Turkish pasha, holding me by the shoulders, and I look like I'm saying, `earth, swallow me'."

"Sure," Mother says, "whenever you want, you know where they are, just help yourself."

Mrs. Krocus keeps the old photographs in a cupboard up high; behind Father's old, bowed billiard cue, and the boxes containing his chess, checkers and domino sets, poker chips, several dog-eared decks of French and Spanish playing cards, his Hohner harmonica, his Dunhill pipe, there is the musty suitcase he used as a traveling salesman: inside, wrapped in cellophane paper, the old photographs.

"Later," says Max; "when you go to bed."

While Max takes his time sucking the gourd dry, she

silently flattens the folds of her skirt with the back of her arthritic fingers. He hands the gourd back to her and while she pours, unsteadily, by spurts, eyes glued to the kettle's shaking beak, she suddenly says, "Jennifer just wasn't for you, Max," and noticing Max's look of stupefaction, she hands him the gourd and explains, "While I was in the kitchen, I was thinking about that."

Max sucks. Maybe if he doesn't say a word she'll drop the subject. Mrs. Krocus has a way with English names. The "j" of her Jennifer is the same sound as the "sh" of her Sharon: for all her command of the subtleties of gesture, her two American daughters-in-law seem to be one and the same person in her mind. Whether it required any effort on her part or not, both times, when Max told her he was getting a divorce, she didn't show the slightest surprise.

"I know about these things as I know you," she pursues implacably: "that woman wasn't for you. She didn't have your very special sensitivity."

"But Mother, how can you possibly know that, if you never met her, never even saw her?"

"What does that have to do with it. It was enough for me to read your letters, to gather how things stood between you and her through you, between the lines, through certain silences, and you won't deny that I know *you*."

Max whines. Mother, the deconstructionist critic. "You would say the same thing about any woman I married, no matter how perfect," he offers, feebly. Max has always suspected that Jennifer didn't quite have his sensitivity. He feels flattered, as he always does when Mother says that he has a very special sensitivity. It's a good thing for a poet to have a special sensitivity.

"No, I wouldn't. You are a difficult man, a very difficult man. But there are some sensitive, intelligent women in the world, and they don't have to be perfect."

"Okay, name one."

"What do you take me for," says Mrs. Krocus without missing a beat, "you think I'm a marriage-broker, a Celestina? Go find your own women. I'm not a *shodkhen*."

They both laugh. Mother keeps pouring maté until Max overflows. It's good to be here, facing Zeide's clock frozen at eleven and the gleaming furniture of Max's childhood — at least what's left of it; Mother among her quiet things. Somewhere, the ideal woman must be waiting for him. The exquisite, supersensitive female who, blessed among all women, would understand him, such a difficult man.

Did you finally get in touch with Fontana?" asks Mrs. Krocus.

"Yes, I did. We'll get together in a couple of days."

Twenty-five, thirty years ago, as university students, they were best friends. Fontana now lives in California, and it's been years since Max last saw him.

"What a coincidence, you and him coming to Buenos Aires at the same time. Do you still want maté? It's washed out. But I could make another one. And how's he doing?"

"Who, Fontana?"

"Yes, he used to be such a *schlemiel*. Open your eyes, he'll try to borrow money from you, as he used to."

"I'd be more likely to borrow money from him, Mother: el Indio Fontana has made a great career, he's a world-renowned scientist, a first-rate mathematician."

"Bah! He too shits, doesn't he," Mrs. Krocus dismisses Fontana's scientific achievements with a brief wave of her arthritic hand. "You listen to me and open your eyes: once a *schlemiel,* always a *schlemiel."*

That's it. He too shits. Since Max's earliest childhood, Mrs. Krocus has instilled in him scatologically based egalitarian views: when it comes down to it we are all shitters (with the possible exception of Uncle Chaim). The act of defecation obliterates any differences due to merit, wisdom or courage; no one can tell a bum's, a schnorrer's turd from Einstein's. When Max was studying Latin in high school, he chiseled it on his desk: *Et cacat.* Later he turned it into Greek: *Kaì kákkai.* A useful thing to remember in any language, especially when confronted with someone else's pretension to spiritual authority: you just tell him, "You too shit," and that should settle his hash.

For Max, keen on the relations between life and ideas, it is a source of wonderment that his mother has always had tremendous problems with the excretory function, despite that universality which she so often proclaims. Enemas, suppositories, castor oil, croton oil and oil of agar-agar, which work on most people, are inert on her recalcitrant gut, and so she has turned, severally or jointly, to milk of magnesia San Pellegrino as well as other less-known brands, to jalap, asafetida, belladonna, barberry, galbanum and gamboge, dwarf flax, bryony, colocynth, rhubarb root, aloes, chicory, curibay, calomel, senna, various spurges, resin of scammony, Rochelle salt, Seidlitz powder, daily infusions from the leaves of the elder tree (Sambucus Peruviana)... It would be grueling to name all of the cathartics and alviducous caccagogues she has relied on over the last seventy years.

Max looks around. Zeide's clock, the handsomely carved, polished furniture, the impeccably waxed parquet. On the table, Max's photograph, in formal suit and tie, framed in silver repoussé. There's no other framed photograph in Mother's apartment, neither of Father, whose bones lie in La Matanza, *extra muros*, at the edge of the pampas, nor of Gloria, with whom the old lady is not on speaking terms. The maté gourd and the kettle, resting on the stool, awaiting the next round. Mother's hands, bony and crabbed, knuckles bent and cramped into impossible angles, grabbing the arms of her rocking chair. Lovingly, Max looks at her ashen face and sparse hair. He's thankful. For the whole rest of the world, el Indio Fontana is a brilliant scientist and Max Krocus an obscure teacher and unpublished poet, someone who may safely be ignored; here only, between these walls and for Mother alone, Max reigns supreme, a prince of sensitivity, a pure flame protected by his mother's vestal care from the harsh drafts of critical inquiry, while Fontana is a *schlemiel.*

"I'm so glad you came, Max," says Mrs. Krocus, laying a hand, frail as a dried butterfly, on her son's wrist.

"I too am glad," says Max in a whisper, for certain words are so true they require a low voice.

4

"This country's a brothel, Max." Gloria, who is sitting across the table from him, gulps down her coffee, puffs from her cigarette and exhales in her peculiar way, a continuous plume directed first upwards then veering down, like a large fan opening out; her elbow resting on the table, she holds the cigarette close to her ear and moves her head in a gesture of disgusted powerlessness. Her nostrils twitch. "A fucking brothel."

Max leans back on the hind legs of his trusty Chateaubriand chair, turns his face away and looks through the moist glass at the traffic on San Juan Avenue. His sister is a grown woman, forty-eight; for him, however, she is still a girl, and certain words are jarring coming from her. Women walk by slowly, arms folded, a plaintive, skeptical downturn on their lips, as if proud of their melancholy. Car taillights shine in the mist. Max's attention is caught by a figure waiting to cross the glistening asphalt, jeans tight as sausage casing and stiletto heels. Buses go by at high speed.

At the center of a hiatus, a Ford Falcon slowly cruises by, the two men inside ogling the woman, hungry for her flesh.

"A giant torture chamber, only recently," says Max.

"Yeah, that too," Gloria takes another puff. "Well, what do you expect, in a giant brothel there's got to be a lot of Jack the Rippers, don't you think?"

"I guess so. Another cup of coffee?"

"Sure," Gloria says. "I won't get any sleep but what the hell, I can do without it."

"Want to eat something?" says Max. "Working two jobs, you must burn up a lot of calories."

"Two jobs, plus, I didn't tell you, the anti-tobacco campaign. That's no joke, coordinating the programs, the promotional ads, the seminars for the whole country."

"You're in charge of the anti-tobacco campaign? Then how come you smoke like a Papin's digester?"

The waiter shouts to the man behind the huge copper machine, "Two espressos, two!"

Gloria shrugs. "Like a what? Anyway, Bruno, my boss, as well as all the people in the line of command, up to the Minister of Health, smoke too. Incidentally, for what it may be worth, I sleep with Bruno."

"You do? Well, fine, as long as you remember that smoking in bed has risks."

"Oh, we are very careful, don't worry. The usual post-coitum cigarette. Ah, smoking can be metaphysical... When else do you find a woman and a man lying side by side, without masks, not trying to impress each other, emptied of sexual drive, quietly talking about life? I've always cherished those moments, and Bruno..."

Gloria pauses while the waiter, lento assai, sets down two espressos, two glasses of water and another ticket. Max

39

resumes, "And Bruno?"

"Ah, Bruno! Bruno's quite a case, you know. Delirious, totally crazy. Pious Catholic background, traditional family from Catamarca, can you picture it? At twenty-two he found himself married to this hysterical bitch who's actually his cousin, and she proceeds to bear him, just like that, boom, boom, boom, twelve children, the youngest eight and a half. Try to imagine the hell the poor guy has been through. He's an MD, but totally revolted by the mercenary ethics of private medicine; he holds a high position at the Ministry of Health, but cannot stomach the corruption; and so there he is now, fifty years old, saddled with a wife he doesn't love and a profession he doesn't have any respect for... On top of that, with his background, every time we make love he feels atrociously guilty. He weeps, calls the roll of his wife and his twelve children, asks them to forgive him. He prays to Jesus and to Our Lady of the Valley to pardon him for fornicating with a Jewess. He asks, do I think he'll burn in hell; but I tell him not to worry: with all he suffers, if there's a hell, to him it'll feel like paradise."

As Gloria lights another cigarette, Max says, "Is that what you call `lying in bed and quietly talking about life?'"

"Well, with Bruno at least it works. I mean, mechanically." She picks a shred of tobacco from the tip of her tongue. "With others, they'll have all sorts of problems. You know, guilt will descend and get lodged in their balls. Ballast. And sometimes, to be fair, it's been my fault. With Marcelo, right before Bruno, I couldn't lubricate. I went to a gynecologist, I stopped my douches, I even stopped using talcum powder. No matter what I did or didn't do or what he did or didn't do (he wasn't very inspiring), I couldn't lubricate. Can you imagine how that made me feel? No, you have to be a woman to understand it. Anyway, I told it to my analyst, and for the past two months we've been elaborating the semantics..."

"Your analyst is a woman, I take it?" Max interrupts.

"No, he's a man. Gastón Panard, right now the best psychoanalyst in Buenos Aires," she says a bit defensively, then adds proudly, "a personal disciple of Lacan."

To soften her, Max tries a little self-deprecatory confession. "I went to a shrink once, twenty years ago, up in the U.S. I never asked, but I think he was a disciple of Groucho Marx."

"You mean you underwent analysis in English?" Gloria seems surprised.

"Why, yes, what's wrong with that," says Max.

"Don't you know that psychic material is like a language? The deeper strata correspond to your mother tongue, therefore whatever you and your analyst were doing in English, you were just scratching the surface, Max. You should have undergone analysis in Spanish."

"I needed something fast, Gloria. It was right after Father's death and I happened to be in bad shape."

"Yes," Gloria says reflectively, "those were terrible times. For me of course much worse, since you weren't here when he died. Three months later, my baby was stillborn." Twisting her mouth in a dolorous grimace, she crushes the cigarette on the bottom of her coffee cup.

"Another coffee?" Max suggests.

"Sure..." Eyes down, Gloria is poking with her spoon the soaked cigarette filters. She seems absent, self-absorbed. Max cannot help wondering if her heavy smoking bespeaks a fascination with taboo. Father, himself a heavy smoker, was dead set against young women smoking, especially in

41

front of their elders; Gloria had it strictly forbidden, and Max enforced the law. Once at a party — she was eighteen and he was twenty — somebody offered Gloria a cigarette. Max looked at her sharply, reminding her of his presence. She went ahead anyway and lit up. With a swat Max sent the cigarette flying, and Gloria left the party in tears. Max wonders if she remembers that. Better not ask.

"You called me on the phone to New York and I vividly remember your voice. Father's dying, you said. That was all. Father's dying. Still ringing in my ears."

The waiter, impassive, napkin-wielding god, brings more coffee. Gloria drinks it in three equally distanced gulps and lights another cigarette. She says very softly, "I used to dream that Father, in his agony, was calling you, Max, but you wouldn't come."

Max drinks up his coffee. "It's natural. Me too, I used to have such dreams. For some reason, in mine, Father always died at table, during a meal. Maybe because he enjoyed eating so much..."

"Or maybe because the coffin was put on top of the dining-room table. That's where we laid him until he was taken away," Gloria says.

"I missed that too." Max shakes his head. "Did you have many mourners? Did you serve sherry or anisette with the coffee?"

"I don't remember, Max. I was pregnant. And I was crying all the time."

"I missed your crying, I missed the caftaned, bearded bum chanting by the open hole over the wriggling earthworms — *Baruch - Atoh - Adonai - Eloheinu*. I flew down and managed to see Uncle Chaim, two days after the burial. He too had missed it," says Max, staring at the space above his sister's hair. "The bastard came in his new BMW, accompanied by Grandma. You think he offered us his condolences? He never uttered, `I'm sorry.' Instead, he insulted Dad. I shall never forgive him."

"Insulted Dad?" asks Gloria. "What did he do?"

"That's right, you weren't there. It was just Mom and me. We were sitting in the living room, when the Bobeh suddenly asked, `What was Onofrio's business?' `Didn't you know?' said the son of a whore, `he was a peddler.'"

"But it's true, Max, Dad was a peddler for the last few years of his life. He went around, even as far as Lobos, selling trinkets on the installment plan..."

"I know, I know, but you should have seen the utterly deprecating shake of his hand."

"Big deal," Gloria shrugs.

"I shall never forgive him," says Max with heroic finality.

He is dimly aware that a mental equivalent of Chaim's dismissive gesture (and not only Chaim's, but also Mother's and the Bobeh's — it's nothing but shit, quick, quick, take it away), may lie behind his own two divorces, the dryness of his soul, his chronic inability to enjoy a lover's mind. But the image of Father's dead body inside a box on top of the dining-room table haunts him. Max doesn't know why. Is it because, as the Surrealists maintained, the more distant the relation between two juxtaposed realities, the stronger the image, the more emotionally powerful and poetically real? No, that doesn't seem to fit. There's something about that image, involving some secret and momentous fact about the world, which he would give anything to uncover.

"Was it open, the coffin," he asks. "Dad's coffin, on the dining-room table."

"I don't know, I don't think so," says Gloria.

"Were you eating at the table, Mother and you, while the coffin was there?"

"Where else," Gloria shrugs.

"You and Mother were carving juicy steaks, breaking bread, sipping wine, while Father was lying there, at arm's length, getting rigid, his tongue cold in his mouth, his body just beginning to putrefy... Was he wearing his threadbare three-piece suit, and in his vest pocket the Parker 51 fountain pen?"

Gloria grabs her purse. "Are you trying to make me puke? Or are you trying to project your guilt? You should have come when I called you back then, if you were interested in the gory details."

Max reaches with his hand across the table and taps her knuckles. "Gloria, don't get mad at me, I'm not trying to make you puke. On the contrary, I envy you. What would I give now, to have been there that day, the day Father died, to have participated in that meal. The Eucharist, don't you see? The messianic banquet, feasting on the flesh of Leviathan..."

She shrugs. "Those things mean nothing to me, nothing at all. You are like Bruno, demented by religious symbols."

"I, like Bruno?" Max is amazed at his sister's insensitivity. "I don't have twelve children. I don't even have a wife right now. And I don't sleep with you."

He has stuck his foot in, and he knows it before he finishes the sentence. Gloria looks at him with her green eyes, transparent, washed out by years of inside weeping. She nods slowly. "Yes, that's the first thing that surfaced in my analysis. Isn't it funny that you bring it up like that, as if by accident, in order to deny it."

Max giggles. "You mean our little capers on your bed, at siesta time? So what. A little touching. Brother and sister playing doctor, exploring a bit. Big deal."

"Says you." Gloria nods some more, each nod a bit more ominous. "I'll never forget your... instructions. Your perverse, sadistic instructions. And the whole thing surfaced again recently with Panard, when we analyzed my dryness. There are three ways to do it, you used to tell me." The words choke in her throat. Her eyes stare tragically at him, horror-stricken, her finger raised, like in Guercino's picture of Amnon and Tamar at the National Gallery. "In the vagina... in the mouth... or in the ass."

Max snickers. "Your holy trinity of holes. Oh, come now, I was twelve and you were ten, it was the whole fucking Argentine civilization speaking through me, don't you realize? It wasn't even me: those were the teachings of our cousin Boris I was repeating. And anyway, I can't believe it was so poisonous."

There is an undertow of indignation in Gloria's voice. "At that age? All I can say is, that's not the opinion of my analysts, every single one of them, including Panard."

Out on Avenida San Juan, they walk in silence. At a crossing, a bus is letting people off, the air reeks of burnt diesel oil, an old bolero is blaring from the driver's radio. *"Doquiera que tú vayas, Si te acuerdas de mí, La pena que te invade, Sol se ha de convertir..."* Silly words, stupid music. Worse: ungrammatical. A bungled effort to start each line with Do, Si, La, Sol, Fa, Mi, Re, Do, like the medieval hymn to Saint John, but backwards. Garbage, pollution of the mind, yet how it churns Max's heart, how it brings back, like a perfume, his adolescence and his youth. Perhaps he should remind Gloria that they used to dance to this song, that he

45

remembers her on the evening of her fifteenth birthday, dancing under the stars, eyes closed, face ecstatic, cheek glued to the cheek of Billar, a high-school pal of Max's notorious for his hairy balls.

Looking at this woman walking by his side, Max tries to bracket the facts, to ignore that she irritates him and that they happen to have been born by the same womb. She walks slightly hunched, as if under some great weight, perhaps the weight of her vaginal dryness. She's grown fat at the bottom, around belly and rump, and the back of her hands are splotchy with the brown spots of age. Max looks inside himself for signs of remorse. He can't find any. On the contrary, he detects a glowing satisfaction.

He thinks he can explain it. With the power for renewal and forgetfulness that's found only in the United States of America, together with the name Krocus, Sharon and Jennifer shed the whole of him. Problem solved, let's move to something new, the next, happier leg of the journey: that, essentially, is what he was told. He has never had the experience of being accosted at a restaurant by an ex-student of his, as he saw in a recent Woody Allen movie, and being told that his Math lectures completely changed his or her life. That only happens to Philosophy professors. As for his poems, they have never been published. Max had to come to Buenos Aires to find a person, his own sister in the event, whose life was devastated and her vagina dried by a few words, a mere few words pronounced by him almost forty years back. This makes him feel warm inside, published, influential, full of energy: to know there was a time when the words out of his mouth had such momentous impact, like those of Jehovah, or of the Egyptian Phtah.

They are not far from Mother's apartment. "Listen,

46

let's surprise her," Max says, grabbing Gloria by the arm. "Come with me, she's probably asleep, we'll wake her up."

Gloria stops and turns toward him. Her eyes are red. Max wasn't aware that she'd been weeping. "Don't even dream about it."

"But why, Gloria, why, just tell me why." He is determined that if nothing else, this trip of his should achieve peace between Mother and Sister.

"Because I hate her," she says as they arrive at the end of the block. They kiss on the cheek, and Gloria goes down the stairs, into the subway.

5

The Bobeh had her own theory about cousin Boris' deformity: it was his mother's — Aunt Porota's — fault. The baby was left to sleep all night in his *dreck*: that's why he didn't grow and why his legs were stunted. The doctors had diagnosed a genetic underdevelopment of the hip cartilage; still Grandma would stick to her guns: it couldn't be that, it had to be the *dreck*. Otherwise, how did you explain that Boris' condition didn't appear until he was two years old? She'd curse her daughter-in-law, first in heavily accented Spanish: "*Puta asquerosa!*" Then, more forcefully, in Yiddish: "*FARSHTINKENEH!*" The Bobeh was tiny, frail and asthmatic, but her words hissed like air out of a crack in hell's top.

Poroto means a bean in Argentine Spanish, and Porota was often given as a nickname to baby girls who were unusually small. Similar reasons must have suggested to the Romans Cicero, Lentulus, Piso. But however apt the nickname of those illustrious men, in the case of Aunt Porota it was definitely a misnomer. She was short but stocky, with formidable breasts, the twin and only reason, according to another theory of Grandma's, why Uncle Chaim, who could have had any woman he fancied, had fallen for her.

Max was eleven, and so his cousin Boris must have been fourteen, when at a family reunion, having feasted on Grandma's *gefilte fish*, while aunts and uncles were playing canasta and laughing at jokes Max didn't understand, he and Boris watched Aunt Porota dancing by herself in the living-room. Her breasts shook like huge soundless maracas, and she seemed oblivious to everything but the song. Max still remembers it, quite a hit that year, a *cha-cha-cha*:

> *"Hay que darle la mamadera,*
> *a mi nene hay que darle la mamadera.*
> *Si el nene no duerme no puedo bailar;*
> *Hay que darle la mamadera..."*, etc.

"Got to give the baby his bottle... if my baby boy does-n't sleep I cannot dance..." Boris was sitting on the sofa, watching her; his legs, too short to reach the floor, pointed ahead, toward his mother. She sang as in a trance, swaying and shaking.

Uncle Chaim had a country house right outside of Buenos Aires, where, free from high rises and beyond the smokestacks, the vast sky was master. Castelar... the name of the town had for Max a grandiose resonance of castles. The house was big, indeed almost a castle, and the lawn, with faucets and croquet hoops sticking out of the grass, was to Max's boyish eyes a royal park.

The Krocuses would visit exactly once a year, for New Year's Eve, which in Argentina falls in summer. This unam-biguous and numerical occasion, unencumbered by the patriotic hoopla and military fanfare of Flag Day or Independence Day, free from the bloodstained menace of the

49

Birth or the Crucifixion, was the only Argentine holiday the family celebrated. At midnight sharp they all had to be together, and during the first few minutes of the year they had to kiss. Reckon: if there were thirty of them, exactly four hundred and thirty- five kisses must have been exchanged. And woe to the foolish child who forgot to kiss his parents! Lesser misfortunes would befall within the next twelve-month, if they should miss an uncle or an aunt.

On the 31st of December the four Krocuses took the train to Castelar, arriving at sundown. Loud explosions everywhere, the swish of rockets and crackers going off. Empty bottles stood on the lawn to hold the sticks of the sky-rockets, and while the girls watched from the porch like scared, excited butterflies, the boys would strike the match, run a safe distance away and see with soldierly pride the thing go up and burst cheerfully in the sky. Max loved the smell of gunpowder. After the explosion he'd go back to the empty bottle and sniff the pale wisps slowly spiralling up the neck. "Come, come!" he would call Gloria and his cousins, Marisol, Pola, Chuchi and Pirula, "smell this, it'll knock you out!"

Searchlights scoured the summer sky, from the Castelar Air Force base or the nearby military barracks... The adults would be watching from the porch, too. Calmly, feet firmly set on the tiled floor, shaking with a rotating motion of the hand the ice in their high-balls, they scanned the exploding rockets and the sweeping light beams, then they looked at the kids running back and forth on the lawn like fireflies, and they smiled. Sometimes, Uncle Chaim would come out to the porch and stand there briefly, like a gener-alissimo among staff-officers, and he'd smile too. They all smiled with obvious satisfaction, as if thinking: "See, see how well protected we are, how prosperous! And this coming year, no doubt, will be even better!"

On one of those New Year's eves Max was, as they say in Buenos Aires, *avivado*, which can be translated as "wised up," but literally means enlivened, vivified, inflamed. They were sitting on the lawn, two or three boys about seven, and Boris, who was ten. All around, explosions, whistles, shouts, the whirl of Catharine wheels, and from the house, the sound of the big-band records favored by Aunt Porota: it was all very jolly. Then Boris broke the news.

Max simply couldn't believe it. "You mean it's like a shot of penicillin?"

"No, silly," Boris explained, "this doesn't hurt at all: on the contrary, they like it, they like it a lot."

"How do you know?" somebody asked.

"Because I've seen it." And to a fascinated audience of three younger cousins, Boris proceeded to tell how he, standing at the door of his parents' bedroom, had seen them lying on their bed, completely naked, furiously wrestling. The idea of Uncle Chaim and Aunt Porota being completely naked and wrestling was too preposterous to be taken without a fit of nervous giggling. Someone asked if they said anything, and Boris told them: "Fuck me, Chaimele, tear me apart! That's what my mother was saying." And violently shaking his head and his stunted legs, he shouted: "Fuck me, Chaimele, tear me apart!"

To this day those heady verbs have remained associated in Max's mind with squibs hissing and the blast of crackers, and with the jerks of a dwarf under a summer sky harassed by searchlights.

*

After the untimely death of Aunt Porota from a brain tumor, Uncle Chaim bought a new flat in the most expensive section of Buenos Aires and took off on a long trip through Europe. For almost a year Boris lived with Grandma, in her apartment, not far from the Krocuses, and during that time Max saw a lot of his cousin.

Boris was nineteen and reached up to Max's waist. He limped badly, dragging his left leg, and his head seemed too big for the rest of his body. Inside the big head there was a good mind: being at the time a second-year medical student, Boris knew the name of everything that has a name within a human carcass. Max felt jealous of the pampering the Bobeh poured on Boris. He would have liked to live in Grandma's apartment himself, to be familiar with so many wonderful old things from the old country: the shiny samovar, the spice tower, the fine silverware inscribed with Hebrew letters. Max would have liked Grandma to cook for him, just for him, her celestial *gefilte fish*; he would have liked her bony, crooked fingers to stroke his cheek as they did his cousin's. But Max was never her favorite.

By that time Boris had acquired a formidable reputation. Most people who happened to know someone from Castelar had heard of his exploits, and the stories of his practical jokes were well on their way to becoming classics. Directing a fertilizer company to dump a ton of manure at the doorstep of some unfortunate neighbors who were away on vacation, was a thing Boris would do casually, as an hors-d'oeuvre, waiting for something better to develop. To an old woman who spent most of the day sitting on a wicker chair on the sidewalk, watching the world pass by, but who would each time avert her face from the misshapen dwarf, he played the following trick: dragging himself close by her, he said, "See if you can duck this one," and broke wind as loud as a tuba trill. Such stories drew from the boys high-pitched laughter, but other, less funny things, and of a darker hue, were rumored about Boris. He was in the habit of playing poker or monte with other boys. One morning Aunt Porota had discovered that some of her silver and a diamond ring were missing. The night before (so the story went), while she and Uncle Chaim were out dancing at Tabaris, Boris had been gambling in the house with a bunch of new boys he had just met, whose last names he didn't know, and who turned out to be thieves.

"Imagine," Mrs. Krocus would say, "inviting such crooks into your parents' house! No wonder," she would add, sadly shaking her head, "no wonder your aunt Porota, *farshtinkeneh* though she was, couldn't bear the sight of her own son doing such things! She's better off rotting under the ground."

Euphemism wasn't a feature of the family's style: if you referred to someone, Aunt Porota for instance, as having "passed away" or "gone to her rest," Max's relatives, especially the women, would snicker and peg you as either a fool or a hypocrite. "Kick the bucket" and "check out" were the softest expressions they consented to, and when Grandma, in her frequent cursing, wished that somebody would die, she would say "May she go under into the ground!" in Yiddish: "*In drerd aráyn zol zi aráyn geyn!*" Hard to imagine sounds that could better imitate the crumbling of our bodies, the turning of earth to earth, dust to dust, grit to grit.

As for the missing silverware and diamond ring, knowing what later transpired about Boris, it is clear that they were not purloined, but were duly betted and duly lost, during a particularly unlucky streak.

The first time the two cousins went out together after Boris moved into Grandma's place, it was to Buenos Aires' biggest amusement park.

"Have you ever been to Retiro Park?" Boris asked Max as they got into Boris' car. It was one of those flamboyant, hardly believable American models, from the years when phosphorescent ties featuring palm trees and female bodies were the height of fashion. Boris favored those ties too, as he did, in general, things loud and outrageous.

Max told him that yes, he had been there as a child, with his parents; that he used to be terribly scared of the ferris wheel, but liked the merry-go-round.

"Well, tonight you'll visit the furry cavern," Boris said with a wink.

Max asked what was that, was it something like the tunnel of love? Boris burst out laughing, banging his hand hard against the chrome ring on the steering wheel, so that for two blocks he drove with the horn going full blast.

"You've got the drift alright, kid," Boris said when he finally calmed down. "We're going to look for a cute little tart I know." Then, noticing Max's bewilderment, with clinical seriousness he asked: "Are you still a virgin?"

Max went red in the face. His cousin had touched the sorest spot, the burning issue, the overwhelming shame of his life: at sixteen, he was still virginal. "Well," he started to say, "you know... I've been sort of necking..."

"No need to apologize," Boris interrupted, "everybody's been a rookie once. Besides, you'll see, Doris will handle you with silk gloves."

For the rest of the trip Max did his best to appear cool,

54

although he had trouble keeping his knees from shaking. He praised the appointments and the power of his cousin's car: indeed, he had never been in such a luxurious vehicle since that trip to Castelar with Uncle Chaim. Now and then, looking through the window, Max praised some woman's behind, or some boobs. His cousin heartily approved of those tastes: "Ah, you rascal, I see you like the stuff!"

When they arrived, Boris took a slide trombone from the back seat. He had been taking lessons once a week, he explained, from one of the best jazz musicians in Buenos Aires. "Girls love a blowing cat; have you seen that flick with Kirk Douglas?"

Max tried to walk self-assuredly, hands in his pockets, into the amusement park. But his heart took a plunge when Boris raised his trombone and right then and there, in the middle of the bustling, straggling crowd, started blowing away. Max fell back a little, trying to pretend Boris wasn't with him. But as some people, not knowing what to do, started holding out money, Boris pointed at Max and shouted: "Thank you, thank you, give it to my assistant," and went on with his deafening blasts.

So Max had a few unwanted pesos in his hands when they arrived at the shooting gallery close to the roller coaster. Boris asked Max to lift him up to the counter, where he ended up crouching like a grotesque gargoyle. From there he tried to get the attention of the attendant girl: "Psst, Doris, psst."

Finally, having handed out a little doll as a prize to another customer, the girl came toward them, and with a perfunctory "hi" gave Boris a gun. Boris handed Max his trombone, put a bill in the girl's hand, and carefully aimed the gun at the stiffly parading ducks, all the while bargaining with the girl. "A hundred each," he said, and shot and missed a duck.

"Three hundred," Doris said, deadpan.

Boris recharged his gun and aimed once more. "Oh c'mon," he said, "what d'you think you've got, platinum puss?" Then bang, another miss.

She had thick, dark hair and high cheek bones, a tight scarlet dress, exaggeratedly rouged lips, and her skin, especially around the neck and bare shoulders, looked gritty and red, perhaps an effect of the eerie light bathing the place. She was saying that it was a very busy night, that she wouldn't be able to leave until one o'clock, and even then... when a blood-curdling scream made Max turn. A group of boys and girls was coming down the roller coaster, screaming their heads off. Boris didn't seem to be disturbed, and this time he hit his duck. The girl gave him his prize, a doll dressed in red chiffon. Max thought it was as if she was saying to his cousin, "There, *this* is what you need: why don't you pick on somebody your size."

But having kissed the doll and Doris' hand, Boris pointed to Max and told her: "See *this* little doll? My cousin Max. Nice guy. Still cherry."

Doris came to where Max was and stretched her arm over the counter. Max thought she wanted to shake hands, and so he extended his, which she ignored; then, for a split second, Max thought that what she wanted was the trombone. But to his utter amazement she put her hand on his crotch. "Hmm..." she said, thoughtfully sizing him up.

After many shots, after another duck was hit and more hair-raising screams had been heard from the top of the roller coaster, after many comings and goings, Boris and Doris were not able to strike a deal. She wouldn't agree to do it in Boris' car, and the boys didn't have enough money to pay for a hotel room, on top of her fee. "Unless," Boris said, "we can get some more money playing the trombone."

Max begged him to desist. Suddenly he felt terribly tired; Boris, on the other hand, seemed fresh, as if just out of his morning shower. On their way out they walked by a tent where a man was blaring: "Come, ladies and gentlemen, come, see and hear the most amazing musical and physiological phenomenon! Ladies and gentlemen: Le Pétomane from Montparnasse! The most powerful, pungent and prolific fart virtuoso in the whole world! He'll play for you La Marsellaise and La Cumparsita in his unique and wonderful wind instrument, ladies and gentlemen — his bottom end!"

A little farther on, another man with a megaphone was calling everyone to watch the most enormous woman in the whole world. A small crowd had gathered to gape at the pitiful, spherical creature, of whom one couldn't say whether she was sitting or standing, or whether the overhanging bulk in front were dugs, a low, drooping, double chinfold or an upper annex of her bellyfat. As soon as he saw the enormous woman, Boris pushed his way through the onlookers, started agitating his arms and bobbing his head in the most ludicrous manner, screaming, "Momma! Momma!" The crowd gasped. The enormous woman saw this misshapen creature coming toward her, and her eyes popped with fear. "Momma," the dwarf kept crying, "Momma, remember the abortion you flushed down the toilet twenty years ago? Momma, here I am! Momma, here's your son!"

The crowd shouted and laughed, wild with joy. The poor woman was seized by convulsions, the huge mass of flesh and fat shaking and sweating, and the manager screaming on his megaphone at Boris: "Out with you! Out! Out!"

On the following days Max masturbated again and again, recalling Doris' reaching over the shooting gallery's counter with her fire-red nails, and her "hmm...", that devilish "hmm..." of hers which sounded like approval, but who could know... He imagined himself and her making love in a velvety red light, amidst a storm of screams and volleys of farts, petards and guns.

One afternoon, about a week after their visit to Retiro Park, Boris phoned Max. "Come over here right away." He was calling from his place, from Grandma's apartment.

What's the rush, asked Max, and adduced the difficulties of his trigonometry problems; but Boris insisted: "Just stop jerking off for a minute will you and get over here fast!"

Max protested that actually, at that very moment, he wasn't jerking off but really doing his math homework; the urgency in Boris' voice was such, though, that he hung up and ran to Grandma's place. He knew that Boris was alone, for Grandma and the Krocuses had gone to the Liniers Jewish cemetery for the unveiling of Aunt Porota's memorial. After which they were taking a cab to the other end of town, to see the progress in Uncle Chaim's new flat. Uncle Chaim, meanwhile, was leisurely winding his way down the French Riviera, the Costa Brava, Costa Daurada, Costa del Azahar, Costa Blanca and Costa del Sol, all the way down to Morocco.

When Boris opened the door, Max saw two women behind him. It took him a while to recognize in one of them the Doris of Retiro Park and of his fantasies. With an expansive gesture, Boris greeted him, "You see? Boris delivers!" And then, slapping the tart's behind, "And Doris dignifies!", in mocking reference to the slogan, "Perón delivers, Evita dignifies," which blared from every billboard and radio set

58

in Argentina at the time.

At the sight of the whores, Max started shaking. He wasn't even aware of Boris introducing him to the other girl who also worked at Retiro Park, at a dart-throwing stand. Her breasts were much bigger than Doris'.

Boris retired with the prize pair of tits to his own room, and Max was left with Doris in the only other bedroom in the place, which was the Bobeh's. He couldn't tell whether their lovemaking was lengthy or short, clumsy or ecstatic. He never remembered anything about it. Max's brain resumed its normal functions afterwards, only afterwards he started remembering. The smell, to begin with.

Herr Doktor Professor Gustav Jaeger, the German biologist, wrote that odor is the origin of the soul, and Heraclitus said that souls sniff as they descend to Hades. Sniffing was the first thing Max remembers doing as he himself descended — his first descent from the high forgetfulness of love, steeper and more abrupt than any roller coaster. It was a sweetish smell. As of violets macerated in sweat. Max was able to taste it too, surely because of the cheap lipstick smeared on his lips.

Doris' back was the first thing Max saw. She was sitting on the bed next to him, putting on her bra: her skin, even here, far from the lights of Retiro Park, seemed red and rough. Following down her spine's concavity, just below the bra's fastening, there was a fair-sized mole, and further down a blackish tuft covered the small of her back. Max couldn't go much farther: the sight of Doris' bottom, that fusty gash, that seat of darkness in tremendous contact with Grandma's white, embroidered coverlet, filled him with horror and stabbed him with guilt.

The jealousies were drawn, letting in streaks of humid

59

light which shone on the brass headboard. On the Bobeh's marble-topped night table, her old atomizer with its bottle of Bohemian crystal and its silk-lined tube and bulb. The silver-framed daguerreotype of her father, a formidable man with a skull-cap and a square beard. A monogrammed handker-chief, a few of Grandma's hairpins. The first thing Max heard was Doris' voice. "C'mon, daddy-o, I gotta go. Give me your little present now. Two hundred pesos."

*

Boris often invited Max to join him and some of his Medical School buddies for a poker game or a session of monte. Max always made some excuse. Cards didn't inter-est him; picking up girls was the only game he liked. And Boris' car made the game easy: big American cars were very rare in Buenos Aires, and few could resist the attraction of that dreamboat, the prestige of those bold aerodynamic lines, the wheeled voluptuousness. Girls would hop into the car, one to the front seat, for Boris, another to the back seat, for Max. Boris would make the introductions, "I'm Boris Vélez Sarsfield," he always said, "and this is Max Anchorena, my cousin."

Boris believed those last names of important Argen-tine families to be much more impressive and effective than their own, Jewish and foreign. And he would go on talking and driving, showing off, but it was easy to detect the front seat girl's double take, the look of disappointment, even revulsion on her face, at the sight of the dwarf's stunted legs, and of the special levers which replaced the pedals. Max would arrange a date with his girl, and if he thought he liked her he would show up, otherwise not. Boris was stood up

60

most of the time. Max felt sorry for him.

They were driving down Rivadavia Avenue one evening, a few months after Max had put an end to his virginity, when he asked Boris about the trombone, not seen since that time in Retiro Park. Boris told Max he had sold it to repay a debt. That brought up the subject of his gambling, and Max said he didn't know what the hell Boris found in it, since gambling was unspeakably boring.

"You don't understand," said Boris.

"What is there to understand," said Max.

Boris became serious. Max had never imagined that Boris could become so serious. "Gambling makes you come face to face with the real thing. Chance is powerful and impersonal. Chance is the stuff, the real stuff of life."

A little surprised at this unusual earnestness, Max suggested that when it came to reality, making love beat gambling any day, that it even beat jerking off, and that one was more likely to encounter the real thing, or stuff of life, or whatever that was, while in bed with a broad.

"Mushy," was Boris' brief comment.

"Mushy? Just get a hold of a nice piece of ass" (it was Max's turn to wax eloquent), "a swell filly, an honest whore, and get right down to business. No bull. What more reality of life do you want?"

"Nah, whores are too sentimental," Boris said with a shrug.

Max asked if he was kidding. "Doris, sentimental?" he added sarcastically.

"Look, you know I'm not queer, I need pussy," Boris said. "That's why I want to be a gynecologist, to have pussy to spare. But you give me a whore, I don't care who, Doris or any other, and I bet you two thousand pesos that in two hours I can convince her that I love her and that she loves me. And you know what's the funniest thing?"

Through the car window Max looked at the church, St Joseph of Flores. The canopied gangway was up, as for a wedding. A priest, his black cassock flapping in the wind, was coming down the stairs. A little farther there was a shopping gallery, a favorite haunt of high school girls or slightly older sales girls, but Boris didn't slow down, and Max, who was waiting to hear about the funniest thing, didn't want to call it to his attention.

"The funniest thing," he resumed at last, "those fucking whores: making love to a cripple like me makes them feel like a saint!"

It was the first time Boris had pronounced that word, "cripple," in front of Max, or said anything about the shape of his body. For the first time he had lifted a corner of the pall which must have hidden his suffering. Max remained silent, looking the other way, at the garishly lit shop windows and the fashionable mannequins beckoning them with gestures full of frozen *joie-de-vivre*. At length Boris said: "Lady Luck, you see, at least deals with me squarely."

*

Before his second divorce Max used to stand in front of his house, on the far end of the driveway, with a justified pride. Larchmont, Belmont, Altamont... To be sure, such places cannot and will never replace Castelar: no English word could bring up in Max's mind so many mysteriously romantic castles. But Max liked to think that even so, his grass was greener, his lawn was better manicured than Uncle Chaim's, and the car in his garage superior to that dreamboat

62

in which he and his cousin Boris used to cruise.

Often, though, he found Jennifer in some fundamental ways as unintelligible as Sharon. Specifically, sex for them seemed uncomplicated. Well, perhaps that's not fair; let's try to be more careful: sex for them seemed to have a softer smell, not the smell of burnt powder inside an empty bottle. And when Max gave Jennifer a bottle of real cheap violets-and-musk perfume, hoping she'd wear it to bed, she did nothing of the sort, but after a single sniff looked at him with a mixture of repugnance and puzzlement.

Boris too moved to the U.S., he too married an American girl, a nurse, and established a prosperous gynecological practice somewhere near Los Angeles. All this Max knew through letters from his mother. She also wrote when Boris and his nurse had a baby girl: two years later she wrote that the unfortunate child had apparently inherited her father's crippling malady, only worse.

When Jennifer's professional association happened to have its annual convention in Anaheim, near Los Angeles, Max went with her and looked up Boris in the phone book. A feminine voice answered the phone, but Max couldn't bring himself to ask Boris who it was, for fear of having to ask about his poor misshapen daughter. He need not have worried: Boris didn't inquire about Max's wife either. As a matter of fact, their conversation could have been the same, word by word, twenty-five years before, when they were still boys in Buenos Aires.

"Max!" Boris exclaimed, "what a coincidence! I was just thinking of you."

"You were?" asked Max, dubiously.

"I was just examining a vulvar fibrous tumor, and it reminded me of your chops."

63

As it turned out, Boris' own professional convention was starting the next day in New Orleans, so they weren't able to meet. Two months later Boris called Max. He was going to Reno on a gambling trip: would Max like to go along. Max reminded Boris that gambling had never interested him.

"You don't have to gamble," Boris said, "they have some of the world's very best brothels over there."

Max demurred, adduced some important commitments, but at last agreed to go.

Boris was shorter, and his gait more disastrous than Max remembered. It was embarrassing how far down Max had to bend when, in the hotel lobby, they kissed each other on the cheek, as they used to do as boys. Max sported a beard then, a Vandyke, impeccably trimmed. Right there in the lobby, pointing at Max's nose, Boris almost shouted: "What indecency! At least you ought to wear underpants!"

It was five o'clock, and they sat at the bar and asked each other about their relatives. Boris told Max Uncle Chaim had invested most of his fortune in the U.S., under Boris' management. Max asked Boris did he remember that night in Castelar when he had "wised up" his younger cousins, told them "the facts of life." He did, and also vividly remembered how terribly pale Max had become. "It was as if suddenly an abyss had opened at your feet, full of hissing snakes."

And how about that scene with his parents in bed, asked Max, did he remember that? Boris, who was sitting at the barstool, turned around, and shaking his head and legs, in a perfect reproduction of that same gesture thirty years before, he blurted out: "Fuck me, Chaimele, tear me apart!"

They had quite a few drinks, reminiscing. Later,

while they were having dinner, they talked about Grandma, who had died the previous year, at ninety-three, senile and institutionalized. Boris knew more than Max about the Bobeh's last years. She was incontinent, and used to spend hours playing with her excrement, fashioning it into diverse shapes, chiefly into patty cakes, and offering it to her visitors pretending it was *gefilte fish*.

Max found in this a kind of poetic justice, remembering that the Bobeh used to call Aunt Porota a *farshtinkeneh*. He told his cousin about Grandma's theory, that Aunt Porota was responsible for Boris' disease, because she didn't change his diapers often enough, and let him lie in his shit. Max immediately regretted having said it, for Boris didn't laugh, but remained for a longish moment in silence, looking at his plate.

After dinner, Boris left for the casino, and Max for the brothel.

Max didn't know if Boris was in his room when he came back, at about midnight. They had contiguous rooms, communicating by an inner door, but Max was too distraught to knock. He locked himself in his room, pulled his pants down, and went over his penis carefully. No obvious signs of disease, not yet, anyway; only a fusty smell. He stood under the hot shower for a while, and washed himself thoroughly with lots of soap.

Without much faith in the prophylactic value of such ablutions, and becoming more and more panicky, Max looked around for something stronger. He considered burning his penis with a flame, like a modern-day Mucius Scaevola, but didn't dare. Finally, he drenched it in after-shave.

Then it was his lips and tongue that started to burn:

65

his tongue, with which he had licked... oh God, how could he, how could he? How was he going to kiss Jennifer, back home? He got up and went to the bathroom, brushed his teeth, then vomited into the sink. All night he had terrible nightmares of being pushed into a ditch where a terrible scorpion lurked.

When he awoke it was late in the morning. He opened the curtains and the window, walked about the room, trying to decide whether to fly back to New York that afternoon, or stay with his cousin, as planned, for two more days. A breeze brought the smell of freshly brewed coffee. He was hungry. If he stayed, he could pay another visit to the brothel. Or perhaps there was another, better brothel.

In the midst of those cogitations he noticed a piece of paper on the carpeted floor, near the connecting door. It was the following letter:

"Dear Max: Don't worry. Except for answering the inevitable questions from the police, you don't have to do anything. You don't even have to call my wife or my father, if you don't feel like it. I've already taken care of that: I've mailed a letter to each. Between us, I've screwed them both real good. I've managed to lose a lot of money — yes, all of mine and most of the old bastard's money too. In this situation, you will understand, it's no use trying to go on with the farce."

"Meanwhile you live it up, and go for twat for as long as you can."

"One last thing: it wasn't like Grandma said. My mother had absolutely nothing to do with this. It was Lady Luck who made me what I am, and it is Lady Luck who kills me now. Good-bye. Boris."

The inner door was unlocked. Boris was lying on his

bed, already cold, like a grotesque puppet. There was an empty medicine bottle on the night table. The air was heavy and quiet, and in Max's mind, absurdly, the words kept echoing: "Fuck me, Chaimele, tear me apart!," as if they'd bring his cousin back to life, as if they could make him shake his head and stunted limbs again.

6

Early each morning, from Mother's balcony, Max surveys the low flat roofs around: under the gentle light they seem eroticized. A clothesline harking, through its cargo of garments, back to those masterpieces of degenerate art: Gloria's panties and Pancracia's culottes, where often, having smoked the forbidden cigarette, he would bury his face. A cement water tank, resting on a pair of props, leaking, either cracked or too full, with that humorous, Kleesque, J-shaped vent on top. A squeegee, long handle leaning against a lime-washed wall, awaiting the doubtless feminine hand, the perhaps beautiful hand meanwhile occupied in other chores, indoors...

At noon he goes out. He walks the streets, roams old neighborhoods, rummages in the second-hand book stores; midnight finds him sitting at a café, reading, scribbling, watching people. Spring lingers, the oppressive Buenos Aires summer heat has not set in, night descends on the city like a spread of dense, heady liqueur.

He stands on the sidewalk, facing Uncle Chaim's old flat, glad to find that part of the city not deteriorated like so much of the rest: the trees, the buildings, the neighborhood, seem as elegant and well-kept as forty years back. The balcony where Chaim held court, and where Marisol once gave an unforgettable performance of hula-hoop... The steady concentration on her face, a little like Aunt Porota dancing cha-cha by herself, yet essentially different. Marisol was only twelve, Max's age, and Aunt Porota was a fully grown woman, but the real difference between them was religious. There was a kind of gratefulness in the aunt's ecstasy, which she seemed happy to share, directed to the spirits that were inspiring her. Marisol's ecstasy was astronomically distant, akin to awe, perhaps of her own lithe, pubescent body, especially of her swaying lower parts, her hips surrounded by the hula-hoop like a shimmeringly haloed presence.

It was a minor halo. On Chaim himself was invested most of the available sacredness, the gold of Mother's adoration and the blue of Father's gaze, Onofrio's timidly admiring gaze, like that of a male animal offering his unprotected belly to the mercy of the dominant beast. Up on this same balcony Max once hid behind a large pot and eavesdropped on Mrs. Krocus and her brother. A plant with a profusion of huge cordate leaves grew out of the pot; beyond, the cane chairs on which Mother and Uncle Chaim were sitting, their backs to Max, and still beyond, the night sky, like a Limoges enamel framed and cloisonné by the elegant mid-rise apartment buildings. Mrs. Krocus spoke in the low, pained tones of a suppliant. "Ten thousand, that's all he needs to get us out of this jam."

"Ten thousand, that's all he needs?" said Uncle

69

Chaim. "And next week it'll be another ten thousand, and next month it'll be fifty thousand." He repeated in slow, snickering motion, "That's... all... he... needs."

"But Chaim, listen to me..." said Mrs. Krocus.

"No, you listen to me," said Chaim. "What will I solve by giving you ten thousand? Onofrio is bottomless, am I not right? No, wait, answer me, he's bottomless, am I not right?"

Mrs. Krocus was silent. Max could see his mother's left cheek, her beauty spot with the carefully groomed lock of hair, and Uncle Chaim's seigneurial, poetic hand, suspended in the air as if waiting for an answer.

"How Onofrio squanders his money is none of my business," Chaim resumed, "but let me repeat what I've always told you: you deserved a better husband. No, I'm not going to give you the ten thousand, and tell him to please stop sending you out with the hat: let him do his own begging."

"All right, Chaim, thank you anyway," Mrs. Krocus got up and left the balcony. For the rest of the evening she kept a dignified, funereal aloofness. Onofrio, on the contrary, cracked jokes with Chaim; they laughed together and slapped each other on the back.

Max walks away from under Uncle Chaim's old balcony wondering about the power of a single gesture or a single word. The airy, dismissing wave of his father's seigneurial hand might have been what made Boris what he was: a tormented chameleon, a misshapen buffoon; Aunt Porota's laziness and the *dreck* in which baby Boris was left to kick and cry had nothing to do with it, nor, in spite of all scientific evidence, had Lady Luck's cruel, genetic impartiality.

Often, reflecting on his having never (to his knowledge) fathered a child, he has felt relief: children, someone said, are hostages given to destiny. And words? How can he want to publish poems when words, like worms, planted at the right moment in a tender mind like Gloria's, can cause a lifetime of unhappiness? Still, how much better he would feel right now, how much more justified before himself and the world, with a book of poems out! Oh, just a little chapbook! He sits on the grass, between the spreading roots of the centenary *ombú* in Plaza Francia. Downslope, by a bush, the statue of Saint Martin of Tours. Looking like a medieval polo player, the patron saint of the city of Buenos Aires, sword in hand, is about to cut a piece of his cloak to clothe the naked beggar standing by his side in adoring expectation. An allegory of Buenos Aires, the pariah Paris of South America, getting a chunk of culture from knightly France.

Ah, *mon Dieu*! Allegory can wait. Max shuffles down the grassy slope.

Unapproachable majesty, impeccable to the smallest detail... That silky perfection, that rare perfume, directly, he could swear, from the rue St. Honoré...

Should he?

Very rarely has he aimed so high... But why not? As long as there is hope, no harm in trying. Follow her on your knees... Beg for a piece of her cloak...

"Madam, I'm lost: would you be so kind as to direct me to the palace of the Apostolic Nuncio?"

"Madam, please... Look, I'm a poet; consent to be my muse a brief moment, only for a sonnet! *Madame, voici mon coeur, qui ne bat que pour vous!*"

She doesn't look at him. She walks erect, arms crossed upon her breast, not a single twitch of acknowledgment.

He doesn't exist for her.

71

Dejected, he crawls back up the grassy slope. What's behind such arrogance? Women in Buenos Aires believe they carry a treasure under their skirt; they haven't heard that the phallus is the only original signifier. Or is it pride in their own virtue, that in spite of the economic disaster they have so far abstained from prostitution? Rather, it's the typical arrogant style of off-duty whores: this broad, deaf to poetry, may have been on her way to her job at a high-class bordello. He lies down next to the *ombú*, and, propped on his elbow, takes another look at the patron saint. Maybe the beggar is Onofrio, and the one on horseback is Uncle Chaim?

"*El viejo hijo de puta*": those were Boris' words, two years ago, the night he put an end to his own life. Yet, ironically, Boris couldn't have gauged how much of a son of a whore Chaim, his father, was. Had he, he might be still alive. For the money Boris gambled away, which was held in a joint account in the U.S. — a life's savings, Chaim had impressed on him — turned out to be a tiny fraction of Chaim's worth. There were other foreign accounts, unknown to Boris, in Switzerland, in London, in Lichtenstein... The day before yesterday, when Mrs. Krocus told him this, Max almost choked with anger. But, using the same word and the same old argument of her brother on the balcony, Mrs. Krocus said, "What could he have done? Had Chaim told him the truth, or given him more, Boris would have gambled away his father's entire fortune. Boris was bottomless, and you know it."

Bottomless. Boris was bottomless. Onofrio was bottomless. And isn't Max bottomless too? Inside him there seems to be a pit — deep, dormant waters — where all forgotten, unassuaged desires, ever since birth and perhaps from before, rot and ferment: each woman who walks by hoists a terrible bucketful. Objects too — faucets, clothes-lines, squeegees, the arabesqued grates on the cellar vents of old houses — squeeze out of the bottomless pit, distilled by absence and concentrated by exile, drops that are an acid for the soul.

Bottomless. And how could one *not* be bottomless? Only if one could find a bottom, a ground where roots can spread into the mud. The sunlight pours down through the foliage and there's a smell of freshly cut grass, edged with whiffs of expensive perfume. The country crumbles, the economy is in disarray, people starve. Supermarkets are looted, public statues uprooted and stolen for their bronze, nervous crowds stand for hours every day on San Martín Street watching on the boards the exponential increase of the dollar exchange rate. Yet here in Plaza Francia, Max can lie on the grass and forget all: the facades and mansards of the *petit-hôtels* look as noble as ever, the fashionable boutiques show the *dernier cri* from the best couturiers, along with tasteful announcements of art exhibits, just like in Paris. A fiacre goes by, driver top-hatted, horse lustrous, lanterns polished, the oval *oeil-de-boeuf* in the rear, so eloquently romantic.

Max walks down the slope toward the Museo Nacional de Bellas Artes with the vague idea of going in to look at the paintings. But he doesn't feel like looking at paintings. What he really wants is to bite into a piece of meat. Remembering the hero of Cortázar's *Hopscotch*, who, first thing on disembarking from Paris, goes to a riverside grill to gorge on beef, he thinks of devouring a thick, juicy steak.

Yet he isn't *physically* hungry. Spiritually, yes: he feels a kind of righteous hunger for low things, for vengeance and for grease.

He walks down Pueyrredón Avenue. Maybe he'll go into a grill, if he finds one, and bite into a *chorizo*, away from Paris and into yummy reality. Max stops before an antiquarian's window — old cigarette cases, fountain pens, chess sets, microscopes, cameras. On an impulse he goes in. Disoriented for a moment by the variety and abundance of objects whose use and name he forgot or never knew, he suddenly sees under a glass, inside a counter, the thing he has been looking for: a small revolver.

The woman who shows it to him has East Asian features. The stock is of mother-of-pearl and the barrel is inscribed with Russian characters. A jewel, a real jewel which might have originally belonged to some Imperial Princess of the House of Romanov, and he can have it for the equivalent of only forty dollars. "Does it work?" he asks.

"Sure it works," says the woman.

"Do you sell bullets?"

"Soon-Bok!" cries the woman, making the Chinese chimes tinkle in sympathy and the Mongolian drums resound, "Soon-Bok, do we sell bullets for this?"

For forty-five dollars Max gets a fully loaded revolver. He goes back into the sun-splashed street holding a gun for the first time in his life, safely inside his pocket. "Just what I need, small but lethal," he smiles to himself. "My Heftpistole, my very own Heftpistole," he repeats under his breath with pleasure, even though the thing is clearly a revolver not a pistol, and even though he's quite sure the German word means something like a stapler. But the sound is just right, grave, heavy with resonance.

74

7

He hops into a number 92 bus, which happens to be empty and which goes (it says so along the top) to La Matanza. That's where his father is buried. Max sits right behind the driver and watches him with fascination while he drives and arranges money bills into neat piles: pink, blue, yellowish bits of paper, crumbling under the finger, greasy, worthless as soon as printed. Ten cents of a dollar is the current value of the highest denomination, yet this grown-up man, perfectly serious, perfectly congruous, mustached, probably married and a father, flattens them carefully, piles them up, lays a metal weight on top so they won't scatter... Max feels like a conquistador or an anthropologist, getting the savages to do what he wants for a fistful of beads.

At Parque Centenario the afternoon sun gilds the tiles of the Museum of Natural History and a few people climb on to the bus. The driver cuts multicolored tickets and gets polychrome bills, like in a children's game. A woman who sits across the aisle, hook-nosed, dishevelled, mouth loosened by lust, fat or frustration, and a first-corporal in the Federal Police who takes his stand right at the driver's side. Max is quite proud of being able to tell, after so many years away, the rank of any member of the Argentine Army, Navy, Air Force, Coast Guard, Gendarmerie, Federal or Provincial Police, by a cursory look at their insignia. Thus, throughout the long exile, he still held on to something of the essence of the country. The guardian of the law puts an arm across the back of the driver's seat, and, knee bent, his booted left foot on the lower footboard. His dark-blue back is right before Max's face. The cop doffs his cap and, holding it by the visor, runs three fingers over his gummy hair and scurfy scalp. Max tries to avoid breathing the dandruff. Then, in search of a better position, the cop moves his service weapon and its leather case to the front, between his legs. Colt '38? 45? Smith and Wesson? Sadly, Max realizes that he doesn't really have much of a hold on the essence of this country. But the Heftpistole in his pocket is a great comfort.

Partido de La Matanza is where he's headed for. Killing Fields County. So named, apparently, because four hundred years ago the country's fathers, mindful of our future appetites, killed in it a whole nation of Indians to make room for cattle. There, at the remotest corner by the lee of the back wall of the Jewish cemetery, lies Onofrio. Max saw the tomb twenty years ago, when it was still new.

Plaza Flores, Rivadavia Avenue, where he and Boris used to cruise in search of idle shop girls. More than once they had to make do with female factory workers, or even lower: house maids.

But Max suspects his father is hiding under the polished black marble of that tomb, biding his time, waiting for his numerous creditors to drop dead, especially waiting for

76

Mother to drop dead too and hoping that she won't be buried on top of him, which would hinder his plans. Then, after so many years, he'll step out sharp, refreshed, reeking of aftershave, looking like the photograph affixed to his gravestone: bushy mustache, wide smile of a bonvivant, three-piece suit, slicked-down hair and wide-rimmed spectacles *à la* Chilean President Allende. Max doesn't know if there'll be stunned sentries with lance and lorica lying by the tomb, and strewn chrysanthemums, as in depictions of the Rising of Christ, but he'll come out, Max is willing to bet, ravenously hungry and wielding his erection as a banner. Down there food is scarce, and as for ass... Max has never been convinced that his father is dead, really dead and forever. Impossible. Father's absence is a most powerful argument for a belief in an afterlife. Father will rise from the tomb and roam the city just as Max is doing now. But what if Father is waiting for *him* to die — Max his son, his rival, his critic — before his triumphal resurrection?

Abruptly, Max turns his head towards the woman across the aisle and catches her looking at him, which gives him no little satisfaction.

When he looks out the window the street has changed. Houses are old, built low. Men in torn undershirts sit on stools on the sidewalk, drinking maté. A pubescent girl crouches on a doorstep, offering herself, if only in thought, to some North-American rock star while a stray cat, fresh from bloody battles atop the roofs, comes and goes, voluptuously rubbing itself against her tender thighs, the raised tail a black question mark against her panties. The side streets are unpaved, cow-padded, burdocked, with here and there a tiny white flower growing from a dung patch. A couple of men on horseback, dressed as gauchos. "NO TO

77

UNEMPLOYMENT AND HUNGER" in big white and blue letters painted on a wall, meaning *"we say 'no'* to unemployment and hunger," as if unemployment and hunger were two devils which must be exorcised, or as if the wealth of the country hung upon a speech-act. And, like a medieval devotional fresco, a mural painting on a dilapidated house: "SPIRITUAL CHIEF OF THE NATION." Evita's image, blond angel on a red background.

As the bus stops at a corner, Max's eye catches the fleeting image of a girl with sweet black braids crossing the street. On a sudden rush of hope and inspiration, he gets out. Right then the traffic light changes, buses and trucks start off, enveloping him in a cloud of black exhaust. He'll have to wait, then run to catch up with the girl.

Meanwhile, what does he have to offer? A choice bit from Rubén? Nonsense: only if he could sing some inane new tune, swaying his hips... "Hey, hey, hey, pretty girl, hey, hey..." only then would he have any hope of success. So what, he'll go down to defeat, but honorably, poetically.

The light turns green, Max crosses the street, turns this way and that, but the girl is gone. He finds himself before a marble statue: "Mataderos a la Madre." The slaughterhouse section to the Mother. Complete with baby in her arms, she looks like a cross between Evita and the Virgin Mary. But her abstract, edifying gesture is not Church style but rather Fascist, Nazi or Stalinesque.

Max sniffs the air: indeed, the slaughterhouse can't be far. More graffiti on dilapidated walls. "Sabina I love you." "María is a whore." Woman, always woman intruding between man and man; always woman with her siren song, seducing him from his duties. He has taken a bus to La Matanza to visit Father's grave. Instead, attracted by a pair

78

of sweet braids, here he is, on Coronel Cárdenas Avenue, only a short walk to the slaughterhouse, as he can tell by the smell. All in all, however, it may have been a smart move. For the slaughterhouse has always been the locus of the essence of the country, the place with the maximum concentration of reality.

"Reality, reality... Easily said, but what do you mean by that?" says a grave, gravelly voice, dear to Max, near Max. By full daylight, his father's specter accosts him, tousles his hair.

"You know what I mean, Dad, don't play the fool. I mean solid, concrete, concussive and conclusive things, no ifs or buts and no kidding yourself. You are what you eat, said Feuerbach." Leaving the bust of the Mother and Child Max starts walking up Calle Tandil.

"Wait, Max! Have you forgotten that the Fuegians didn't perceive Magellan's ships? Having never seen any boats but their own coracles, those bulky caravels were invisible to their aboriginal eyes. And have you forgotten about Hannibal's elephants, and about Dr. Kinbote's cuff links? Above all, have you forgotten about the Relativity Theory and the Quantum Mechanics I taught you? Where does that leave what you just called "reality"? Or have you become a gross, naive materialist, like your mother? I've never put much stock in reality. Come on, buccaneer, visit me... Can't you see that I've been waiting for you? It's horribly lonely, you know, under the sod."

"Father, Father, I will. Be patient. And no, I haven't forgotten your lessons. Funny thing. I just was in Plaza Francia, before your brother-in-law's old place. Remember? Nothing but order and beauty up there, luxury, calm, voluptuousness... Reality? Think of where you are, Father: La

Matanza, the tanneries, the smell of sewers and meat-packing — and think of where he is, in the arms of houris. From him to you: *voilà* reality, at its most precipitously tragic. No, Father, the direct trip would be too much for me, the connection too strong. I'll visit you after I visit the stinking place where cows are killed."

Talking thus with his father's ghost, Max arrives at the main gate of the Municipal Slaughterhouse, where there is a statue of the Drover on horseback, five flagpoles, and the coat of arms of the Republic. The colonial-style facade, the arcades, the balustrades, the five flagpoles, the coat of arms of the Republic, the statue, the commemorative plaques, the jacaranda trees — all that reminds Max of grammar school. And again, for a moment, Max is a boy, a fifth-grade boy in white school duster, in the class of angelic Señorita Arenaz, standing at attention, intoning the ringing strains of the National Anthem. "Harken ye mortals the sacred cry: Liberty, liberty, liberty! Harken ye the noise of burst shackles..."

"Hey macho," says Vergara standing next to him, holding in his hand a photograph, "hey, macho, speaking of burst shackles, how would you like to bust her butt?"

Shaking off that uncouthness Max proceeds south on Avenida Tellier, then turns left on Avenida del Trabajo. By the cattle ramps, four men are milling around, smoking and sipping maté, waiting. Max too decides to wait. What for? He doesn't know. It's impossible to hear what the men are saying; they often spit on the mud. A black cat comes by, arches its back, looks at Max with wary yellow eyes, goes away hugging the wall. A hag shuffles along the sidewalk opposite, cuddling a bloody parcel against her cringing bosom. Crooked-billed birds circle overhead. Clattering,

80

honking, a truck slews around the corner of Murguiondo Street: it's of the stake rack type, with a tinted windshield visor. As it rolls by Max notices brown muzzles and pink nostrils sticking out between the railings. Young muzzles, moist-lipped, with thick, virginal threads of saliva hanging. Calf's eyes, large, placid, with delicate, seductive eye-lashes.

The four men come out, signal the truck to a stop with its back abutting on the entryway. The tailgate goes down; somehow a snag develops. The men run up and down the flanking steps, goading the animals with rods and screaming, "*Hijas de puta! La puta que las parió!*" Two calves emerge in terror and start running down the gored, mud-splattered gangway. The whole truckful then follows with a long, mournful "moo!" and a clatter of slender hooves.

Slowly, sadly, Max walks back the way he came. Avenida del Trabajo, Avenida Tellier. How cruel, how absurd, calling cows and calves whores. Besides, why tongue-lash the victims. Like in the U.S. courts, when, after slapping a life sentence or death by frying on a poor devil, the judge regularly inflicts on him a high-falluting moral sermon on the evils he did. Melancholic and slow, Max finds himself back at the slaughterhouse's main entrance, facing the equestrian statue, the flagpoles and the coat of arms of the Republic. The afternoon sun paints on the colonial-style facade a tawny distemper. The drover, hatted and cloaked in his poncho, seems to have left all hope behind, and gazes at a darkening, indifferent horizon. The bronze horse too seems sad. Some people, real Argentine men, Father for example, although not Uncle Chaim, have eyes like that... The antique gaze toward Jerusalem? No, many *Goyim* too: one would say these men have been exiled... A weaning brash? Is that what ails the cattle driver and his horse? Why

81

do they look so drunk on a heady cocktail of solitude and moos? Should we hypothesize some far-off Rancho Lost? This much is certain: cattle on the hoof lurks behind that sadness. The fact of being a horse, the fact of being a man. Being a man on his horse, cows all around. Those are awesome facts, and it is a terrible privilege, driving cattle, leading them from behind, pushing them to their destiny, shoving them into those gates of doom. Cows, calves and heifers are stupid and don't have a clue about their destiny; they're only able to switch their tails, flutter their eyelashes and carry their own delicious brawn on slender hoofs. But the drover and his horse know where it all stands and where it all must end, and they must bear a heavy rod and an enormous burden of responsibility. "A thinking reed," that is said easily. Reeds are lithe and graceful things, and flexible: they rustle and whistle with the wind. A thinking rod is something else again, the heavy staff of prophets and philosopher-kings.

Max is facing the statue of the Drover when suddenly, some fifty yards down the street, the sweet glint of those braids! He rushes up, his heart at a barbarous gallop, his brain rehearsing: "Señorita! You probably don't know me, but I've met you half an hour ago, on Coronel Cárdenas Avenue, and haven't forgotten you ever since. Will you marry me? Wait! Before you answer: I'm in good health, divorced, I have a Ph.D., and a little stack of dollars to buy us a nice, cozy nest where you can pour maté for me..."

But the sweet braids have dissolved. The *conventillo* whore balancing herself on her heels, Doris in her tight red skirt, Pancracia buffing Father's study floor, angelic Señorita Arenaz, Marisol, aunt Porota... Scores of housemaids, grammar-school teachers, part-time drabs, shop girls, slubbing machine operators, typists, once desired but long forgotten, crowd before his eyes, a mirage, the illusion of a growing herd. He recognizes a few faces; he can distinguish their rumps and legs but not their faces; they trot unsteadily away on muddy patent leather pumps, swaying long horns, milk-white: Isises in search of their Osiris, gadfly-tormented Ios... Moo... Out of the growing herd, a low murmur arises, a sorrowful moo, the adieu of humble goddesses stampeding...

His abdominal muscles twitch, his blood stirs. All of a sudden he feels a crazy urge to rampage through the pampas screaming and shooting.

Drive them! Ram them! Rod, prod, goad, *hijas de puta*!

He's got a painful erection.

8

Section 3, Division 55, Square 172, Grave 69. Out of the main desk, donning a black yarmulka, Max repeats the coordinates of his father's corpse like an incantation, so as not to forget them. It's a long way, if he remembers well, to the place at the southwestern end of the necropolis, past thousands of low and middle-class sepulchers (the well-to-do Argentine Jews rot segregated in a smaller plot, in sweeter-smelling Liniers). "¡Rujl!" "¡Mamá!" "¡Bélbele!" "¡Zeide!" "We will never forget!" "Always in our hearts!" Protestations in bronze. The anguished cry of the quick, carved in the dumb marble of the tombs. On the ledger of a girl dead at age 14: "Celina! We shall always remember you! Your friends and classmates, First Year, Division 1, Lyceum 2." Behind the death-denying rhetoric of that "You" and that "Your," behind the prolix numbers, Max guesses the terror in the souls of three dozen adolescent girls, their secret conviction that Celina went on a long voyage and that their polished, laurel-wreathed metal plaque was just like a hair barrette or a bracelet, a beautiful, fashionable gift, only more solemn and expensive. An invitation to a dancing party, sweet fifteen, on bronze not paper. But did Homer, Dante or Shakespeare do any better? Black palace of eternal night... Can anyone do better than use the ridiculously inappropiate language of life to try speaking to the dead?

Max recalls Mother referring to Aunt Porota: "croaked, kicked the bucket." Chaim preferred subtler expressions like "Joined the silent majority," which is blatantly false, for there are more people living now on this planet than the sum total of all the ones who've died. A fact that's called, by definition, exponential growth, and just going by Statistics, an argument could be made out of it that we're immortal, since more then 50% of us haven't died yet (and as for the minority who have, that may be because they were born too early to benefit from the recent miracles of Science). Frightening thought. Section 3, Division 55, Square 172, Grave 69. Now the Church taught that Christ had descended to Hell to save some of those who had croaked too early to be helped by Her sacraments: will Science do the same, show equal charity? Will She return to life some of these carcasses? Which? The ones who could solve, in their prime, Schrödinger equations? Or will Her divine justice summon peer committees and choose according to lists of publications? A group of people standing around a freshly dug grave, a bearded cantor mutters Hebrew prayers, the women weep. What a miserable thing to be buried among women howling. Drunkards carousing is what Max wishes for, drunkards and whores. A newly opened section, the tombs yet unmonumented, unmarbled, a stench rises from the ground. $C15H14N2$, pentamethylenediamine. By a little twisting of the molecule, soon someone will come up with a drug which injected right after death will make corpses smell like fresh linen.

This sea of tombs is like the top of an iceberg: what goes on underneath? Underneath no coordinates, no numbers. The dead have no zip-codes. Section 3, Division 55, Square 172, Grave 69 is only for the quick. We depend on ledgers, records, sum totals, the kind of thing that made Father miserable during his life time, and perhaps he's happier down there, in the realm where accounts don't have to square, with crowds of unchaperoned women of all ages, all styles, all dispositions. The dead, though, are beyond sex... Who's to say? Rosso Fiorentino painted Pluto and Proserpine french-kissing... Max is lost. He has arrived at Section 3, Division 55, but cannot find Square 172. He approaches two workers, gives each a fistful of colorful bank notes, and they dilligently take him to Square 172, Grave 69, just ten meters from where he was. And *le voilà*, Onofrio Krocus, 1912-1969, a bunch of Hebrew characters carved and gilded on black marble, a photo.

"I bring you this vase, Señor," says one of the men, grabbing a tin flowerpot from a tomb nearby, throwing away the old, dry flowers in it, and setting it on Onofrio's ledger.

"And here, some flowers too," says the other man, pilfering some fresh gladioli from another location.

"Let us wipe the marble, Señor... Do you want the letters repainted?" they say almost in unison.

Max sends them away with another fistful of worthless paper, and the two leave bowing and swearing that Grave 69 is their favorite charge, their model tomb, that from now on it will sparkle and overflow with the choicest blooms. Max sits on the ledger and looks around. Over the curve of the wall (bare brick, no romantic ivy, glass shards on top), a railroad signal arm declares the way is free. Not for passenger trains, though: this track starts from La Tablada, right by the Cementerio Israelita, to end at the slaughter-house. Exclusively for death-bound cattle.

"What's the matter, scalawag, you don't like my neighborhood?"

"On the contrary, Dad: you and your neighbors get a privileged view, from below, of cattle being carried to slaughter. The underside of their hooves."

"Oh, cows, cows... As much as anyone, I used to enjoy a good barbecue. Now, see, the cattle feed on me. Or rather fed, to be truthful, for there's too little left of me to feed on now. But you come, if I understood correctly, from the old dwelling of my ex-brother-in-law? How is he doing? Above the ground or under it? Feeding on cattle or being fed upon? Ah, the vile, dandyfied toad! For, you must know, he was my nemesis, my wrecker, and the immediate cause of my undoing."

"But Dad, I thought you died in a car crash..."

"True, but listen how. I needed five hundred thou-sand pesos in a hurry to make good three bad checks; no other way to get the money; so I go to him, explain the situ-ation, promise to repay, but he says no, not even a thousand in his wallet, no cash flow... bullshit, of course. What was five hundred thousand pesos to him? Nothing. But, see, to me it was all. Max, you know that Buddhist thinkers, Neoplatonic philosophers, Deschamps who was a French Benedictine monk, and the arduous disciples of Hegel, among others, preached an identity between Nothing and the All. Which, I don't dispute it, may well be true from a strictly metaphysical point of view. From a financial point of

87

view, however, there is a world of difference, and for me, strapped for money as I happened to be, those five hundred thousand pesos represented the only possibility of salvation. I was too old, buccaneer, to spend another spell in jail, and that's where I was headed for sure, unless I could come up with the dough. That's where things had come to. The next day, coming back from Lobos, where I used to go once a month to collect moneys owed me and to visit some customers, I'm worried, distraught, all the time asking myself, 'What for? What's the whole purpose? In a week the lid will have blown up out of the pot and I'll be sleeping in jail...' when suddenly I realize I'm passing a truck, and there's another truck coming at me full speed on that narrow, two-lane route 205. I can avoid it, I can step on the gas, get ahead of the truck at my side in no time: the Torino Gran Turismo I'm driving has 400 horsepower — you should have seen it, you should have driven it, it was a terrific car. But in that split-second decision, with my foot ready on the gas, when all I have to do is to press hard, those What-fors? and To-what-purposes? and the smell of jail all creep into my mind, clouding my judgment, and so my foot goes limp and listless. Horrible, Max, horrible, most horrible."

"What you say doesn't surprise me, Father. I suspected as much, especially since Boris, Chaim's son and my cousin, killed himself two years ago, in Reno, because of my uncle's avarice."

"Poor Boris, so young... well, not really much younger than I when I died... Tell me, Max, what does Chaim think, that he can carry his wads down here with him? Let me disabuse him: he cannot. No legal tender rules, no coinage circulates amongst us. But tell me too: does your mother live? Does she still idolize Chaim the way she used to, something that caused me, when alive, keen suffering? Is he still the pupil of her eye, the model and mirror of all manhood? Tell me the truth, guttersnipe, don't blunt or soften it."

"Truth is, Dad, she does, he is."

"Smiling beast, sweet-lotioned villain! Max, you must swear you will avenge me on my ex-brother-in-law, for who else is to do it if not you, my true son? As for your mother, spare her, I don't want you to give her a rough time, she has already suffered much. But Chaim, ah, Chaim! On him you must avenge me, Max."

"See, Father, this is the Heftpistole I bought just for the purpose. Here, I lay it for a minute on your tomb, so you can feel its loaded, fatal weight, and so I take an oath: I'll seek revenge! From now on, my thoughts be bloody, or I'm not your son!"

"You are, you are my true and only son, clapperdudgeon, and I know you'll take good care of your mother, of your sister Gloria, and of my just revenge, like a gentleman."

"I will. But now you tell me something, Dad, which I've been meaning to ask you. Mother says you were a philanderer, that you lavished your money on other women, which was why you were always broke. Chaim too (I heard him say so myself) told Mother she deserved a better husband, because of your multifarious love affairs. These pebbles I see here, strewn on your tomb, make me suspect that Malvina, your late lover, the woman who cried on Mother's shoulder when you died, may have been here periodically. Perhaps other women too, who've kept, throughout the years, a sweeter, gentler memory of you than Mother has. Tell me, Dad, is there any substance to those rumors? Or are they just the flatulence of jealousy and ill-will? I'd like to know, Dad. Dad, you've become silent. Are you still there? Dad, dad..."

9

"Hello, come, sit down," she says, waving expansively toward the empty chair.

She tells him her name is Gaby, obviously a *nom de guerre*. She smiles, showing solid teeth, Pancracia's cheek bones and flat nose, Doris' smile, the swarthy complexion of the *conventillo* whore: nice combination.

"And what are you doing," she asks, "just hanging around?"

"Hanging around," Max shrugs.

For close to an hour, before making his move, Max was sitting next to a mirror, watching. Gaby, as it turned out. The other unattached whore, sitting at the opposite end, by a window: plump arms, haughty poitrine, hair dyed yellow-green. The two coupled whores, each with her john. From his vantage point, these look prettier, less pathetic, than the solitary two: the market's invisible testicles keep only the least attractive whores in circulation. First john: fortyish, bearlike, obviously enjoys caressing his whore's arm and telling her earnest and confidential things, perhaps about his business problems or about his wife's lack of understanding; when the waiter brought the whisky, they clinked their glasses and drank to what seemed nothing less than a long life of domestic happiness. The second john is in his sixties and talks quietly to a whore who cannot be a day over fifteen. Then there is Max. Is he too a dirty old man, the third one, *Jean le voyeur*, sitting and watching? *Pas du tout, Madame.* He's doing it for art's sake. He figures he's at a Parisian café, Le Dôme, Flore, La Rotonde or La Coupole, like so many artists of this or the last century, like so many poets and writers, or at the more up-to-date Royal-Jussieu or Saint-André, gathering material for a poem. The whores? Kiki, or Bijou of Montparnasse. To those who maintain that whoremongery is a disorder having to do with low self-esteem or oppressive social conditions, to bloody Puritans who, bowing to Mars rather than Venus, believe that women ought to fly fighter planes rather than sell blow jobs — to all those one must reply that it would be impossible to imagine the history of art or, indeed, of civilization, without the distilled products of whoredom. In fact, whoreless theologies are Calvinistic wastelands: leaving out the Ten-thousand Virgins, more than half of the Catholic Church female saints had been prostitutes. Max took a piece of paper out of his pocket and his pen, made some notes. La Negra, or swarthy one (Gaby, as it turned out). The big-breasted one. He drew arrows in between those words. Both women kept throwing quick glances at him which he surprised on the mirrors, and they smiled when he looked back at them. Apparently they thought he had potential as a customer. La Negra. Big-boobs. A heart around, an arrow. Big-boobs, La Negra.

He felt desired, he felt good. He knew, of course, that the whores were after his money. So what's wrong with that. Why insist on making love instead of buying it ready-made? There was a time, in his youth, when Max approached a whore as a sinner approached Our Lady in a medieval miracle play, with trepidation, amid petards. Now Max can sit at this versaillesque salon, sip coffee, relax and be the women's cynosure, like a pretty baby doted on. Who knows, the two prostitutes may have found him more attractive than the run-of-the-mill, middle-aged john. And, anyway, being the focus of amorous attention, like a huge phallus growing at the center of the mirrored salon... Far from Max to claim any understanding whatsoever of Lacan's *Stade du Miroir* (leave that to his sister), or the post-structuralist inextricable galleries of mirrors, but being looked at so solicitously by Big-boobs and la Negra, by la Negra and Big-boobs... Ah! And between those two, sharp glances of jealous, competitive ill will flying back and forth... Max felt blessed among women, Max, the unworthy fruit of Mrs. Krocus' old womb!

But choose he had to. He was forced to decide because their interest in him, keen at the start, was wearing thin, as is natural. Piety explains why Max went for la Negra, a.k.a. Gaby: even though his cousin Boris is no more, he'd have appreciated Big-boobs, and Max offered her to his cousin in a sacrificial gesture, as one offered the largest fruits to the ancient gods.

Gaby tells him she's from Salta. Salta is a yoke-shaped province in Northwestern Argentina.

"Yes, you kind of look from Salta," Max scrutinizes her.

She smiles. "You like women from Salta?"

Her dark complexion could have hailed from any of

many northern provinces — Chaco, Jujuy, Tucumán, Santiago... But there is something in her thick skin that suggests Salta, a thickness apt to protect her against the insects of the Amazonic jungle. And there's still something else in her skin that points to Salta and its metallic mountains: golden, red and green beetle-like reflections, reminiscent of Darwin's observations on the coleopteron, the insect that's attracted by the oversize Hymenophallus. There's something coleopterous even in her small eyes, golden, grabbing and astute, eyes that belong in the night of Salta's mountains and jungles, rather than in a bar of downtown Buenos Aires...

"I don't know," says Max, "I've never been to Salta." He could have told her, "Oh, yes, I love women from Salta," but Max is basically a truthful man.

"You don't travel much?" She seems intent in starting a regular conversation, but Max isn't inclined to help, and why should he. She's the one who has been sitting, waiting for hours sipping soft drinks, like a swamp flower waiting for an insect; she's the one who is supposed to spread her fragrance in the air to attract the man, to seduce him, and then to open up her petals and her innermost stamens to his sting. For a fee, of course.

"I never moved from Buenos Aires," says Max. He doesn't want her to suspect that he comes from the U.S. and carries dollars in his wallet.

"You married?" she asks, and then tells that she has been married too and has a child up in Salta, a real little angel, but her husband left her one day, just like that, he disappeared, and no, he never sent any money for the boy's support, are you kidding, and he was a terrible loser anyway, good riddance, besides he was a drunkard, but the dear little angel is still in Salta, with her parents, yes, she misses him, what do you think, very much so, and she's the one who sends them money every month, rain or shine, for the boy's support, but the old folks have no inkling of how she earns it, they think she has a regular job, poor souls, as well she might, for you mustn't suppose that she's like most girls in her line of work, who can hardly read and write and have no converse with polite society, no, believe it or not she's a cultured girl, she has even started on a university career, and would have finished it except that she has to support her little angel in Salta.

"Oh yeah?" Max interjects, "what university career?"

"Midwife," she says.

"Midwife." Max nods and struggles to remain serious. Phaenarete, mother of Socrates, maieutics. "You would have made a first-rate midwife."

The waiter is standing there, waiting for Max to order. Max was drinking coffee at his previous location, but moving to another table starts the whole process anew. Max looks the waiter in the eye, searching for a spark of derision: he has witnessed Max's fall, his moving from drinking coffee in noble isolation on his marble-topped *guéridon*, observing and taking notes, to sin and a whore's table. Max looks into the waiter's eyes, in an effort to witness his witnessing, but finds brown boredom and absolute indifference. Good waiter. He also serves who only stands, waits and doesn't give a damn. Max orders a ginger-ale.

"And so I moved to Buenos Aires," Gaby-la Negra goes on, "and to support my little angel, I worked as a housemaid."

"You did!" From midwife to housemaid to whore: now she's talking! An interesting development indeed, making la Negra look a lot more enticing and domestic.

94

"In the first house I worked there were two teen-age boys, and between them and their horny father, I couldn't sleep at all. Night and day one or the other would sneak into my room and expect to be serviced. The creeps. Until one day, right when the old goat was in my bed..."

"Don't tell me," Max interrupts, all excited. "One of the sons came in."

An image of himself as a boy going into Pancracia's room and finding Father in her bed. Does such a scene have any basis in reality, or is it one of those memories hovering between fact and dream, or one of those dreams which, because so often repeated, finally acquire the consistency of fact? Don Onofrio's life can only be explained in terms of quantum mechanics. You could never say for sure that he was entirely here or there, at this or that time, a member of a particular family, but was always a messy superposition of several locations and of many masks. Even as a ghost Onofrio turned out to be quite slippery. Max's recent fascination with the idea of his father's dead body lying on top of the dining-room table can be seen in this light to be entirely scientific and to have nothing to do with vague Freudian constructs like the Oedipus complex. It is rigorous Physics. For finally the indeterminacy collapsed, and it was decided once and for all that Onofrio was right there, that he was that lump of matter on top of that table, at that particular time. Father was thus reduced to Classical Mechanics.

And a good thing too. For God doesn't like to play dice, being subtle but not malicious, says Einstein, and in difficult matters one must believe the experts. What is most remarkable about these insights into God's and Max's minds is that they came to him while in the company of a whore. Why should that be? Because whores are closer to the ori-

95

gins, much more so than midwives. Closer to the land when there was nothing, no cities, no trees, no horses, no cows. Pythias of remote origins, victims made into monsters, their job is to slither into and clog our brain pipes so that the whole repulsive mess up there backs up and settles, unglorified, before us.

"No, his wife," says la negra.

"His wife?" says Max.

"His wife came in, and saw us. We were lying on my bed, naked, all sweaty; she barges in, and you know what? This you won't believe. She looks past us, through us, as if we were transparent, made of air, fumbles around, leaves, and never says a word. I'm telling you, they were creeps."

"You mean they didn't fire you?"

"No, that was later. The day she fired me," says la Negra, gnawing on a lemon wedge that came with her diet cola, "it was because she found some hair in the soup. What could I do, I've always had lots of hair, like now, long, and by the way: do you like it? Beautiful, isn't it? But she was convinced it was hair from my crotch not from my head. She was convinced I was laying some hocus-pocus on her men, can you believe it, when all I wanted was to shake those three oafs off my bed. She was screaming, and it was pea soup I had made. I told her to shove it and poured the whole hot kit and caboodle on top of her head."

"Wow," says Max, "good for you!"

"Yeah, I'm not one to take such things lying down, no sir. Anyway then I went to work in a hotel. Thirteen rooms I had to make up every day, all by myself, plus wash all the linen by hand. Ah, what a son of a whore that owner was. Always making passes at me, the fat disgusting pig."

"I don't blame him, you're too attractive," Max butts

in.

"One day I was at the tub, washing the linen, when I feel my skirt going up and something pushing right into my ass. I turned around, and there he was, my boss, cock in hand and a smirk on his fat lips. I tell you, I let him have it, right on the kisser I slugged him. So what does he do? He gets mad and fires me."

Ah, Gaby! Such a harmony as there was till now, such beautiful, touching domesticity, and you had to destroy it! Such stupid violence, too. But why, why? "Well, as you probably know, it is the great obsession of Argentine males," Max observes with hypocritical, anthropological detachment.

"Yeah, all they want is to fuck you in the ass..." She wags her head sadly, twisting her lips.

"But especially, you see, while you're washing, and most of all if you're scrubbing on a washboard," says Max.

"Really? I didn't know that. Had I known, I'd have worn pants not skirts when washing. Anyway, as I said to myself, what are you doing, you're working your ass off for a miserable bed and a few bucks, you might as well be mounted for a decent fee. That's how I started."

"It was a wise idea. And how much do you charge?"

"Forty thousand."

Forty thousand australes is roughly forty dollars. "Forty thousand! I'm afraid that's way, way over what I can afford. I'm not a wealthy man."

"Well, it's a matter of talking it over, see how much the customer can afford. The customer is always right, right? How much can you afford?"

"Five thousand, not an austral more," says Max.

"Hm... Can't you stretch it a little... Five thousand...

97

Not so much because of me, you see, but I've got my little angel... Make it eight thousand..."

She's willing to go to bed with him for eight measly dollars. But he isn't interested. Her tits are flattened against her thorax by her tight, black jersey dress, like an insect's hard shell. Max turns around and looks at the other whore, Big-boobs, still unattached, bored, looking through the window. *Those* are tits. Boris would have loved them. At least, they are mammalian, not cockroachy.

"How about rubbers," he asks, "have you got any?"

She eyes him suspiciously. "Only foreigners wear rubbers. What do you want them rubbers for? I'm clean. I go to the doctor every month, as a matter of fact I went there last Friday and he found nothing, spic and span, except he removed a polyp the size of a small rutabaga. I have the certificate right here in my purse to prove it."

Haven't Argentine whores and johns heard about AIDS? They must have, but either they think they are immune to it, or they like playing Russian roulette. What are the chances that this stewball should test HIV-positive? On what imponderable intangibles one's fate hangs! On a mere gesture, thumbs up, thumbs down. The sad wagging of her head, the deprecatory twisting of her lips: that saved him. Suppose for a moment that instead, after telling the story of her misadventures with her boss at the hotel, she had smiled bewitchingly and said something like, "He startled me, the son of a whore, while I was at the washtub, but you know, I'm not always that sulky." Or better still, "Now, when a real gentleman hoists me off my sandals from behind, ah, then..." What would Max have done then? Spend the rest of his life worrying about his visit to unspeakable places.

"But if you want to wear rubbers, it's okay with me,

98

they sell them at the hotel desk," says la Negra.

"Really," Max answers with his mind elsewhere. He remembers the recurring theme of Verdi's Falstaff: *Bocca bacciata non perde ventura.* A mouth is not spoiled by being kissed. But how about a cunt. How about a swamp where grows a rutabaga.

He looks around the mirrored salon. The bearish guy and his whore are still drinking whisky, clinking their glasses, no doubt making plans for their half hour of happiness. The older man has walked quietly out, and presently the teenage whore gets up from her table and walks out too. She's wearing a purple miniskirt, and Max puts on his glasses to follow her progress down the street. After a few yards, she meets the old man and, arm in arm like grandad and granddaughter, they hail a cab. Max's thoughts wander and he remembers something he read last night in a book by Lévi-Strauss, one of the many books left behind when he moved to the U.S., which have been gathering mold in the depths of Mother's cabinet. "The indefinable grandeur of man's beginnings." Indefinable grandeur! Look at this scaraboid whore, imagine her little angel. Where does the son of a whore come from? From a certified, public uterus whence a polyp was just removed, the size of a rutabaga. Is it worth five dollars or even five cents, a tour of such a public place? Why, her lowness happens to be her only attraction, her hailing from the dark, from the jungle, her having served as a housemaid. That hotel owner, her ex-boss, had it figured out exactly right. Her cunt! The origin of the little angel who, twenty or thirty years from now, will make a fine, dandruffy first-corporal in the Federal police, a virtuoso of the electric prod perhaps. Indefinable grandeur! What madness. The clubby madness of the intellectual who, in the depths of the Amazonian jungle, sees only the canonized writings of previous intellectuals.

"Well?" says la Negra.

Max smiles, absently. He's in no hurry. No, human beginnings are always low, nauseating, a latrine, and only myth lends them "grandeur." Well, fine, that's, after all, what myth is for. Births of nations are too low and too horribly violent and in any case impossible to be told at a remove, for any truthful telling would require words that were obliterated and lungs and tongues that were too long ago ground into the soil. The truth of the beginnings is too horrible to behold. Ah, if he, Max, could be a conquistador, a rapiered rapist, begetting nations of bastards upon a few thousand slave cunts! But he lacks the balls. So what's left to him? Art. In art, beginnings may be clean, and a case can be made for the sinless begetting of the Dolce Stil Nuovo, Flemish oil painting, Masaccio's impassioned depiction of the human shape, or Haydn and the string quartet, and even, in all modesty, his own poems...

La Negra gets up and ceremoniously announces, "I am repairing to the powder room."

For the first time Max sees her legs: spindly compared to her full *túkhes* and to the rest of her, the whole precariously balanced on steep heels. A steatopygic statuette to be stuck in the ground of paleolithic caves. South America, narrowing down, bracing her feet against Antarctica. She got up and "repaired to the powder room" to show him her swaying behind in all its barbarous splendor, so as to persuade him, at the right time and with a supreme gesture, to part with his eight dollars. Such artistry touches Max in the heart, as he has been touched by Sviatoslav Richter accenting certain bass notes in the last movement of the Appassionata

Sonata. Maybe he should be a patron of the arts, and spend eight dollars on la Negra.

Max looks behind him. Big-boobs is still sitting at her table, alone. She twists her lips and shrugs, as if saying, "What are you waiting for?"

Yes, he should give la Negra those eight dollars even if he doesn't go to bed with her, just on aesthetic grounds. Whoring is a sort of art, involving both illusion and risks, as well as certain dangers. In both whoring and art one gets paid to deliver a pleasure, and in both, the pleasure follows from a shameless make-believe, from getting the customer to feel in touch with his beginnings and their "indefinable grandeur." That's why — Max suddenly understands it — that's why Boris used to say that whores were "mushy" compared to Lady Luck, and that's why he liked to use the same word, "mushy," to describe a lot of things, from Tommy Dorsey's or Harry James' big hits, to Lester Young's solos with Billie Holliday, and he would have said the same of most classical music, had he condescended to listen to it. This Negra, frustrated midwife, ex-housemaid, ex-hotel-maid and present whore, Boris would have considered the pits of slushy mush, because for him only pure randomness and chaos carried a breath of fresh air, free from the stench of human wishes. Organized existence choked him as it is: how much worse existence organized as art.

"It's seven thousand five hundred and twenty-two australes." The waiter is standing there, shuffling a bundle of little tickets.

"What? For one coffee and one ginger-ale?"

"Yours is nine hundred and forty australes," the waiter reckons, "and hers is six thousand five hundred and eighty-two."

101

Max looks again into the waiter's eyes. Brown, bored and indifferent.

"You don't have to pay for hers if you don't want to," says the waiter.

"That's not the problem," says Max. Seven or eight dollars: big deal. He won't go hungry. The problem is, it now appears that la Negra "repaired to the powder room" not to show him her butt but to have him pick up her tab. Such lack of artistry pains him. Still, paying for a woman's drinks is a gentleman's duty.

Max gives the waiter a ten-thousand australes bill, tells him to keep the change, and leaves.

10

As a boy, Max liked to play dead. He'd lie under the dining-room table, close his eyes and imagine himself in the grave, banishing from his mind all other thoughts. Slippery ideas kept creeping back, it couldn't be helped, the most insidious being that of Mother coming out of the kitchen into the dining-room, finding him there and crying out, "He's dead, oh god, he's dead, the poor little angel!" In her distress, she called Father and Uncle Chaim, and they too cried, forgetting their rivalry for once, "Yes, there's no doubt, he's dead. What a pity, such a beautiful, such a brilliant, such a promising boy." Then Gloria, and the Bobeh, and Pancracia too: they'd all come to cry around his lifeless body...

Getting a foretaste of his own absence, trying to put the world between brackets, practicing for the ineluctable moment... No one knew for sure when that moment would come: it could be long, protracted, his last few seconds asymptotic, lasting as centuries — or sudden, abrupt, like the endpoint of a closed segment in the infinite line. From the kitchen came the sounds of Mother chopping on the block: before the next thud of the knife against the pile of meat, bread crumbs and egg yolk, his whole being could stop. One couldn't know: time is uniformly dangerous, homogeneously abyssal. Time's an ever-pregnant womb. Such games, as is evident at a forty-year remove, prefigured a poetical vocation. André Breton and Paul Eluard played dead in well-trimmed, comfortable coffins, and Petrarca, the famous Francesco Petrarca, would lie down, say a *Pater Noster*, whisper his Laura's name a last time and picture himself so vividly as a corpse that he'd jump back up in horror and disgust.

But it wasn't horror of nothingness that awakened ten-year-old Max back to life; it was Pancracia's familiar cloppety-clop. Opening his eyes, from where he was lying on the rug, under the table, beyond the clawed chair legs he'd see her furrowed heels, hardened, split by sun, water, bleach and hard labor. She would be polishing the sideboard, or winding the vacuum cleaner cable, unaware that Max was there, studying her feet. He'd forget all about death, and concentrate on the frayed vamps deformed by bunions, on how the heels became more calcareous and chapped as one approached the lighter skin of the sole. He would wonder how they'd feel to the touch, how the leather of the old slippers, buffed like suede, right under the heel, by wear and rub and flapping, would feel under his nose.

A question — but it wasn't a question really, nor was it an idea; rather a dreamy, wordless, never explicit musing, only a vague association of sounds and spaces, echoes fusing: between Mother's meat chopping in the kitchen and the *conventillo* whore's heels tapping out in the street, Pancracia seemed to hover and mediate, with her old slippers, her rags, her duster and the whine of the waxing machine. Pressing his cheek against the table crossbeam, he'd ask himself what manner of thing was woman, who could tread with such poignant precision, clop-clop, point after point after point out on the sidewalk, and who, at the other extreme, could chop meat in the kitchen so single-mindedly and often slap him on the face all of a sudden, whenever she decided that he had misbehaved. Women seemed, like time, rhythmical, flowing, and uniformly dangerous, abyssal.

Ten-year-old Max couldn't begin to understand the difficulties attendant to such thoughts. At an age when we are closer to the uniqueness of our origin (even if actually it is already impossibly far off), he felt that if he would only dare extend an arm and tickle that secret, light-skinned sole which detached itself from Pancracia's slipper as she wiped or polished the upper reaches of the cupboard, somehow he would make himself safe from the dangers of time and lurking nothingness. He didn't know that we cannot do it; we cannot touch another's sole without a recoil of horror and repulsion (keener than Petrarca's before death) which shows, as lightning in the murk of night, the abyss between I and her, between I as I am now and I of the forgotten birth. To ten-year-old Max, playing dead under the table, Pancracia's feet and shoes looked soft, warm, and far more inviting than the grave.

One morning the chopping knife was quiet, Mother out shopping for food, and the maid was giving the last touches to the dining room. Thinking herself alone, she took a break and sat on one of the two richly carved, damask-upholstered armchairs against the back wall. This was so extraordinary and untoward, it couldn't fail to attract little Max's curiosity: slowly, slithery, he crept from the foliage at the center of the carpet out toward the forest of chair legs.

When he finally raised his head, he got his first glimpse of the mysteries under a woman's skirt — mysteries which have kept getting hopelessly deeper and more entangled with the years, ever since. Pancracia was sitting unaware, knees apart. Max lay on the floor shaking, open-mouthed, fascinated. Suddenly she saw him and jumped up. "Get outa here! You scared me!" She resumed her chores, and Max never played dead again.

Now, at fifty, he stretches his right arm and touches the wall. Mother is beyond that wall, her head is on her pillow, her blanket lit by the soft light coming in through the shutters, and under the blanket her womb, the womb that bore him, the old womb which (as Mother was telling him only yesterday) fulfilled her chief purpose in life, producing a son after two years of special medical massage. Is she awake? No, of course not. She would have called, "Is that you, Max? Are you back? Are you okay?" Mother would never pretend that she was sleeping; like the Cartesian God, she would never dissemble or mislead him. Max is lying on a line parallel to the wall, Mother is lying beyond and along a line at right angle to it, but on a more elevated plane (she being on a raised bed and Max on a mattress, on the floor). They are lying, therefore, on lines that never meet. On any two such lines there's a unique point on each where a minimum yet positive distance is attained. The existence and uniqueness of the two points is an elementary geometric fact, not hard at all to prove, but Max, lying in the dark and unable to sleep, finds it quite remarkable. There seems to be something stupendously momentous about it. When, out of an infinitely long separation, two beings come closest to each other, yet do not touch as it would happen with intersecting lines, but, after casting a brief, intense, loving glance at each

106

other, they go on and diverge forever, silently. He's not about to touch the soles of Mother's feet — as far as he knows, he never did. Yet he feels that at no time was he closer to Mother than at this particular, quiet moment, tonight. Max lays his hand flat on the wall as if affirming this closeness, a closeness interrupted when he left for the U.S. Twenty-six years and two divorces later, the old Zeide's clock stopped at eleven, the old furniture, the old books inside the cupboard. There is the wall, Mother's wall with Max's hand resting on it, and there is Max, lying on the floor. All those memories, long dormant — Max at ten, under the wooden firmament of the dining room table, Max playing dead — flow softly back to him before the onset of sleep. It is as if besides the dihedral angle, wall and floor, the rest is only a dark, receding dream. There is Mother on her bed and him on the mattress; there's the wall, the floor which is the negation of the wall, and the line shared by wall and floor, the almost invisible line under the baseboard, synthesis of both. He tries to concentrate his attention on this line, almost invisible, so humble that only an insect or a worm would consider it noteworthy. He's too sexually excited to be able to sleep.

107

11

At siesta time Lezama Park is deserted, except for a
bevy of little girls. Nine or ten year-olds, black-haired, they
all wear skirts (no jeans!) and sneakers, and each has a
sharply individual style. The lanky one with spindly legs:
her hair, held back first by a ribbon on top, then by a
descending sequence of elastic bands, and her blue,
diaphanous dress which in spite of the short skirt has something of the peplos, lend her an Aegean allure. She is taking
slow, measured steps away from the group, as if reckoning a
distance or absorbed in her thoughts. The one who squats,
inspecting something on the ground, apparently some pebbles or some shells, with the seriousness of a Marseillaise
boules player: as she argues the score with the other girls, her
two ponytails shake from their butterfly-shaped barrette.
Another girl slowly turns around, on tiptoe, arms extended,
clapping a pair of imaginary castanets. Max sits on a cool,
shade-mottled stone bench.

Nowhere in the United States do little girls seem so

sharply different. When he was their age, he must have looked at similar little girls the way Prince Paris looked at the three competing goddesses: as the prefigurations, embodiments and weavers of divergent fates. It isn't a minor loss of the exile that to him little girls look mostly alike.

The sun is high, the shadows along the graveled avenue are of tall palms and their foliage. The shorter trees cast small, southerly patches, as do the urn-shaped pots on their pedestals, with their yuccas, their green tufts or dwarf palms, lining the avenue. There's only the sun, the trees, the alternating urns and empty benches, the little girls and Max in Lezama Park, and he feels drowsy after a sleepless night. A night in which, after a quarter of a century spent in a search so vain that it all seems now like a moment, the true place was revealed. Here in Buenos Aires, next to Mother. He should stay here and take care of her.

Down the road, the bronze-and-marble statue of Pedro de Mendoza, the founder of Buenos Aires. He stands alone, the only bronze amidst a mass of marble, in high boots and Spanish cape, grabbing the pommel of his naked sword. Behind him, carved in a huge marble slab, a woman opens up. Spread-eagle, her conical tits point down toward Don Pedro, her ecstatic Indian face heavenward. Fifteen minutes ago, when he discovered it, Max was struck dumb by the revelation. He had never seen that monument, even though it has been there since before he was born. The most notable thing about the carved Indian woman is her abdomen: a baroque muscle structure, one may think; but no, on a closer look it is her guts, the outline of her intestines, visible through her skin. The sculptor has made sure that we would not miss it, for the Indian woman symbolizes the land before the origin, before the Spaniards arrived, the virgin land opening up to the sword. The ecstasy on her face bespeaks her orgasmic reception of the Christian Truth. And her intestines? They refer to the prosperous Argentine country, the bounteous fatherland, the amazing fertility which Don Pedro and his men impregnated and imbued. Through her rectum, of course.

Ah, the conquistador's erect posture, his noble solitude! Beneath him, carved on the pedestal: "Buenos Aires is his immortality." Max asked *sotto voce*: "But did you tell her you were syphilitic?" For Don Pedro was a dying man when he founded Buenos Aires, one of the earlier victims of the AIDS of his age, caught in the bloody orgies of the sack of Rome. And the city's father from his bronze sputtered: "Me tell her? Fuck her! La puta que la remilparió!"

Here, too, in Lezama Park, was the first African slave market, property of the French Guiana Company. He feels drowsy but happy. On the bench beside him, a little present for Gloria: *marrons glacés*, daintily gift-wrapped. Not a breeze moves the spidery shadows of the palm trees, but from the river side comes the amphoric sound of a tugboat's horn. The girls are playing hopscotch. One of them, with the grace of an impish Nausicaa, hops on one foot from square to square, bends down to pick up a pebble at heaven, and comes back hopping down to earth. What would they say if Max asked to play with them? Would they think he's hopped up, or an old degenerate?

Just in time to save him from finding out, Gloria arrives. She comes up the graveled avenue with her impeccable, puffy hairdo in the style of the sixties, her heavy gait, her bulky handbag hanging from her shoulder. Max mentions the elegant stockings. "You won't find a well-dressed woman in Buenos Aires without black stockings," says

110

Gloria.

"I'm under the impression that you're already the best-dressed woman in Buenos Aires," says Max, giving her the present, "and now you'll be the best-fed too..."

Gloria unwraps the box of chestnuts. "Oh, I love *marrons glacés*! But God, think of the calories... And what's the occasion?"

"Nothing, just like that," Max shrugs, modestly.

"Well, thank you..." She's a little confused. She stuffs the box of chestnuts and the wrapping inside her bag, rummages some, takes out her cigarettes and her lighter, offers a cigarette to Max.

"I quit smoking ten years ago," Max reminds her.

"Hm, that long ago. It's incredible, how time goes by." She lights a cigarette, draws deeply and exhales her characteristic plume, which repeats in the air the ground motif of the palm's shadows.

"But I'm not sure it was a good idea," she continues. "Oral and anal fixations, you know, have a constant total sum. You quit smoking, and you either eat more and grow fat, or else..."

"Or else you shit more and grow thinner?" Max laughs. "But you're right, alas how right: time flies."

"I tell you, Max, I can't believe how fast these last years have passed. You don't realize it until it brutally confronts you. Just now I saw Rucha Rússovich — remember her? I was trying a new lipstick at a drugstore in Santa Fe Avenue and she was trying the same lipstick but in a different color on the mirror next to mine. At first I didn't recognize her. All skin-and-bone, grey-haired, she looks like an old witch. Scared me. So much so that I didn't say hello. I tell you, it wasn't a merry encounter, it left me horribly depressed."

Indeed, it's hard to believe. Rucha Rússovich used to be poignantly beautiful. Max muses, "She used to be a beauty so daunting that I wouldn't even entertain the thought of dating her: way, way above my league..."

They fall silent and think of the passing of youth.

"And how about Mary Burgos," he asks about another high-school friend of Gloria's whose looks used to impress him. "How odd that Dad, so jealous, always so terribly tyrannical with you, his immaculate daughter, was so keen on getting you engaged to Mary's brother..."

"What do you mean, odd. It wasn't odd at all: Jorge Burgos had no sex, he was the most unsexed man I've ever met, and that's precisely why Dad liked him for me."

"Funny, I had thought it was because of the Burgos' money," says Max, "but your explanation is plausible..."

"Oh God," says Gloria.

Max follows her gaze. The little girls are squatting, crouching, leaning down around impish Nausicaa, who's holding something in her hand that makes them giggle and chirp... a used condom.

"They were playing hopscotch," says Max, "they must have picked it up from the ground. Gloria, please, go tell them to drop it, it's dirty!"

But Gloria just sits there, smoking and staring at the little girls. Max feels he cannot do it himself, telling the girls to quit playing with filth: had they been smoking cigarettes, he could have intervened, but a used condom is something... between women. Little Nausicaa holds it up to the light, the stock image of a scientist peering into a test tube.

"It's dangerous..." he insists. Gloria seems interested but unwilling to intervene, like an ecologically savvy person

112

watching a snake in the act of swallowing a frog.

Little Nausicaa passes the whitish thing around. The girls touch it, giggle, investigate. The pretty *boules* player finally throws it away into the grass. Gloria drops her cigarette on the gravel and puts it out with the tip of her shoe. Her black stockinged knee gleams under the sun.

"You should have stopped them," says Max.

"Come on, don't be so nervous. I was younger than they, I was at most eight or nine when I handled the real thing, not the rubber ghost. I was with Mother, on a bus."

"Which bus?" says Max.

"Number 132, the one that goes up Carabobo and turns on Rivadavia. Mother was sitting on the seat behind me, I was next to the aisle and this guy was standing next to me. My hand was on the handle and suddenly I'm touching something under his trenchcoat. At first I thought it was a finger, but no, I couldn't find the nail. The guy had quite a hard-on. We went all the way up to Córdoba Avenue, where I had to wipe off my hands on my school uniform. Now you know why they make those school uniforms white: cum doesn't show."

"And Mother never noticed!" says Max, admiringly.

"No," says Gloria.

The little girls are jumping on and off the stone benches, playing puss-in-the-corner. Screaming and laughing, they jump in and out of the spidery shadows on the ground. Suddenly but vaguely, Max remembers a dream he had this morning, when he finally fell asleep for a while at about five o'clock. He was facing the opening of a stone canal or sewer into which he was supposed to climb, but the entrance was narrowed by a row of iron spikes.

"Speaking of adventures on buses... I too remember

one," says Max. "Once in number 40, one of those small, silvery buses which used to go from Primera Junta all the way to La Matanza, you know, where Father is buried. But back then of course he wasn't... Anyway, I was standing next to this girl. The bus was quite crowded. I looked at her face. She was about eighteen or twenty, swarthy, poor. I was fifteen. I had been hearing so much about it from the other boys at school. They all spoke about their exploits on the buses, but I would have never believed it until I saw for myself. I had to try. You cannot imagine how nervous I was, but I took the plunge: I planted my right hand smack on her behind. The boys at school were right: she acted as if nothing was happening. Incredible, don't you think. For the rest of the trip, down to Flores, where I got off the bus, I explored her ass, no questions asked, not even a glance."

Max feels that Gloria's bus story is brighter than his. The episode with the condom, such girlish purity and grace coming in contact with filth, has put him out of sorts, and he is angry with Gloria for not having stopped it. And although Max is not given to the popular error of judging past deeds by present moral standards, he has found, on re-telling, his actions on bus number 40 seriously wanting, even repellent. This may be, of course, because of his long, too long stay in the Calvinistic North. Anyway, he is mostly angry with himself, at thirty-five years remove, for having gotten off the bus without saying a word to the nice, patient girl.

Gloria lights another cigarette. Max takes another risky plunge: "What would you say, sister, if I propse a graver crime?"

"What do you mean, a graver crime?" She sounds surprised but intrigued.

"I mean, jerking off a guy in a trenchcoat, or goosing

a poor little blackhead: that's petty malfeasance. We are grown-ups, we should graduate to something bigger, don't you think?"

"Well, it certainly *sounds* exciting," says Gloria with a little nervous laugh.

"The problem is, how do I know I can trust you," says Max.

"Oh, by nature as well as nurture, I make a perfect partner in crime, Max."

"And you won't tell a living soul, ever, either about what I'll propose to you, or about the deeds which may ensue, should we agree to perform them?"

"I promise."

"Not even to your shrink?"

"Not even to my shrink."

"Swear it."

"I swear never to tell anyone, not even Panard, of what you are going to propose to me or of anything we'll do. And if I don't keep my word, may evil lightning strike me dead right then and there."

"Good enough. Then here it goes: let us kill Uncle Chaim."

Gloria blows out a jet of smoke toward the sky, then, after a long pause, another jet tangential to her stockinged knees. Finally she says, "I can't believe you're serious, Max."

"Why not?"

"What would we get by killing Chaim. With Boris dead he's childless, true, but you're not expecting to inherit his dough, are you?"

"Of course not. That's not the point. We want to kill him to exact vengeance. He killed Dad."

"Chaim killed Dad? Where did you get that notion?"

"Dad himself told me."

"No fooling."

"Yes, Gloria: believe it or not, yesterday, at his tomb, I heard his voice, clear and distinct as when he was alive, telling me how Chaim's repeated refusals to help him were the cause of his becoming desperate, and how his desperation caused his fatal accident. I had suspected the same long ago, but Dad confirmed it."

"Amazing, truly amazing. You say we're grown-ups, but you're still a small child. Blinded by Oedipus. Scarred by Oedipus. So much so that you hear voices and consort with ghosts."

"I did talk to Father's ghost, but I know I won't be able to persuade you. Anyway, bear this in mind: killing Chaim, we'd rid the world of one of the worst whoresons who ever lived."

"To kill the whoresons, we'd have to kill off half the country. Chaim's no worse and no better than the rest of them."

"So you are not game?"

"I'm afraid not," says Gloria, "not for that."

The little girls have all run off to watch two mounted policemen, who are parading themselves and their horses. The girls turn around the jack-booted cops asking questions, admiring the horses, the saddles, the whips. Max remembers a bit more of his dream. With superhuman force he tore the iron spikes off the stone at the sewer, screaming, "This is not what you think! This is an asshole!" Having scraped those iron spikes, it wasn't hard to creep up to a secret attic full of books. He doesn't remember any further. And now the cops leave and the girls run again after each other, a little farther off.

116

"If what you want is murder," Gloria resumes, "why don't we play Electra and Orestes? Oedipus had no sister."

"Ah, that's horrible, too horrible to think about! When was the last time you saw Mother, Gloria?"

"I'd say about a couple of years ago. When I threw her out of my house."

"A couple of years! Gloria, do you realize that she doesn't have that long to live, that in another couple of years she might not be around..."

"Oh, she'll hopefully die sooner than that," Gloria corrects him with clinical detachment.

Max grabs his sister's arm. He strokes her hand. "But why, tell me why..."

"Why what."

"Why you won't visit Mother. Why are you so unforgiving. Why do you hate her so..."

"I don't love her, that's for sure. I don't think I ever did."

"Nevertheless, she is your mother, isn't she. And one has certain obligations... how should I put it... of a biological nature..." he finishes rather hesitantly, dropping her hand. He dislikes his own tone of voice, but is determined not to drop the matter. Gloria has always been a sentimental absolutist; for her, people are created to either love or hate each other, as if we had no choice and no possible intervention in the matter.

"Then why don't *you* move back here, Max, to take care of her? You are her son..."

"I'm fifty and my life is built and organized up there, in the United States. Nevertheless you're right, I am her son, and I'm giving the idea serious thought."

"Well, I'm glad to hear that. Keep thinking it over,

then. I grant you, it *is* a tough problem, Max."

He stretches his arms, stretches out his pectoral muscles, breathes deeply. Ah, how much he would appreciate a good word. Gloria lights another cigarette. He would also appreciate a smoke; he's dying for a cigarette. The little girls have left. But matters cannot be laid to rest simply with the acknowledgement that he's got a tough problem.

"Suppose Mother died without you seeing her, without you visiting her... You'll feel bad, Gloria, believe me. You'd feel terribly guilty."

His sister looks at him, enveloped by the smoke and the leafy shadows. "I want to know one thing, Max. Why do you feel so damn superior? I've been keeping a tally: first you tell me I should have saved the girls from touching a condom, as if they were about to eat the forbidden fruit; then you determine Chaim is evil incarnate; now you're telling me I'll feel terribly guilty if I don't visit Mother. Who gave you a lease on the high moral ground? You know what I think? I think that after all these years you're Yankeefied. You're bloody-minded, but want to make everyone optimistic and happy. You go around preaching, telling people, people smaller than you of course, how to behave. Just in case you hadn't noticed it: I'm *not* a banana republic."

"You banana republic, me Teddy Roosevelt, how absurd!" Max shakes his head. "If anything, you could call it the older-brother syndrome... Me a preacher? No, that's unfair..."

While they walk up Calle Brasil toward Constitución, Max sulks. He a preaching bully? He forgets to show Gloria the monument to the city's father Don Pedro de Mendoza. He'd like to persuade Gloria that he doesn't despise her. And why should he despise her? Actually, he envies her easy familiarity with those things they both grew up with, something he, as an exile, had to relinquish. Silly things, like going into a bakery and knowing by name each of the many different pastries, or being able to go to the same hairdresser in Chacarita twice a week. He envies her for having witnessed the most awful events, Perón's second coming, the terrorists, the tortures, the lost Atlantic war, the crumbling country, the recurring nightmares, the innumerable deceptions. If Max told her that he envies even her despondency and her sadness, she probably wouldn't understand. All his life, since he was a little boy, he wanted to get out. He used to go to the airport just to watch the planes take off, imagining himself aloft. Having succeeded in getting out, he now wants his place in the collective grief.

"Are you really thinking of moving back to Buenos Aires?" Gloria asks at length. She sounds skeptical but conciliatory.

Yes, he thought about it carefully last night, since he couldn't sleep. At fifty he's old enough to go back to his origins, old enough to bite his tail and close the cycle. He's always found circularity fascinating. Bach's Goldberg Variations. The Musical Offering. *Schumann's Frauenliebe und Leben.* Circles are more spiritual than open lines. Perhaps no one understood this better than Beethoven in the Theme and Variations of his piano sonata opus 109. "*Andante molto cantabile ed espressivo.*" And at the end, when the Theme is repeated: "*Molto tranquillo (quasi religioso.)*" "Almost religious! Just think," says Max while putting a hand on his sister's shoulder, "what could be nearer the original meaning of 'religious' than − after the exile, after the vast and heady crescendos, the trilling avatars, the stormy fugato parts − a tender re-reading of the original Theme?"

119

They've arrived at the Constitución train station, and he holds Gloria's arm while climbing the steps. "I have a fantasy," says Max. "I'd like to come back and buy one of those big old houses — with a patio, a lemon tree, a jasmin — a big old house for the three of us: you, Mother and me."

Gloria snickers. "Two women and a man? We would be always competing to be the one who pours maté for you, Max. I'm afraid you'll have to count me out."

They kiss, and with the glazed chestnuts in her bag she goes down the subway stairs. Her impeccably coiffured hair disappears into the hot, dim, electrically charged air.

12

A few minutes later, el Indio Fontana gets off a train and the two men bear-hug amid commuters and clouds of burnt diesel oil.

"When did we see each other last, Max? Was it in Chicago, seven years ago?"

"No, no, in New York, ten years ago."

"Was it? Then let us start from the latest, as in a CV: where were you this last year?"

"Where?" says Max. "Mostly at home. Mostly tormenting Jennifer. And you?"

"Half the year in Pisa, at the Scuola Normale Superiore, the other half in Paris, at the École Normale Supérieure, mostly doing mathematics."

"You don't seem to have grown up," says Max, and it is true, in a sense, although his gray dishevelled hair, bushy mustache, and the wrinkles all over his tanned face make his friend look like an ageing guru.

"Age shows when I pee, Max. Have you noticed how

the older we get the longer it takes to shake off the last drop?"

Max agrees. But see, the same mechanism makes older men better lovers.

"Really? Hmm... You'll have to fill me in the physiological details. Are you going anywhere in particular?"

They walk out of the station heading South on Lima Street. It feels good to be again walking the streets with el Indio. Is there a more spiritual pleasure than to walk in the company of an intelligent man through places full of common memories? Max realizes he has been spending too much time with women, Mother and Gloria.

They walk and chat. Yes, he has received most of the postcards el Indio has sent him over the years — an uninspiring lawn and a barrackoid building in the background, with the caption, "University Library"; others of a more exotic kind: Rio de Noite, La Torre Pendente di Pisa, Les Champs Elysées. Another source of pleasure: Fontana, like him, is an exile; they both look at the city with artistic eyes, with the detachment, acuity and freshness that only distance makes possible.

"Do you enjoy life, Max? I do. I like the taste of bread and wine, I like exotic lands, music, mountains, grand old buildings. And I like beautiful women. There was a time when I envied Kistheimer for his asceticism — remember? — when he and I were together at Princeton, from my bed I'd spy his lit window at midnight and say to myself, 'The son of a bitch must be proving some astounding new theorems!' But I've been lucky. After every trip and every adventure — and you know how dangerous the call of the diverse is, how one risks drowning in chaos — after every journey of enjoyment, I've always been able to return to Math. And tell me:

with his asceticism and all those midnight watts, what has Kistheimer done that's so earthshaking? His work on complex analytic spaces, to be sure. Not bad, but it was almost immediately superseded and circumvented by Grothendieck's results and mine."

Fontana's fundamental theorems. Modern analysis would be different without Fontana spaces, and there is much to be proud about being his friend. Max feels he was wrong, however, in thinking, just a moment ago, of a fellowship in exile. If Fontana is an exile, he is so in a fundamentally different way from Max, for Mathematics is Fontana's true fatherland, his ubiquitous Ithaca, his universal language. He, unlike Max, has no distance to heal. Distances in space, the incurable distance of time, the insidious distance between the name and what's named: such gashes do not occur in Math. Fontana may be an exile, perhaps, but of a special kind: banished from the world of distances, an exile from exile; this is what makes him such a pleasure to walk with.

They stop by a shop window. *Rotisería. Lechón al spiedo.* A piglet is slowly rotating on the spit, blistering and exuding brown juices from the cracked, crusty skin. How Onofrio loved to eat roast suckling pig, what a joyous feast that crackling was for him!

"Yes, Don Onofrio liked the pleasures of the table; he had, shall we say, a definite tendency to embonpoint." El Indio makes a barrel-shaped gesture with both hands.

Max adds that Onofrio also liked to bullshit, to borrow beyond his means, to go spectacularly bankrupt and to screw around.

"Well, you shouldn't complain," says el Indio; "remember, a man without vices is like a dog without pee, he doesn't leave any traces. That's what my uncle Teófilo used to say anyway. He left fifty children by the official count — unofficially of course it is much higher — and was rigorously plastered most of the time. But tell me, Max, seriously, what have you been doing lately? I mean, besides tormenting Jennifer."

Max cannot lie to his friend. "For close to ten years I've been writing poetry," he says, afraid that he will be humiliated and devoured forthwith.

Max's fears are not entirely unfounded, since that's how Fausto Roberto Fontana got "el Indio" for a nickname. In their first semester at the University of Buenos Aires Max and el Indio had a crusty, old professor of Calculus by the name of Díaz de Solís, same as the Pilot Major of Spain who discovered the River Plate in 1516 and ended up eaten by the Indians. The Calculus he was acquainted with, Fontana used to say, was also from 1516. That was an exaggeration: Prof. Solís might not have been brilliant, but he had a passing familiarity with simple integrals and derivatives, besides being a respected member of the Argentine Academy of Sciences and of the country's cultural elite. Often Fontana would interrupt him, to offer a proof, a method, a solution, ten times shorter, incomparably more elegant and infinitely more general than the one Solís had proffered. It was clear to all that each time, with each lecture, Solís was fighting for his life, but then, Fontana was fighting for Youth, Truth and Beauty, and the students naturally sided with him. Solís pulled a few strings, tried to have the seventeen-year-old prodigy thrown out of the class and formally disciplined "for academic insubordination." The dean would not go along with this. Finally, cornered by genius and youth into shame and ridicule, Solís reported sick, stopped showing up for class, and a year later retired from his chair at the University. The students declared that Fontana had "devoured" Solís, "just like the Charrúa Indians devoured the other one." The name stuck.

And now Max is afraid it is his turn to be devoured. A fifty-year-old man, writing sonnets...

"Poetry... hmm..." says Fontana while they walk, hands in pockets, on the tiled sidewalks. "Difficult... It may be even more difficult than math. I imagine you must work very hard."

Max assents reticently, with his head.

"As a profession, I mean, it must be harder," Fontana goes on. "A mediocre mathematician has a lot to contribute — small, partial results can go a way to motivate a great theorem... But a mediocre poet, what's he good for? I don't mean regarding you, of course, but in general."

"You're right," Max laughs. "But I don't have that problem. I'm a great poet: inspired, orphic, essential."

Max says this with a resentful, self-directed sarcasm that grows out of isolation, fed by a steady regimen of rejection slips and frustrated expectations, but Fontana takes it literally and replies, "That's good!"

"Anyway, I have fun," says Max after they've walked silently some fifty yards. "Dealing with smells and sounds and special light effects... Poetry is not ascetic like mathematics..."

"Oh come now. People imagine that a great mathematician ought to be some kind of anchorite like Kistheimer," says Fontana, "or like Hilbert, who was totally unfamiliar with the features of the town where he had lived most of his life because those were things his wife and the housemaid were supposed to worry about. There have been great mathematicians who didn't renounce bodily reality. Caratheodory loved a good cigar, and didn't Oka live in a tree house and write about the Japanese feeling for spring? Between you and me, I happen to have a penchant for beautiful young females."

"I'd be the last person to blame you," says Max.

He's aware that the dishevelled eagle at his side is very much an animal to be feared. They stop by an old-bookshop facing Plaza España and browse in the sidewalk stalls.

"Hey, Max, listen to this." Fontana holds a thin, yellow paperback and reads: "'His work, mediocre and plagued by foreignism, from which only the well-studied titles shall remain, is raised to the pinnacle of glory by the commercial press, which, at the same time, condemns to silence the names of free and progressive writers.' Do you know which poet this critic was talking about, circa 1955? Jorge Luis Borges."

Fontana buys the pamphlet. "For only twenty-five cents!" he whispers in Max's ear, "I've got a first-rate collection. You should come to my house in San Francisco just to see it. Some remarkable items. An attic-wide imbecilities depot. Or would you like to keep the book? I'll let you have it for fifty cents. A 100% profit. Might help you keep your critics in perspective..."

Max refuses on the grounds that nothing could help him keep his critics in perspective. He's not completely at ease in the company of a man with a knack for discovering nonsense wherever it might hide, with a passion for bringing it up to the unflattering light of reason.

They walk without a definite aim. Max's divorce from Jennifer comes as news to Fontana. He says, "I'm sorry, Max, although I know most divorcés prefer to be congratulated."

As for his own wife, Haydée, she's doing fine. It's on her account they often come to Argentina, to visit her relatives. They've been married now for twenty-five years, and they have one grown-up son. "Haydée is the ideal wife for me: easy-going to the point of complaisance. Unfortunately, those same virtues became serious defects when applied to bringing up Ramiro, our son. He's spoiled and doesn't feel like doing anything in particular. At twenty-two, he only smokes pot, watches the tube, and is going deaf with rock-and-roll."

Max says he's sorry for Ramiro, and congratulates el Indio on *his* recent successes, which he has read about in the newspapers.

"Are you referring to my becoming a member of the U.S. Academy?" Fontana smiles. "You'd think they are intent on turning me into a honorific old fart. But returning to you, Max, why did you give up math?"

Max hesitates. He cannot say that it was because he suddenly got mysticism, like Pascal. Was it his father's messy life and death, his body on top of the dining-room table? Or his invisible daimon, who whispered in his ear, "Max, Logic and Math cannot do justice to you or me; try poetry..."? Who knows. Although he has thought about it over the years, he has never been able to formulate it, and perhaps there is no formula. Why am I here? Why are you? Why is the universe? Why must you always be asking stupid questions? Max doesn't give voice to these objections; he just replies to his friend, "Hard to say; it is mysterious."

"Do you remember old Kunihito Kodaira?" says Fontana. "I used to walk with him around the pond at the Institute in Princeton, talking mathematics, and to every question I raised he offered but two answers: it was either,

'Most mysterious' or, 'Most obvious'."

That's it. Max wants to know whether his friend, his old classmate who's a reason virtuoso, would interpret conversing with one's father's ghost as a most mysterious happening or as a most obviously imaginary phenomenon. "You who are a scholar, Indio —"

But Fontana interrupts, "Do you know where we have arrived?"

Max views the long, uninterrupted wall. Glass shards along the top, and running barbed wire. About a hundred yards down, at a place where the wire is cut, a figure, a man, arms over and across the top of the wall, is hanging like a piece of cloth from a clothesline.

"This is the place where the people who sincerely want to stay in Argentina are kept securely lodged," Fontana says with a laugh.

Behind the wired and sharded wall stands the Municipal Neuropsychiatric Hospital, the Buenos Aires madhouse. Max looks at el Indio, el Indio looks at Max: they both remember Schamberg.

13

Thirty years ago Fontana and Krocus visited Schamberg at the madhouse where he was committed after he had smashed furniture, banged his head against walls and drank a glass of chlorine bleach. His family was not wealthy and could not afford an expensive private mental clinic. Max and el Indio found him sitting in the madhouse patio, arms limp, head hanging, unshaven. He looked gaunt, dehydrated.

Schamberg did not return their greetings, didn't even raise his eyes. To an awkward transmittal of best wishes from Llorente, Capricoll, and the rest of the Math Faculty, he responded with grunts. Obviously he was in a world all his own, oblivious to the madhouse's brueghelesque environment. He was sitting on a tree stump and the two visitors were standing, not knowing what to say, terribly uncomfortable. One feels safer before a talking madman than before a silent one. Then el Indio had a brilliant idea: he had a book with him, Felsönhör's "Linear Partial Differential Operators," recently published in the U.S. and hard to get in

Argentina. He offered the book to Schamberg saying, "Here, we thought this might interest you; we imagined that you would want to keep in touch with the latest developments."

Schamberg's eyes lit up. He leafed through the book eagerly, as through the text of some final revelation, drooling, mumbling, "Thank you, dear friends, thank you." When he got to the last page, he started leafing backwards, mumbling all the time, "Thank you."

"We can leave you the book if you want it," said Fontana. "Just tell us what happened, how come you ended up here."

Closing the book, vaguely looking at the eucalyptuses and at the loitering male nurses, "Yes, you are probably wondering why I'm here..." Schamberg muttered, then sighed, "It's because of three lovely, lovely holes."

"Holes, Schamberg?" "Three?" the two visitors, in turn and after decent pauses, pressed him.

"Yes, T.L.H., Three Lovely Holes," said Schamberg, "that's how she was advertised in an American magazine."

He opened the book again, read Theorem 2.4.2 aloud in a solemn, nasal tone of voice. After a silence Max delicately insisted, "Who was she, the one advertised in an American magazine?"

"Tee-el-ache," said Schamberg in a whisper. "I had my uncle bring her from the U.S."

Schamberg sighed. He dropped his head and looked at the ground. Max and el Indio waited.

Without raising his eyes, Schamberg whispered, "She came with a fluffy blond wig, high heels, a frilly negligée... The options I had ordered."

"So," said Fontana, "what did you do?"

"What did you want me to do? I pumped her up."

130

"You pumped her up? What are you talking about?"

"I followed the directions," said Schamberg. "They said to pump her up to the desired plumpness then to push the valve down into her navel. That's exactly what I did, with my bicycle pump. But her eyes didn't open and close as I expected. No, her eyes were just painted, and as I pumped, her expression slowly changed... the more I pumped the more she looked astonished, I suppose at finding herself lying on my bed. My friends, do you think I made a terrible mistake? Do you think I should have left Tee-el-ache flat in her box?"

Max and Fontana were astonished. What could they say? A doll! For there could be no doubt that was what Schamberg was rambling on about. An artifact, a mechanical lover. What a lunatic idea! But, on second thought, and as Fontana remarked later, who is to judge? He didn't mean who's to decide on what is right and what is wrong, or who is crazy and who is sane, which are relatively simple matters. He meant, especially after Turing's classic paper of 1950, who's to decide on who is a human lover and who is a machine. True, in Turing's thought-experiment it was a man, not a woman, who couldn't be distinguished from a digital computer. But, as is well known, Turing had peculiar proclivities...

But right then, in the patio at the madhouse, Fontana and Max were astonished and didn't know what to reply. An old man sitting on the ground was alternatively scratching the sole of his right foot and picking something from it which he then took between thumb and first finger up to his eyes to be examined. A long-haired young man who seemed lethargic suddenly barked twice. The eucalyptus leaves rustled in the breeze. The male nurses were leaning on the trunks and smoking.

"Her mouth, ah, her mouth!" Schamberg wailed, breaking his long silence.

"What about her mouth?" asked the visitors, grabbing the chance.

"One of her three holes," said Schamberg.

"We gather that. What about it?"

"No teeth. No tongue. She had a voice, though. Ah, my friends, that voice of hers, that harsh, pitiless voice of hers!"

"What did she say that was so pitiless, Schamberg?"

"'Do it harder!' She would always say, 'Do it harder!' no matter how hard I applied myself. Well, I didn't mind that; I can appreciate a tough task master; you know that, my friends, you have seen me going in one week through four chapters of Wittaker and Watson... No, the problem, the real problem was... And last year, didn't I do every single exercise in Coddington and Levinson? Do you remember that?"

"We do remember it," Max and el Indio assured him, "but what was the real problem? Tell us."

"The problem was," said Schamberg, "Tee-el-ache would lose air. Wouldn't you say American industry makes better products? Each time, at first her eyes would open wide, but soon they'd lose their luster, wrinkles would appear on her face, her charms would fade, and she became emaciated. Ah, my friends, have you ever gone through the experience of taking a lovely bride into your arms, only to find, ten minutes later, that you have married a shrivelled hag?"

"You could have tried the water test for punctures," said Fontana.

"Yes, I thought of it," said Schamberg. "But what

about her delicate vibrating parts? And what would moisture have done to her voice?"

"So, what did you do?"

"I set her on all fours and I attached the bike pump to the valve in her navel, then I tried to pump air into her while at the same time —" Schamberg's face reddened.

"Well, did it work?"

"Ah, my friends," Schamberg face turned into a tragic mask, "you can't imagine how hard it is, keeping up with two independent strokes while someone is constantly prodding, 'do it harder!'"

"Yes, I can well imagine it," said Max. "It's exactly like playing on the piano Schumann's Concerto without Orchestra, trying to play two different rhythmic patterns with the two hands, while the score tells you to play as fast as possible, *Prestissimo possibile*, and then, only a little later, believe it or not, still faster: *Più presto*."

Max regretted having said it, for Schamberg immediately reverted to a hostile silence. He fidgeted with Felsönhör's book for a while, then, nodding approval, he intoned, "Lemma 3.3.1, lemma 3.3.2, theorem 3.3.6, corollary..." as if murmuring an incantation. He was ignoring the two visitors, until Fontana had a second inspiration: he snatched the book from Schamberg's lap, and told him that if he wanted it back, he had to answer their questions.

"But you must be patient, you must be patient, my friends... I've been adversely affected... you must understand... listen, it's too tragic for words..."

Max and el Indio promised to be patient, but told Schamberg that if he wanted the book back, he had to tell them his story to the end.

"The end of my story... Well, fortunately Tee-el-ache

was under warranty. You have to grant it to the Americans: they give good warranties. My uncle was returning to the U.S., so I asked him to take Tee-el-ache back and exchange her for another doll of a different type. Ah, my friends, those two months! How impatiently I awaited her! Finally, my uncle arrived with a large box and a bag full of stuff. Some kind of plastic, rubber foam or styrofoam or sponge, I am not really sure. As you know, I have studied some chemistry, a couple of semesters — I'm sorry, probably I should have studied more, but I am no chemist, my friends, as you well know, I'm just a mathematician."

"We know, Schamberg, go on."

"I followed the instructions carefully. I filled her carefully with the stuff in the bag. I decided to call her Gudrun. Once filled, she looked like a Gudrun. I gave her all the clothes I had bought for Tee-el-ache. Do you think that was wrong, giving Tee-el-ache's trousseau to Gudrun?"

"In your place we would have done the same. But go on, what did you do with Gudrun?"

"Whatever your tastes, wherever your fancy may take you, whenever you are ready, she'll go along, humbly, selflessly, no questions asked. Make her yours. Now. I'll never forget that American prospectus. Ah, my friends, I shall never forget it... The glossy paper and the perfect English. But how could I possibly describe to you... How could I... Gudrun... Corollary of my life... Ah, how I wish I could write in English like that, on such glossy paper!" Schamberg started mumbling incoherently.

"Tell us," they coaxed him. "By letting it out you'll feel much better, it'll be a weight off your heart. Tell us about it... if you want to have Felsönhör's book back."

There was a prolonged silence. Max looked down at

a eucalyptus sprig on the ground, the long-haired young man barked. Another man, who was squatting on a bench, clucked.

Schamberg came out of his reverie. "This semester, as you know, I'm in charge of the practice sessions of Real Functions II, in the afternoon... After that, well, on Tuesdays and Thursdays anyway, I go, like you — don't you? — to Szmalcownik's seminar: it's very important, a very important seminar, don't you agree? A very powerful method for partial differential equations, I would say... a very powerful method..."

"Yes, yes, Schamberg, and then, after Szmalcownik's seminar... back to Gudrun?"

"Yes, my friends, after a bite to eat, I would go home and Gudrun was always there, lying on my bed, waiting for me. Oh, Gudrun! Oh, my lovely companion!"

"What happened, did she also collapse, like Tee-el-ache?"

"Oh, no. Quite the contrary: each day she seemed to grow plumper," said Schamberg.

"Strange indeed," said the two friends; "and then? Go on, Schamberg, if you want to get Felsönhör."

"One evening, as I spread her legs apart, out of her — well, this is unspeakable — a creeping thing came out and started down her thigh!"

"Jesus, man, you must have been stunned," said el Indio and Max. "How did you react?"

"I stood there. Then a second thing came out. What would you have done in my situation? I had to investigate it, don't you think?"

"Of course you had to investigate. And what came out of it?"

135

"I pulled down Gudrun's zipper. You cannot imagine what that was like. The tee... tee... teeming pull... ull... lation... The ex... pl... osion... Tell me, I'm sorry I am no biologist, no chemist, but do you think it's possible, that all that, all that horror, could have been started out of styrofoam?"

"Could be, who knows," they said. "What did you do about it?"

"What could I do, what would you have done in my place? I took her out to the backyard, together with the bag and the box. I doused the whole thing in kerosene and put a match to it. I incinerated her! My love, my Gudrun, I burned you like a pile of garbage!"

Schamberg started up and took his hands to his face, as if trying to wrench it off his head. At his hair-raising scream, from behind the eucalyptuses two burly male nurses in white aprons came up and took him away, kicking and punching. Fontana picked up the Linear Partial Differential Operators book from the ground, and walking sadly, slowly, he and Max went to talk with the asylum director.

The doctor received them in his office, a dusty room with a desk, calendars on the walls and white aprons hanging from pegs. Max and Fontana explained that they were Schamberg's classmates at the University. The medical prognosis was not good: the only hope left for Schamberg was electroshocks. And as the two friends were leaving, paternally resting his hairy hands on their shoulders, the doctor delivered, in a hushed voice, a barbarously simplified diagnosis: "An excess of masturbation, that's the real cause... You say he's a brilliant student? Mathematics, uh? Too bad, with the electroshocks he may forget it all..." And patting them on the back he concluded, "Don't follow his example, boys..."

*

Eventually Schamberg did get out of the madhouse, his brain unscrambled enough to get a Doctorate in Math, and then, a little later, to get married to a fleshy, real woman. Meanwhile, in thirty years, absolutely nothing in the Municipal Neuropsychiatric Hospital has changed, not a single glass shard on the wall el Indio and Max are walking along. The figure hanging like a rag from the top of the wall asks for the time. It is five thirty. "Ahhaha!" the madman rubs his hands, "not too long to suppertime!"

"His wife finally left him; they say that's what did him in," says Fontana. Then, as an afterthought, "Pity, he was a fine mathematician."

"Who?" says Max.

"Schamberg," says Fontana.

"Why do you say, 'He was'?"

"He killed himself three months ago, didn't you know?"

No, Max didn't know.

"He jumped off a thirteenth floor."

Max isn't shocked. He receives it as a resolution; in a way he feels relieved, as when, after a series of harmonic shifts, a musical piece is finally brought to an end in a tonic chord. "Poor guy," he mutters, shaking his head.

"Yes, poor guy," says el Indio. "Yet, he proved one good theorem, and so a bit of him will be remembered."

"Remembered!" Max chuckles.

"Well, yes, a bit. It was Hardy who said that Archimedes will be remembered when Aeschylus is forgotten, because languages die but mathematical ideas last forever? Schamberg was no Archimedes, nevertheless his one little contribution, Schamberg's theorem, will be remembered."

They walk by a house with a small garden. A woman is making cascades of tremulous rainbows with a hose around a jasmine bush. Max feels he's been taught a hard, bitter lesson in mathematical meekness. Archimedes/Schamberg versus Aeschylus/Max: the ratios and proportions seem clear enough, and even though he was deserted by a wife (one, not two, like Max), even though he jumped off a thirteenth floor and his guts spilled out on the street, Schamberg ends up ahead. He will be remembered a little; Max, probably not at all. Languages die, mathematical ideas don't. Could Max reply that he may have eschatological justifications too? He hopes to rise from the dead on the day of the last judgment and tell God, as did Jean-Jacques Rousseau, to judge him by his writings. But el Indio would reply that Max is joking, that he knows full well that his friend Krocus doesn't believe in God, nor in an afterlife, much less in a last judgment.

"What I don't understand is those dolls. What did he find in them? I mean, subjection and submissiveness are fine up to a point, but I want to see some desire, hidden or overt, in the eyes of the animal I'm making love to, some yearning for me, or some fear of me, don't you think?"

"As far as I'm concerned, you're right," says el Indio. "But that may be our weakness, yours and mine, and the cause of a lot of useless complications. Making do with dolls, maybe Schamberg had more free time to think about important stuff."

"Sure," says Max. "And to end up in the madhouse and then jump from a thirteenth floor."

"And you, Max, are jumping to conclusions. We don't

know those fucking dolls were the cause of his suicide, do we? Maybe it was his having married, maybe if he had stuck to dolls he'd still be among us, proving theorems."

14

Over the bed Max shared with Jennifer there was a lamp. While she slept (she snored, softly in the summer, loudly during the cold, dry winter nights), he stared at that lamp for so long that he would have sworn it would be impossible ever to forget it. There was a ceiling lamp too over Sharon's bed, and another in the room Max shared with Gloria as a child. Having looked at each of those three fixtures a million times, yet he's unable to recall them. He has been sitting for hours at Mother's dining table, writing, seeking rhymes, woolgathering and counting syllables, now and then raising his eyes and looking at the chandelier illumining the composition of his poem. His mind is totally exhausted, but this one must be preserved; Max takes a three-by-five card and puts it down in writing:

Suspended from the ceiling by two links of chain, concave rows of glass beads run down to a bronze ring encircling a lower hemisphere of beads; a faceted crystal globe hangs from the bottom.

If only his present happiness could be as precisely

described: delving deep into his mother tongue, surrounded by Mother's things, bathed in her tender atmosphere. The poem is dedicated to his friend Fausto Roberto Fontana. There is no other way to explain to him why Science and Math turned out not to be enough. Max rises from his chair, stretches his arms, lies face down on the floor and does ten push-ups. He goes to the kitchen and drinks a glass of water. From the kitchen cabinet he pulls out the old enameled pot where Grandma used to cook *gefilte fish*: she passed it on to Mother, who cooked in it her own simplified version. Lovingly Max caresses the outer surface, the handles, the inner concavity, the tiny cracks. Then he carries the oil-cloth-covered stool to the living room and climbs on it to reach the upper closet. Under Father's billiard cue, under the boxes with his chess and checkers sets, at the very bottom, the frayed suitcase he used as a peddler. Inside, wrapped in crunchy cellophane, three stacks of washed-out photographs. Max unwraps them with the trembling hands of one stripping his lover after a quarter-century of forced celibacy.

Mid-twentieth-century Falstaff in unbuttoned shirt, Onofrio smiles under his bushy mustache from inside a circle of fawning seamstresses. His heavy, hairy hand rests on Max's shoulder, who slouchily crouches on the grass, at Father's feet — a seven-year-old in short pants, jacket and tie, slicked pompadoured hair, wincing, on the verge of tears.

In the next one Father seems younger. A banquet. A banner: *Unión Industrial Argentina*. A score of gentlemen sitting at table, shirt collars, cuffs and three-peaked handkerchiefs peeking out of formal dinner jackets, competing with tablecloth and napkins for the acme of starched whiteness. The tops of the siphon bottles gleam under the chandeliers,

141

counterpoint to the cufflinks and wrist watches. At one end, Chaim flashes his seigneurial smile. Onofrio sits near the opposite end, eyes fixed on Chaim: yearning but frightened eyes, facial muscles relaxed in animal submission. Max gets the definite impression that his father married his mother not because of her but because of a fascination for her brother Chaim.

Next one... Max is about to pick another photograph, when he notices a sheet of paper, a bill of lading from Father's lingerie shop, with its logo, a big O and a smaller K inside a hexagon. Father's handwriting. The first letter is a florid capital O. No, it's not an O, it is a zero.

"0 is supposed to be the symbolic expression of Not-Being. However, as soon as we begin closely to examine this concept on which the vast imposing Edifice of Mathematics rests as on foundations inexpugnably secure, a cumulus of contradictions and absurdities springs forth to our view. In effect, are we capable of distinctly intuiting such a notion? I submit that we are not. Let us imagine, for a moment, the annihilation of all matter and the suppression of motion: we are left nevertheless with the intuition of an empty space (the idea of extension), and the flow of time (the empty sequence). Assuredly this is not Not-Being: for undoubtedly those two ideas are still present. But let us annihilate space and time altogether (assuming this is possible, a highly dubious proposition); shall we then have achieved the idea of Not-Being? Not at all. We would still be left with the very idea of Not-Being, which is indeed something in itself, and therefore we would be far from any intuitive grasp of that notion. Zero stands, therefore, as the symbol of a self-contradictory idea, undoubtedly undermining, like a worm, the entire foundation of the Mathematical Edifice."

A worm. Indeed. A cigarette-burnt hole near the bottom is not the least pathetic thing about this document. Next to the hole there is a date: 1957. Max's first year as a math student at the University. Poor Father: zapping zero he was zapping his son, or so he thought. But since he could have attacked Max so easily on so many truly vulnerable fronts, why did he have to attempt the only one that was impregnable? Foolish, demented, quixotic! And perhaps the secret of his unrivalled achievements as a loser.

Max imagines his father sitting on a throne (a gilt, rhinestone-studded barber chair), Emperor of the Realms of Thought, in possession of the awful secret: zero is a fraud, and therefore all of Mathematics, and therefore all of Physics, Astronomy, etc., all of Modern Science, are built (like all of Father's businesses) on a fraud. The whole thing's worthless, and he's the only one who knows it. Yet Science has proceeded, canker-free, along her triumphal road, while a convocation of philosophic worms has eaten all that's left out there, under the mud in La Matanza cemetery, of Father's body.

One thing Max cannot understand: if Father really believed in his discovery of the worthlessness of Math, how could he be so fascinated by his brother-in-law? How could he, in the possession of such momentous knowledge, admire a simple millionaire? The obliqueness of his desire, his disguising it into thought and philosophic humbug... Why couldn't he declare it directly? "I, Onofrio Krocus, am immortal, all-devouring and bottomless!" History is littered with the tortured corpses of obliquely desiring men. To triumph, one must be direct — infinitely subtle but direct... Sniffing and rereading the yellowish piece of paper, which is crumbling at the edges, Max feels an intense surge of pity for the mud that was Onofrio, the lumps that were his testicles, the mess that was his brain, for his scattered mustache.

143

Jealousy, resentment, fear and desire is what's behind all those Beings and Not-Beings, those howevers and therefores; those pretensions at love-of-wisdom hid a scream, and Max is grateful for the gift of poetry, for being able to do what Father couldn't: turning the fullness of his passion into words, without having to kill it first and stretch it on the racks of conceptual thought.

The fourfold sound of the elevator doors, opening then closing. Enter Mrs. Krocus, bearing friar's balls in one hand and in the other her cane. "I found a piece of paper scribbled by Father, pretending to prove that mathematics is all wrong," Max shouts because his mother went straight into the kitchen.

"Aw, he was always into that kind of stuff. Gibble-gabble, quack, quack. All he could do is talk. A mountebank. Uncle Chaim thinks that your father..."

"Mother, I think Father had more intelligence in his little toe nail than Chaim ever had inside his numb skull."

"I'm not saying that your father was stupid," says Mrs. Krocus from the kitchen, "only that he liked to talk. How do you think he dazzled me in the first place, the very day I met him. Blah-blah, that's how. He stupid? Naw... The stupid one was me, for listening to him."

"You mean you should have listened instead to your dear brother..." says Max, with vehemence and sarcasm.

Mrs. Krocus isn't offended. "No, Chaim was never a mountebank. You can't compare. Oh, he could talk when business called for talk — you don't make millions if you can't talk — but he never had to resort to blarney with women. *They* had to talk *him* into it. Like bees to the honey they flocked to him..."

"Bees flock to the honey?" says Max.

144

"What did you say?" asks Mrs. Krocus from the kitchen.

"Nothing," says Max.

"He was sixteen, I remember. We were so poor we lived in a *conventillo* on Portela Street, and in the apartment next door there lived a Catalan couple. A tall, magnificent woman, you should have seen her bearing, and she fell head over heels for Chaim, who was only sixteen. Her husband, a man who packed a pistol, wanted to kill him: Chaim had to hide under the bed... And even today, even though he's over eighty..."

"Even today," Max blurts out ferociously, "I'd shoot him." Easy, easy. Max checks himself, having decided to avoid confronting Mother on the subject of Chaim. She must know nothing, suspect nothing. Every night, after roaming the streets, Max hides the Heftpistole at the bottom of his suitcase so Mother won't come across it.

"I don't see why, Chaim has always been nice to you. More so than to most people. Usually he's not so nice. When Onofrio was in jail Chaim took you with him to Castelar. You can't complain. Is it hot enough? Should I turn off the stove?" says Mrs. Krocus, handing Max the maté gourd.

"It's fine." Max sucks the gourd empty and hands it back to her. "But I don't think you appreciate how touching it is, how admirable and how pathetic, that Father, with a tenth-grade education, would confront singlehandedly the whole world of science, of thought, of mathematics..."

"He used to read a lot. That he did. After he died, out of curiosity, I opened the book he had been reading. Max, I couldn't believe my eyes: it was pornography!"

"Oh, for God's sake, Mom! I remember the book. It was Brantôme's *Damas Galantes*, a sixteenth-century classic!"

"Classic? I can tell smut when I see it. Classic my foot. Filth! Yeah, read he did."

Mrs. Krocus pours another maté with a shaking hand. "And don't you remember the bewitched math book? No? But you must remember, Max, that math book your father used to read in bed..."

"No, I don't remember. A math book? Bewitched?"

"Of course you remember it! The book had vanished. One day, I went into Pancracia's room when she wasn't there, to sift through her things — you can never be wary enough; it takes a gimlet eye to keep them honest. Born thieves. So I go through her room and what do I find? At the bottom of a drawer, hidden under her stuff... the math book."

"Absurd! What could she want a math book for? She didn't even know how to read."

"That's the thing," says Mrs. Krocus, leaning with a haggish chuckle toward Max. "She-didn't-even-know-how-to-read. What could she want the math book for?"

"Well?" says Max.

"Well! For a *gualicho*, of course."

"A *gualicho*? But Mother, *gualicho* is supposed to be a witchery, something a woman puts inside the maté to get a man to fall for her. A sort of love filter, like in Tristan and Isolde, or like they say Caesonia gave to Caligula, or Madame de Montespan to Louis XIV."

"You always bring up kings," shrugs Mrs. Krocus. "Sure, some crazy women put their pubic hair inside the maté, or their menstrual blood, or even their *dreck*, if it comes to that. But, you know, it doesn't have to be with the maté: they'll do it with anything a man wears, anything that belongs to him, and since your father was reading the math book every night, what better object could she get. Ah, the way it smelled, when I found it in her drawer..."

"It smelled? Like what?"

"Do you expect me to give you the precise chemical formula? It smelled strange, that's all. Maybe she had it fumigated." Mother hands Max another maté saying, "I can't believe you don't remember that math book, Max. How we laughed! You wanted to take it to a priest, to have it exorcised, don't you remember that?"

"I'm telling you, Mother, I don't. It smelled, uh? Fumigated... like an anthill?"

"To get the big ant-eater," Mrs. Krocus replies with a guffaw.

"You can't trust anybody these days," says Max; "how do I know there is no *gualicho* in this maté?"

"Ha, ha. Yeah, sure, the powders of Mother Celestina. Poof, poof, hocus-pocus. Rest assured, Max, your mother is not bewitching you. But by God, when one thinks about those poor people... in this day and age, such ignorance, such stupidity, such superstitions..."

"Why, Mother, do you think *gualichos* don't work?"

"Come on, Max, are you serious? Back then I couldn't help laughing at the fool, who thought she was going to get Onofrio into her bed... He stalked better game; he liked younger, prettier women. *Oi wei*, do you remember what Pancracia looked like? I've been stupid in many ways, but *that* way I was always smart: never did I hire an attractive housemaid. Well, back then I thought Onofrio wasn't going to fall for her for all the *gualichos* in the world. If you ask me now, I wouldn't be so sure. He was an unbelievably dirty old man, Onofrio was. Into any filthy hole..."

Father, the dirty old poker...

"In any case, the book should be still up there, in the

147

leftmost cabinet," says Mrs. Krocus from the kitchen, where she is warming up water for a fresh maté.

Max climbs on the stool again. A pile of musty books. The humidity of Buenos Aires is a killer. Malet's *Historia de Roma*, Sartre's *La Nausée*. Well, at least here one isn't startled by electric sparks as in the dry, cold North. *Tristes Tropiques*... lots of textbooks from high-school... And here it is, Silvanus P. Thompson, F.R.S., *El Cálculo Infinitesimal al Alcance de Todos*. He sniffs it. Mildewed, like the others. Max detects no mystic stink, no pythonist pother, no charmer's reek, no difference. White letters on a taupe, distempered cover. Yes, he faintly recalls having seen it on Father's night table.

More vividly he recalls Father's underpants, invariably carved with grungy brown glyphs, lying by morning on the floor, on his side of the big bed. Like the bloodied sheets, in the old days publicly displayed, of newly married girls. It is quite possible that he intended it, those dirty boxer underpants, as a challenge or perhaps even an insult, the way he burped at table, or when he wrote that zero is a fraud and mathematics worthless. And it is possible that push did come to shove between him and Pancracia. Later on, dirty son of a bitch, he must have grown tired of her, or maybe he found something better, even lower, and Pancracia was left to the young son.

Max lets out a groan. Was it in wakeful reality that he fucked Pancracia, or was it one of those dreams haunting the rooms of the old Flores house? He sniffs various sections of the book. Differentials, Integrals, the Curvature of Curves: theoretically different concepts, but to the nose exactly the same.

"Let's see the book... Yes, that's the one, I'm pretty sure," says Mrs. Krocus, returning from the kitchen.

"It doesn't smell like anything though," says Max.

"Do you expect hocus-pocus to last forever, like some kind of radioactivity?"

As a matter of fact, yes, that's what he expects. They sit down to another round of maté. In between bites of friar balls, Max reminds his mother that her birthday is coming up. He would like to take her out to a nice restaurant. He would also like to invite Gloria.

"You know very well that I will not accept to see Gloria or go anywhere with her; thank you anyway."

"Mothers and daughters, mothers and daughters!" Max grasps his head.

"My birthday!" Mrs. Krocus says contemptuously. "She looks forward to the day of my death, expecting to get half of my savings. But you, Max, promise me this: don't let yourself be gypped."

"Mother, stop it, stop it, I can't stand such talk!" He sucks maté in surly, reflective silence. "When all is said, at the very bottom, it's clear to me that the one thing you hold against Gloria is that she walked away from her marriage. Don't deny it."

Mrs. Krocus smiles. "How wrong you are. On the contrary, that's the one and only thing I admire her for. I should have done the same: I should have left Onofrio long ago, while the going was good."

Max puts the Calculus book on the table, by the silver-framed portrait of himself, says thank you to his mother, meaning he's had enough maté, and picks up his poem where he left it. Only a few last touches are needed. Made up of hendecasyllables and heptasyllables in a ratio of three to one, the recondite stanzaic structure not given away but rather hidden by the larger spaces between lines. The assonantal rhymes are strict, but so faint and far apart as to be perceptible only to an acrobatic ear. It is a narrative poem. The poet has died, an exile in a far-away country, and his soul flies all the way to Buenos Aires. She (for, it is agreed, a man's soul *must* be feminine) makes a first stop at Uncle Chaim's, flits about the elegant balcony, then heads down to Flores, to the old family house. On flowerbeds and roses, on dried leaves, on the housemaid's musty mattress she alights, then proceeds southwestward, toward La Matanza. Amid the foul smells of slaughterhouses, meat-packing plants and tanneries, she arrives at the Café-Bar "La Academia," close to where Father is buried. A not uncommon name for a Buenos Aires café, and a clever allusion to Plato's Academy: a delicate suggestion that what we have here is a re-telling of the myth of Er in the last book of The Republic (anchored deep inside literature Max feels cozier, secure). At the farthest corner of the café-bar, among a bunch of old, sad, broken men in caftan, the dead poet's soul encounters Dad's. Free of the flesh and its lures, finally at peace, the two souls play dominoes, and in the very last line (this has just occurred to Max, prompted, perhaps, by his reading of the essay on zero), Father opens the game with the double-blank. Two zeroes, father and son, facing each other. Death a passage, a dark line between two nothings: the one before and the one after. Max hopes his friend Fontana will like it.

He reads it once more from beginning to end under his breath, and is quite pleased. "Mother, what would you say if I told you that I'm thinking of coming back to Buenos Aires for good?"

Mrs. Krocus has finished cleaning the maté gourd, and is returning her old English china to the cupboard. "What would I say? I'd dance the polka on one foot. And I wouldn't believe it for a minute..."

"Why not?"

"Son, please, don't take me for an idiot. What would you do here? Everybody's trying to get out, like rats from a sinking ship, and you, you of all people are going to come back? Sure. Any day."

"Well, believe it or not, I am thinking of returning. I'm applying for a teaching position at the University. Schamberg, remember him?, just killed himself, and Fontana promised to help me get his job. With Fontana's influence, it's as good as done."

"*Der sof iz git*! Are you serious? You aren't pulling my leg, are you, Max? You wouldn't play such games with an old woman who has a heart condition, because if that's your idea of a joke, let me tell you, I'm never going to talk to you again, I swear to God by what's most holy." Mrs. Krocus is standing in the center of the room, hands joined over her bosom, cheeks flushed, lips trembling.

"You'll sell this apartment, and with that money, plus a portion of my savings, we'll buy a house," says Max with mounting enthusiasm. "A big old house, with ten rooms, and gallery and patio, with a fig tree and honeysuckle all around..."

"But darling, I'm much too old to be cleaning a big house..."

"Why should you do the cleaning? Naturally, we'll have a housemaid." But this time, he secretly determines, he'll be the one to choose and hire.

15

This evening at seven o'clock Fontana is lecturing at the University; Max wants to be there and present him with his poem, moving evidence of the spark, the tiny but unique spiritual thing that is Max; the spark which, being beyond the world and prior to it, cannot be approached by Math. At one o'clock there's plenty of time to visit the old house in Flores; there's even time to go back, after that, to Father's tomb. And there's a good reason to do both, for such is the journey of the soul as described in Max's poem, and one should never miss an opportunity to make life and literature agree.

Max inscribes, "To my old and admired friend Fausto Roberto Fontana" on the top of a long-hand copy of his work, puts it in an envelope, and says good-bye to his mother, who is about to turn in for her siesta.

"Where are you going," she asks.

"A walk through the city, as usual, and then to see el Indio."

"You'll be back for dinner?"

"Maybe, I'm not sure," says Max.

On the bus Max reflects how strange, having been in Buenos Aires for over a week, he hasn't visited the old family house. Often, during his years of exile, he has remembered it, and recalled, one by one, those windows not seen in more than twenty years, walked in his imagination through each of the rooms, upstairs, downstairs, terrace, balcony, patio, and lain in the shadow of the garden, by the roses. Shortly after Max left for the U.S., the house had to be sold to pay debts: it was either that or Onofrio back into the slammer.

Fontana too had lived some happy hours in that house. El Indio would spend more time in Max's house than in the cramped Fontana apartment. After their daily dose of triple integrals and sundry math and physics problems, the two young men would open a bottle of wine and proceed to translate a tango into macaronic German, or compose an absurd cha-cha-cha (boleros being too hard, the words impossibly sentimental). They'd propose to each other *bouts-rimés* with the most outlandish words, or plan a cookbook *more geometrico*, which el Indio, proud of his reputation as a cannibal, insisted on heading with the motto, "We eat what we are," and where one would find axioms such as, "There exists an eggless omelet." Some of the theorems were inspired by Spinoza: "Nothing can be cooked, except by a cause hotter than itself," or, "The human stomach has an adequate knowledge of the eternal and delicious essence of the cow."

Occasionally Don Onofrio would join them and, from a dense cloud of cigarette smoke, would try to convince them, on the basis of Fichte's self-positing Ego and other

153

metaphysical shenanigans, that minus one times minus one can't be plus one, and that the imaginary numbers are unnecessary nonsense.

There were also parties for ten or twenty friends, and the house resounded with the ferocious screams of Gesualdo Costa imitating King Ubu, and with everybody's laughter at Consuelo Regueiro and Rolo Santón going at each other in a battle of grimaces, like in Gombrowicz' *Ferdydurke*. When they played "exquisite corpses," their collective texts were (so they thought) most clever and avant-garde. Once Tina, who had a wooden leg and limped badly, arrived late at a party and apologized, "Sorry friends, I tripped over the 35th parallel." At the wee hours, they'd all sit quietly and listen to Schubert's *Winterreise*.

A truck with a green-streaked, elliptic-cylindric septic tank runs parallel to the bus, racing, until the bus stops for passengers and the truck rushes ahead. Max calls the roll of his other, almost forgotten friends: Guillermo O'Brian, Tina Brescia, Lucio Cimascek... Even Schamberg showed up at the house for a party once or twice. All of them were eighteen or nineteen and felt like culture heroes, Prometheans who had discovered the keys to freedom and immortality. Those keys were mostly Formal Logic and the Literature of the Absurd, both equally opposed, if from opposite ends, to the middle jargon of officialdom. Against the many who wielded slogans — Marxist, Freudian, Peronist, Catholic, Nazi, Argentine Nationalist — they responded with infinitely more powerful weapons: Jarry's *baton of Physics* and the *baton of Finance*, Gombrowicz' disgusting anarchizing of the compote, the word "Critic!" uttered as an insult by Beckett's bums, and most irresistible of all, the fact that the slogan-mongers had no idea what a tensor product of modules over

154

a ring was, and *they* did. With mathematics as an ally, those boys and girls were waging an aristocratic war against stupidity, bombast and conformity.

Then Marceline appeared. A ravishing freshman, she was waging no wars. She didn't have to, for she was naturally elegant, cradled in refinement, and seemed to know exactly what she wanted. Max fell in love with her right away, and invited her to a party at his house. At first his friends were mistrustful. The newcomer was too well dressed, a whole year younger than they and just taking Calculus I, but admiration sprouted on all sides when she wittily dismissed Hollywood movies as "anemic cinema," and it knew no bounds when Marceline, with typical nonchalance and perfect accent, showed them the French distich:

Gal, amant de la reine, alla, tour magnanime,
gallement de l'Arène à la Tour Magne, à Nîmes.

"Who is that girl?" asked Fontana, dazzled.

Max whispered in his friend's ear, "She told me her father is the best French poet alive and that her mother owns the best art gallery in Latin America."

El Indio, who at eighteen was shy and had never yet had a steady girlfriend, whistled. "And you... and her..."

"Love" was not a word Max could utter in seriousness. "For her I'd swim to the moon and back... For her I'd solve Riemann's conjecture... For her..."

Marceline Quimperlé was Max's first true love. Her face was lovely, and reminded Max of Nadar's photography of twenty-year-old Sarah Bernhardt. The shop girls of Rivadavia Avenue, Doris of Retiro Park, all those one-night-stands had receded into a paleolithic past. By that time Max didn't see much of Boris, who was too busy with his medical studies and hospital internship, and anyway Max would have been too embarrassed to introduce his cousin to his friends. It would have been a gaffe, a shameful anachronism, like slipping a medieval buffoon into a salon of the Age of Enlightenment. Between Math and Marceline, the beautiful daughter of the poet and the *marchande d'art*, Max was seraphically floating on the most refined symbolic systems known to man.

Not that it was easy; perhaps nothing worthwhile is. Like Faust, Max would sit in the dark, wishing Satan to appear on the armchair before him so as to strike a simple deal: his soul for Marceline. She proved to be harder to grasp than topological spaces, and six months and many fervid declarations, presents, movies and dedicated lines went by before she consented to kiss him. That was the beginning of a difficult period, for Max had no experience with virgins. With skill and patience, though... But the toughest, most intractable part had been Mrs. Krocus. She hated Marceline. Max could never figure out why. The girl's refinement, her beautiful, fashionable clothes, the traces of a French accent? Or the fact that she was never able to respond to Mother's Yiddish curses, that all those calls for cholera into her belly and fiery plagues into her bones just left her puzzled, open-mouthed, and she didn't even understand the awful meanings of "*Gei in drerd aráyn*"? Max suspects that it would have been the same with any steady girlfriend, that Mother wanted him to be a Don Juan, masterful and cruel to women, unattached to anyone but her. Mother wanted him to be her exclusive and vicarious *schlong*.

From the back seat of the bus, jolted by the rough ride, Max twitches his nostrils. Amazing thing, the human brain.

How far is Marceline? Three decades and many degrees of longitude and latitude apart (long ago she moved to Paris, married, divorced, married and divorced again, like Max). Still, as vividly as if they were making love right now, by sniffing his own mustache he can smell her singular combination: her soap, her vaginal sweat, and her perfume, *Femme* by *Rochas*.

He gets off the bus with a strategy: he'll approach the old house stealthily, obliquely; he'll follow the same path he used as a twelve-year-old coming back from school.

The kiosk is no more, and Max doesn't mind it much, since he quit smoking. But the *conventillo* is still there, the long corridor, the black and white floor tiles, the skystrip, and he stands at the threshold as he did forty years ago, receiving on his face the cool, moist air carrying a hundred smells. At siesta time the place is quiet, and a big woman swabs the floor: she could well be the daughter of the giantess, the whore whose gait so impressed his boyish fantasy, now grown to her mother's girth. Time courses on, tricky and sly, battening lithe whores into swabbing mastodons, only to fell them later and spread their fat to fertilize the pampas. Age and a mustache, however, have not made him any braver, for he still would run if the big swab raised a threatening broom.

The barber shop is there too, but how different! The spiralled stripes are gone, the tin basin has rusted off and the barber is someone else. "So young," thinks Max, and immediately realizes that his barber, who chewed on a *toscano*, was probably not older than this one, who's chattily clipping a customer: younger than Max himself is now. The old barber — old! — was probably no more than forty-five! "What have I done with my own youth?" he mutters. "You lazy bum,

157

killer of time, now time is killing you, and it is only justice."
And the café has been remodeled. It seems smaller, and on
the section where the billiard tables used to be they've
opened a couple of shops. Sport clothes. Video rentals. On
the window, a large poster of a huge ape carrying off in his
arms a well-endowed, frightened girl, bikini-clad. New tech-
nics, new fashions, but some myths never change.

Then, at the turn of the corner, across the street, as if
carved with a razor out of his own eyes, where the old house
used to be, there is an empty lot.

16

Oatgrass and burdocks where the roses grew. The iron grille, uprooted. Gone, the palm and the avocado trees. The house, tiled roof, rooms, balcony, stairs, carved oaken doors, stained windows, all erased. The shock is so violent that only after a moment he starts noticing some of the traces left. Pipe ends sticking out of the side walls. A few brightly colored tiles where the library was. Loose bits of wallpaper adhering to the mortar, a darker band between what used to be the master bedroom and the children's.

Schamberg's three lovely holes. Gloria's three dry ones. Vergara's dirty asshole. The capital O of Onofrio. Jell-O, Dran-O, Odor-O-No. Blank images flood his brain, like that time when he was twelve and arrived home to find that Father was in jail. Zero. The double blank. He is filled with fury against his father. How can the manifest everpresence of nothingness be denied? His sophistry, his show of empty logic, was intended to camouflage the fact that it was he, nobody but he, Onofrio Krocus, the pope of nihilism, the architect of nothingness; he was the one responsible for the house being sold, demolished, turned into a void; it was he, nobody but he, who was the cause of his own death and disaster; he who was to blame for every hole, and for the fascination of the holes in Max's soul. And it is he, as a disembodied voice, who's seducing Max into the nothingness of vengeance, the red, automatic impulse to redress a balance of wrongs, which is another name for not-being. Chaim, instead, with all his criminal selfishness, stands in Max's sulphurous soul surrounded by an aura of desire, of perfumed life and sensual happiness.

Max reaches for the envelope in his pocket. He intends to destroy his poem, for it is a reconciliation, and with his father none is possible. After death Max will refuse to dwell in the same shadows. He touches, instead, the cold metal of the Heftpistole. Before he searches his other pockets he notices, against the remotest wall, some pieces of masonry still intact. Door hinges, blackened pipes, the remnants of a water tank. The rests of the servant's room and bathroom: the meanest part of the house the last to go.

*

The doors and jealousies were open, letting in the breeze. From the balcony side, the acid smells of acacias, of joyful gutter rivulets and decayed leaves; from the terrace, whiffs of soap, bluing and bleach, and the vapors of an incipient pot-au-feu: marrow bones and onions boiling somewhere, in the same pot. The smells merged while the housemaid moved between the beds. Max approached and laid

160

the palm of his right hand on her buttock. Nothing more. Pancracia was wearing a brown skirt over her draft-animal rump. She looked at her young master, and raising a monitory, minatory finger, scoured by bleach and ammonia, red-capped with chipped nail polish, said, "Cut it out or I tell the Señora."

For days Max trembled; the thought of Mother's reaction filled him with abject terror. But after some time it became clear that Pancracia hadn't squealed: no one had been told about Max's shameless *Jeu de Paume*.

Then, on a warm late afternoon, Max opened the jealousies of his bedroom and tiptoed into the terrace. The usual laundry smells, the late-afternoon sounds of doves cooing in a nearby dovecot, of the woman next door watering her gardenias, the springy leaves resisting the downpour, and of a distant radio soap, two voices smothered by passion: "Julio..!" "Graciela..!" A faucet dripping docilely into a drain. The sun was low, red and enormous. Max tiptoed to Pancracia's door and listened. Not a sound. He tiptoed back to the bedroom, ran all the way to the head of the stairs, went down six steps, put his ear to the wall. From that point one could hear every sound from the maid's room, the clink of the iron against the ironstand, the fainter thud of the iron against the pad. There he stayed, hearing nothing, for a while.

He rushed back to the terrace, tiptoed to Pancracia's room. The sun pulsated a fiery redness upon the dying day. Silence. Only one way to find out. He pushed the poorly fitting metal door, which opened with a screech. That screech lives in Max's mind as a bird's augural cry before the commission of a crime, and those exposed hinges on the farthest wall are the last holdovers, the only remnants of his domes-

161

tic world. Standing on the sidewalk, facing the void that was his house, Max marvels at the poetic subtleties of destiny.

Pancracia was lying on her cot, in her slip. Max was standing at the door in his pajamas.

"What you doing here," she said.

He was shaking too violently to answer.

"Get out," she said.

"I came... to keep you company." His throat was so dry that the c's and k's hurt. "Why don't you tell me about El Caburé..."

Pancracia didn't seem surprised. She hailed from El Caburé, a God-forsaken place on a corner of Santiago del Estero, near the border with Chaco. At twelve, an illiterate orphan, too homely to be sent to the brothels, she was launched on her lifelong career as a housemaid. Rolling over the cot to crush her cigarette on the tin cover of a bottle of tomato paste, she exposed her thighs. Ten years before, from under the dining room table, he had studied Pancracia's furrowed heels. Now, naked, right there, in front of him, those heavy, sturdy thighs, her dark, abyssal flesh...

"What if the Señora comes in," she said, anxious yet strangely calm; "Get outtahere right away!"

Her concern with Mrs. Krocus interrupting was in obvious contradiction with her professed wish to get him out of the room. Her leisurely crushing of the cigarette contradicted the urgency in her words. Repulsive as it is to logic, there is nothing more exciting, sexually, than contradiction. But there was no doubt that Pancracia was worried. "What if the Señora comes!" she kept repeating.

"She's left," said Max, supremely excited by the housemaid's fear. "She won't be back for three hours."

"How about the Señor?" she inquired, still a bit worried but visibly relieved.

"He's out, and Gloria too; we are alone in the house."

Pancracia smiled, showing her rotten teeth, the embattled fortification of her mouth. By now Max had acquired some confidence and was shaking less. It was clear that he wasn't unwelcome, and so he was about to ask her for a cigarette and settle down to a bit of chit-chat. He was going to sit at the edge of her cot and talk. Surely there could be no lack of topics for conversation between two people who had lived under the same roof for any number of years, yet had never exchanged a word besides "bring the bread," or "your shirt is ironed." There could be no lack of insights to be shared about the family, more interesting for coming from opposite points of view. But Pancracia wasn't into conversation. Max was surprised when, raising herself from the cot, Pancracia reached at once for his crotch.

"Mmm..." she said.

She said "Mmm..." and stroked him, just like Doris. His legs yielded and he fell on top of her. Before he glued his lips to her gums, Max whispered, "I've been wanting you for a long time..."

"I know," she said, opening herself to him.

But once inside her he felt limp, nauseous. There seemed to be something opposed to the consummation of the act. Her cunt was vague, enormous, viscous. It stank. The young man who came out of the maid's room five minutes later, as the sun was setting, looked not like a conqueror. And now, thirty years later, it all flows back.

Several days went by. At first, whenever their paths crossed, Pancracia would purse her lips, or wink an eye. He would pretend not to notice. One afternoon he was sitting at his table, exploring the abstract labyrinths of a mathematical treatise, Bourbaki's *Structures Fondamentales de l'Analyse,* when she approached stealthily and whispered, "Come to my room tonight." It was as if a dragon, foul and concrete, had suddenly breathed fire on his neck.

He spent that night with Marceline. In her arms he strove to dispel the nightmare of his visit to the maid's room. Pancracia appeared in his dreams as a sewer, as the mouth of a dark tunnel at the top of a sheer cliff, her genitals a loathsome granular lump of yellow suet. The boundaries between dream and reality had become fluid: no longer could he be sure whether a scene, a texture, a smell, originally belonged to one or to the other. With Marceline, the sweet-scented daughter of a *marchande d'art* and a poet, he could enjoy the delights of the flesh on a level of equality, of perfect comradeship: theirs (Marceline used to say) was the ideal love between a man and a woman, free of bondage, a love of the kind the poets Rimbaud and Laforgue had longed for. Marceline didn't suspect that if it had occurred to her boyfriend to love like a French poet, it would have probably been rather like Baudelaire, by mortal jumps between the High and the Low, traveling on a sulphurous sky-rocket like the ones he used to launch on New Year's Eve in Castelar; and how could Marceline possibly imagine that while he was with her, as he heard her, in the height of pleasure, call him *mon chouchou, mon p'tit lapin,* as he half listened to her explications of de Beauvoir's latest book, Pancracia's coarse refrain kept resounding in his ears: "What if the Señora comes!"

What had happened to him? Perhaps, following Rimbaud's advice (Marceline might have ventured), Max had succeeded in making his soul monstrous. If so, it was a sorry, bungled monster, an amphisbaena, the reptile with two opposite and opposing heads. With Matisse in his eyes, a song by Reinaldo Hahn in his ears, and her Parisian perfume still clinging to his nose, reeking of Culture and Art, after making love to Marceline he'd walk the elegant streets of the *Barrio Norte* like a wounded beast, hating himself for being an intellectual and not a butcher or at least a corporal in the Federal Police like Pancracia's son, wishing he were *macho* enough to pin her to the cheap armoire or to the screechy metal door, and possess her stinking cunt: make her sputter Indian curses and holler between pleasure and pain, between fear and delight.

He neglected Marceline, forgot to call her for her birthday, made love to her absent-mindedly. They quarrelled. "You came to this country when you were only three; how come you still have a French accent?" Max irritably asked. "I wouldn't be Marceline Quimperlé if I didn't," she replied, which was true enough, but unhelpful. By March 1959, Marceline had enough of Max: she dropped him, and took up with el Indio Fontana.

Max didn't mind it much. He immersed himself in theorems. As a relief from the levels of abstraction of Bourbaki's treatise, he read Spinoza's *Ethics* and Kant's *Critiques*. Mathematics and Philosophy were a refuge for the mind, a *sanctum* from which contradiction, his daily tormentor, was excluded: indeed, contradiction was *La Grande Exclue*; anything, anyone else might be admitted, but not her. His heart, however, looked upon those symbolic adventures as upon children's games having little to do with reality. Reality had heavy thighs and was up there, tremendous, behind a screechy door, lying on a cot, smoking, waiting to be ravished, fertilized, and no amount of bloodless abstraction could assuage Max's heart, or compensate for his failure to act like a master and take absolute possession of Pancracia.

In his heart he dreamed of being a conquistador, a cruel, raping brute, but apparently he could be but a scholar, a scribe! Gradually, in the feverish pauses between theorems and corollaries, an idea started taking shape in Max's mind. The idea had some mathematical and philosophical underpinnings: often, when confronted with something absurd, it is enough to turn one of the terms around to obtain a perfectly viable result. Namely, while "p and not p" is certainly contradictory, "p and p" need not be. And here was another reason: how many times have we admired in the great philosophers the courage to push an idea to its utter, often bitter, end. Why not imitate them. Max was attracted to something which he found repulsive. *Eh bien*, let him try to experience it *at its most repulsive*. Maybe then... And there was this proposition from Spinoza: "If we conceive that a thing, which is wont to affect us painfully, has any point of resemblance with another thing which is wont to affect us with an equally strong emotion of pleasure, we shall hate the first-named thing, and at the same time we shall love it."

It became clear to Max that in order to escape the painful contradiction in his mind he had to eliminate all such points of resemblance. Pancracia was not like other women, and should be approached in a different way. One might say that ontologically and logically, Pancracia was prior to Woman. She was a dark continent waiting to be evangelized and exploited, and if he was to succeed, Max had to abandon all civilized habits and ideas, all pretensions of comradeship, mutual pleasure and consent that worked relatively well with Marceline. Expecting to have a conversation with Pancracia! How stupid could one get? He should behave like a master. To start with, the conduit to her womb must

166

be canceled, condemned. He had as little intention of collaborating with Pancracia in bringing forth a future Federal policeman with a Jewish nose as of helping her do the laundry. To be in any way connected with her uterus (even with a condom) meant a descent from the level of the all-powerful master to that of the slave: only through her anus could Pancracia be fundamentally possessed.

Armed with these insights, he went into her room. She was standing at the ironing table. That pleasant afternoon there was nobody else in the house. The doves cooed, the terrace faucet dripped, there was a smell of freshly pressed linen. Max lifted her skirt and groped about her buttocks. She let him grope without a word. He fell on his knees and started kissing, licking, biting those buttocks, slobbering all over them. Then, suddenly, pressing his forehead against her flesh, he wept.

"What the hell you doin'," she grumbled.

"Pancacha... Pancacha..." Max sobbed. He had heard her son, the corporal in the Federal Police, call her that.

She had stopped ironing and was wriggling her behind. Arms around her belly, hot cheek pressed to hers, eyes closed, he let himself be rocked. For a moment it felt like paradise. "Don't cry, baby, don't cry," she crooned a lullaby, "tell your momma what you want..."

Max bestirred himself, got up, pulled down his pants. "What you lookin' for," she laughed at his feverish poking.

"Pancacha... Pancacha... *ahí*, Pancacha..." he babbled, poking and groping.

With a belly laugh she bent down over the table, reaching out to him, stretching herself, trying to be helpful. Right then he came. He couldn't help it. For a moment he stood watching her. She was still bending down, elbows on the ironing table, wriggling a bit, waiting. Those heavy, hairy buttocks, wet with his own saliva, his tears and his semen... The painful absurdity of the whole thing. He pulled up his pants, turned around and left the room.

He went downstairs, among the books. His mathematico-philosophical idea had not worked. That, of course, did not detract in the least from the idea as such, as an idea *an sich*, but he was left in the old, painful, contradictory lurch. Actually, now it was much worse. He felt abject, as one who has committed a foul crime; a burrowing worm who has been undermining the foundations of his own house.

Looking at the books he felt a little better. The laureled L of *Editorial Losada*, the winged wheel of *Santiago Rueda, Editor*. The f of Gallimard's *nrf*, graciously surging like a siren from the paper's pure whiteness. The running torch-bearer of *The Modern Library*. The pelican, the penguin. The cartouched N of *Nelson, Editeur*. Here and there, the leather-bound, gilded binding. He opened the bookcase door. How sweet the squeak of the bronze hinges, and the smell of wood, old paper and leather... Max opened a book. It was an old *Garnier* edition: he rested his eyes on the title page and soothed his agitated mind with the beautiful balance, "6, Rue des Saint-Pères, 6." Then he saw her. She had come barefoot from upstairs and was standing before him, wearing only her slip.

She smiled. "I came to keep you company..."

The book fell from his hands. He backed up and took refuge behind the desk. Pancracia in the library, with her lewd, humble, beseeching smile, repelled him.

"If you want, I can pour maté for you..." Like a serpent, through the Pompeian-red reflections of the walls, she moved toward Max's corner. He moved too, making sure the massive desk stayed in between, unable to utter a word. "Why so nervous..." Her voice was hoarse and thick with rut. "We're alone, ain't we... Up there in my room you made me hot, you know, real hot... Come, don't be silly... Come 'ere, Max baby, with your momma..."

After one and a half turns around the desk, Max was close to the door; he bolted out of the library, out of the house, until he found himself in the street, standing on the opposite sidewalk. Exactly where he is standing now, thirty years later. Back then, when he stopped and looked back at the house, it seemed to him that he had pulled a hidden plug that wasn't supposed to be ever pulled and that the abyssal waters were pouring out, an unstoppable flood. He had awakened a monster. Now it is hard to understand why he was in such terror, to the point (one memory evokes another till it all comes back) where for weeks he was obsessed with avoiding Pancracia, until he succeeded in persuading Mother to dismiss her. Two of his valuable American math books had vanished (Max lied) as well as his gold cuff links. Clearly the housemaid had stolen them, as she had previously tried to steal Thompson's Calculus. With a false accusation was Max finally rid of the unendurable presence.

In retrospect, it might have been his own actions and not Father's that brought ruin down on the House of Krocus. Max pictures Pancracia raising her scoured, fearful finger, uttering terrible Quechua curses. *Gualichos*, wax dolls transfixed, blasphemous brews; he had falsely accused her, and what's worse, had failed to perform, failed to assuage her savage female heat: this hole, littered with debris, is the result. He's guilty, as was Dad; liars both, hypocrites, timid sexual misfits. And now Max feels closer to Father than ever, ashamed that he blamed him only a moment ago. Dad, who tilted against zero and unassailable windmills. How could he live like that, blindly, without urgency, or die in any kind of fulfillment? His eyes fill with tears. Facing this house-hole, the obscene obliteration of his past, Max has touched nothingness like Thomas touched the risen Christ. Had he gone to La Matanza and found a café near the Jewish ceme-tery where he could play dominoes with the dead; had he ascertained that souls are truly immortal, his joy wouldn't have been greater; rather less, for he finds it impossible to imagine any post-mortem arrangements more sovereign than nothingness, or any prospect that could give a stronger meaning to his life. It is an inebriating, joyful sadness. Musical. The thought of past lust, cowardice and lies, of his own guilt in the erection of this palace of not-being, gives him force; his will has been purified, and he is certain that a more resolute and reverent life, and greater poems, shall yet come out of it. As for Chaim, whether he loves him or hates him, Max cannot say.

17

Three boxy, dismal buildings on a treeless plain strewn with debris and garbage, standing by the side of the river which poetically minded Argentines call "lion-hued": to a prosaic eye it looks mud-brown. University City, *Ciudad Universitaria*. Back in the early 1960s, when there was less garbage on the ground and in the air more hope, Max worked here as a Math Instructor. A quarter of a century later, the halls where he used to strut are bustling with young suitors after scientific knowledge, but none of them smiles at Max, nobody knows him. Fewer ties and more blue-jeans than in his time; like in the U.S., more sneakers. Still, there are differences. In the U.S. students produce shrill buzzes from their heads, a sort of harsh, grating stridulation, and they will suddenly startle you with an explosion, like monstrous caterpillars of the Malayan hawkmoth. Here, electronic devices for avoiding the dreaded misery of silence are fewer in number, as are the devotees of bubble gum. Plus, of course, in the U.S. they have wonderful facilities, labs and libraries, clean bathrooms, a stunning amount of information at everybody's fingertips.

But what might be in the minds of these science students of the Argentine backwater? Although he was one of them once, Max has no clue. They walk and move as if they knew where they go. So did Max at one time, so did his friends. Until, after the military coup of 1966, the police were sent into the University with orders to smash or puncture a few heads, too full of science for their own good, and the generals in power, perhaps mistaking it for Psychoanalysis, classified Vector Analysis "subversive."

A group of students comes noisily down the stairs; one of the girls looks like an up-dated version of Marceline; one of the boys looks like Schamberg. They charge ahead laughing and joking, as if life were a bed of never-wilting roses. With a shudder of envy, Max wonders how much he'd give to be that boy with longish hair whose arm is around the pseudo-Marceline. At times he would give everything, yet, at other times, he wouldn't want to be that young again, that foolish.

They strut by without noticing him. As children, they've lived through nightmarish military regimes: the students of only ten years ago, those who were grabbed and taken directly from this same Student Center, from the mimeograph machine where they printed their demented pamphlets, to a protracted death in secret torture chambers, are they still remembered around here? These merry boys and girls seem to have forgotten everything and to be placidly awaiting a new round. Max suspects there isn't much in their heads, other than dates, dancing clubs and designer clothes. Or nothing at all: blank, zero, *pace* Onofrio.

But down by the windows some students are talking,

172

and from a distance at least they seem intelligent, unfashionable. Max is willing to accept the possibility that they may have come to study science here for the same reason he did, thirty-odd years ago: for the marvelous oasis of clear language, an escape from the repulsive, pervasive, recursive, nauseating Hispanic hydra of mendacity.

Walking along the main hall, involved in this reflections, Max comes upon a man whose face he recognizes. Squat, completely bald except for carefully flattened, sleeked slices of grey hair along the sides of his pate... that Tyrone Power mustache... but of course, it's Escobar! Though he must be pushing sixty, he hasn't changed much. Max stands, smiling, while Escobar, too busy to notice, is talking to an aproned, younger guy. Max calls him.

The little brown eyes scan Max up and down, firing quick signals to the brain, which matches, compares, sorts, elicits, tries to recover a face from face-filled decades. But as soon as Max mentions his own name, they fall into each other's arms. Escobar slaps Max's cheek, Max slaps Escobar's pate, and the young janitor watches from a respectful distance.

"Where have you been, all this time," asks Escobar.

"In North America, mostly."

"No foolin'! What you been doin' down there?"

"Good question," says Max. "But I've decided to come back."

Escobar explains he is now Chief of Janitors, in charge of all three buildings. Taking him by the shoulder, Max asks does he remember when he was in charge of washing glassware at the chemistry lab, back on Perú Street. Does he remember how he used to whisper into Max's ear the name of the chemicals he was supposed to identify? Later, when

173

these dismal buildings were built, Escobar was transferred to the Math Department, to make coffee and clean bathrooms.

"I don't clean bathrooms no more, but I still make coffee," says Escobar. "Come, let's have some. My treat."

In Escobar's office there's a cracked wooden desk and a swivel chair. Electrical switches cover a wall. A board with a hundred keys. Above the coffee machine, three pictures: Gardel holding a guitar, Perón wearing the white and blue presidential sash across his plastroned chest, and Maradona stepping on a ball. Escobar explains that he supplements his paltry salary making coffee. He classifies the faculty not by rank, or field, nor by age or prestige, but according to the generosity of their tipping. Benzadón and Llorente are at the top of the list, both great guys; Lucas and Capricoll are so-so, and Kuligovsky seems not to have noticed that there is galloping inflation: his tips haven't gone up for a whole month. "What d'you expect," Escobar explains, "he's a Jew."

So is Benzadón and so is Max: doesn't Escobar know that? Try to tell him that Jews are not what he thinks: it wouldn't make any difference. Max asks about el Indio.

"Fontana's a good man, good tips, but he don't drink much coffee. Too busy with the broads, I reckon," Escobar concludes, winking an eye.

What does he mean, says Max.

"A superbroad is what she is, Vanessa Satanovsky. What, you never met her?" Escobar whistles low. "Quite a bitch, if you ask me, but man, the way she walks..."

Escobar offers a grotesque imitation of her swagger, and Max laughs. "She a student?" he asks.

"Sure," says Escobar.

"And Fontana and her..." Max prods him.

Escobar makes a rubbing gesture with two fingers,

174

followed by a vigorous, reciprocating motion of his right fist at belly level. "Everybody's knows it," he adds; "our friend Fontana don't waste no time. Hell, he's here only for two months, ain't he? Reminds me of a gaucho I met, who couldn't watch a horse's rump — you know, when the tail rises 'cause the turd's just coming out — without getting a hard-on."

Escobar puts a cup of coffee before Max, then suddenly remembers, "Hey, lemme treat you to somethin' good." He opens a desk drawer and pulls out a bottle and two glasses. "To celebrate your return. It'll make your ears tingle. Caña from Paraguay," he says, pouring. "Here's to you."

They touch glasses, take a sip, and Escobar asks, "So you've been moving around?"

Max tells him about foreign lands. At Florence, Pisa, Rome and other Italian cities, the mathematics institutes are generally provided with an espresso coffee machine. Anyone can make coffee, but most professors ask an orderly to bring it. The situation in France, at places such as the École Normale Supérieure, is basically the same, except that some of the orderlies are women. Escobar shakes his head in mild, wondering disapproval. Now, in India, at a research institute in Bombay, each professor is assigned a man who crouches in a corner of the office and waits. No, he doesn't bring the coffee; he just waits there until you drop a piece of paper or a pencil: then he jumps forth, picks it up and hands it back to you. That's all he does, all he's supposed to do. One can tell that Escobar is impressed. But in the United States coffee machines — no pressure, mind you, no steam, just the paper filter kind — are usually at the department secretary's office, or at the faculty lounge, and there are no janitors, no orderlies to bring a cup of coffee to a professor's

175

desk. Escobar can't believe it. Well, yes, there are janitors over there, somebody's got to clean, but they work in the evening, once the professors have left. No, they are not supposed to serve professors directly in any way; if you want a cup of coffee, you go get it yourself. So people like him, decent men but without much of an education, don't they ever work during the day, Escobar wants to know. Yes, a lot of them do: computer operators, key punchers, mail sorters, lab assistants, boiler maintenance people... Many machines need to be served night and day. Escobar scratches his pate; he seems nonplussed. He gulps down his caña, Max does the same. "You never stop learning," Escobar says.

As Max takes his leave the Chief Janitor asks, "Did you hear about Schamberg? What a shame, from a thirteenth floor, sunny side up, with a spatula they had to pick 'im up. They say his wife left him, and that's what pushed him to the edge. Women... Still, those were the good old days, when you were here, and Fontana, and Schamberg, and Costa, and all the other guys; remember those drinking bouts, remember them barbecues? And the jokes! Students nowadays... a bunch of sissies."

They hug again. "And remember," says the Chief Janitor, "anything you need, here's Escobar to serve you."

Max goes upstairs, to the Math Department office. Behind a desk, a young woman is typing. There's no one else. She doesn't look up and he doesn't want to interrupt. Her hair is tied in a ponytail. Her long nails are polished something opalescent. Max always marvels at long-nailed typists: this one does it with two fingers, hunt-and-pecking. He clears his throat; she goes on. That door goes to the chairman's office. Who's the chairman now he doesn't know, but he'll have to find out if he's to apply for a job. Where this girl

176

is sitting another girl used to sit whom he once asked out but was refused. She was pretty and clearly a fool. He clears his throat again. The typist doesn't register. A man comes in (Max recognizes him immediately: it's Professor Llorente) and says, "Tell Capricoll I'll be back in an hour; the Dean wants to see us."

"Sure thing," the girl replies without raising her head, and Llorente rushes out, without recognizing Max, who used to be his assistant.

Max takes the opportunity to slip in, "Excuse me, but could you tell me where the mailboxes are?" She raises a totally blank face. He adds, "I'd like to leave this envelope for Professor Fontana."

"He's not here," says the girl.

"Do you know when he'll be back?"

She shrugs and shakes her ponytail. "He's teaching a class right now."

"Where?"

"How should I know. In one of the classrooms, I guess."

18

Max enters unobtrusively through the back door. The class has not started: Fontana is erasing from the board the dusty corpses of prior performances. Out of ten students four are women; Max wonders which is Vanessa Satanovsky: two might qualify for Escobar's superbroad, and he bets on the freckled one who looks Jewish. The other, a pert Andalucian type, wears large ear-rings amid cascades of lovely locks.

Fontana slap-dusts his hands, arranges his notes, breaks a piece of chalk. Hush. A world's about to emerge. A u appears on the board, upper left. What will befall this u, which in its solitude and humble stance elicits our immediate sympathy? For starters, it acquires an Indochinese-peasant-style hat. On a different stage, say at a French class, the sign over the u would be called a circumflex accent; here, in Mathematics, it is called a hat. Next, û is propped up, provided with protection, anticipating God knows what perilous adventures. Fontana draws a bodyguard on each side:

| û | . The plot thickens, new characters appear, including a suspicious, foreign-looking one, a Greek lower-case xi. And a long serpentine thing, like a cobra rising out of a charmer's basket:

Then all hell breaks loose on poor u-hat. After being bracketed, squared and variously tormented, it reappears, like a battered Pulcinella, with its hat upside-down. "U-check," Fontana calls it now, an "inverse-Fourier transform."

How many Math lectures has Max attended in his life? Two thousand? Three? He doesn't remember realizing until now how much they resemble a theatrical performance. The classroom, with rising ranks of seats, reminds one of a small theater, yet Fontana doesn't "act" at all, on the contrary, his style and his tone of voice are unemphatic. Since Max happens to be familiar with this material (odd word here, Mathematics being the incorruptible paradise of matterless form), he does not have to pay close attention and can indulge in the fantasy of thinking of symbols as actors in a play. There seems to be only a difference of content, not of form, between saying, "let u be a smooth function with compact support," and "Enter Ghost in his night-gown," or "Enter two Clowns with spades and mattocks."

A male student with a funereal profile and a dirty collar interrupts to observe that there's a minus sign missing somewhere. Fontana stops, inspects the board, strokes his chin.

"No, no, it is all right; that factor over there becomes e-to-the-i-pi, equal to minus one." The Gipsy girl. Her earrings tinkle to the soft, tropical breeze of her own speech. There's mastery in her voice, like a manorial habit of command; and withal, a sweet, moist, pleading undertone. Another Sonja Kovalevska, another Sophie Germain?

179

Fontana has noticed his presence, waves at him, but Max is absorbed by this amazing phenomenon, this blending of Pythagoras and Thais. The beautiful Gipsy girl looks at him with mirth rippling around the corners of her lips, and for a split second, Max thinks: she wants my soul — then realizes that not only she but every one is looking at him, and hears el Indio's voice, "Hey, Max, welcome back to Math."

He blushes. When he first arrived in the United States, Max was amazed that in the streets of New York women avoided eye contact. Didn't they see that he was a clean, sensitive, spiritual young man, wearing shoes of the best Argentine leather? How could they be blind to the obvious? Once he was standing in Washington Square, by the Arch, with nothing much to do, when he saw a beautiful, mink-coated woman with silver-spangled eye-lashes flashing bewitching glances. Heart thudding against his ribs, he timidly approached, and found himself at the center of a circle of people. "Hey mack, move over, will you," said a man holding a light meter. The woman was a fashion model, and her smile was meant for the market, not for Max. Come down from outer space, Max. Welcome back to Math. Stick to the play that's being staged, don't try to change it, or to become an actor.

And what a play it is, marvelous, far superior to anything on Broadway. No crazy passions here. No old men stabbed behind the arras, no young philosopher's wife turning into a whore, no Heliogabalus knifed and thrown into the sewer. Review the theater from Aeschylus to Beckett; what do you find, but the frightful or comic spectacle of Reason's humiliations? Here u-hats, and now v-hats, phi-hats, a whole company of hatted or bareheaded letters, play their passion-free and exemplary roles with humble, selfless perfection. And Fontana, Max, the Gipsy girl, the funereal boy, all the others, are not merely spectators but participate as commentators, a Greek chorus. This is our celebration of Reason, her triumph not her humiliation. You don't have to suspend your disbelief: on the contrary, you're welcome to sharpen it, you are begged to wield it to the best of your ability. Exercise your skepticism: you shall be persuaded anyway. Reason's High Mass, enacted at every Math class. The kind of theater Jean-Jacques Rousseau wished for: one is amazed he never hit on it, although Giulietta, that skittish, beautiful Venetian courtesan gave him good advice, "Jack, let women alone and study Math." And, of course, it is useful to boot: you don't merely get uplifted, or purged, or catharsized, or tickled blue, or whatever else you are supposed to get at a theater or at a brothel: you learn how to think, how to build jet planes, or figure the orbit of Saturn. If you are told, "Math's too specialized, how many people understand it?" you may reply: more than those who ever saw a Greek play back in 400 BC.

"But Math doesn't speak to us of the human condition." No? Are you sure? Take a look around, at things and space and shapes, nature and artifice, and you'll see that she does, perhaps more so than any of the so-called Humanities.

"How about love, and suffering and death: Math doesn't speak to us about that." No indeed, Math does not speak to our puny fears and desires, and why should she? She's got too many important things to do.

Occupied by these thoughts, Max has missed a good chunk of the lecture. Fontana mentions a theorem called "the Minimax." In vain Max scans the boards looking for a statement; perhaps el Indio has already erased it. Maybe "Minimax" is the name of the guy who first proved it?

Someone named Max, but frail, short and consumptive, hence the "mini". Of course he's kidding: he knows the name is a synthesis of the terms "minimum" and "maximum," as "oxymoron" means both sharp and dumb, and although Max has a recollection of having seen a Minimax theorem in his day, honest to goodness he doesn't know what it's supposed to do. He tries to retrace a couple of u-hats and v-hats back to a point where he can remember what they were up to, but he is lost. The rest of the audience seem to be following, everybody takes notes. The freckled girl gnaws on her pencil, the hair of the Gipsy grazes her notebook. Max suspects that neither is wearing a bra. Ah, to be young again, and powerful!

Obscurities accumulate. The Closed-Graph theorem, the Fredholm alternative. In the past, Max has published papers on such things, yet now he is unable to attach any precise meaning to those names. Frightening, as if one suddenly found one can't recall the first couple of bars from Beethoven's Fifth. The two beautiful girls, the other two, the funereal and the other boys, all seem perfectly comfortable with Minimax. They are all oxys, Max the only moron. Any of these young students is better equipped to fill Schamberg's position than he. What could he possibly teach them? They could be teaching him. Ah, it was foolish to apply for a University job: he should be teaching high school, bored to death, making fifty dollars a month, or working as a janitor under Escobar, living with Mother not in a big old house but in a small *conventillo* room. Instead of being the choragus at the noble Theater of Mathematics, he should be the lowest bum, a Vladimir or Estragon...

Leaving all decorum aside Max fixes his gaze on the Gipsy girl. Forget the u-hats, the phi-hats and the integrals:

182

he should persuade el Indio to go out on a double date, he with his freckled Vanessa Satanovsky, and Max with *her*... Why not? Indeed, when we say, "Let x be a real number," or, "Let u-hat be the Fourier transform," that's it, *fiat lux*, what we've said becomes a mathematical fact. Then why can't Max simply say, "Let that beautiful girl fall into my arms," or, "Let her be mine"? Why aren't these "lets" as effective? Why is it that only in the realm of pure thought mortal men can play god? And conversely, Max muses, perhaps Plato's god, who used to geometrize all the time, non-stop, is a more human god, more to man's measure, than the Christ of flesh who died on the cross.

Whitney's embedding theorem. Max used to know what it does, he used to know a dozen different embedding theorems, he can remember none. What's happened to his brain? Oh, shame, shame! Embedding is just what he would like to do to the Gipsy girl. If Max were a god, or merely an oriental despot, he wouldn't spend all his time geometrizing. Oh no. At sundown he'd command, "Let that beautiful maiden be conveyed to my bed." Abstract thought is what's left when all else has failed: magic, prayers, sacrifices, *gualichos*. U's let themselves be Fourier-transformed more docilely than beautiful girls let themselves be taken to bed. Isn't she peeking at him right now out of the corner of her eye, to see if she can catch him looking at her? But Max is looking straight and intently into the board, at the u-hats and the integrals.

Why would such a girl want to go out with a guy like him? El Indio is the same age, he's got prestige, and the poise that goes with it. Young ladies like wreathed brows on older gentlemen: the tremendous sex-appeal of laurel leaves. And isn't it astounding that the successful exercise of mathematics, which is only a *pis-aller* born out of disillusion and the failure of magic, should end up having the effect of a love potion? Look at Fontana, with what self-confidence he takes a step back and ponders at his formulas, how he contemplates his students like a benevolent god who condescends to showing them only a tiny portion of his thunder. And Max, what could he show, what power? What famous theorems has he proved, what famous poems composed?

And now the board is a sea of disconnected signs, and el Indio's phrases are random gibberish to Max. Should he sit down with paper and pencil and slowly, painfully, sign by sign, try to decipher: definition, lemma, theorem, corollary? Years, years of hard mental work. He's grown old and his brain become addled, softened by rhyme and wishful thought. When he was young, there was time both for love and for deciphering; he doesn't like whining at life, yet he can't help asking: why has his smartness left him, but not his longings?

Things are not so glum though, there is still enough brain power left in him to solve elementary problems; and so if by some miracle heaven were to bestow on him this beautiful girl, here's what they'd do: whenever a climax should loom close they would take a step back and think of integrals. He'd ask her to integrate sin x times e-to-the-two-x, she'll ask him to do the hyperbolic tangent. They would keep it simple yet challenging: that way they should be able to hang on to delight all night long. Nothing like a little computation to keep climaxes on hold: old Pythagoreans knew the trick, and the influence of Hindu math on Tantric techniques is a little-known fact about which Max may write a learned paper. "Pauca cupit qui numerare possit," a Roman poet said: as long as one is capable of arithmetic, passion will not overflow; and the English bard, contrarywise, "Number there in love was slain": you stop counting when you finally come. Kipling, too, has Kim escape the influence of hypnosis, first cousin of sexual climax, through the simple expedient of remembering multiplication tables...

All stand up. The lecture is over.

"Had I known you were coming, I would have asked you to my Faculty Seminar, earlier in the afternoon. Poor Max, bored to death by this elementary stuff!" says Fontana as Max approaches the lectern.

"But it was extremely interesting!" Max protests.

Leaning over confidentially toward Max, Fontana says, "You know, most of these kids are not that well prepared, so I have to start from scratch, from the basics."

"Going over the basics is never a waste of time, Indio, and you make them perspicuous..."

"Will you join us for dinner?" says the mathematician. "We're just going across the street."

"I came here mainly to deliver this little poem, dedicated to you," says Max.

Fontana thanks him and puts the envelope in his briefcase, together with his math papers and notes. Max finds it odd and embarrassing that his poem should cohabit with the u-hats and the Fourier transforms. It is like Doris' fusty gash in intimate contact with Grandma's sheets, that far-away first time.

"Have you met Vanessa Satanovsky," asks el Indio, introducing Max to the Gipsy girl.

Max is already quite intimidated, and the unexpected reversal flusters him: he offers her a limp hand. She smiles indifferently. His beautiful Gipsy turned out to be Fontana's lover.

185

In the hall they meet Professors Llorente and Capricoll: they do not recognize Max, but greet Fontana and Miss Satanovsky effusively. Her earrings clink, which makes Max inexplicably sad. As they walk, Fontana says to the old gentlemen, "But of course you remember Max Krocus."

They go down the stairs into the main hall and out into the dusk. "Oh, yes, Max — Krocus — But of course — So many years — where have you been all this time? — Well, truth to tell, you don't look the same — We're getting old, aren't we all..."

19

From the Municipal Airport all the way to the University, a hundred restaurants dot the riverside. Once those were trailers carrying a few tables and a barbecue grill; as they prospered, they shed their rails and raves and wheels, but since there was a limit to how much trailers could expand that way, they were finally torn down, burnt, and out of the ashes sprung capacious restaurants well anchored in cement. The low hiss and the smoke of broiling beef hang over road and treeless fields, and people come from all over the city for fleshy feasts. Stray, eternally hungry dogs ramble about, and bums too, palm cupped at hip level, who will hail a cab for you or open a car door. Students and faculty only have to cross the street from the School of Science to enjoy carnose carousals the likes of which have not been seen since Homeric times.

Of the students, only Vanessa is invited. Professors Llorente and Capricoll, fresh out of their meeting with the Dean are, to judge from greedy glances toward the grills, ready to tackle a whole cow. Two of Max's old classmates, Gesualdo Costa and Consuelo Regueiro, join them at the door. Max hasn't seen them for two decades; they hug, they kiss. "Hey, you're still a kid," and, "You haven't changed at all..." Gesualdo is accompanied by his daughter, a lanky girl of sixteen, and two foreign mathematicians: a young Italian, Luciano, and an American, Alan Sanders.

Max calls Mother on the phone to say that he won't be back for dinner. *"Oygn!"* she utters somewhat mysteriously, as if she were calling Prinz Eugen to defend her from the Turks. The Yiddish word means "eye," "keep a sharp eye," that is. Coming from his mother, Max interprets it to mean, "Watch out, I know you well: no monkey business at Retiro Park." Mrs. Krocus may not be aware that Retiro Park doesn't exist any more.

A place has been saved for Max at the round table between the Italian topologist and Consuelo Regueiro. While he unfolds his napkin, Max looks at Consuelo. He remembers her hair always pulled back into a chignon. Someone has been cruelly turning on that knob, making her hair and face tauter. Those wrinkles cannot have been drawn merely by time; rather, he suspects, by daily wincing, and the bitter downcurve at the corners of her mouth bespeaks long familiarity with sarcasm. Consuelo used to be Max's friend — never lovers, always confidants — until she married Rolo Santón. Out of the orphanage, penniless, as soon as he entered the University Rolo climbed on the shoulders of giants — Newton, Gauss, Cauchy, Einstein — and began scanning not the vast horizons of Science, but the unattached wealthy females. Consuelo's father was a well-to-do wholesale grocer, but in a few years the grocer died, the fortune vanished, the couple separated, and Rolo rolled away towards Germany and a younger heiress from Stuttgart.

"El Indio won't let his best disciple stray far," says Consuelo in Max's ear, pointing with her chin (there's poignant hair on it) to the point on the table diametrically opposite, where el Indio is sitting next to Vanessa Satanovsky; "you're stuck with me, Max; the two old divorcees, left-overs from a bygone era."

El Indio must have spread the word of his divorce, or she may have noticed it herself on Max's face; she knows him pretty well. Or perhaps she's referring to Sharon, his first. "Let the little Satanovsky sit where she will, there's no better place for me than next to you, Consuelo," says Max, while secretly wondering how long el Indio intends to keep his affair going, whether he'll take Vanessa with him and his wife back to California, keep her as a pet, or will he leave her in Buenos Aires, an erotic *pied-à-terre*...

"What courtly manners! Right out of Versailles! And I thought you lived in North America... But you know, with me, after the board there is no bed."

"That's all right, I'm celibate. Ascetic. I've been sleeping on the floor, at Mother's place," says Max.

"What's *chinchulines*?" asks Sanders, the American mathematician, pointing into the menu. "Chinese food?"

"A calf's braided duodenum," says Fontana, "a typical Argentine delicacy, salted, braised, and roasted to perfection. Piping hot."

"Is it the duodenum? I thought it was the hind gut," says, in his grave, Balearic English, Capricoll.

"The hind gut! Look here, one must distinguish. There's the duodenal *chinchulín*," says Llorente, bringing the edge of his hand down decisively upon the tablecloth, "and

189

there's the jejunal *chinchulín* (he repeats the hand gesture a little further down). It's like with sweetbreads, you know, there are two different kinds..."

"What does 'piping hot' mean," Gesualdo's daughter interrupts with her adolescent soprano.

"Piping hot is the same as sizzling hot," explains Gesualdo; "two favorite words of U.S. ad-copy writers."

"But up there they are used differently, Gesualdo," says el Indio; "meat may be piping hot, sizzling hot could be a bikini, a novel, or a Caribbean vacation."

"I'll have those chin-chu-whatever and a steak," says Sanders; "how do you say 'steak' in Spanish?"

"White wine for me," says Vanessa, *"Blanc-de-blancs, bien frappé."*

"White wine with red meat?" asks Llorente, who is sitting next to her.

"I never drink red, it gives me a headache," says Miss Satanovsky with a gesture that Max finds delicious, and Llorente evidently too, because while he looks at her drool runs down his gray goatee.

"Something to start nibbling on," Fontana says to the waiter. *"Matambre...* roasted red peppers... and let's see, how many *provolettas?"*

"What's a *matambre,"* asks Sanders.

"Too involved. Not in this syllabus, Sanders: wait until next semester," says Luciano.

"But going back to *chinchulines,"* says Llorente, "you know, it was African slave women who came upon the idea. The *negras* would go to the slaughtering field, and while they waited for some choice chunk of beef or pluck to come their way, they'd pick, just out of boredom, some offal from the ground, some useless guts, and start braiding."

190

"Doesn't it remind you of those women who knitted by the guillotine, during the French Revolution," says Gesualdo's daughter, and Capricoll interjects:

"I've read somewhere that Rosas used to throw his enemies to the tender mercies of those *negras*, and so his henchmen would eat barbecued 'Unitarian' *chinchulín*."

"Nonsense!" says Llorente. "Where did you get that story? From the madman Sarmiento?"

Luciano stops chewing on bread to say, "In Dante's hell Mohammed stands with his intestines out, hanging between his legs, and that's why the Commedia is banned in Muslim countries. They're afraid people will get the idea of making *chinchulín* out of the prophet."

"You have spent all the time in this country, never gone away?" Max asks Consuelo.

"Five years in Spain."

"Still got family there?"

"I left Buenos Aires just in time; they caught my brother — tortured, killed; Father died of a broken heart; I was next."

"Jesus," says Max. And after a silence, "Nevertheless, you came back." Consuelo shrugs.

"Incredible, the American obsession with numbers," Gesualdo Costa says. "What do you think their best-selling book is? The Bible? Shakespeare? No Sir. A collection of numerical records, the stupidest you can imagine, like who said 'motherfucker' the most times without breathing. While I was at the University there, they had a game of musical chairs, with more chairs than ever before, so as to appear in the big book: even the President played, and it was the most memorable thing that ever happened there. During the Vietnam war, they tried to keep the public happy with numbers and body counts. Why do you think *Time* and *Newsweek* always give you the age of a person right after his name? Because they can't write more than two words without spitting out a number, that's why. How good a lover are you? How attractive? How smart? See your score, page 48."

"Why do you find it incredible, Costa?" Professor Capricoll speaks gravely, as usual, separating his hands in a grand, curtain-opening gesture. "It's clearly stated in their axioms. How does it go? We hold this truth to be self-evident: all men are created equal. Being stripped of all essential distinctions, men become mere elements of a set, exactly as in Hausdorff's *Mengenlehre*. And what do you do with sets? You take unions, intersections. You take complements. But mostly, you count them. Not much else to do with them, is there, Costa. You mix them up and recount them. And so for North Americans, both Theology and Anthropology are branches of Statistics."

"And what is this, 'barbecued *ubre*'?" asks Sanders, still studying the menu.

"Udder. Cow teats. From the Latin 'uber' as in 'exuberant,' meaning either milk coming out of the teats, or teats coming out of the brassiere, I'm not entirely sure." Llorente makes a round, capacious gesture over his belly bend.

"Like Saint Agatha," says Luciano, "who had her tits cut off for refusing to go to bed with a Roman centurion: one wonders if he had them roasted and if he ate them too."

"I guess back then, in those dark ages, anything was preferable to losing one's virginity," says Gesualdo's daughter, contemptuously shrugging her bony shoulders.

"Sure, sure. *Vergine d'avanti, martire di dietro*, like the Pope," says the Italian topologist.

"What did he say?" asks the girl.

192

"Nothing, nothing," says Gesualdo. And turning back to Capricoll, he adds, "I'm convinced that's why Americans are so concerned with their body weight. If you are looking for a continuous variable with an ample enough range to make it interesting, and if it's got to be more or less subject to will power so as to fit both their obsessions with numbers and with self-control, what's better than body weight?"

"Well, there's blood cholesterol," says Capricoll.

"Salud!" Llorente raises a glass of wine.

Everyone proffers, "Salud!," except for Gesualdo's daughter, who's still asking what Luciano said.

"To the health of our distinguished visitor, Fausto Roberto Fontana," Capricoll toasts.

"Our truly distinguished visitor is sitting right there," returns el Indio pointing at Max with his raised glass; "Max Krocus, who's not just a mathematician but a poet too. He touches both extremes, you might say he burns the candle at both ends."

"Really," intones Llorente.

"Indeed," echoes Capricoll.

What proportion of irony there is in el Indio's words Max cannot tell. Fontana takes irony as a duty, and except when he talks Mathematics, irony seems to infect his every phrase. But Vanessa's look of interested curiosity is enough compensation. And when, lifting his eyes from his slice of *matambre*, Max encounters again her burning eyes across the siphons, the bread baskets and the bottles of wine, he cannot hold her stare, and his heart goes berserk.

To hide his agitation, Max starts telling Consuelo of his vision at the slaughterhouse. How, facing the statue of the cattle driver, he saw hundreds of women being driven

193

down the muddy road, like cows. Consuelo doesn't seem to be horror-struck or particularly impressed. "The Argentine cow and the Argentine woman are in the same predicament, wouldn't you agree?" says Max.

"Oh, no! Cows are in much better shape... They're left alone, to chew their grass and look at the passing trucks... until they're killed. But they are not expected to love their killers, or to mend their socks, or wipe their little asses... Cows are happier... Moo!," she concludes, smiling bitterly.

To Max's left, Luciano is having a tête-à-tête with Gesualdo's daughter. They talk about Vivaldi. "Orphaned teenage girls by the hundreds, *ragazzine* abandoned by their families, secluded in a convent for life... He taught them music and turned them into lovely singing angels... Some people accused him of being a dirty old man — nowadays he would be called a sexual harasser — but, I ask, having helped those poor girls ascend to the harmony of the heavens, would he have done his duty as a teacher if he hadn't taught them how to love?"

"Tra-la-la, my dad told me about Perón and his high-school sweethearts, he taught them how to ride moto-scooters..." laughs Gesualdo's daughter.

More meat is brought to the table. A hissing, portable charcoal grill is laid next to Max, with the short ribs he ordered, and the *morcilla*, the glistening blood sausage. Black but comely, ye daughters of Zion.

"Can't compare! Vivaldi left five hundred concerti, a musical treasure," says Luciano, sticking a corner of his napkin under his collar. "What did Perón leave? A sorry mess, *un casino*. Look at this poor country now."

"What does Perón have to do with it," says the young girl, petulantly. "It's the rich countries, Europe, Japan and

194

the Yankees, who are killing us, keeping us pastoral, prostrate."

"And the International Monetary Fund, and the World Bank," Gesualdo pointedly reminds his daughter, and goes on explaining to Sanders, "A lamb that's never chewed on grass, you roast it very, very slowly. Use a square grill; for the first half-hour have only four coals, one at each corner. Then add four more, like this, see, at the midpoints. Only then, after another half-hour let it have a few small embers at the center..."

"Do you know the one about the doctor doing a rectal exam?" Llorente asks Capricoll. He waves his hands in the air with the expression of intense enjoyment of a child driving his bike: "Look, no hands!"

Max wonders how his poem is faring inside el Indio's briefcase, in the company of those Fourier transforms. This country is a big brothel, Gloria says. Okay, but add: a giant cattle-ranch. The question is, what will they do with the embittered, aging women. If they ever organize, their revenge will be terrible. The young girls, that's no problem: just send them to Luciano. Suddenly, out of Sanders' plate, something hot squirts all the way across the table and grazes Capricoll.

"Fucking duodenum," says Sanders. "How did you say it was called?"

"You must exercise caution with *chinchulines*, Sanders; they are always overfilled with juices, very treasonous," says Capricoll, gravely wiping his earlobe.

"The more I see people eat meat, the more I consider turning vegetarian," says Vanessa.

"Why do you think that eating plants is less evil than eating animals," says Llorente, who is sitting next to her.

195

"Plants suffer less," says Vanessa.

"That's your surmise. Just because plants don't go 'moo'," says Capricoll.

"Plants must bear the historical guilt of our devouring each other," says el Indio.

"Really? How is that?" says Llorente, refilling el Indio's cup.

Fontana takes a long draught, then wipes his mouth with the back of his hand, an uncultured gesture done in self-deprecation to compensate for the little lecture coming up. "You see, at the beginning, life was going on with just sunlight and the minerals around. Nobody ate anybody: it was the garden of Eden, the Golden Age..."

"You mean Eden really existed?" The little soprano voice of Gesualdo's daughter.

"Without any doubt, it's a scientific fact," says el Indio; "but there were no people in it, only bacteria."

Gesualdo's daughter makes a wry face. "Science always comes up with wonderful facts; only they've got nothing to do with us."

"That's life, my dear," says her father, laughing.

"Go on with it, Fontana," says Llorente; "what happened then?"

"Then plants came along with a new and more efficient idea: noncyclic photosynthesis. But here's the catch: the waste-product of this process is oxygen, and plants were so successful, they produced so much oxygen, that the atmosphere changed and high-energy ultraviolet rays were screened out. To make a long story short, the planet became covered with the plants' gaseous excrement. This made it harder for nitrogen to combine with hydrogen into ammonia, something all living beings must have, so the alternative was either to disappear, or to procure those nitrogen compounds ready-made, from other living cells: in other words, to start eating each other. You see, plants are the original sinners."

"Morally, then, the Brazilians and the Indonesians are doing the right thing," says Gesualdo, sawing deeply into his thick steak, "cutting down the forest, settling old scores."

"Hey, we ought to cut down all trees, all bushes, and uproot the grass. I refuse to eat any more of this salad. The war to end all wars: war to green stuff!" says Consuelo.

"I should say, inasmuch as possible we ought to be using those ozone-killer spray canisters, that healthful ultra-violet may shine through upon us, and usher in a second coming, *donec finiatur mundus corruptionis*," says Capricoll, gravely proud of his Latin.

"It's the only moral course open to us, the only way to stop the ongoing carnage," says Llorente, helping himself to another sausage.

"Methane would help too, methane's fundamental: so let's all fart, fart, fart, hooray!" says Sanders, raising a fist holding a fork and a piece of *chinchulín*.

Vanessa is saying something in el Indio's ear. She gets up and walks away. To the bathroom? No, she goes out through the front door. Max overhears Luciano speak softly, in Italian, to Gesualdo's daughter. Verses! The bastard is reciting verses! And the tender girl smiles, young sister of Ginevra de' Benci. Consuelo, hand on Max's right forearm, asks if he wants to try her sweetbreads. It's now or never. Max says, "No thanks," gets up, half of his meat still on the portable grill, and walks out.

Outside, the night is quiet, velvety like a bat's soft fur, humid and deep. He walks past the cars parked at the curb, past the sleeping attendant sitting on a bench, limp arms hanging, hand frozen in a begging gesture while on his transistor radio a singer complains of women's treachery. He walks across the empty boulevard, towards the riverside. Vanessa is leaning over the balustrade, her black hair half covering her face. Max leans, elbows on the dewy stone, next to her. Beneath them, the river, the dark water lapping the wall. She says, "Hello." The word hangs in the stillness, suspended around them, like those halos around the distant lights dotting the fishermen's wharf.

"I was looking for you," says Max.

"Well, now you've found me," she whispers.

20

How can some be so blind as to deny there are miracles? What is a miracle, after all? Out of ordinary wakeful experience, we formulate certain laws, on the basis of which we proceed to figure probabilities. Open a phial of essence of violets: the molecules hop out, bump around, rebound, a few get into our nostrils, hit nerve endings — in other words, perfume the room. The likelihood of all of them returning to the bottle is close to nil, maybe ten to the minus thirty, but not zero. After we die and are buried, our old cells, proteins and ions will not be likely to organize themselves back into anything resembling ourselves, but such a resurrection is theoretically possible: we would call it a miracle, *the* miracle, no doubt. A whimsical, elitist god could have given his children back to Job, but such capers, benefitting only one man, or one man and his family, would hurt the vast majority, making weather prediction, allocation of resources and modern civilization impossible: the practice of Statistics is based on the systematic rejection of miracles.

Yet miracles, now and then, do occur. Max repeats the name, Vanessa Satanovsky, over and over under his breath (Mother is in the kitchen, listening to the radio, but her ear is keen). Vanessa's warm, Napoleonic eyes, meant for command and the ushering in of new epochs, for invading the cold steppes of Max's heart... Vanessa Satanovsky: silken name, like her laughter, taffeta interwoven with gold; her adorable Mediterranean nose; her Sienese madonna forehead. Yes, miracles do occur: at fifty, gray turning to white, to begin loving! After that first affair with Marceline, then more so with the passing years, he had become a shrunken, fearful conservative, content to live in the shade among the shadows, resigned and cynical. Love had ceased to be life's promise and had become a mirage or, as for Proust, a mistake. Later, love was the red heart and the turtle doves of U.S. postal stamps and bumper stickers, the "I love ya'll" of the TV evangelists, the candied commodities of Christmas and St. Valentine's day, a ploy to sell neckties, handguns and cosmetics, a false promise of health, protection and simplicity. Love had ceased to exist.

And now, suddenly, melodious, marvelous like the best production of a master poet, that kiss... Wise combination of labials, dentals, palatals, voiceless or softly voiced, fricative, delicately aspirated, with just the space to breathe at the caesuras, those delicious enjambments as lips cross without breaking touch. As some lines in Homer join a human music to the chaos of the sea, Vanessa's kiss has returned to Max Spirit as Woman and the world as delight.

Disloyalty to his friend Fontana bothers him. But what's this girl, really, to el Indio? Obviously a divertissement, a diversion from math. Besides, thirty years ago Marceline left Max for Fontana, and it is only fair that now

200

Vanessa leave Fontana for Max. But has he a right to expect such miracles? Why he? Why should Max Krocus, not particularly deserving, be saved by a fantastically lucky chance, while cousin Boris had to die in a Reno hotel room because one night Dame Roulette refused to favor him, on much, much better odds? This image bothers Max most of all, Boris dead, lying on his bed like a puppet. The ridiculous, rigid corpse seems somehow to be his, Max's, stretched out in his mother's apartment. He's grateful for this second opportunity at love, rapturously grateful for the miracle of that kiss... yet it *is* an upsetting fact: miracles are unfair, they ought not to occur in a democracy.

Fair or unfair, he is determined: this time there will be no darkening, no explosion of the Low, no awakening of slumbering snakes. At fifty, he's in charge, his monsters have been tamed. Max gets up from the mattress. "Mother, do you remember why Pancracia left?" he asks Mrs. Krocus, who's in the kitchen, listening to the news.

"Who? Pancracia? The *gualicho* fool?" asks Mrs. Krocus.

Food riots in Santa Fe. Supermarkets looted. The Government, having recently confiscated all bank accounts, is encouraging the people to open new, special accounts in U.S. dollars: these, the Government solemnly assures, are guaranteed and will not be touched.

"No, I don't remember. I don't think I fired her though," says Mrs. Krocus. "I guess she must have left on her own. You know how hard it is to fire those people, ever since Perón? A month advance notice, and a bundle on top."

Officers of the thirty-third armored regiment in Santa Rosa have threatened to take out their tanks and drive on to the capital unless their salary requirements are immediately met. The Archbishop has offered to mediate in the dispute.

"Why do you ask?" asks Mrs. Krocus.

"No reason. Just thought of it," says Max.

"Are you going to have breakfast?" Mrs. Krocus is eating her morning yoghurt.

"In a little while."

Max paces the room, rummages in his jacket which is hanging from a chair, finds the piece of paper with Vanessa's phone number. Eight in the morning, too early to call. He grabs the phone anyway, sits on a chair and dials the first two digits. If he lets it ring just once, he'll be able to hear the sound of Vanessa's phone ringing, which is already a part, even if a tiny part, of her domestic world. No illusions; no doubt in his mind that she will not want to see him; she will adduce other commitments, will say that she's got to study math; nonetheless... He dials the third digit, then changes his mind and hangs up. His heart is pounding.

Judges, from the Supreme Court on down, are going on strike, starting next week. And that's the news. Mrs. Krocus turns the radio off, washes the yoghurt spoon, and goes into the living room. Max is sitting on the chair next to the phone. She looks at her son and sadly shakes her head. "Max, where did you go last night?"

"I told you, Mother, to a restaurant."

"To a restaurant... with whom?"

"Fontana, Costa, Llorente, Capricoll, and a bunch of other people," Max shrugs.

"A bunch of other people... women too?" asks Mrs. Krocus.

"Women, yes, there was Consuelo Regueiro, remember her? And Costa's daughter. She's sixteen. Why do you ask."

"Consuelo, yes, and Costa's sixteen-year-old daughter... But who's the one who turned your head — fliff-floof." The old lady accompanies her last word with a vortical motion of her hand.

"Mother, for goodness sake, where did you get the ridiculous notion that a woman turned my head? What, do I look... fliff-floof?"

Mrs. Krocus smiles. "Well, yes, you do." She sits on the chair next to Max. "Did I ever tell you how much I wanted a son, how I had to undergo treatment: special diets for a whole year, massages of the womb, until finally I got pregnant? And when at last you were born, my God, I went completely crazy, talk of a fliff-floof! Onofrio used to laugh at me; 'He's just a baby-boy, not the Messiah.' And I would reply, 'To me, he *is* the Messiah.' I don't exaggerate when I say that feeding you, rocking you, kissing you, bathing you, wiping your dirty bottom, was my whole life. I lived for nothing else. Certainly not for Onofrio. Day by day I saw you grow into a man, a strong, intelligent, handsome man. Yes, yes, you don't have to be modest with me: strong, handsome and extraordinarily intelligent. And did you think I wouldn't notice what's going on inside your heart? I know, you think I'm being arrogant, but tell me: is there anybody in this world who knows you as well as I do?" She lays her frail, arthritic hand on Max's arm. "Now, you may choose to confide in your mother and tell her about this woman, or you may not... But don't take me for an idiot and tell me that I'm wrong."

Mother's moles; Mother's white, spindly legs; her warm hand on Max's arm; the morning sun reflected on the white enamel of the stove top; everything's so soft... Why not?

"Her name's Vanessa, Mother... She's a math student... She's amazingly beautiful... and very intelligent... She's... Mother, what do you want me to tell you, I have never seen in my whole life a girl like her!"

"Max, you make me so happy, so happy you can't possibly imagine."

"But wait! There's nothing really yet. She's much younger, she's only twenty-something, we've only met yesterday, and we have only kissed!"

"Only kissed, only kissed! In my time people got married before they ever kissed."

"But I've no idea whether she wants to have anything further to do with me, no idea at all!"

"If she's so intelligent as all that, she'll understand that with you she's hit the jackpot," says Mrs. Krocus.

Mother and son are sitting next to each other, hushed for a moment. Ah, may she be right! Her buckled, crooked hands are on her lap, the hands which used to caress him and wipe his little bottom, half a century ago. God knows, she may be right, for Mrs. Krocus isn't often wrong. Max smiles: "You may be interested to know that she's Jewish..."

The phone rings, next to Max. He hands it to his mother, who holds the receiver with a trembling hand. "Hello. Hello, Chaim? How are you. *Vos makhs du epes?* Me? Great spirits, but about the body don't ask: a piece of shit. Yes. Yes, I hear you. Uhu. I see. Sure, why not. Good, whatever you say: you certainly know best. Max? Oh, he's fine, fine. Thank you, Chaim. *Zay gezúnt!*"

"That was Uncle Chaim," says Mrs. Krocus once the phone is hung up. "He sends you best regards."

"Best regards! The bastard. May he soon be farting under the sand: *Zol er gich fortzn indrerd!*"

"I really don't know what you've got against your uncle," says Mrs. Krocus. "He behaves like a prince. He called to tell me he's moving my dollars to one of those new special bank accounts."

"What? You must be kidding me," says Max.

"Why would I kid you; do you think I've no better things to do? The interest they're paying is fantastic."

"But Mother, who in his right mind would put twenty cents into those bank accounts? They'll confiscate them, as they've done with the others!"

"Do you think Chaim doesn't know that? Do you think he was born yesterday, that he's sucking his thumb up on cloud seven, like Onofrio used to? He's got friends absolutely everywhere, as high up as you want: when there's danger, he'll be the first to know, he'll move the money out. Meanwhile, I'm reaping a windfall!"

"That's why this country is bankrupt: only corrupt bastards make a killing," Max grumbles.

"Can you tell me what's corrupt about this?" asks Mrs. Krocus.

"Since when has your brother been administering your money?" Max somberly asks.

"Listen, Max, I want to make this perfectly clear, because I want you to understand," says Mrs. Krocus rising from the chair with difficulty and standing before her son. "When Onofrio died he left me in the street, literally, in the gutter. Worse — I had to hide: three loan-sharks and fifty angry creditors were after me, ready to murder me. You know that: after all, he screwed you too. Who helped me then? Was it you? I'm not blaming you, I know you didn't have money. Was it Gloria? Ha! She's just waiting to inherit the little I have got. No, it was Chaim. Chaim helped me then with his advice, and with my efforts and his experience, I was able to get where I am now. Not rich, but comfortable. Peace, at long last, in my old age. Chaim's always done superbly, like a king, by me. Now I said what I wanted to say. Not one more word about it. If you want maté, I can pour it for you."

Mrs. Krocus goes back into the kitchen. Max stays by the phone, boiling and fuming. Father the loser, Father the sucker, Uncle Chaim the king. Father rots under the ground, while Chaim rolls in shameless luxury in his *Barrio Norte* flat. And now Mother has the last word. Isn't life unfair enough, she's got to make it worse by siding with the winner? There must be some way, short of waiting for the improbable Last Judgment, to make Father come out on top and Uncle Chaim at the bottom, deep in hell. There must be a way, at least, to show Mother...

"Max, you were asking about Pancracia," Mrs. Krocus says from the kitchen. "I suddenly remembered. She came to see me once, many years ago — it was before Onofrio died — she was all gussied up and told me, very proudly — ah, you should have seen her — that she was living in Berazategui, with a man. Then she says — listen to this — that her man was better than my men. In those words. What do you mean, I asked. '*Más hombre, más cojones*, more balls than your husband and your son, Señora,' she says. I thought she'd gone completely nuts."

"What did you do?" says Max.

"What did you want me to do? I was watering the roses; she caught me by surprise. I said maybe she was right since her man apparently could stand both her stinking self and the stench in Berazategui, then I told her good-bye and don't show your face at my house ever again. I told Onofrio.

He agreed with me, the woman had gone mad."

Berazategui! That's where the city sewers discharge into the river Plate. The embarkment to the sewers of Cythera... Truth is, Max has missed all chances of love. He's missed all boats — the ones consigned to mud, to the peaceful beaches of domestic happiness, to the islands of refined, voluptuous luxury. Teeth clenched, angry with the world, in an act of desperation, like a gambler who has lost everything and throws his last chips on the gambling table wherever they may fall, Max dials Vanessa's number. It is she who answers. Perhaps it's too early to call, was she asleep? — No, not at all — Could he see her today, perhaps? — But of course, she'd be delighted — Where? — How about seven o'clock, at her house — Can he bring something, like a bottle of wine? — No, just himself — Just himself, is that all? — Oh, and those shoes he was wearing yesterday (she laughs); she should like to see them polished.

21

Don Onofrio has been survived by his old shaving brush and tarnished tin mug. Swirling the soapy bristles on his chin, Max decides five minutes is the minimum for a thoroughly soaked beard. Vanessa, so fastidious as to reqire polished shoes, will not like a face streaked with cuts. And who could blame her? This is the shave of your life, Max old boy: prior ones were just rehearsals. Last painterly touches on his Adam's apple.

Going over his image on the mirror, he notices that with a lathered face he doesn't really look fifty, if it weren't for some sagging neck skin and double chin, plus those thick hairs on ear lobes and septum. Van Gogh wasn't crazy: he was just getting rid for good of old-man's hair. Anyway, he, Max, surely looks an awful lot like Father. And in just a short time he'll be Dad's age when death changed him finally into his quiet, undissembling self.

Yet, as a boy, Max's looks were ambiguous. People saw in him Chaim's features, which made Max proud. Even

Aunt Porota used to say there was definitely less of her husband in Boris than in Max. But with the years Chaim's part drifted underground. Not a trace of it left. Onofrio surfaced in its place. Chip of the old block, Dad's spitting image.

"What are you up to buccaneer?"

"Nothing much, Dad. Shaving, as you see. With your old brush and mug."

"Nothing much! Have you so soon forgotten your word? You lay that pistol on my tomb and swore a solemn oath. 'From now on my thoughts be bloody, or I'm not your son.' You swore. Yet look at your thoughts now: broads, broads, a brothelful of broads. Meanwhile Chaim, that whoreson, disposes not only of your mother's heart but of her savings too. Everything is in his hands!"

"Father, stop. Today's theme is not revenge, but love."

Like sunlight piercing through angry clouds, Vanessa's reality floods Max. Sweet kiss! The water splashing at their feet... "Let's go back inside," she said afterward, breathless. And today he's going to see her at her house! Max could be just a whim, her ephemeral whim, and he probably is, he *most* probably is; but never mind: her noes will only fan the fires of his passion, her reticence will be the sauce of his autumnal love. Max pictures Vanessa's jet-black hair, her pouting, juicy lips, her ears and her tingling earrings. Will she mind the gray hair on his chest? "It's so distinguished," she'll say. She's young, and he is old. True. But look at Picasso, bald-pated, seventy-years old, turning the heads of young girls with his renown and glowing eyes; look at Paul Eluard, the Protopapas of Poetry, reeking of Stalinism and Gauloises, sitting next to a beautiful woman, thirty years his junior, who right away falls at his feet; look at Casals, marrying at eighty a girl of twenty-one. Look at Goethe and Bettina von Arnim. If only he had a solid, sexy reputation, like Picasso, Eluard, Casals, or Goethe. Or like his friend Fontana.

Steady hand now, steady hand. Above all, no cuts today. That's it: stretch the skin, then slowly, carefully... Damn it: in fifty years he could have acquired some kind of solid reputation. If only he wasn't such a concrete, practical man. Solid reputations accrue to men floating in the symbolic and sailing on the abstract — ideas and beliefs, stocks and bonds, words, numbers, formulas. But Max has always gone for unmediated comforts. The womb and the soft bosom. Men with solid reputations flock to Camp, Campus, Church, Bank, Executive Office; Max has stuck, concretely, to the Female. Therefore he's innocent, he's never raped, never murdered, like Pedro de Mendoza or Uncle Chaim. Hence too, he has accumulated no power and accomplished nothing. And as a third corollary: having no power, females couldn't care less for him. A paradoxical result, but, really, a logical consequence of having stuck to the Female, who's more accesible to, and readier to be conquered by, the self-possessed Male, the one who's after something else, not her. Anyway, why does he always shave in exactly the same way, from left of neck to Adam's apple, then right of neck, left cheek? He showers too in ways rigidly set. Routines are poison to the spirit. Also, why a disposable safety razor? Max feels he ought to be using a straight razor, neither safe nor disposable, sharp, dangerous, like his old barber, like Joyce's Buck Mulligan, or Marlon Brando in "Last Tango in Paris."

On a sudden inspiration, Max goes to his suitcase and gets the Heftpistole. Back in the bathroom, before the mirror, the cold Russian-inscribed muzzle against his lathered cheek, he feels this is now the true level, the only vital level of risk.

As a boy, Max used to marvel at how confidently men reclined on the barber chair and abandoned their lathered necks to a barber's razor; now he realizes that the truly amazing thing is rather how men trust themselves to their own hand. Once they reach a certain stage — once they realize that this is it, no progress, no improvement, no salvation; that they'll have to bear themselves along like a heavy, familiar, rotting corpse, for the rest of their lives — the truly amazing thing is how, at that point, men can resist the temptations of suicide. The only real question is why not do it. Press the trigger and be no more. What better opportunity? Right now he's full of hope, full of love, riding high. Fine moment for an ending. Tomorrow it might be too late. Why fool himself: one bad word from Vanessa, and the world will darken. Better to die inside a brightly lit, sumptuous palace, like Delacroix' Sardanapalus, than in the scorched garbage fields of depression. Or should he wait, like Father, like Boris, like Schamberg, until he's totally crushed? No. A bit more pressure on the trigger...

What will Mother do? When she hears the BANG, will she come into the bathroom, screaming "Max, Max!"? And when she sees his blood all over, his brain splattered on the ceiling, will she drop dead on the spot of a heart attack? It's possible. But if she survives, will she call the police? No, more likely she'll call Chaim. As in every crisis, Chaim will come, inspect, reconnoiter, ponder and decide.

"That's exactly what I've been trying to tell you, buccaneer: he holds everything in his hands — your mother's heart, her savings, everything — even your bloody carcass if you were to pull that trigger. Death is no escape. Broads nei-

211

ther. Stop wasting time on death and love and petty non-sense: concentrate on revenge!"

"Father, you're a remarkably obsessive ghost. But let me ask you something. Can the dead perceive beauty? Do your hearts, like our own, at once expand with joy, tremble with marvel and dissolve with pity at the sight of mortal beauty, the body of a girl like Vanessa Satanovsky? Or do you at least remember what it was, while on earth, the triple wound?"

"There's no joy among shadows, and from below nothing seems marvelous. As for pity, we shed it off together with vulnerable flesh. What we need, what we greatly crave for, we the dead, is peaceful rest, for which we must achieve equality, balance and redress. Justice, not beauty. Symmetry, not love. Avenge me, Max!"

"Justice! I'm afraid I owe much on that score. Tell me, Dad: has Pancracia gone down? Have you seen her among the dead? Is she roaming the dismal cellarage, calling for revenge against me, spoiling my happiness, frustrating the blooming of my love and my success? Or is she still alive and shitting in Berazategui? And out of curiosity I'd like to know: did you fuck her? Tell me, Dad: did you fuck her when you were alive? Dad? Silent again..."

Max puts the Heftpistole back in his pant pocket. There's time enough to die, time enough — indeed, a whole eternity — for balance, equality and redress. But Vanessa is the fruit and ruler of the present moment. The miracle of her kiss, the hope of miracles and kisses yet to come, bathe and illumine Max like the golden, wine-hued light of a Poussin *Bacchanale*. The lather on his face has dried up. Max pours some more hot water and soap into Dad's mug, works up new lather, dabs it on his face and starts shaving again. He doesn't mean to forget justice and revenge, only to postpone them for a while. All his attention must be concentrated on the present miraculous, Vanessian moment, and for this, Father's limp, ghostly resentment must be put aside. For the nonce it would be far, far better to adopt the elegant self-assurance and conquering airs of Uncle Chaim.

There, a clean shave. A fresh face, ready to tackle happiness. Oral hygiene next. Toothbrushes look pretty safe, no muzzle, no sharp edges. That's a wart growing on his left eyelid, never noticed till now. Lastly, a careful mustache trimming. For the last half of his life, through thick and thin, Max has sported a bushy mustache, unkempt and Nitzschean. Today he'll tidy it up. Vanessa should find his lips clean, easy to reach, user-friendly. He must remember to have his shoes polished, too. Apparently she finds men's shiny shoes attractive: Max is perfectly willing to go along. He has never been able to understand why Jennifer, for example, refused to wear his favorite black stockings, garter belt and high-heeled sandals on account of wanting to be loved the way she was, *au naturel, sans poivre*. By the same token, Aphrodite and Athena should have refused their epithets from Homer, and nouns and verbs should stand everywhere clear of adjectives and adverbs: imagine, then, what would become of writing.

Max trims the ends and the excess at the edges, and combs his mustache forward, *à la* Stalin. "*Tovarishi*, I'll let you know all about the objective interests of the Proletariat! All of you will be taken care of by the *Generalnoie Upravlenie Lagerei!*" Not bad, not bad. But every time he delves into his mustache he uncovers more white hairs: he cuts them at the base but, like Hydra heads, others keep popping up. No need to appear older than he is. He keeps trimming, up and

213

down, right and left, deeper. By now the thing is a shadow of what it used to be. Max pauses, scrutinizes his face on the mirror. Nothing he can do about that wart, but about his mustache, yes, he's going to cut it off completely. In the first place, he originally grew it to have one bigger and bushier than Dad's, but now he is not going to follow Dad's example. In the second place, Chaim never had a mustache. No need for a mustache. Vanessa, poetry, love, beauty will save him from Dad's pitiful destiny. Go on, cut it off. No mercy.

He starts by shaving off both ends. "Heil Hitler. *Ein Volk, ein Reich, ein Führer*! *Alles geyn in drerd aráyn*!" Good. Then he clips away. And Father thought one couldn't imagine nothingness: look at what he's doing now to his mustache. Max lathers it and shaves it off, then rinses off the cream (aloe and lanolin for a smoother, touchable face), and there he is, clean, bare, zero. He is surprised at the helplessness of his upper lip. The feminine contour of the outer edge draws a Cupid's bow, and the inner arch seems to be hanging in terror, as if crying out for a nipple. Max grins, pouts, wrinkles his nose and bares his teeth, produces umlauted u's and circumflexed o's, kisses the air. The naked truth is, those are the schmalzy lips of a clown, and Max is tempted to paint them orange, white and red; to smear his face all over with Mother's lipsticks. Perhaps it wasn't such a good idea to be left this open, vulnerable, unprotected.

But when he puts on his tie and jacket and goes back to the mirror, he's satisfied. He feels refreshed, finally defatherized, un-Onofried, much younger. "Mother, I'm leaving!"

"Where are you going?" says Mrs. Krocus from the kitchen.

Max prefers Mother not to see his face so drastically

changed: it might scare her, a dangerous thing for a weak heart. Later, of course, with more preparation and more leisure. "First to see Gloria, then to visit Vanessa. I'm probably not going to be back for supper."

At the door Max stops as if he had forgotten something. He hesitates for a second, sniffs the air. Onions. "Oh, and incidentally, Mother, if your dear motherfucking brother had exercised the same princely generosity he shows you now back when Father was alive, Father might still be here with us."

Out in the street, Max is satisfied. His face and upper lip feel pleasantly tingly, and at the very least he had to say *that* about Chaim. Justice, truth and filial duty required it.

22

As soon as the door of the Chateaubriand swings open, Max can tell that Gloria's day has not been smooth. Her eyes shift toward the usual table, register her brother's presence, but aren't lit up by the slightest twinkle. Sculptural hair-do, letter-quality make-up, tasteful color coordination of her skirt, sweater, and scarf. Several idle men turn their heads; Max gets up, pulls out a chair. He's going to be considerate and gentle; he's not going to insist that she make up with Mother. Why mention Mother at all. He's so happy and excited, thinking of the imminent visit to Vanessa. Anything Max can do for his sister he vows he'll do — little things, little gestures. He wants to treat her to Campari with cheese. No, she'll have a Coke. A Coke? Are you kidding? Gancia, Cinzano, Fernet, artichoke Cynar, Porto Ramos-Pinto, Ferrochina... How about Uzo, Suze, Dubonnet, *apéritif à la gentiane*, Picon, Kir... No? Then Pernod, Pastis, Cassis, Byrrh, *vin généreux au quinquina*, Punt e Mes, Pineral, Clacquesin, Hesperidina... All those wonderful apéritifs from civilized ancient shores, now standing at the bar, quietly waiting for her bidding... and she wants a Coke. Like passing up Chartres, the Alhambra, Venice, for a visit to Disneyland!

"I just want a Coke," Gloria shrugs.

"Rough day?" says Max.

"A bunion in my right foot's killing me. Besides, in this country every day is rough." Her eyelashes are smeared with black; splashes of ochre overflow the concavity of her orbits, and under a veneer of beauty creams her furrows glare. Max is reminded that Gloria is forty-eight, twice Vanessa's age. "What have you done to your face," she asks.

"Shaved off my mustache. What do you think?"

Gloria squints at him, shaking her head. "Makes you look older. Anyway, I'm just back from the salon. I ask the girl shampooing my hair, 'where's Pedro?' — Pedro's been my hair-dresser for ten years — and she tells me he died last Wednesday, while doing a customer's hair. Dropped with the curling iron in his hand. A heart attack."

"You must have been in shock."

"The suddenness of it. Two weeks ago we were gossiping, laughing, cracking jokes, and now, just like that..." Gloria snaps her fingers. "It brutally awakens you. You realize how fragile the whole thing is, how awfully fragile... Makes you rethink your whole life. At least, that's the effect it's had on me. Plus, Pablo, the other hairdresser, is really no good; see what he did to my hair... makes me look like a gorgon..."

"What are you talking about; you look beautiful!" says Max.

Gloria lights a cigarette. "Shock after shock. The one at the salon was not the worst. The worst was a couple of days ago, with Panard."

"Panard?"

"Gaston Panard, my psychoanalyst. I'd been on the couch for only five minutes when he cut me off and threw me out. Do you realize how that makes you feel?"

"What do you mean, he threw you out."

"He interrupted the session, that's what I mean. He told me, 'Señorita Krocus, I will see you next time.'"

"Did he return the money?"

"Don't be absurd. Lacanian psychoanalysis is like that: the session may be interrupted at any point. That's one of the ground rules. An important part of the therapy: I know it, I understand it. Analysis should be as much as possible like life, and since death is always there which can cut it short, analysis should keep you off balance, on the edge: I accept that. But do you realize how it feels when it actually happens? Especially since I had just begun talking about a very, very painful experience of a few days ago... No, you have to be a woman to realize how it hurts."

"I think I can understand it without being a woman," Max interjects.

"No. Women suffer from *coitus interruptus* much more keenly than men. Once his erection subsides, a man is basically back to normal, but an aroused vagina is something else: it refuses to quiet down, it makes you miserable, it ruins your whole day, your whole week..."

"But with men too," Max protests; "a situation like that can be quite a pain in the nuts."

Gloria seems absorbed in the stirring of her Coke, thoroughly homogeneous, as it is, down to the molecular level, from the factory. She wields her straw with thumb and the two fingers holding her cigarette; the straw is of the colored spiral kind, a skinny barber pole, a glassmaker's punty dipped into the sparkling dark.

"I found out the waiter's name," says Max, leaning confidentially toward his sister. "Basilio."

"So?" says Gloria.

"Basilio means 'king'," Max whispers, and Gloria shrugs. She doesn't seem to be in the mood for etymology.

"Yesterday I met a wonderful, wonderful girl, Vanessa Satanovsky," Max tries again, partly to distract his sister from her gloomy reflections, but mostly because he can resist no longer: he must pronounce that name.

"Satanovsky?" Gloria is suddenly interested. "By any chance the daughter of Cecilio Satanovsky?"

"Who's Cecilio Satanovsky?" says Max.

"You haven't heard of him? He's the rival, the arch-enemy of Gaston Panard. Their squabbles have been all over the news for the last couple of years. Max, are you sure you haven't read about it? Didn't they report it in the United States? To make a long story short, Satanovsky provoked a scandal, accused Panard of unethical behavior, of distorting the true syntagmatic function of desire, and of adopting a naive, spherical view of the psyche instead of the correct Lacanian view, which is toroidal. Satanovsky and his friends split the Lacanian Center of Buenos Aires, and now they say he's the true continuator of the Master. But it's all bullshit: he's the one who's spherical, and besides, he hasn't ever undergone analysis with Lacan himself as Panard has. The fact is, most of the better analysts in Buenos Aires have sided with Panard. Satanovsky has only succeeded in making a complete fool of himself."

"Did he make a bundle in the process?" says Max.

Gloria shrugs. "Actually, he charges more than

219

Panard. But how did you happen to meet Satanovsky's daughter?"

"At the University," says Max; "she's a student of Fontana, do you remember him? I am desperately in love with her; she's barely over twenty, absolutely spectacular... And she has brains! Can you believe it, beautiful and brainy! So now the question is: how do I get her to fall in love with me? Not an easy project, Gloria, for an ugly, stupid, fifty-year old fellow, don't you think?"

Gloria doesn't seem touched by Max's having fallen in love at fifty, nor does she seem overly impressed by his modesty; her face darkens almost to the tint of her Coke. "You know, Max, I think you ought to undergo psychoanalysis."

The straw is being twisted, wrung, split and rent, torn into small pieces. Her voice is pricklier than a late-summer artichoke. "Serious, Lacanian analysis I mean; not like whatever it was you did up there in North America."

He laughs. "That was twenty years ago; but now I wouldn't do anything that could interfere with my poetry, as I'm afraid psychoanalysis would."

"Nonsense: if André Breton and Michel Leiris and many of the writers you admire were analyzed by Lacan, you could certainly be analyzed by his disciples, without much risk to your poetry."

"Those are not my favorite writers," Max objects. "Besides, if I move back to Buenos Aires, do you expect me to have enough funds to be analyzed by Panard?"

"I don't expect anything," Gloria replies. "It's your problem, not mine. It's just that your incredible lapses and repressions — I prefer to call them neurotic lapses and not sadistic impulses, although I'm sure there's a lot of sadism involved — cannot fail to affect your poetry as much as they hurt the people around you. You're a Marquis de Sade with a baby brain. You hurt everyone around you, but refuse to register."

"Hurt the people around... You mean... like when I slapped you in the face for smoking?"

"Slapped *me* in the face? When?"

"You don't remember? It happened when I was twenty and you..."

"I've no idea what you're talking about. I'm not your psychoanalyst: I don't have to go all the way back to when you were twenty to dig up your neurotic lapses."

"Lapses?" says Max.

"The most recent example. How could you possibly have forgotten that many years ago I was involved with el Indio? Not that it ever amounted to much — partly, at least, because your jealous male exclusiveness wouldn't allow me to interfere with your beautiful male friendship. But we did go out several times, and talked a lot, although, in case you're curious, we never went to bed together. Do you remember now?"

"To tell you the truth, no, I don't," says Max; "I guess I have totally forgotten."

"Of course you would," says Gloria. "And that's why, the other day, when you were about to meet el Indio in Constitución, you first had me safely dispatched down the subway tunnel. Your sister was always the little turd, too insignificant and foul-smelling to introduce to your friends. Things haven't changed: at fifty, you go after twenty-year-old girls; at forty-eight, I'm the dried-up piece of shit to be flushed down the subway tunnel. I was so hurt I couldn't stop the tears from flowing, all the way home. If you want to know, that was the painful experience that I started telling

221

Panard, when he cut me off."

"But Gloria, Gloria..." Across the cigarette butts and the bits of plastic straw, all the way up to the glass full of sparkling Coke, Max reaches for and holds her hand. "I didn't think... I should have, I know... It was my fault. I just didn't remember the thing between you and el Indio. But believe me, there was no conscious intention on my part. I didn't want to exclude you, or to deny you the opportunity of talking with him." Max pauses, furrows his brow and twists his lips, as if searching for some way of communicating an embarrassing fact. "And anyway, you know, el Indio is a married man..."

"I can't believe my ears," says Gloria, "you, of all people, telling me, 'el Indio is a married man'? You, with your record of broken marriages because of your philandering? You're a hypocrite, Max."

After a while, their hands are too damp for comfort, but neither one is willing to be the first to retreat. "Gloria, I think you're too quick to take umbrage," says Max.

"Me, quick? After forty-eight years of continuous bombardment?"

"Come on, Gloria, you *are* quick, and you know it. Otherwise, you wouldn't have thrown Mother out of your house."

"I never threw Mother out of my house."

"That's what you told me the other day."

"That's not what happened at all."

"What happened, then?"

"We were sitting, Mother and I, in my living room and, out of the blue, she says that she's sure I want her dead so as to get a hold of her dollars. I've always known Mother has a terrible anal fixation, but this... this was too much."

222

"What did you do?" says Max.

"I told her, 'Mother, you may be right, but it's strictly up to you to act so that I would rather wish you alive.' She got up and left without a word. No, I didn't throw her out; she left of her own accord."

"That was two years ago, and you have never seen her since," says Max, removing his damp hand, now cold, from his sister's hold.

"Never again," says Gloria.

"How absurd, how thoroughly absurd," says Max.

"Absurd? Wait until she does it to you, we'll see how you react."

"Does what to me?"

"Her thing. Her fecal aggression," says Gloria, "Wait until she hurls the shit at you," and both hands free now, she tears up the paper napkin. The slender barber-pole of a straw has already been shredded. Her glass of Coke remains full, and two flies are feasting on it.

"I'll tell you what," Max resumes. "For New Year's eve, I'll buy a bottle of champagne; you'll come to Mother's place, give her a kiss, we'll drink, the three of us, to your reconciliation, and that will be the end of it."

Gloria gets up and grabs her purse. "Excuse me, I have an appointment with Panard at six o'clock."

"Wait, listen. I'll call you tomorrow or the day after, and we'll arrange a meeting, the three of us, you, el Indio and I... and perhaps Vanessa Satanovsky. A double date, how about that," says Max, ebulliently. "Unless you object, of course — but I hope you won't."

"It's fine with me," says Gloria, kissing her brother good-bye.

Through the window, Max watches his sister cross the

avenue. He tries to imagine Gloria's foot, a callus on the underside of the big toe... A bunion... There is a grammar, somewhere, of the lines of the sole — is it called reflexology? — as there is a grammar of the lines of the soul which is called psychoanalysis: everything in this world, down to the soles of our feet, must be interpreted and re-interpreted in a never-ending rehash, a scramble for meaning and sense itself as meaningless, cruel and endless as the braiding and recycling of proteins in our animal flesh. Not even one's balls can be treated as a simple, natural fact. A shoe-shine boy, dark and dirty, comes into the Chateaubriand with his box and his tiny stool. Max suddenly remembers and calls him. Shiny shoes for Vanessa.

The boy sits on his stool and brushes ink all over Max's right shoe. "You're a hypocrite, Max." *Hypocrite Maxeur, mon semblable, mon frère.* Bah, he should have asked Gloria how can hypocrisy be avoided in a world where everything must be interpreted, analyzed and explained: the only real hypocrite is, on reflection, the rascal who believes himself to be sincere. Or does she think she's being sincere, with all that ochre around her eyes and blacking on her lashes? Don't make him laugh. Neurotic lapses! Etruscan haruspication on a couch, the inspection of the *chinchulines* of her brain: evidently she expects that any moment now the hot juices of meaning will squirt out and hit her and Doctor Panard in the eye. Should Max tell her that it's all laborious illusion, that her brain is as dry as her vagina, that, mathematically speaking, human life is a non-integrable vector field of desires pointing to no exit, enveloping no object and along no certain path? No, he oughtn't. Gloria is not prepared for the truth, she is too sad and too dry. As for him...

A tap on the tip of his right shoe; the turn of the other

224

one. Max leans back on his chair and abandons his left shoe blissfully to the boy. He must be doing pretty well, the brat. Here in Buenos Aires there are few sneakers and more leather shoes than in the U.S., because men are more formal, and not likely to pass over the oportunity of killing cows. As for himself, the whole world is a feast — masks and per-fumed water, confetti, flowing champagne. He can accept life as it is because in an hour's time he is going to be kissing Vanessa; because, in a very real sense, he's got himself a sun: a central, massive gravitational object toward which all his vectors point. She's about to be his: can one imagine any-thing headier and more focusing? Max throws a cheese cube into his mouth, works a toothpick in between two molars and looks at the boy from high up. He's perfectly aware of repeating a gesture he's seen his father perform a hundred times. An awful lot like Father. *Hypocrite — mon père.* Yes, but never, never in his sunless life did Father enjoy a woman like Vanessa. You're talking about two entirely different lev-els. Had Father known such happiness, he would have been more alive, more focused... Certainly he wouldn't have killed himself.

When the boy finishes his shoe-shine job, Max gives him a thousand australes bill — a whole dollar. "Keep it," and enjoys watching the incredulity on the bituminous face.

"Enjoy, enjoy! This world, m'boy, is a hugely joyous feast."

"Yes, sir!" says the boy, smiling, showing his toothless gums, and giving Max, with his free hand, a perfect military salute.

23

His silhouette against the night sky, a roaming spark, pausing, brighter, before his face, then, again, hovering like a crazy planet; the stars above; his strange and solemn gestures. Max the Knight, Max the Great surveying from the parapets the vastness of his battle field: the universe. Cigarette smoke rising in eddies and twists, like the smoke of guns around a warrior, completing his glory: that is Gloria's most vivid memory of him. She still smiles at her brother's naiveté: he would get up from bed, fumble in the dark for the pack of cigarettes he'd hidden inside a box of soccer cards, and go out to the terrace on tiptoe; but she was awake and saw his every move, and what she didn't see she guessed; she would get up too, crouch down by the door and watch him smoke, out there under the stars, and when he turned on the faucet just a tad to put out the butt, that gave her enough time to scramble back and dive under the sheets. Every once in a while, twice a week maybe, she would take a cigarette from Max's box, but he never noticed it. She'd go down the block to Amelia's house and the two girls would sit on the maid's bed; Amelia's maid would tell them about her boyfriends while they smoked Max's cigarettes.

"Oldie but still yummy, uh..." "Wow, look at those legs..." Two smart-alecky bums standing before the post office. The younger one is darkly handsome, around thirty, shy. She could still teach those assholes a thing or two. These formidable Italian pumps never fail to attract male compliments; nor do they ever fail to hurt her feet: her bunion is killing her. "Señora, you should not walk on those heels," the podiatrist is always pleading. Try to explain it to him... The guy's serious, never made a pass at her, never touched her above the ankle: wears a wedding band, wonder if his wife wears high heels, maybe she does, but just for fucking. What may have become of Amelia? Her parents were Greek, they say Greek women have hot buns, which was definitely the case with Amelia from a very early age: she wanted Max so bad, that must have been why, come to think of it, they had a falling out, because Gloria wouldn't introduce her to Max. Wonder if she's still alive, Amelia, still smoking. It pisses her no end that Max quit. He sits there, at the café, rigid, virtuous and clean, horribly Yankeefied, despising her while she puffs, as if it wasn't all because of him, because of him and his smoke rings and his silhouette and his mysterious, unforgettable gestures against the dark-blue sky. Of course, Dad too, who sat her on his knee and sang to her Italian opera, who tousled her hair and said, "Who's my little girl?" Dad's lapels were steeped in cologne and tobacco; but Dad, she is convinced, was secondary: if it hadn't been for Max she wouldn't be smoking today. Once he slapped her in front of everyone — wham, sent her cigarette flying — she wasn't supposed to light up in public even

227

though she was already eighteen, how utterly absurd. Evoked by Max only an hour ago, that scene she had almost forgotten: repressed, no doubt. Now it flows back. Even though Max had hit and punched her many times before, that public slap was shattering. Yet somehow she didn't mind it nearly as much as Max having quit smoking on her: the slap was a crime of passion, but quitting is betrayal. And being a quitter makes him feel superior? For God's sake. Gloria's shoulders shake, a harsh and bitter laugh; she stops walking, rummages in her bag, lights a cigarette, draws savagely, until her lungs are full, then, throwing her head back, ejects the smoke in a long plume.

Up there in the sky is Pedro. Not the whiny patron of Rome holding the keys, but her hairdresser who dropped dead last Wednesday, Pedro who attended to Gloria's progress from strategically placed highlights to discrete overall dye, through so many different fashionable styles, each one linked to a different stage in her life. Pedro, who not being interested in women, only in their hair, used to be like an oasis, peace and calm always flowing from his professional fingers right into her skull. And now Pedro too has abandoned her. Pedro smiles at her wistfully, apologetically from heaven. Fuck him. Why are men such a bunch of quitters? Bruno, her boss and lover, is just about to leave her too, like all the others. She can tell from certain signs. His erections come a little easier now, and he doesn't weep as much as he used to over his damnation to hell as an adulterer. He's getting used to it, the son of a bitch, and guilt has lost its sting. It means that pretty soon he'll look for greener pastures, if he's not already found them, and it means she'll have to start looking for another part-time job. She doesn't really mind: her salary from the Anti-Tobacco Campaign hasn't

228

gone up with inflation, and as for Bruno's erections, they are not particularly enjoyable without the heady sauce of joint sin and damnation. The desperate, whining thrusts, his somber determination to keep it up, as if to force down, to abase his own sagging spirit in the abject but nutritious depths of her cunt, and, when he manages it (by no means always), his final sob and his weeping like a child — no, not like a child but like an old, dying man, a wasted man with the body of an asparagus attached to a pumpkin paunch — all that makes her feel powerful, goddesslike if only for a little while. She wouldn't have any use for a jaunty, guiltless Bruno. The thought of Bruno as a Latin lover is so preposterous she laughs. On further thought, she wouldn't have much use for any man. In a recent British magazine she saw a catalogue of battery-powered vibrators, the most varied shapes. Short and thick, long and straight or curved upwards, smooth or fluted, they are so easy to handle and run at different speeds. Why put up with precarious egos and precarious erections, why put up with men at all, who only want women as nurses, to change their mental diapers?

A perfect, gorgeous evening, unusual in December, truly an evening for romance... Gloria crosses the street and walks into an elegant crowd going to Mass at Nuestra Señora de la Merced. The idea of Max with that young, beautiful girl nettles her. Where will they go? Certainly not to that dive, the Chateaubriand. To an expensive restaurant, to a boîte in Olivos to neck and dance, then to a hotel, to fuck. At his age! And why not? He's still handsome, still interesting, even though he's such an asshole. Older men become more attractive, older women become hags. Life is unfair, terribly unfair. The bells are calling the faithful to Mass; Gloria lifts her eyes toward the belfry and prays, "Please, please, don't let Max fuck the Satanovsky girl."

She visited Max in the U.S. only once, ten years ago. Right after his divorce from Sharon and before he met Jennifer. Gloria had saved enough for the ticket and for a stay of one month, and had placed much hope on their encounter, but she found Max strangely distant and aloof, cordial on the surface, yet keeping her at arm's length, as if afraid of close contact. The place too, the whole country harmonized with Max's attitude: cordial on the surface, but forbidding. He had taken her to many places, famous places, he said, but she has no memory for English names — a skating rink in the midst of skyscrapers, the oldest ale-house in the U.S., neighborhoods haunted by drug pushers and painters. It was January, winter there. He took her to several university campuses, showed her many impressive edifices, but it all seemed to her terribly distant and cold, and she missed the old, dilapidated Buenos Aires buildings and the seedy offices where she worked. At one point she asked Max how he could live in such a country, so cold. "So you prefer the heat and the torture chambers of our dear Fatherland?" he snickered. In a way he was right, it was the terrible time of the military regime, but Gloria knew her brother well enough to see he was pissed by her not duly admiring his adopted country, his appliances, and his living arrangements. She went back to Buenos Aires. Three years later, during the war with England, Max wrote her a sarcastic letter, mocking the Argentine rights over the Falklands and the mettle of the Argentine armed forces. How dared he, while so many of our boys were fighting and suffering in the South Atlantic. She had replied with an impassioned and patriotic letter, after which their correspondence came to a stop.

Years passed. New wrinkles, more gray hair, belly

and breasts kept sagging; one shrink superseded another; many times she changed jobs, bosses and lovers. On the other hemisphere, Max went through another marriage and another divorce. They hadn't communicated, except for the occasional birthday card: they had become almost strangers. Still, when Max phoned to say that he was coming, her heart first stopped and then raced ahead, and she felt again like a young girl, like the first time she was asked to a dance. How is it possible? How often must he betray her before she says, "This is it, don't you ever show your face again"? As soon as he arrived, he moved into Mother's apartment rather than stay with her, then, to add insult to injury, he suggested that all three move into the same house! Finally, to top it, he proposes a cockamamie crime: to kill Chaim. Either he's gone completely mad or, more likely, he's trying her, teasing her. Making fun of his little silly sister.

Before the mirror on the elevator to Panard's office, Gloria touches up her makeup and messes up her hair a bit. Panard once told her, "Why are you so perfect? Not even a hair of yours is out of place. Why don't you let some chaos into your life?" and ever since, as soon as she approaches the analyst's office, Gloria remembers to follow his advice. (Panard's style is a carefully monitored breeziness, his mono-grammed shirt showing the proper wedge of gray-haired chest, and on his book shelves always a Séminaire Lacan slightly out of alignment.) Gloria kisses Graciela, Panard's secretary, on one cheek, and notices that she's wearing yet another silk scarf. How does she manage it, on a secretary's salary? Every time (three a week for the last year), Graciela has been wearing different accessories. Gloria sits down, picks a magazine, *Turismo en la Patagonia*, and leafs through it. Hotel Llao-llao. Isla Victoria. *Arrayanes* are rose-red colored trees, as if painted by Gauguin, which grow only in Patagonia and Japan. "I will see you next week," he said, and that was it, nothing for her to do but get up and leave. Still smarting. Why did he cut her off like that, right when she had started talking about such important stuff, the memory she had just recaptured, the first breakthrough since July? For the first six months analysis with Panard had been a fantastic voyage of discovery, ten times more intense than with her previous analysts. They had explored her Electra in ways she had never thought possible. The basis of her anger and her hatred for Mother, her anger towards Dad (why didn't he leave his wife, why did he go and die on Gloria?) And those dreams, back in March and April, one after the other, frightening, perturbing, yet at the same time, how exhilarating! She, Gloria, taking a shrunken Dad in her arms, rocking him like a baby, humming to him Italian opera! When she woke up she would burst out crying, and those weren't tears of grief, but of joy and gratitude. Even Panard was impressed when she narrated that dream, and made some fascinating comments on the syntactical displacements and semantic condensations at work in her oneiric discourse.

Lago Futalafquen, Provincia de Chubut, best trout fishing in the world. The majestic spectacle of the glaciers at Lago San Martín. Then, a long period of draught, a large and arid plateau, until the day before yesterday, when, reading the Sunday Cultural Section of *La Prensa*, she suddenly remembered having spied on Max while he was in the bathroom. She started telling it to Panard, "I was reading about Sartre's 'other,' the other person's gaze transforming one into an object, you know, when it called to my mind that I too, had once peeked through a keyhole." That was when Panard stopped her dead. Why? Why precisely at that cru-

232

cial point, at this long-awaited breakthrough? She had remembered everything: Max sitting on the john, her own reactions, her fear of being caught. Actually, she's not absolutely sure it was while she was reading the newspaper that she suddenly remembered; it actually seems to her that she has always remembered her peeking through the keyhole, that she has even thought about it explicitly from time to time, only not with the present focus and intensity. The knowledge was always there, but half-conscious. Except she doesn't know if Panard will accept the category, "half-consciousness." Probably not. Anyway, the newspaper has something to do with it, as has Sartre, even though it isn't completely clear what. It all happened at roughly the same time, the same traumatic epoch, not long after Dad went to jail, and Mom and she went to visit him and bring him food. Dad would stroke her face and call her my little girl, my beautiful little angel, and Mom and Gloria would cry, that time seems thoroughly soaked in tears, and Dad would say not to worry, that in a couple of days, once the police mistake was cleared up, he'd come out and deal his accusers a severe blow, take them to court, and with the award he would no doubt be granted for defamation he'd buy a mink coat for Mom and for Gloria the best pair of crepe-rubber-sole shoes, and Gloria was sure the shoes were more expensive than the fur coat. Where was Max all the while? Gloria doesn't remember him during those tragic days. Has she blanked him out? She must analyse that with Panard. But only a little later, with Dad out of jail and strapped for money more than ever (no crepe rubber shoes, furniture and chandeliers seized for debt, Mother throwing daily hysterical fits), Max destroyed her innocence and fired her imagination, pouring into her childish ears all that poison, all that talk about the three holes, the three methods. He showed her his limp penis and told her that it was much bigger when excited, but that Vergara, the policeman's son, had a still bigger one, monster-sized. Max seemed impressed with Vergara's cock, and after that, she too could think of little else. She told Max about her clit, that it was shaped like a half bean, a *poroto partido*, a fun thing to touch, but Max refused to try. She has always associated Aunt Porota with the clit, perhaps an instance of what Panard calls syntactical displacements and semantic condensations, or perhaps because she, Gloria, had always seen Aunt Porota as a kind of sex symbol. Dad too used to stare at Aunt Porota with strange eyes, the same way he stared at big Cadillacs. As for Cousin Boris, he frightened her. Gloria is not sure why. A gnome. A faun. No, she always felt he knew too much, he could tell her things that would ruin her life, let her into some godawful secret about her not being a real woman but a perverted fraud. But maybe even this, genuine as it feels to her, is a post-facto construction, a back-projection, triggered, much later, by Boris's having become a gynecologist; on the other hand it is perfectly possible that the laws of cause and effect, of time before and time after, just don't apply to her psyche, that she felt what she felt about Boris *because* much later he was to become a gynecologist. Or maybe the two facts are unrelated. Whenever Gloria reflects on her psyche, she gets lost in a dense forest, a thicket of symbols from which nobody but a very skillful man would be able to extricate her. A woodsman, sure-footed and wise. Unfortunately, it could not have been Dad, too ineffective, a loser, Dad never mentioned crepe rubber shoes again, Dad stupidly clung to his wife, like the foolish father of the story of Hänsel and Gretel; no, she was always in need of a clever man like Hänsel, to mark her

234

way with pebbles or breadcrumbs. Visit Santa Cruz and see the penguins. Someone to lead her by the hand, someone to teach her the three methods. Tierra del Fuego, beautiful bottom of the world. Ushuaia, southernmost town. A leader, a man who's got it all figured out, the ropes of the universe, the ways in and out of the forest. In fact, back in those days, when Gloria, like all twelve-year-olds, had to join the U.E.S. (*Unión de Estudiantes Secundarios*), she fantasized about being noticed by General Perón, being invited by him to the Presidential Residence in Olivos, and having him at her feet, in full military regalia, licking her clit in front of the other girls, the President's aides-de-camp and his ministers of State.

No, Max didn't stay with her. He left her a prisoner in the witch's house, in the midst of the madmen and the torturers; he ran away, saved himself, became a Yankee, and now he faces her from his non-smoking superiority, pretending to be a poet, ah yes, better be careful, don't rub him the wrong way, *el señorito* is a lyric poet, asking what did Dad look like, was he a distinguished-looking corpse, was he wearing his three-piece suit, his Parker 51, were the torture chambers painted blue, tittle-tattle, gobbledygook, just to put it all in rhyme, a pretty sonnet, pretending to have fallen in love with a ravishing twenty-year-old, pretending to be a fucking poet! She gives out an explosive snickering snort, Graciela stares at her. No one else in Panard's waiting room. Gloria stares hard at the magazine, pretending she's come across some really funny region of Patagonia. Max the lyric poet. She still keeps the old letter in her wallet, she has learned it by heart, the letter dated May '75 in which he announced he had become a poet. "I know it sounds ridiculous, but I feel my life is running out, I'm getting old to no purpose: at some point one must risk all." That phrase haunted her: in December 1975 she decided that she too would risk all, and so she hastily married Pancho Locro Revuelto, her boyfriend at the time, in a desperate attempt at happiness. But if as a boyfriend Pancho had merely been a humorless bore, as a husband he proved to be a cretin whose favorite occupation was to get drunk, and when he started beating her, Gloria decided she had had enough: the marriage lasted exactly seven months. There was no divorce law in Argentina at the time, which meant that Señor Locro Revuelto owned everything and Señora Krocus de Locro Revuelto nothing at all. She had risked all, and had lost. Now, whenever she remembers her brother's letter, she pictures him standing on the terrace, at night, enveloped in smoke, surveying the cosmos, and she is gripped by grief.

"I was reading" — No: "I was re-reading Jean-Paul Sartre," yes, that's how she'll start. Why mention the rather low-brow Cultural Supplement of *La Prensa*. "I was re-reading Sartre, *Being and Nothingness*, you know, when, coming across the guy who's caught eavesdropping, it all came back to me, in a flash." It's very unlikely Panard will interrupt her twice in a row. He never does that. "I suddenly remembered I once peeked through the keyhole while Max was in the bathroom. I was eleven or twelve. You must understand, this happened shortly after Dad went to jail, the most traumatic period in my life. And right after my brother gave me that lecture on his three methods. I guess it was natural for me to be curious." She can picture Panard's every gesture, the slant of his head, the French dubitative pout. "Max was sniffing a piece of clothing. My soiled panties." Pause. Panard would raise his eyebrows, ever so slightly. "I had left them there, on the *bidet*." Pause. Then, an octave lower, "On

236

purpose." After some time in analysis, one starts feeling a certain pride in confession, one ends up convinced that knowledge is the supreme ethical value. "His penis was big and he was stroking it. My first impulse was to go away, but I couldn't. Then I decided I was going to go in, the bathroom door had a keyhole but no key, and I was going to tell Max, 'Here, brother, have *me*, why bother with the giftwrap, which method do we use, all three?' I was just going to do it, when I heard the maid coming up the stairs, and ran away."

In her mind, Pancracia was a strict, fire-breathing dragon, enforcer of morals and of God's commandments; once, when Gloria had given Mom a snappy answer (she was about six), the maid upbraided her, "You hussy, is that how a daughter talks to her mother?," and there had been other, similar occasions; Gloria feared Pancracia's tongue as much as Mrs. Krocus' angry slaps. And now she ponders, it was Pancracia who saved her from awful incest, by coming up the stairs. She might have been looking for a rag, or a vacuum cleaner brush left in a bedroom. On what imponderables one's destiny hangs. And so she, Gloria, went on, unpolluted, intact, until at seventeen she had her first lover, Eustaquio, whom Max called "Aconcagua," a short, epileptic boy who had a grand mal seizure the first time they made love, his convulsions and his foamy mouth the only image surviving in her memory. She had gone on to other lovers, other foamy fragilities, in their diverse styles all quitters, some sooner, some later, and at age twenty-nine, shortly after Dad's death, she lost a child, her womb removed, the whole kit and caboodle. Had she gone into the bathroom that day, her life would have been different, and Max's too. Hard as she had tried, she could never blow smoke rings, like Max, but had she walked into the bathroom, one thing is certain: even at that early age, she would have known exactly what to do. She would have shoved the old witch into her baking oven. Guilt? Breaking the taboo: to carry inside, to be heavy for the remainder of your life with such a secret! Gloria has always felt, vaguely yet keenly, that there is something naturally dirty and evil in herself; she knows many other women who feel the same. Probably cultural: patriarchal society, Judeo-Christian ethics, bourgeois mentality. Incest would have focused that guilt, given body to the ghost; at least she would have known why she was dirty and in what way she was evil; all in all, incest would have made life easier for her.

And Max wouldn't have escaped so easily either. With the years he has become invulnerable, unreachable. Now she means nothing to him, less than a half-bean. But incest would have followed him all the way to the U.S.A., to graduate school, to Disneyland, to the remotest wilds where the buffalo roam. Partners in crime will stay together, and who is to say, perhaps they would have returned together, like in the fairy tale, to find the stepmother dead, and to make Dad rich with the precious stones and treasures of the baked old witch. To live happily ever after. Hänsel and Gretel has always been Gloria's favorite story, the image of Gretel pushing the evil witch into the oven gives her great joy, and now the thought occurs to her for the first time that it was not her marriage to Pancho Locro Revuelto but the moment before that bathroom door: yes, that was the occasion, the one occasion in her life for risking everything. That was her opportunity, and she missed it.

But she's not sure she wants to tell it that way to her shrink. Panard is big on Hegel. The first time she met him was a couple of years ago, at a seminar on the dialectics of

238

lord and bondsman which he was conducting, and she was so impressed — overwhelmed is the word — that she immediately wanted to undergo analysis with him. There was a waiting list, and she had to wait a whole year, but it was worth it. And so that's how she'll wrap up her narration if, God forbid, she's not interrupted a second time: her childish admiration for her brother, her love for Max (if that is what it was in fact), has, with the years, turned dialectically into its negation, its opposite. Or better still — what was that word Panard often used, that German word, *auf... auf...* The hounds of recollection bark in vain: Gloria has a terrible memory for German words. Anyhow, this is what she will say: both love and loathing have been subsumed, lifted and preserved into a feeling for her brother which is neither one nor the other, and which, she realizes, is too complex and ambiguous to figure out and analyse by herself. Panard will understand and will help her throw light on that whole region of her psyche; he, more than any one else, should be able to help her out of the forest.

24

She stopped peeling onions and grabbed the sink with both hands. "My God, it's the heart!" she thought at first. The pain slowly receded. But then she could hardly breathe. Was it the heart? Or her old asthma, as so many times in the past, whenever something upset her? She sat on the stool and tried to quiet herself. "It's psychological, all in the *kopf*; a little pain, I get scared, that makes it worse... then more pain, I get more scared..." The oil cloth wrapped around the stool top, the sheet of plastic wrapped around the oil cloth, her taffeta gown, her satin slip: layers between the quiet wood and Mrs. Krocus's scared, trembling flesh. Inside the kitchen sink, a knife and two large Spanish onions; one glistening, the other half-peeled. She tries to breathe rhythmically, in and out, elbows on the sink flange, and the onions make her weep.

She doesn't want to weep. God knows she's had more than her share of weeping. Enough. *Shoin genik.* One after the other, she picks up the onions and throws them into the garbage pail. Max is not coming for dinner anyway; didn't he say so? Onions! Dinner! Idiot! All her life peeling onions, making dinner, all her life in the kitchen: what for? To be treated like a *shikse*. He's not coming for dinner, the shithead. And if Chaim had helped him, Onofrio "might still be here with us." Here with us! Still fooling around, lying to her, swindling everyone, splashing his *dreck* on her, wasting any money coming his way and devouring her dinners. Thank God he's rotting under the earth and not here with us!

Anyway what's the difference: Onofrio kicking above ground or kicking under, she is still in the kitchen, isn't she, peeling onions and crying. Married woman or widow, still a slave. It was in the kitchen too, at her parents' house when she was twenty-four, that she yielded to his heavy pleading and surrendered herself and her virginity to Onofrio. While she was fixing maté he lifted her skirt and forced her to bend down on the counter. After much effort and a lot of pain he penetrated her. She was biting on the dishcloth to stifle a scream; they had been trying for weeks, but Onofrio was too broke, too cheap to take her to a hotel. That night she had her first asthma attack; lying in bed, thinking of the violence done to her, of her virginity gone, he wanted a proof of love and now what, will he marry her, she suddenly found herself unable to breathe, gasping for air. Dad, poor Dad, had to take her to the hospital. The next day everybody knew; perhaps, semiconscious, she had told Dad at the hospital, perhaps they noticed the trail of blood all the way from the kitchen to the bathroom, the irrecoverable blood of her virginity. She couldn't wipe it off, no matter how much she scrubbed with scouring pad and steel wool.

Together with the image of blood and rape and a dull pain in the temples, flashes of that other woman, Malvina

Cildáñez, who came to see her after Onofrio's death "to cry together." "At least you have the children," she had said, "me, he left me nothing, all my savings he took, I'm destitute." She must have expected a hand-out, the fool. "You richly deserve what you got," Mrs. Krocus had told her, "don't complain, and don't ever bother me again." That visit finally opened her eyes to the awful truth. The catalogue of Onofrio's many lies and love affairs began to unroll. The other day she saw that slut Malvina at the butcher's, and she regrets not having spat on her. With her own hands she should have strangled the bitch. That one? Ha! And how about all the others? The one across the street, for example, married and with five kids. Or the owner of the notions store at the corner of Ramón Falcón. And how about the ones she didn't know of? Who, back in Flores, didn't see Señora Krocus bearing horns? *Cornuda*! Walking back from the market, loaded like an ass with provisions for the master's repast; a horned ass with bells on her head and a placard, "Kick me, I'm an idiot." The thought of having been a dupe all her life is unbearable. And why the hell should her brother have helped them? For years she was stupidly blind, refusing to see what was under her nose, but Chaim clearly saw what kind of dirty game was Onofrio's, what kind of husband she had been saddled with. Chaim was never a fool. Vain, yes, and maybe, on occasion, cruel, but no one, man or woman, could pull the wool over his eyes, and no one in this world has — except, that is, for her. Many years ago, at a party in Chaim's house, he refused to lend her ten thousand pesos that Onofrio needed desperately to cover a check, but that night, back home, she said to Onofrio, "Chaim won't lend to us, but what if tomorrow I go to his office and tell him that I'm following his advice, that I'm leaving you for good

242

and need his help? I bet you he'll give me the dough."
Onofrio thought it a brilliant idea. And sure enough, Chaim
was glad to oblige. Of course, after a time he realized the
whole thing was a scam, but he never complained and never
mentioned it. As far as she knows, that was the only time
Chaim was taken, and whenever the thought comes upon
her that she, an uneducated woman, was the only person
who ever bested her brother, the smartest man in the world,
a grin appears on her face, and a sudden bubbling of mis-
chievous laughter tickles her trachea and assuages her pains.

But with the first kink of hilarity, a stab at the base of
the skull and down the neck, as if she had been pierced with
a hook. Taken! That time it was she, she was the one who
was taken, not Chaim! Her brother's trust lost, and Onofrio
in unencumbered possession of the ten thousand. Onofrio
had cause to grin; he, not she, could have a good laugh!
Laugh, laugh, laugh under the earth, you rotten bastard!
Mrs. Krocus raises a trembling fist, deformed by a lifetime of
injustice and anger. She was always such a dupe, so blind,
so incredibly stupid! Why didn't she follow Chaim's advice
and dump Onofrio? No, no, it wasn't merely because of her
willful blindness: it was because of the children, yes, it was
especially because of Max. A separation would have
destroyed the sensitive, high-strung boy, and it was only for
his sake that she bore the burden of her marriage in silence,
year after year, until the bastard died and she was free. And
now, twenty years later, her dear son, the fruit of her long-
suffering womb, comes all the way from North America to
tell her that if only Chaim had forked out some more money
Onofrio "might still be here with us"! Max, of all people!

Clenching her jaws, Mrs. Krocus grabs the dishcloth
and wrings it till her crooked fingers go white. What does he

think he is, the scholar, the great professor, making pro-
nouncements? Is he blind he can't see the pain that's filled
her life? *Groise knacker*, great shitter, to his own mother, who
used to wipe his dirty little ass! Where would he be if it
weren't for her? And she had told him, hadn't she warned
him, don't say one more word about Chaim! But he had to
do it anyway, he had to tell her from the door that it's
Chaim's fault that Onofrio is not farting around. And it's not
because of love for Chaim that she's seething with anger. As
far as she's concerned, Chaim too can go in *drerd aráyn*, he too
can drop dead and rot under the mud. Always a despot to
her, ever since she was a little girl, controlling her every
move, she will never forgive his interfering with Finkelstein
(last spring, when the new phone book arrived, she didn't
find his name, always preceded by "doctor"; he must have
passed away). Doctor Isidoro Finkelstein, who was a lawyer,
an important lawyer, not a shyster, and who was interested
in her, smitten after seeing her only twice, even though at the
time she was only seventeen and he was thirty-something.
And Chaim had to go and formally demand from Doctor
Finkelstein, on behalf of the family, an immediate declaration
of matrimonial intention. Understandably, after that she
never heard from the lawyer again; he must have thought
they were all nuts. If it hadn't been for Chaim's meddling
(prompted, she's certain, by his envy of Finkelstein's education), her whole life would have been different: she would
have married a doctor instead of Onofrio, who had barely
finished tenth grade, and not just a doctor but a cultured man
of delicate feelings, a gentleman. She has never been interested in luxuries, big houses, furs, cocktail rings; with
Finkelstein her life would have flowed tranquilly and happily, with no more than a normal quota of human grief: was

that too much to ask? Looking back at her past she sees it layered: frustration upon mockery, upon shame, upon impotence, upon hoax. An enormous rotten onion, stinking to heaven. And that punk, her own son — ah, why didn't she abort him while still in her womb! — comes and tells her that if only Chaim had coughed up more dough, Onofrio would be alive. He speaks his mind, goes out, and leaves her peeling onions. What is it that gives him the right to the last word? Is it that *schlong*, that piece of dung hanging in between his legs? To have the last word Max threw his shit at her and ran away, the coward! What is he afraid of? Why can't he accept that she has suffered for him? In a fit of rage Mrs. Krocus rises from her stool and throws the wrung dishcloth into the garbage pail, to join the onions.

In her scream there is anger and the effort of a constricted, cosmic defecation. Out, out with him! Out from her life! She has freed herself from husband, daughter and parents; she has no friends left in this world: now the time has come to unburden herself of her son. Out with the oaf! She doesn't need him, she doesn't need a soul; she's got enough in her bank account, thank God, the dollars she's saved these twenty years, since Onofrio died; she can pay a nursing home for herself . And even without the money, even if she were destitute, an invalid, she wants to be left alone! Lying in the gutter, sharing a watermelon rind with the rats, but alone, she's slaved enough, alone at last! There is savage, desperate defiance in her cry, the cry of the warrior hopelessly charging against a hill where the enemy — the quick, the dead, the whole world — are entrenched: **IN DRERD ARAYN ZOL ZI ARAYN GEYN!!**

245

25

Vanessa is dressed in shimmering silk satin, her dark hair gathered up with a leopard-spotted scrunchy ribbon and falling down her neck in curls and wisps. There she is, his dreamgirl, two yards away, smiling tentatively. Her bracelet, alternating sections of lapislazuli and gold, shines under the light of the entrance-hall chandelier. Max is about to rest his hand, like her, on the console-table, but the marble top seems too precious, her arm too sumptuous and the dream too fragile to bear the burden of his proximity: he slips his hand into his pant pocket. Vanessa takes her hand to her hair, as if to right a rebel ringlet. Max succeeds in closing his mouth, succeeds even in smiling, but only briefly. His heart has stopped. She says, "Hello." He says, "Hello."

"Well, come in," she says.

Max follows her into the living room. He walks on tiptoes, afraid to break the spell, the magic of the *hic et nunc*. Wood, tapestries, upholsteries, vases, oil paintings, lace, ivory, silver... she's been soaking into these objects, and they,

in turn, have acquired her soft, organic, blood-suffused over-
tones. Those wild ringlets, inked by some Chinese painter on
the pure porcelain of her neck, the crepuscular light, rippling
and foaming, shimmering on the fabric of her *peignoir*. What
is she wearing on her feet? Lord, ballerina slippers! But of
course! On what else would a lovely nymph saunter among
her treasures?

"What can I pour for you, Max? Wine, whiskey...?"
she says.

"With my mother I drink maté," says Max; "with
you... how about some wine?"

"Your mother doesn't drink wine?"

"No, the doctor forbade it."

"Is she sick?"

"Well, yes... old age, you know, all kinds of complaints... arrhythmia, arthritis, arthrosis, asthma... She does-
n't sleep well, she doesn't breathe well, and she doesn't —
well, anyway, she's not supposed to drink wine."

"What a shame," says Vanessa. "How old is she?"

"Seventy-seven," says Max.

"She's not that old," says Vanessa.

"No, not that old," says Max.

"When you consider," says Vanessa.

"Yes, nowadays that's not that old," says Max.

"Yet she can't drink wine. Does your father drink
wine?"

"He used to, but he died long ago."

"Then your mother lives... alone?"

"There's Gloria, my sister, but they don't speak to
each other."

"So, your mother lives alone, and she doesn't drink
wine... what a shame," says Vanessa.

247

"Bah," Max shrugs, "she drinks maté."

How in heaven did he get into this stupid conversation about Mother and her beverages. Vanessa has gone to fetch the wine. Max gets up, walks to a window, presses his hot forehead against the window pane. Outside, dusk is gently settling on the architraves and courtly facades along Avenida Alvear, the choicest neighborhood of Buenos Aires. Across the deserted street, a lamp post, an elegant *reverbère*. She didn't seem to notice the vanishing of his mustache. Or maybe she did, but didn't think it was worth mentioning, and, anyway, how can a bunch of bristles make any difference in the supreme enchantment of this moment. Somehow or other he's got to astonish her, make her shiver and shudder. He's no artist if he cannot seduce her, just a puny poetaster who can't shine at this most critical moment. All this beauty around, if only he could possess himself of it... Possess himself? No, be mastered by it; just let himself go; if only he could get the lowly worm within, that tiny, lazy, bland animalcule to come out and take on wings under the splendid light of beauty! Beautiful form can arouse the soul from slumber, old Platonists taught. But he's too nervous, and it's not clear to him how to enchant a twenty-year-old girl, the daughter of a wealthy shrink. Perhaps a *laissez-faire* attitude... Why not relax and let her charm him? Let the young girl seduce the old man. The bottle of wine she brings in is of such a rare kind that Max cannot help asking, "Do your parents know we're helping ourselves to it?"

"My mother doesn't live with us," says Vanessa, pouring the wine. "As for my father... you should take a look, there are so many of these down in the cellar..."

"Then your father has a fortune lying in his cellar!"

"You think so?" says Vanessa, with a coquettish twist.

"I'm sure of it. What does he do for a living?" Max feigns ignorance.

"He's a psychoanalyst: the most renowned, the best psychoanalyst in Buenos Aires, and therefore in the whole world."

"He must make a lot of money, then," says Max, unsure whether there's a tinge of irony in Vanessa's hyperbole.

"Money! Money! Always money! The eternal pretext... Often Dad will listen to an analysand in silence while counting out piles of dollar bills. Lacan himself used to do that. Jacques Lacan, you know, the genius. Some people become enraged, which is all to their good, because it shatters their repressions and speeds transference along."

Irony there seems to be, but Max doesn't know what to make of it. "How old is your father?"

"Forty-eight."

"Forty-eight! Then he's younger than I," says Max, "I am fifty."

"You're fifty... Well, physically, I must say, you are pretty much like Dad. Especially your voice..."

They sit at the two ends of the sofa, in silence, holding their wine cups, Max looking at Vanessa's pink ballerina slippers, Vanessa looking at the tip of Max's shoes. Why do parents keep coming up? First Max's mother, now Vanessa's father. Is it because they feel embarrassed to be thus by themselves, surrounded by luxury? Max hasn't seen such private wealth since his last visit to Uncle Chaim, and that was many, many years ago. But Uncle's luxury was fogged by Max's guilt and Krocusian jealousy and envy, while this is gentler, like a visit to a delicious museum. He searches in his mind for some subject at the antipodes of both Mrs.

249

Krocus and Mr. Satanovsky. The leather of Vanessa's ballerina slipper is puckered under the toes. The word "puckered" brings up unpleasant associations. Mentally he brushes it off, as if chasing away a pestering insect. Vanessa raises her gaze from the tip of Max's shoe and says, "A ta santé!"

"A la tienne!" says Max, responding in kind, and they take a sip. An evening walk on a country lane lined with eucalyptus, the moisture of the air holding a tinge of wood smoke. The tang of lemon peel, still green, on lips and tongue and fingertips. Wild, purple grapes hanging from a rusty arbor. The smell of cedar or acacia released as one opens a drawer. Max looks at Vanessa. Is she too, like him, facing an tidal wave of childhood memories?

"Mmm... Good, isn't it?" she says.

"Good? My God, this is —" The delicate curtains redden and swell with the sighs of the dying day. Vanessa's hand holding the crystal cup, her bracelet, the soft, perfect contour of her arm... her lips, wine-moistened, kisscharmed... "This must be paradise!" Max concludes.

She laughs. They drink in silence, as one should drink in paradise. Why is this girl so good to him? Is she the long-awaited guide, the psychopomp? It is not even clear who he, Max, really is right now. In paradise we can't preserve our identity: how could we possibly dwell there if we remembered the individual sadness, the personal misery? And why he? He hasn't deserved paradise by desiring it fervently enough, as one ought to, nor, for that matter, by being indifferent, disinterested, cool, which is the surer way. Beauty? Yes, he has, now and then, here and there, felt the prestige of form; not a stranger to music, mathematics, painting, poetry, or beautiful buildings. But fervently? No, his most secret fervors have been only for ugliness, for mud, for sewers and low whores, Retiro Park, garbage dumps and ramshackle huts in Berazategui... Oh God! The image of Boris' shaking limbs... "Fuck me Chaimele, tear me apart!" Boris lying dead, like a grotesque puppet... Even here, in Paradise, dwells the Low, a poisonous snake lurking in the manicured lawn! Out with you, ugly worm! Max empties his cup.

"Say, Max, do you like to play?" says Vanessa.

"To play — you mean, like playing music?" There's a grand piano in the Satanovsky's living room, and if Max could only play Chopin like he used to, it could be the straightest way to this ravishing nymph's heart.

"No, I mean playing, in general. Playing as opposed to being serious. Most grown-up people are terribly serious — why do you think that is?"

"There might be various reasons," says Max; "different reasons for different grown-up people, I imagine."

"Come on, can't you propose a more general theorem?"

"Well, I guess most grown-ups want results — if they do something, it is always in the expectation of something else coming back to them later on... I guess it's part of the definition of growing up..."

"Yes," says Vanessa, "that's why my dad is serious, for example. But pure mathematicians, who are supposed to specialize in playing — isn't pure mathematics an intricate sort of play inside our minds? At least, that's what we are led to believe, and that's why I got into it. But when someone like Professor Fontana..."

"Is he very serious?" Max interrupts.

"Oh yes," says Vanessa bashfully, pouring more wine.

"Well, I'm afraid I am not," says Max; "I'm hopeless: you'll find in me an utter lack of seriousness wherever you

251

care to look. Hegel, another dreadfully serious professor, said that the full-grown man devotes his life to labor for an objective aim, which he pursues consistently, even at the cost of his individuality. I find the idea repulsive; for nothing in this world would I relinquish my individuality; to be perfectly honest with you, Hegel makes me puke. Nietzsche, instead, says that the true man wants two things, danger and play, and that's why he likes woman, the most dangerous plaything. Serious people play only in order to get more energy to go on getting results, as one lets an ox out to pasture before the next day's tillage. Every year come September I get a memo from the president of the university: 'I hope you had a restful and productive summer...'" Max snickers. Then, suddenly he lunges, "Vanessa, do you know to what kind of labor I've devoted my life?"

"No, tell me," she says, pouring wine into Max's cup.

"I've done nothing besides staying alive. For fifty years I've been stalling, gaining time. What for, you may ask. I've been waiting. For what? For whom? For a playmate, Vanessa, for a lovely, intelligent playmate who'd give meaning to it all. Now, with hindsight, it is clear: I've been waiting for you..."

Vanessa laughs. "Seriously?" Her voice overflows with mirth. "You mean you want to play? Just play?" She shakes her hair and flutters her eyelashes. "Are you truthfully saying that you came to this place without any thoughts of... a result? Do you promise that you will leave contented even though you get no results?"

Max drinks his wine slowly, thoughtfully. Not daring to look at her face, he aims a little higher, at the leopard-spotted scrunchy ribbon and her hair. "No, I cannot truthfully say that I came here without any thoughts of a result. I con-

fess I had thoughts of... well, you know, of seducing you...
kissing you, you know, making love, that kind of thing...
Mea culpa! But then, you see, as soon as I entered this beautiful place, I knew I was in paradise. As soon as I came in
and while I've been sitting here, all along I knew I was in paradise. Still, little dirty thoughts, stupid thoughts, kept
intruding like worms, spoiling my bliss. And now I realize
why... Do you know why? Because I was expecting results!"

"And so, now..." Vanessa's lovely sealskin eyebrows
arch.

"And so now I'm not expecting anything. Do you
remember Faust?

'*Ich bin zu alt, um nur zu spielen,*
Zu jung, um ohne Wunsch zu sein...'
I could never understand that."

"Me neither, I don't understand Yiddish," says
Vanessa.

"I mean, one can never be too old to be content with
playing. What else is there? Being here with you, drinking
this nectar, looking at you among your things, breathing the
air that grazed your skin — that's enough. I want no more,
and I'll treasure this moment for the rest of my life."

"You promise?" says Vanessa.

"I promise."

"And you're still willing to play?"

"I'll play anything you want, anything you propose,"
says Max. "Volleyball, hide-and-seek, rummy-canasta, you
name it... I'll even play dead under your dining-room table
if you want me to."

26

"I used to stay here for hours on end when I was a little girl..."

Vanessa's voice, soft, wistful, comes from under the desk in her father's study; Max is sitting on Dr. Satanovsky's Eames chair: they are playing (it was her idea) "psychoanalytic session."

"The peace, the sense of holiness... this is my favorite place. When they asked me what I wanted to be when I grew up, I always said: a psychoanalyst like Father, and have an office like this. The books, the paintings, the rug, the leather chairs and the couch... I can smell it from here, the leather of the couch, mixed with the other leather, the book bindings. The smell of Dad's attaché case, Dad's perfume, Cuir de Russie... Once, I was twelve, I fell asleep right here, under the desk, and when I woke up I saw Dad's feet. One of them was dangling close to my face, before my eyes. Could you place your right foot... Yes, that's it, that's just right. Thank you. Well, I was about to jump out and kiss Father hello, when I heard a woman's voice. I realized she was one of Dad's analysands. I couldn't see her, she must have been lying on the couch. Her voice I will never forget: low and hoarse..."

"Go ahead; what was she saying?" says Max, making an effort to sound like a shrink. He wants to be a sport and play by the rules, but he has a nagging image of himself as a fat, sweaty Catholic priest hearing the confession of a beautiful and wealthy penitent.

"The woman was telling my father about her own father... she was saying that he used to fondle her when she went to bed — he would sit next to her and fondle her, 'just to relax her,' he'd say... and she'd lie motionless, terrified that her mother or someone might come into the room..."

"But what did *you* feel," says Max, professionally.

"More than what she was saying, what I found fascinating was her voice... something in her voice... steaming, oozing sex... hard to describe... it was as if — "

"It was as if — ," Max insists.

"As if she was a spider wrapping around my dad cobwebs of sex, viscous and sticky... No, it was like a flood, an avalanche of sex..."

"And what did your father say?"

"Father didn't say much, just an ahem! now and then, and his foot would swing a little faster. The session wasn't long. At the end Father said, 'I'll see you on Friday,' and that was the end of it. I decided that on Friday I was going to be here, under the desk, again."

"Brava, Vanessa!" says Max.

"No! Goddammit, don't say 'Brava Vanessa'. Just say 'What did you feel', and 'Go on'."

"Go on, Vanessa, please go on," says Max.

"On Friday I hid under the desk, and then the woman came, and Dad sat on his chair and his feet were right there. Swing it a little faster. That's it, good. The woman said that the night before she had had a dream, and in the dream she was lying in bed, with her father sitting next to her, as usual, fondling her, and she was terrified, as she used to be when she was a little girl, but then, she said, all of a sudden everything changed... it wasn't her father who was fondling her, but her analyst, my father..."

"Go on, and then? What did you feel? Go on..." says Max.

"Then... there was a silence. Have you ever heard the expression, pregnant silence? Then Dad asked, 'What did you feel.' And the woman said, 'I felt good... wonderful... I felt at peace...'"

"Go on, go on, what did you feel?" Max insists.

"Then Dad asked her, 'What else did you feel," and the woman said... ah, that voice, like a gurgle from way down inside her guts... 'I felt intensely happy,' she said."

"Go on, Vanessa, go on."

"Then Dad said, as from a thousand miles away, `Go on... What did you do?' And the woman... that horny bitch..., 'I was guiding your hand to the most secret recesses...' And..."

Vanessa is moaning. Max bends, crouches and tries to look under the desk. But the sun has set, the lights are off. Something, however, a bit of a smell... "What are you doing?" he asks.

"What do you think I'm doing..." she moans; "c'mon, keep talking, keep swinging your foot..."

"And what did you feel," Max asks, affecting, with stupendous effort, a far-away clinical tone.

Vanessa sighs. "I was guiding your hand to the most secret recesses..." Her voice is now different, hoarser, as if she was possessed by the other woman, her father's patient. "You touched me at the very center of my being, you found the spring of my life... You caressed my sun... my secret... my center..." She's breathing faster now, hot and moist upon Max's shin, through his sock. "I never felt like that before... I never will... Cecil... my love..."

"Vanessa, why don't you let me..." says Max. "Why don't you let me help you..." He bends down and gropes under the desk, in the dark.

"Don't you touch me!" she shrieks. "Don't you dare touch me..."

"Vanessa, Vanessa... Please... I'd love to..." Max mumbles.

"Keep swinging your foot, you dirty old geezer, keep asking what I felt," says Vanessa.

The odor of her genitals now dominates over the leathery smells of the office. "What did you feel," says Max, swinging his foot and about to break into a sob.

"The most secret recesses... oh, Cecil dear, your hand... I never felt anything like that... never... you reached down to my very center... oh, Cecil, come, give me your hand now..." Vanessa's voice thins out, a high-pitched dying murmur. "Then Daddy got up, and I heard..."

Silence. Max waits. The place is now completely dark. Not a sound from under the desk, just the strong odor. He shuts his eyes tightly. When he opens them, an oblong yellow patch — a cigar, a paramecium? No, a dirigible, the Hindenburg, ascends along a straight line from right to left and suddenly explodes. Again, everything is pitch-black. He has forgotten about moving his foot. He swings it a little more, then stops, clears his throat. He feels like a little boy, but very old.

"Leave me alone now," Vanessa's voice comes from under the desk.

"Won't you come out?" says Max.

"I beg you, leave me alone," again Vanessa's voice, aloof, impersonal.

But how does one get out of a dark and unfamiliar place without tripping over and crashing against the furniture? Suddenly the room is flooded with light, and a man appears at the door, who shrinks back upon seeing Max.

Max and the man stare at each other like two cats across a flower bed, judging distances, volumes and intentions. "Who are you," says the man. Such territorial boldness can only be due to his being the master of the house, Vanessa's father, Lacan's distinguished disciple. Dr. Satanovsky's hair is black streaked with gray, like Max's. He's about Max's height, of similar weight and size, and his nose is fairly Jewish, very much like Max's. He's also wearing brown oxfords.

"My name's Putzpine... Dr. Honoré Putzpine, from Paris, to serve you," says Max, with fast lucidity and effrontery born out of desperation. "Dr. Satanovsky? Nice meeting you," he adds, extending a cordially outstretched hand across the massive desk.

Ignoring the gesture, Dr. Satanovsky asks, "Have I ever met you? Are you one of my patients?" He is obviously unaware of his daughter's presence under the desk, behind the modesty panel.

"No sir; at least not that I recall, and I certainly hope not," says Max. "I'm a Lacanian inspector, *Inspecteur Lacanien, monsieur*, and, as you must surely know, it would

258

be highly unethical for either a patient, an ex-patient or an acquaintance of yours to be put in charge of a surprise professional inspection of the transferential transparence of your office. As I am sure you also know, such inspections must be unannounced and done in complete darkness, both from the patient's couch and from the analyst's *fauteuil*: that is why you found me sitting here, in case you were wondering. *Voilà*. Now, as regards my report, which is the really important question, *n'est ce pas?* I got an excellent impression, Dr. Satanovsky, for which I must congratulate you. One can breathe transference in this place, one can feel the flight and frothing of the signifiers, sitting at your desk; believe me, I wish I could say the same of Dr. Panard's office, but unfortunately I cannot. Between ourselves, and in the strictest confidence, I found a stack of dirty magazines tucked away in the bottom drawer of his desk. Most unprofessional. Anyway, I obtained an excellent impression at your office which I will not fail to convey to my colleagues at the *Ecole de la cause freudienne* in Paris. And now, I'm sorry, *je suis désolé, mon cher ami*, but I must leave. Will you conduct me to the door. You live in a beautiful place, excellent taste. *Mes compliments*. Please, don't ask me to stay; I'd love to, I really would, but, believe it or not, I must do two more inspections tonight. *C'est la vie*. Nice meeting you. Congratulations. *Au revoir, monsieur.*"

259

27

Life's meaning is a spider web, and Max was foolish enough to stretch it between a tree and a pissing dog. From lamp post to handsome, fluted, acanthine lamp post, a long-legged shadow sneaks up, slides ahead, shrinks and darkens, breaks along the wall, then lengthens again and disappears, only to reappear, gray and long-legged, before the next lamp post. Max's polished oxford shoes fall on the impeccable tiles. Before the palace of the Apostolic Nuncio he stops and howls, "Son of a whore!"

The question begs for an answer while he goes on walking: whom did he howl against? who is the son of a whore? Not the Apostolic Nuncio, perish the thought. Dr. Satanovsky? The wealthy disciple of Lacan didn't strike him as a nice man, but there was an intensity, a bitterness that caught Max by surprise and that he can still feel in his mouth, something so radical, so desperate in that howl, someone as accessory as Satanovsky cannot be held for its main referent. It cannot be Vanessa either, for what Max screamed was son, not daughter of a whore. Masculine gender, definitely. Fausto Roberto Fontana? That seems a bit more plausible. There's a degree of hatred reserved for those whom we betray, the keener when we do not succeed. The thought of el Indio climbing into Vanessa's bed, when all Max could do was sit on her father's Eames chair while she played with herself... The thought of those two, teacher and student, enjoying each other, and afterwards, as dessert, or in between peaks of delight, Vanessa offering, "Your friend Max imagined he was going to succeed you." Then Fontana, "I know; and he gave me a poem he wrote about meeting his father in a café-bar — what a drag." These are not pleasant thoughts. Yet there was something so primitive in that howl, which can be described only as the terror of a baby animal that's been left alone, a cub that's been exposed... Maybe Father's the son of a whore. Don Onofrio Krocus, beloved father of Gloria and Max, devoted husband of Berta, upright member of the Jewish community, indefatigable entrepreneur, typical Argentine hypocrite, his remarkably pointless life a source of inspiration to us all. What business had Onofrio Krocus shooting his semen up into his wife's womb, so as to perpetuate his failure by starting the cellular proliferation, the rotting in abeyance that is Max? Why couldn't some other man, a winner not a loser, do the dirty job? The duc d'Antin, the only legitimate son of Mme. de Montespan, couldn't forgive his father, M. de Montespan, for having sired him, instead of King Louis XIV; for him it meant being just another regular duke instead of a prince of the blood royal.

"Dear cousin, you were more than a duke, more than a prince of the blood: you were the King's only child, the Dauphin! Yet you lived and died like a buffoon, and your stunted bones lie now in California, waiting for the end of time, or for the earthquake that'll set 'em shaking again. You could have inherited the earth. You blew it. Why?" Thus Max expostulates as he reaches the end of Avenida Alvear. Today he's got proof, if further proof was needed, that he's not welcome on this earth. Beauty — tapestries and ballerina slippers, crystal chandeliers, rare and expensive wines, precious perfumes, the soul-healing harmony of sounds and the vivid colors of baroque skies: all that's Chaim's realm, the Middle Kingdom. Max is excluded from the charms of sense: to set his longing there is sinful, treasonous, and anyway he has no business *on* the earth, his business is infernal. His place is where his father is, the stinky plains of la Matanza. Under, under, further down! The sewers are his habitat. Rat! Old mole! A harem of dark housemaids, too old to tempt any conquistador, should smother him under their excrement. Torturers and prod-wielding meat workers will be his guard of honor.

Do you find that disgusting, ladies and gentlemen? Are you looking for a heaven, a salutary refuge, a third and higher place, above the earth and far removed from hell? Of course, Messieurs-Dames! You may have not one, but many. You may choose, from the wide variety of sign systems, the one you like the most — chess, painting, math... — the way you choose toothpaste at the drugstore. But Max has been expelled from all those heavens, and angels with turning, fiery swords...

At the Five Corners of Juncal, halfway to the Retiro Railroad Station and the old amusement park where he got his first whore thirty-five years ago, Max finally understands his cousin Boris' buffoon wisdom. Besides air, light, protein, glucose and several metallic ions, besides water and food, to

262

sustain life you must have a faith, a devotion of some kind. It matters little which: you'll always find other nuts of the same confession. And since choose you must, of all the varieties, which is simpler and healthier than the purely numerical? Faith in God, in Progress, in Humanity, in History, in the Spirit: one after the other, all kaput. Faith in words too has of late been exposed as the worst floccinaucinihilpilification: they only refer to other words, in an idiotic, infinite regression. Faith in friends? What lunacy. Friends are fine, so long as you don't hang a faith on them. As for faith in beautiful women, in the charms of voluptuousness... all you're left with is a whiff of their sweat, of their *odor de femina* (Vanessa's private molecules haven't stopped hopping, like cruel gnats, in and out of Max), and the bitterest aftertaste of humiliation. "Mushy," Boris used to say, and right he was, how right! Numerical faiths are the only reasonable ones, and a gambler's is as good as any, maybe better than most.

Max is standing at the crossroad of the Five Corners of Juncal. Behind those windows, by the amber glow of that lamp, perhaps an old woman is reading Ronsard, lamenting the passing of her charms, regretting the young poet she once laughed at and drove away. Smartly dressed couples in taxicabs, going to a *dîner en ville* or perhaps to a quick fuck out in the suburbs. Onofrio always drove too fast, but that night a truck... Screech! bang! crash! Darkness. Nothing. Impossible to imagine. If we ask, accident or suicide?, difficult to tell, or to assign numerical values to each likelihood. He thinks of Boris sitting at the casino gaming table, that fatal night in Reno, his stunted legs hanging, dangling, sweat on his brow and above his lip, eyes glued on the roulette wheel. *Rien ne va plus*! Boris' life hangs on it: he has placed all that's left of his money on a neat pile *en carré* on 31, 32, 34 and 35. What are his chances of winning, and coming out alive? Far from a rhetorical question. The answer, quite precisely, is 4 out of 38, or 0.105263157894736842..., the eighteen digits forever repeated. As it happened, Boris lost, went back to his room and put an end to his life. He might have won, in which case he might be here today, beside Max, merrily standing at the corner of Juncal, Quintana and Libertad, blowing his trombone, farting, frightening the passersby. But that's not the point. Winning or losing, being saved or damned, it is our destiny and sooner or later it must befall each of us; the question is how, in what manner: the question is really one of style. Boris had faith in the sacred impartiality of chance: no mush, no mud, no bull. Madonna Fortuna, Tyché, Lady Luck. 0.105263157894736842... probability of staying alive; 0.894736842105263157... probability of having to die. Harsh, indeed, but what austere simplicity! What dignity! Boris the trombone-blowing clown died with style, while he, Max, survives lamentably, shamefully, ridiculously. Onofrio died in a car crash, and Uncle Chaim is alive and living like a king. That murderous and long-lived *roi soleil* deserves to be called a son of a whore. Chaim's the only real *hijo de puta*. His uncle, the tempting Satan, the prince of light behind Krocusian desperate desires, must be shot. Max has not forgotten that, nor does he doubt it. But what kind of punishment would it be, merely to bring death to interrupt that long career of delight? No: first Chaim should be brought down, dragged through stink, misery and hopelessness. He ought to get a little taste of hell and of the monsters that lurk under the earth, before he's killed.

Gambling, however, is not Max's destiny. About to die, Boris put it concisely in his last letter: "Go for twat for as long as you can." At the time, Max had interpreted those words as a *carpe diem*, an injunction to enjoy life each day while you're alive, to gather roses while you're young, but now he realizes that they were meant literally, as a statement of fact: his destiny, his vocation, is twat. Not randomness, or power, or truth, or beauty, or mystical awareness. Twat. Ass. Low ass.

And so it is a pious duty toward his cousin: he must follow his star. Max starts walking down Calle Juncal towards Retiro in search of la Negra, the cheap whore. He now walks at a good clip, and doesn't stop to expostulate or howl. He searches his pockets for australes. Two hundred thousand total, and he can have her for five thousand, although tonight, out of sheer melancholy, he's willing to pay eight. But what if la Negra is not available? It isn't very likely, after all, that she will still be sitting, waiting, in the same spot. But Aristotle was right: walking tonifies the brain: if la Negra is not there, why, there's Big-boobs, and if neither la Negra nor Big-boobs is there — which is already less likely: the probability of that being the square of the previous one, assuming equal probabilities for both whores plus independence, i.e., non-collusion between them — then he will pick a third whore, say Milonguita, or Ace of Spades, or Muskrat. And the good news is, as you increase the number of whores, which has practically no upper bound, the probability of not finding any approaches zero (barring whores ganging up together, establishing a union and going on a general strike).

Occupied with such thoughts, Max briskly walks the few blocks and in no time he is standing before café Versailles. And lo! behind one of the windows he discovers Big-boobs; behind another, la Negra. They are sitting at the same two tables, placidly, patient as spiders, exactly as the other day. Figure out the probability of such an event. If cousin Boris had had this kind of luck, he'd be alive, a wealthy man. All excited about this unexpected good fortune, like a child before a roomful of new toys, Max hesitates. Should he approach la Negra again, or go for variety and accost Big-boobs? Not an easy question. La Negra or Big-boobs? Both look equally cheap, gaudy and vile. Big-boobs or la Negra? Max stands on the sidewalk before the two whores like Buridan's ass between the two haystacks. Negrita... Boobsieboob... He rubs his hands, his mouth is watering. Big-boobs' exuberance is tempting, but la Negra comes from Salta, and she's dark and Indian-looking, which is equally tempting. On the other hand, the other day he got the impression that la Negra was somewhat insensitive to the needs of the Argentine male, while Big-boobs' lewd lips are very much like Pancracia's, and her hair too, if only Pancracia's had cared to dye hers yellow-green. One way or the other, he's got to decide. He is about to walk into the café and choose one of the two whores on the random spur of the moment, when he hits on a brilliant idea.

With all the attention recently lavished on cognitive science, and specialists in creativity working around the clock, no one truly understands how this thing works, how and why or when we get a dazzling insight. If we could only trigger it, muster it, if we could only control it, the world economies would be in far better shape. Gauss was eighteen when one fine morning, while still in bed, undecided to leave the warmth of his mattress, he suddenly saw how to construct a 17-sided regular polygon with compass and straightedge, a discovery that made him famous. Descartes and Kekulé build their whole careers on a dream, and Henri

Poincaré had the idea of the relation between non-Euclidean geometries and Fuchsian functions the minute he stepped on a bus at a place in La Manche whose name I don't want to recall. A similar sudden illumination now descends upon Max, while he's about to enter the café.

Why choose? He doesn't have to choose, he can have both! For the measly sum of ten thousand australes, ten dollars, he can go to bed with two sluts for the first time in his life, thus opening new, unsuspected sexual vistas! Think of the possibilities, the bizarre combinations, the ways it could be generalized: three, four... n... An immense bed full of beautiful, sadly phosphorescent flesh, like in Delacroix's *Death of Sardanapalus*. Amazing that it did not occur to him last time he was here, a few days ago.

But as soon as he enters the café, ready to summon the two tarts to a conference, he finds himself unexpectedly facing a third woman: Consuelo Regueiro. "Max! What dirty business brings you here?" she asks. "And what have you done to your face?"

"I have shed my mustache," says Max. "Regarding your other question, I need to go to the men's room. I was just walking by, but I'm pissing my pants. What about you?"

"I'm not pissing my pants," says Consuelo, "nor have I shaved my mustache. I was sitting over there, having a drink, between those two ladies of the night. I wasn't aware it was *that* kind of place. I don't mind *them* so much, but all these mirrors... Having to see my face no matter where I turn..."

"What's wrong with your face, Consuelo? You look great!" says Max. In fact, Consuelo's taut face (making abstraction of her widow's peak and her chin hairs) has always called to Max's mind Picasso's portrait of Gertrude

267

Stein. Why doesn't she get rid of those hairs, Max has asked himself over the years: that would eliminate if not the gravest, at least the most tractable of the problems she presents to the eye.

"Well, thank you," says Consuelo; "I feel flattered, the more so because it comes from you, who compliment so rarely..."

"Do I smell a faint odor of reproach?"

"My God, no! What? Am I going to reproach you for last night, at the restaurant? For not paying me the least attention after not seeing each other for twenty years?" Consuelo laughs. "You had eyes only for the little Satanovsky."

Max blushes at the mention of his all-too-recent wound, which Dr. Satanovsky would have dubbed *narcissistic*. Shrugging, taking hold of Consuelo's elbow, he says, "Come, let us get out of this place."

"But weren't you pissing your pants?" says Consuelo.

"Isn't it odd," says Max, "the joy of our encounter makes me forget my most pressing needs."

28

Johnson Fireclay Co Ltd Stoke-on-Trent. Waiting for a few drops before the urinal, Max has a little confidential talk with his penis. "Sonofabitch, today you and I were going to visit the Satanovsky paradise: that didn't work out. Then we were going to visit hell with la Negra and Big-boobs: that didn't work out either. As I bear with you you'll have to bear with me... grin and bear it..."

Above the urinal, above Johnson Fireclay and the rusty stains, someone has scribbled, "99% putas" Or is it "99% putos (fags)"? "Kill 'em all," a little to the side, and farther, "Wash your balls with Moisheol." It takes Max a while to decipher that one. Moishe = Jew, ol = alcohol. One doesn't usually wash one's balls with alcohol though. No, not alcohol, rather German *öl*, oil, the umlaut dropped, omitted or washed off. Typical Argentine humor, an allusion to Auschwitz, human fat saponified. Laugh, laugh if you're macho enough.

"You and I were lucky after all," Max whispers, shaking off the last drops. "Within a year we'd've been blind, or demented, or wasted and sarcomatous through you, because of you, sonofabitch. No, you've never been the same, since that terrible night in Reno." The idea comes to his mind: grab the Heftpistole in his pocket and blow off the whole kit and caboodle. "You've certainly deserved it," he concludes, "but it would be too messy."

As he leaves the mirrored salon, Max throws a last glance towards the two whores. La Negra shrugs, Big-boobs smiles. He thinks: there goes my chance to die like Sardanapalus. Out in the street, Consuelo says, "Honestly, I can't understand why a man would pay to lie anywhere near something as repulsive as those two..."

"It's an acquired taste, I suppose," says Max, "like smoking cigars, or modern painting."

They start walking, and Consuelo says brightly, "Well, Max, how does it feel to be back in Buenos Aires?"

"Strange: I'm thrown into a most exalted mood," says Max, "as if I were a kid again, but with the whole cargo and realm of an adult. Do you see what I mean?"

"No."

"You're a mathematician, you know about fundamental structures — sets, groups, topological spaces, and so on. Well, here in this city, in the paving stones, the humidity, the shadows of palm leaves, in that gesture of your hand or in the way you walk, Consuelo, I reencounter the fundamental structures of what we call Max Krocus."

"Hm... interesting... in the way I walk?"

"I don't know how to explain it any better," says Max. "I should add, I'm planning to move back to Buenos Aires."

"You? I'm surprised. Why would you do such a thing?"

"My mother," says Max. "She's old and she's sick. I've got to take care of her."

"I can't believe you are serious."

"Why, sure. What do you want me to do, put her in a nursing home?"

"But don't you have a sister?"

"Mother and Gloria are not on speaking terms."

"Then why not take your mother with you to the U.S."

"Mother to the U.S.? No, that would be impossible. She doesn't speak a word of English. Anyway, she wouldn't move from this city, she never has, she totally refuses... Buenos Aires is her place."

They are walking along Calle Florida, deserted at this hour: shops closed, public employees gone home, bums lying in doorways under cardboard boxes. Consuelo asks, "I heard Fontana mention that you became a poet?"

"Yes, but definitely not a famous one, as he claimed," Max blushes.

"But surely you remember what happened to Don Quijote, who mistook knight-errantry fiction for fact?" Yes, of course Max remembers that. "And you also remember," Consuelo continues, "what happened to Madame Bovary, who read too many romances and took them to heart?" Yes, of course, Max remembers that. "Well, it must be an occupational disease or something of the kind," Consuelo concludes; "I think a similar disorder is affecting you."

"You mean I'm reading too much? Too many poems, too much literature?"

"No, I think you must have been listening to too many tangos," says Consuelo, "I'm afraid tangos have softened your brain, Max. This talk about returning... Returning to Buenos Aires after twenty years, hair snow-white, wrinkled

271

brow, eyes feverish with disillusion, the pale glow of street lamps... Jesus Christ, you're even talking of returning to Momma, first love and true, your only one!"

Max laughs. "Look who's talking. You lived in Spain for a number of years, didn't you? What brought *you* back?"

"No, with me it's different," says Consuelo, as they walk up into Plaza San Martín. "Oh, I could tell you about this widowed aunt of mine who lives in Barracas and whom I love very much... I could tell you about this guy I had left here in Buenos Aires whom I also loved, and who loved me too, or so I thought... oh, I guess I could tell you..."

"Another sonofabitch, Consuelo?"

"Sonofabitch, him? No..." She shrugs. "He was the one who denounced my brother to the military. Actually the son and grandson of a bitch... Aren't all of you Argentine men of the same noble genealogy?"

"You may be right, but in that case, why come back?"

"That's precisely the thing: because of it. Because I need them, those sonsofbitches. Because I'm a masochist: is it possible that you have never noticed? I'm a true, full-blooded Argentine woman, therefore I'm a masochist, I enjoy being a slave. Q.E.D. There's a simple implication, an analytic *a priori* judgment. What can I do about it? I've had friends, women who moved away, to Spain or Venezuela or to the United States, who stayed away, and who apparently became free, clean, almost healthy, hard as it is to believe. Didn't Marceline, that old girlfriend of yours, move to Paris? But she wasn't a true Argentine woman, really, she wasn't like me. She didn't need to be treated like shit. That's why I always knew she wasn't the right girl for you, Max."

Most lamps in Plaza San Martín are shattered. Consuelo and Max take a path among the trees.

"And you, Max," says Consuelo, with a different tone of voice, kinder, caressing, almost loving, "What finally brings you back? Is it your sadism?"

Max stops dead, as if he had been slapped in the face. "What do you mean, my sadism?" He peers into the dark ground around his feet, as if looking for something that could be construed and marked off as *his sadism*. A twig, some pebbles and bits of gravel, a piece of foil from a pack of cigarettes, a stray ant, a hairy worm. He vaguely remembers splitting those with a spade and watching the severed sections shrink and writhe. He also remembers dissecting cockroaches, their legs twitching, their innards bathed in milk-pale blood. There was the sick, mangy cat, the one he poked in the ribs with a broomstick. Memories from childhood. Do they prefigure a tendency, an ethos, a perversion? One that's now noticeable enough to come to Consuelo's attention? Suddenly, with a horselaugh, Max slaps his thigh. "I get it! That's your occupational quirk: as a mathematician, you're obsessed with symmetry, Consuelo. And since according to you, returning Argentine woman implies masochism, then returning Argentine man must imply he's a sadist, right? Quite a theorem! Ha, ha, ha!"

Consuelo doesn't answer. She's a few paces ahead. Max walks up. She's talking to a man who's sitting on a park bench.

"I arrived today," the man is saying. He speaks with a sing-song; a recent arrival by train to Retiro Station.

"Where are you from?" asks Consuelo.

"From Paraguay."

Baroque Jesuit churches, orange groves, cruel dictatorships, green oceans of maté plantations! Hell, yes, but a bucolic hell, and infernal Arcady peopled by innocents! The man's face, brown and smoked, is hard to distinguish in the dark. "Do you speak Guaraní?" Max asks.

"Up there at home I do."

He speaks Guaraní! He must drink maté of course. Hot or cold? Does he drink it together with his barbecue or afterwards? Does he put orange peel or Arabian jasmine inside the gourd? Does he live in a hut made of wattle and daub or in a masonry structure? Does he by any chance remember, back when he was a boy, the Great Chaco war? There are so many questions Max would like to ask. But the man is the first to ask, "And where are *you* from?"

"We were both born here, in Buenos Aires," says Consuelo.

"Then maybe you know," says the man, taking a piece of paper out of his shirt pocket, "where this is..."

With the help of her cigarette lighter, Consuelo reads an address on Arenales Street. "Is this a one or a seven?" she asks.

"I don't know, Madam, I can't read; this is where my daughter works. I've come to see her."

He came all the way from the tropics to visit his daughter, and he doesn't know how to read. Consuelo says, "It's very close, in that direction... a ten minute walk. We'll go with you and show you the way."

The hundred-year-old ombú, the gravel, the plaza's benches, the nostalgia of those benches where Marceline and Max used to kiss... The man walks silently in his old, dusty clothes, a little behind Consuelo and Max. What can the tallest buildings in the country, seen from here — the Kavanagh, the Sheraton Hotel — mean to him? He doesn't even raise his eyes. Perhaps he hasn't noticed the skyscrapers, like the Indians of Tierra del Fuego didn't notice the tall

Spanish ships. When they get to the building on Arenales Street, Consuelo gives him back his piece of paper and tells him to take the elevator to the sixth floor, apartment C.

Soon the man is back: he doesn't know how to operate an elevator. He's never seen one before. Together they go up to the sixth floor. The Paraguayan is visibly anxious, like a bird used to the bush getting its first taste of the cage. They ring the bell of 6C. From inside, a woman's voice: "Who's that?"

Max nudges him, and the man from Paraguay intones in his slow, hopeless sing-song, "Is Dionisia in? I am her father..."

"Her father..." says the voice from inside, "if you're Dionisia's father you should know that these are not hours to come to a decent house. Come back tomorrow."

Max looks at his watch: it's eleven o'clock. "Madam," he proclaims, "this man has come all the way from Paraguay to visit his daughter."

"Come back tomorrow." The voice sounds annoyed.

"Madam," Max insists, his voice self-righteously aflutter, "no decent house would close its door to a man who's wearied after a long journey, a father who wants to see his daughter!"

A drop of a full, ominous octave. "Leave right away or I'll call the police."

Back on Arenales Street, the man from Paraguay asks, "Will I be arrested if I sleep on a bench?"

The blessed park benches on which Marceline and Max used to neck!

"You might be," Consuelo says. "Besides, it wouldn't be comfortable."

"Come, we'll take you to a hotel," says Max.

They walk back toward the river and Leandro Alem Avenue, the Paraguayan following behind Consuelo and Max, who reminisce. Remember Patricio O'Fallon, who was a *capo* of the Communist Party cell at the University? Well, he's now one of the chief economists at the International Monetary Fund. And remember Carlo Fantoni, *il Conte Rampante*, who wore the most elegant and fashionable suits and declared himself an anarchist? He went back to Italy and is high up in the government. El Indio Fontana joined no party, but nevertheless, what a trajectory! Remember when Marceline took up with el Indio? Oh, that wasn't serious, it was just to spite you, Max. You think so? I'm positive. Marceline's career too has been meteoric: director of the Institut des Hautes Études Mathématiques at forty five. And us? You and I? We have been left behind, haven't we? Obscure but happy. Obscure yes, but as for happy... On the other hand, look at poor Schamberg, jumping off to his death, after fifty-plus years of precarious surviving. And poor Gesualdo Costa, didn't you know? His wife left him. She finally came out of the closet — a lesbian, and by the way, that lanky girl, his daughter, too.

When they find a hotel that looks suitable, cheap though not one of the seediest, the Paraguayan says, "But I haven't got money..."

"Leave that to me," says Max. He opens the door and ushers the man in. At the desk, after paying for a room, Max takes his hand and shakes it. "Don't thank me," says Max, "but keep an open eye: this is a big city, and not everyone you will encounter is going to be nice."

Back in the street, Max explains to Consuelo, "For eight thousand australes we'll feel much better, you and I, and the poor fellow will sleep on a fairly decent bed." He adds to himself: And I was about to pay as much for a couple of flea-bitten whores...

"Listen, I have an idea," says Consuelo on an impulse. "Let's hire another bed in this same hotel, for you and me. This one's my treat."

Max is taken by surprise. He stares at his old classmate, friend and confidante, he looks at her face taut like a Japanese nô mask, at her widow's peak and the hair on her chin, yellow in the light of the hotel's entrance hall.

"I've always liked you," she goes on; "I felt attracted to you when we were students, even when you were going out with Marceline. You might say I had a yen for you. One of those things, you know, today they call it chemistry... a special sexual affinity..." she concludes with a shrug.

"But Consuelo... You and I..."

"Wait, don't say anything, let me explain. I've known you for many years, practically since we were kids. I know exactly what you are and what you want. Where will you find a woman who knows you as well as I? You can treat me like a whore, like a mare, like a piece of dung... and that's exactly what I like. You can't imagine how you aroused me last night, telling me about that fantasy of yours at the slaughter-house: women as cows, and you the cattle driver... You ride me, spur me: I'll moo for you, Max."

She looks at him expectantly. Her heavy eyelids, her chignon, the wrinkles around her eyes, her hairy chin jutting out as she says, "I'll moo for you, Max"... Her face, her waxy hands glowing under the hotel's yellow light... There's a smell in the air, maybe from the gutter... from the hotel entrance-hall... from some latrine upstairs... maybe from her mouth... "I don't know if I... It comes as a surprise, Consuelo."

"What do you have to lose... It's just a one-night stand, and I promise I won't be pestering you afterwards... I'll give you my ass," she whispers.

Max straightens himself and shakes his head. "I'm not into that kind of stuff. And you are completely wrong: I'm not a sadist. I like you very much, Consuelo, I really do — but..." He now looks directly into her imploring eyes. "But you're too much like myself. It would be no good. I love you... like a sister. That's why I can't make love to you." Tears roll down her cheeks, like drops of wax rolling down a church candle. "You're a female copy of myself, you see what I mean? You aren't a cow. Come on. Be serious. You can't be a cow. You're an intellectual, a mathematician. It would be no good... Too equal, you understand? How could I possibly go to bed with my own sister..."

29

His soul returns to his body, runs to his eyes and clashes: light! Sunlight fills his realm. Still whole, enormous, Time, all around. Outside, the bellowing of city buses and the chirping of birds; inside, sounds of Mrs. Krocus in the bathroom, taking an early shower. How do they hop, these sounds, merrily atop the still soft yellows of tender beams of dawn! *Mater Matuta.* Mother Dawn. He is lying on the mattress. Yesterday... it all comes back by chunks, acquires solidity. Vanessa, Gloria, el Indio, Consuelo, the two whores, the man from Paraguay: one by one they appear, low in the horizon of Max's consciousness, like inauspicious planets of yesternight. Dawn chases them away with fresh, glittering arrows. How warmly the new sun shines on his forehead! The day is intact, and Max is still the sinless Adam. Anxious to get up and sit down to new work, ready for the greatest enterprises: a new poem, imbued with faith in life and in the ultimate power of light. He looks at his watch: December 21st, longest day of the year.

But it's not yet six o'clock: too early to get up. Max pulls the sheet over his face and lies quietly, legs stretched, arms alongside, bathed in the milky sunlight through the linen. He feels the quiet pulse of his blood, the quiet flow of his thoughts, the quiet rhythm of his breathing. A chrysalis in its cocoon, at the right moment he might emerge in dazzling, brilliant new wings. Thursday. He'll drink a few rounds of maté, chatting with Mother until eight or nine, he'll eat a couple of left-over friar balls. In the late afternoon he'll go see Capricoll, over at the University, to talk about Schamberg's job. In between, he'll work, he'll get started on something, maybe a poem full of the tensions between the High and the Low.

The shower has stopped running. Max imagines his mother drying herself with the large towel. Footfalls, then the sharp sound of the toilet cover coming into contact with the seat. Clapping, slapping. Mother's frail body, enveloped in a cloud of steam and talcum powder. She hovers above the sheet covering Max's face, in a white aura of milk and talc, like a protective spirit of light, a sort of Ahura Mazda.

Twelve twelve-line stanzas, each based on a different word. The word "quilombo," to start with. Originally, in Brasil, it meant a self-ruling village of fugitive slaves: here it means a brothel, and, by metonymy, a disorderly mess. High, free and noble for the African slaves; vile, despicable (and supremely fascinating) for their masters. Something should come out of that. The word "galpón," second stanza. From the great hall of an Aztec palace, it came to denote a shed or hangar. The ruins of the High survive as the haunts, the ghettos, the dung heaps of the Low. Third: the word "coya." The Queen of the Inca Empire, now a woman of the lowest class.

280

No more Vanessas, no more ridiculous infatuations. Sex as a hygienic activity, sure, nothing against it; one has to eat, etc. Max is no cenobite, certainly no puritan. But no more emotional involvement. Work, work and only work: the new, the unexpressed, is waiting to see the light; Max's essential oil is still untapped; poems are waiting to be written. Work, and caring for Mother. Work, hygienic sex — lubricated condoms, no kissing, no whores, just young housemaids from the northern boondocks — and caring for Mother. Mother will pour maté and he will write. Max digs with his little finger inside his ear and considers the bit of yellow wax. He smells it. It smells like curdled milk, like a baby.

Another word. "Tambo" once referred to an Inca royal inn or caravansary, now to a dairy farm. The word "kiosk" in the East, in Persia and Turkey, meant a palace; now, in the enlightened West, it means primarily a newsstand. Five so far, seven to go. Incidentally, the Heraclitean fragment, "The way up and the way down is one and the same," would do well as an epigraph. The bathroom door opens and Mrs. Krocus walks in. She is dressed and combed as for going out, her lips rouged, her face powdered, the gray hair of her beauty spot wetted into a perfect spiral. From Max's viewpoint, lying as he is on the mattress, she looks vertical, forbidding. She goes into the kitchen, without saying a word or throwing a glance in his direction.

"Good morning, Mother," Max's voice is easy and bright, "are you going out by any chance?" She doesn't answer, and he tries again, "It sure seems like a beautiful day to go out. It would be sinful to stay indoors."

Water running, china clinking: she must be about to eat her usual morning yoghurt, toast and tea. "Mother, listen, if you're going out, would you do me a favor? Could you buy the paper for me?"

Heraclitus, so it is said, ended up on a dung heap, under the strong sun of Ephesus. Devoured by the dogs. Or roasted in the dung, like *pollo al barro*. The way up and the way down. Eternal return, universal cycles. The spoon against the saucer, Mother eating her yoghurt. But the intervals in between are far too long, ominously long. As if she were taking a spoonful only when her mind, occupied with weightier things, condescends to breakfast. The intervals in between clinks, the pregnant, spooky silence...

"Mother, is there anything wrong?"

This, at last, produces an effect. Mrs. Krocus emerges from the kitchen. She moves slowly, and sits on a chair not far from Max. Her air is solemn, as on the very great occasions. The day when Max came home from school to find that Father had been arrested, she struck a similar attitude. Tragic. Hieratic. But, strangely, it makes her look much younger. Finally, she speaks. "I have a favor to ask of you," she says, and Max finds her voice surprisingly sweet, like heliotropes.

"Sure, Mother. Anything."

A stifled stridulation, as in a high-voltage line swung by a winter storm: "Could you please leave me alone."

Her shoes, flat-heeled, tongued, laced.

The clawed legs of the sideboard.

The Zeide's pendulum.

Her socks, reaching up to just below the knee.

"I don't know if I'm making myself clear." Her tongue is like a poisoned chisel. "Could you vacate this place, please, could you move out of this apartment." She gets up and disappears in the kitchen.

Large squares of sunlight on the polished floor.

A long band all the way across the ceiling.

When he was a boy he fancied some day he'd make a bundle — not a pecuniary one, just a few belongings wrapped in a pack tied to a stick to carry on his shoulder — and leave home and Krocuses behind. That's about what he did at twenty-five, when he moved to the United States. But he never imagined, never dreamt in his worst nightmares that Mother would kick him out. Out, to the street. Derelict, orphaned, exposed. Ridiculous. Absurd. It can't be real.

A joke? It's a whole week until December 28, day of the Massacre of the Holy Innocents and Roman Catholic April Fool's day, when one's supposed to make jokes.

No, this is no joke. She's being almost, but not quite, in earnest. For some reason she's mad at him, and as always on such occasions, she's trying to make him pay for it: just wait a bit, and it will clear up. But why? What did he do? Could it be his suggestion that she call Gloria for her birthday? At the time, she dismissed it out of hand and said, "Don't even mention it." She didn't seem offended. No, that can't be it. He must have forgotten something. These last couple of nights he didn't kiss her good-night. But in the past, when Max was a child, that kind of omission would at most put her in the pouts: nothing worse. Did he forget an important date? A birthday, an anniversary? Perhaps, unwittingly, he called her by her first name? (She never did like that: lack of respect). Might she have resented his unobliging words yesterday about Uncle Chaim? But damn him, Chaim's only her brother, Max is her son! No, it probably was Max's discovery, two days ago, of dirt under the cupboard. Showing her his grimy fingertip. But she knows it's only a game: how many times have they played it, and they both ended up laughing. Heavens! Didn't he leave his work on the table, the other night? She must have read it! The poem about playing dominoes with Father in the café-bar... male bonding between the living and the dead behind her back: pretty nasty. No, that was two nights ago: yesterday the table was clean and Mother was happy...

Suddenly, like an avalanche of mud: it was his masturbating in the bathroom, last night, before going to bed. Of course. He must have left some semen on the toilet seat. She must have noticed it. Cleaning it. Or, oh God sitting on it. He should have checked, he should have wiped it off. And the puff! Didn't he powder his penis, didn't he twiddle his glans with her puff? That's it! Just now, she was powdering her cheeks when something sticky... What is this? Whose is this? How? Max... That soft puff, that subtly scented puff. Oh shame. Oh crushing shame. Since the days of his boyhood, Max whines, "Momma!" whenever he feels ashamed. In the U.S., he'd be driving along the Interstate when, out of the blue, remembering some particularly shameful incident of his past, "Momma!" erupts from the depth of his gut to the top of his voice. But what is he to cry now, under this most profound and absolute shame? Accursed light. Infernal sun on his face. Darkness is what he needs, where no one can see him. He would like to be blind. He ought to gouge himself blind, like the smart-alecky Theban.

He pulls the sheet back over his face, but the light shines through. The filtered light in which he was basking a moment ago seems now even more odious than the naked product. He covers his face with the pillow. Think of something. Make up something. Example of a continuous function of bounded variation which is not absolutely continuous. A catalogue of North-South streets of Buenos Aires between the River Plate and Congress Square. More examples of Amerindian words gone to seed. The dialectics of the High and the Low. Impossible: his brain resists all ploys. He is alone, defenseless, like a baby at fifty, confronted with his shame. Through the pillow Mother's voice reaches him. Holding on to the pillow he peeks at her. She's standing by his feet, younger than ever in her terrifying verticality. "Please do get up. I'd like you to move out as soon as possible."

She goes into her bedroom, closes the door: she does not want to be in the same room with Max. Trying to get up he is amazed at his own weakness. His body seems lead-heavy, and when he leans on an elbow, his arm shakes uncontrollably. He lies down again. He says to himself, "Relax, relax, everything will be okay," but space feels impossibly dense, as when he was a child and ran a high fever, and the walls, the furniture seemed to slip into his mouth like huge chunks of unchewable food. He's afraid his body won't respond to his will. But his will, where is it? Is there anything inside or outside him that could pass for "his will"? Pretty soon he won't have it in him to ask such questions. The beads of Mrs. Krocus's chandelier taunt him with a million reflections. "Out, out with you, out with you, bum!" they glitter. He has no right to be in this room, no right to the light. He rolls over and lies face down on the mattress. But the mattress too in its warmth, in its very softness, rejects him. His own smell on the pillow says, "Out, out with you, masturbator!" He raises himself until he's on all fours. Outside, the solstitial sun shines gloriously. Not a sound. Mother is in her room, waiting for him to disappear: if he doesn't, she'll return and inflict on him her merciless verticality. Somehow he finds himself standing, getting dressed.

There is not much to pack, Max travels light. His shoes, his papers, and his books. His shirts, and ah! the one that's drying in the kitchen. A stray pair of socks, under the cupboard. The Heftpistole at the bottom of his suitcase. Max considers whether to leave it there or put it in his pocket. He's never started a life with his dick, nor has he killed anyone with this gun. Useless both. Rusted scrap. Mere masturbatory tools. He slips the gun in his pocket. His toiletries and his umbrella are in the bathroom. Max stops for a moment before his mother's door, then, very softly, knocks. She doesn't answer. "I have to get my stuff from the bathroom," he whispers in the jamb, and opens the door. Mrs. Krocus is sitting on the chair by her bed, hands resting on her lap, gaze focused on a tragic void.

In the bathroom, he goes very carefully over the toilet bowl. Mother has had, of course, ample time to clean it, but there's no trace of stickiness. Next he opens the powder box and takes out the puff. As virginly dry and pristinely powdery as it ever was. He flushes the toilet and washes his hands. Then, umbrella on forearm and toiletries in hand, he opens the door and confronts her.

"But why, why? Can't you at least tell me why?"

It takes a while. Without deflecting her gaze from the poignant void, Mrs. Krocus says, "You know very well why."

Max finds this exasperating. Not only does he not know why, but he always makes a point of not knowing for sure anything at all. "Listen," he says, trying to contain his temper, "I have no idea what you have in mind, not the slightest. I don't know what I'm supposed to have done. But if you kick me out, I will not come back, I will not visit you, that'll be it between us."

"I see," says Mrs. Krocus very slowly. "You think this way you wash your hands. You cannot wash your hands."

"But then what *can* I do?" Max is about to burst into tears.

"Keep them filthy, keep them covered with shit," snarls Mrs. Krocus with sudden, vicious violence.

The word "shit" can be, through over-use, harmless enough, but at this juncture, exploding out of the old woman's mouth, its crushing weight is too much. A fifty-year-old umbilical cord is torn, and Max suddenly sees his mother as her own mother's heiress. Grandma, in her old age, innocently kneaded excrement into imaginary *gefilte fish*; now Mrs. Krocus wants to knead him, Max, her son, into raw excrement! Under the weight of the word "shit," fifty years of fear finally explode. "It's not me, it's you who's covered with shit," Max hurls back at Mrs. Krocus. "Like your mother before you, like your grandmother, like a whole line of constipated bitches, there's always shit in your mind, nothing but shit!"

He goes back to the living room, throws his toiletries into the suitcase, grabs it and shambles to the door. "Father was revolted by the smell of you, you repulsive piece of shit, and so am I!"

He carefully avoids slamming the door, which would be an anticlimax. On the street, he puts down his suitcase and looks around. He's shaking. He's more on his own than ever before. Where will he go? How did he come to such a fix at fifty? But there was nothing else he could have done. Leaving meekly, without a word... no, that was impossible; after she hurled that "shit" and that hatred at him, how could he live as a human being?

He picks up his suitcase and starts walking, alone for the first time in his life. He starts walking slowly, a little awkwardly because of the suitcase, because of the utter novelty of the experience and because there is a hole all the way from his throat down to his anus, as if someone had bored through his guts, where the tender, bodily memory of Mother's cheek against his used to be.

30

Earth, o Earth, old place of brown and heavy bondage! Too long you have been our prison. Trees, plants, peasant women, ploughmen, so many slaves to seasons, sunshine, rain or storm, lifelong-stuck to the soil, impotent to choose new and exciting sites for its, or his, or her development. And you yourself, o Earth, what are you, in the final analysis, but hard rock and dumb, coarse dirt? Freedom must be fluid, wanton: a free person must be able to sail or fly to distant shores, just like light, or like the wind. Free is he or she who, in the unsullied air over his or her fair share of freshly-cut suburban grass, far from the swamp and dung of the inner city, is electronically networked to the whole world; freer still if his or her talents and ambitions carry him or her farther up, to a towertop office, amidst the clouds and the roar of jet planes. And freest of all when he or she acceeds beyond, to the boundless, empty space which Pascal's timid soul feared so. There, unattached, independent, uprooted, regardless of faith, race, gender, ethnic origin or sexual quirk, he or she becomes able to soar high enough to be inmune from Father's disasters, safe from Mother's excrement. Let us therefore leave our earthly dwellings, you free spirits and brave souls, let us flee earthbound bondage and plagues; let us, with glad and hopeful hearts, start the trek toward the Promised Emptiness!

"So, this is where you hang out?" says el Indio once they're sitting at the usual table in the Chateaubriand. Here, glancing at the same sidewalk tiles through the same window panes, elbows resting on the scrubbed marble, before the cracked coffee cups and grungy panelled walls, Max finds it easier to feel that no change has occurred, that in spite of the dreadful appearances the world is basically, essentially the same as yesterday.

"You always liked low-class joints," says Fontana. "What shall we have? Too hot for coffee, too late for croissants, too early for apéritifs. Odd time to come to a café. Incidentally, I talked to Capricoll about you taking over Schamberg's job; he seemed surprised — pleasantly surprised, I thought."

Grateful as he is for this favor, Max doesn't think he's going to stay in Buenos Aires, this stinking dungheap, this swamp.

"So you are going back to the U.S.?"

Maybe. He doesn't know. True, that is the voice of reason: go back to the North — but here or there, does it matter? And since el Indio gives him a worried, quizzical look, he apologizes: there's so much emotional turmoil, such a mess in his mind, he can't think two moves ahead. Patience. It'll get better, he hopes.

"Two coffees! Right?" says Fontana, first two words to the waiter and third to Max. "And two glasses of Holland gin! Eh, what do you say to that? Ice? Heavens, no. Straight up. Remember, Max, when we were young and spent hours talking, proposing math problems and drinking gin? What was the name of that joint? *El Comercio*? *El Progreso*? Chief effect of ageing: one remembers only the inessential, and forgets the really important stuff."

Max tries to smile and manages an oblique grimace.

"It doesn't make much sense," el Indio resumes after another worried look at Max, "believe me, it doesn't make any sense at all to pine for her. I can well imagine how you feel, and it may be rather presumptuous of me to tell you to forget her. But you must. Look, I wouldn't go as far as to call her loony, but she is wacky; quite talented and intelligent, but flighty as a smoked-out bat. I'm afraid some day she might end up like Schamberg. She's so pretty, though, she's turned quite a few heads, and she has a penchant for older, prestigious men."

Up to the last sentence, Max thought all this referred to his mother. But it would be gross and foul flattery to call Mrs. Krocus pretty; now he doesn't know who his friend is talking about.

"Vanessa Satanovsky. She told me you had a fling with her, and of course I don't mind it — can you imagine? — but for you to become despondent over her, that's ridiculous... that I *do* mind."

No, Vanessa Satanovsky is not responsible for the mess in his brain. Max smiles at his friend's generous mistake. He thought it was love-sickness, a case of the old man falling for the young coquette to the point of madness, of trying to stay near her, in Buenos Aires. Does el Indio know about the humiliating *mise en scène* in Satanovsky's office? Max shrugs: no point in telling him. Vanessa's version, whatever it was, is good enough.

The Holland gin is brought in its brown earthen bottle, drinks are poured, and the two friends touch glasses. El Indio's concern, joined to his lack of possessiveness, is moving. A true, a genuine friend. But how about him, didn't he fall for Vanessa's charm? Wasn't his head turned?

"Oh, with me," shrugs Fontana, "it just adds a little spice. I like beautiful women, and I'm as vain as the next guy. Haydée doesn't care to find out about my dollopings and spicings, and even if she did I don't think she'd mind it much. But as you know, my only real interest is math. An elusive theorem might turn my head, never a woman. If I remember correctly, however, you were extremely susceptible to the feminine."

Susceptible to the feminine... Funny way to put it. That's the main reason for Max's admiration for his friend, precisely: his success in those two levels at once, the heaven of mathematical form and the earthly paradise of voluptuous flesh. Funny concept, though, "susceptible to the feminine." Why not? But should be stretched a bit if it's to include his present predicament. This very morning, his mother has thrown him out. She has given no reason; no, Mrs. Krocus has given no justification at all for her strange conduct. Yes, just like that, out of the blue. Thrown out. Max empties his glass, wipes his mouth with the back of his hand. Is it possible to conceive of an event less graspable by the understanding? A mother casting out her only son, her fifty-year-old son, for no reason at all! If there's a *mysterium tremendum* in this world, this is it, this must be its terrible manifestation.

"Hey, hey, Max, aren't you letting yourself be carried away by your own rhetoric? How ready you poets are to cry, 'Mystery!' There are many possible explanations for your mother's behavior. You may have unwittingly offended her. How? How should I know. Perhaps you forgot her birthday, or some anniversary; old people are very touchy when it comes to dates. No? Then perhaps in some other way... I notice you shaved your mustache: that may have bothered her. Waiter! Pour us more of this stuff! Didn't you tell me of your mother's rancor against your father? Well, there: you are Don Onofrio's spitting image, so, since your father is dead, your mother takes you for the object of her hatred. A metaphoric substitution, a Freudian *Verschiebungsersatz*, I think it's called, deplorable, but entirely understandable. Lastly, and most likely, your mother may simply be crazy. How old is she? Seventy-eight? Senile dementia. Gaga. Here's to you. C'mon, cheer up."

Okay, but the problem is pain. The problem is, he loves his mother above all. When he arrived home to find that his father had been taken to jail: that's the closest thing, the closest pain he ever felt. A burning lack, a searing absence. Suddenly the world as he knew it crumbled. Building a world is what a father is for: good fathers are good architects. Max is convinced of this. Sure, some men would rather run the world into the ground — the film clip of Hitler at Nuremberg, shouting, *"Zugrunde!"* with a forceful, downward stab of his forefinger. And his own father, for that matter... A couple of days ago he found the old family house in Flores razed, gone. Onofrio, Great Shaving Razor, King Gillette: only weeds and burs sprout where he trod. Yet, terrible as is the view of one's own world in ruins, this present pain is worse. He never dreamt the American Dream, motherlove was all he aspired to: why did this happen to him, this removal of the ground under his feet? The soul retreats into one's innermost and doesn't dare to venture out into a public space without a father-world; without a mother-ground there *is* no inner side, the soul hangs out, on a dungheap. Without your mother's *placet*, without her smile of unconditional approval, your soul recoils in horror before itself, and dares only desire its own demise. There you have a vague idea of mother-pain. Max doesn't think he'll be able to survive it. He doesn't think he has the will to survive it.

Fontana laughs. "You talk of worlds and grounds, of souls and dung so eloquently, so poetically, that one thing, at least, is evident: what's ailing you, *Abgrund* or *Mutterschmerz*, does not involve aphasia. That unspeakable pain you just described, that mother-pain: is there any way of knowing that the effect of removing mother-ground shouldn't rather be bliss? I mean, like the happiness of a bird let out of the cage. I'm not being captious. In fact, my guess is that removing the ground, the underlying, dead gravitational mass, should allow you to fly. Expelling you from her place, your mother has done you a favor, raising you *out* of the dungheap. The scales have fallen from your eyes. You should be glad, you should feel free now, Max."

Thanks. Max appreciates his trying to cheer him up. But the pain is still there. His love, the bleeding love for Mother is still there.

"Let's have another glass of this so we can go on with our analysis."

Analysis! Max's face turns crimson. Mother-grief a subject of analysis, as if it were an unknown chemical, or a well-formed sentence in some language, or some complex function of which we want to find the zeroes and the poles! But that's what he's been trying to say: Max's pain, mother-grief, is bestial, elementary, prior to everything, before all logic and analysis.

"If you're going to confront me with an absolute, an ineffable not-beneath-this-level, go ahead, but do so by yourself, or seek the society of some Germanic doctor of philosophy: here we part company. Come, Max, consent to let holy mother-grief be analyzed by a friendly mathematician. Are you going to tell me next that nothingness nothings, mother mothers and openness opens or some such helpful rant? Don't make faces. Believe me, this is not the end of the road for you. Waiter, a refill! Careful: you spill any on the table and it'll bore a hole through the top! That's it. Here's to you again. Ah, doesn't it look and taste like nitroglycerine? But topologically you're all wrong. It's not so much a ground you're lacking, but space, space around and above you. I don't mean Newtonian or Euclidean space, I don't mean R-to-the-three. More like, perhaps, what painters call pictorial space, an ideal, structured locus where you can draw your designs, things that are personal and at the same time meaningful and interesting to others. A public space for you to walk erect, knowing that you're informing it. This is what I noticed first, meeting you after all these years, Max: you don't walk proudly, you trudge close to the ground, as under a winter storm. And you know what I thought when I saw you? I thought, why has he quit mathematics. What? Yes, I know: now you write poetry. True, it is a space, of a certain kind. The problem is, of what kind. The poem you gave me... Did I like it? As a poem? What can I say, I've got a tin ear and no discernment for metaphor; I'm into math, not literature; only competent to comment on the topological aspects of the thing. The guy dies — 'I died by night and in a foreign country,' you write. Breaking away from its body cocoon, the soul flies 'towards the blue debris of Buenos Aires.' From then on it's all downhill, until finally the soul finds herself at a café-bar near the Jewish cemetery: the low-est point, if I remember correctly, your father's resting place. Well, what can I say... This kind of space looks very much like a shaft, vertical, one-dimensional. No spread, no public parks for other people to mill about; there's shoulder space for just one man rigidly standing, arms alongside, between heaven and hell. The space of choice for a poet or an artist, perhaps? I wouldn't know, but personally I doubt it. Certainly not the right space for a scientist. I bet you share with psychoanalysts and many modern artists the old Gnostic belief that self-knowledge is to be found somehow in the lowest of the low. Why? Give me one good reason why it should be so. The elusiveness of pleasure, the universal presence of pain... Sure, I grant you that. But why should we be concentrating on the pee and the pooh instead of studying information theory, say, or artificial intelligence, or the theo-ry of circuits applied to nervous systems? Man's heart is bent on contradiction, you've replied often in the past, like Dostoevsky. I've lived for as long as you have, Max, and in my experience men are pretty damn consistent, especially when they are being naughty, rebellious, and bent on con-tradiction; and when they're fascinated by the dizzying dis-tance between heaven and hell, by what you call the abyss, why, then they are the most readily predictable. Dostoevsky's Man from the Underground says that two plus two is five. Big deal. It follows therefore that two plus two is also six, and seven, and whatever number you will — and so addition loses all meaning, and your poor Dostoevskian character must start looking for something else, some other logical constraint, to pound on and bang his head against. But, my friend, only where there is form, only where logic rules, can there be a possibility of beauty, of marvel and spir-

296

itual surprise. And don't tell me that a poet doesn't care about these... Max, are you okay?"

Max looks at his friend with blank amazement. He assures him that yes, indeed, he is okay.

"Then, how come you didn't even notice the beautiful girl who just walked in?"

The last thing Max needs right now is beautiful girls. As a matter of fact, Max wants to have nothing at all to do with women. He's scared of them, to death. Especially of the one who carried him in her womb. But... actually, did she? Max has hit on a conjecture, a bit surprising, a bit hard to believe, but of great explanatory power. His mother carried him in her colon. Why not? She's always telling how hard it was for her to get pregnant. Perhaps the medical profession came up with an ersatz solution, the better since Mother seldom moves her bowels. Max was *colonized* by his mother, just as the American Indians were colonized by Colón and the other conquistadors — words offer us a clarity all their own. And that is why, too, Max's soul, like his cousin Boris' body, like Latin-American nations, has stayed stumped, underdeveloped. The shrinking power of *dreck*. And that is why, finally, his mother has ejected him and flushed him down the toilet.

"Oh, come on now, forget that shit and cheer up! Always touching the extremes. Let me tell you an old Gnostic story. When Jesus arrived in Heaven, he looked down the long shaft he had ascended, and on the waters at the bottom he saw reflected his own face, with which he fell in love: that face was also Satan's. Such seems to be the dream of all of you, vertical people. A monstrously narcissistic anal fantasy. Ah, this juniper juice goes down fast and hot! Divine liquor. You know, it's not every day I talk about these things; the people I deal with for the most part have ampler spaces. Some live in valleys surrounded by mountains, many limit themselves to an elegant room, and a few are truly oceanic; but I've met no scientist yet who stands inside a mine shaft; they have better things to do than spend their time shuttling between the high and the low, or closing the circuit between celestial glory and the abyss. Take Pascal, who was blessed with a pretty good mind: you've read the stuff he wrote when he turned himself into a mystic: enough to make you weep. I feel like shaking him by the shoulders, yelling, 'Blaise, somber imbecile, no, your greatness doesn't reside in fathoming how vertically miserable you are, but in your theorems, the only part of yours that will survive. Meanwhile, rest content with being mortal, take a pleasant break at the beach, go to Provence, bask in the sunshine... Space, more space is what you need, not more faith or hope or rotten charity!' Do you think he would have listened? Probably not. But you, dear Max, old Max, you who have been just weaned by your mother, squeezed further down the tube, will you listen to me? Okay, I'll tell you what; but first we'll have to have another — a last shot of *ginebra*. Waiter! Refill! Damn him, what is he waiting for? How much do you say it is? Eight thousand? Here, keep the change. Listen, I'm leaving Buenos Aires on the 28th, but I'm stopping in Brazil for ten days. No, just by myself: Haydée's flying directly to the U.S. Have you ever been to Rio? No? You can be on Copacabana beach on New Year's eve, watching the fireworks; sheets of fire fall from the top of the Hotel Méridien, the crowds go wild. Brazilians are pretty good at those things: did you know they're the ones who trained the Iraqi missile engineers? Exploding firecrackers are everywhere dense; people light candles, throw flowers into the

298

waves and pray to African goddesses for a prosperous new year and even better fucks. I don't particularly go for that kind of stuff, but you can guzzle beer, munch on greasy sausages, fried shrimp and shishkebab, smell the sweaty throngs all around you: real low, I'm sure you'll like it. You'll watch the flaunting buttocks: they are everywhere, like the firecrackers. Buttocks of every age, in every shade of brown, wiggling, jiggling, gyrating, apple-shaped, pear-shaped, melon-shaped, plump, well-turned, smallish, enormous: anyway, who's to tell what the fruit of the Fall actually was? I won't be scandalized if you drift away on your knees behind some sambaing goddess, your tongue hanging out, adoring the miracle of the bumps and the grinds; no, I won't hold it against you; to each man his religion and his weakness, and if I know you as I think I do, dear Max, it'll come to you as a revelation: I always wondered how you, a Jew, are more of a mystic than I, a *goi*. You had a passion for Kierkegaard, Unamuno, Shestov: marginal philosophers of disease and Slavic or Hispanic poets who pretended that if only one's desire is infinite enough, then anything is possible. Truth, for them, is to be won with passion, like a woman; truth is a whore, redeemed, made intact and deified by their delirium. Well, I'll let you into a little secret: it's the other way around. Moderate desire, sly and scheming, patient, disciplined, is what makes us reach our goal, with a little luck. Infinite desire longs for itself most of all, and succeeds only in killing its object, like Orpheus when he looked back at Eurydice. Infinite desire is a viscid tunnel; that's what the vertical shaft around you seems to be made of, Max: infinite, inefficient, self-digesting yearning. You want a miracle. But tell me, you who know more Latin than I do: where does the word come from? *Miraculum*: from *mira*, he

299

admires, and *culum*, the buttocks. Isn't that so? See? Q.E.D. And how can one cure the incapacitating yearning for a miracle? Obviously, by turning it into an everyday event. Here in Buenos Aires such things are seen as through a glass darkly; they're only muttered of. But in Brazil, Mecca of the buttocks, they are openly proclaimed, and no one trembles before a bottom as Pascal used to before the lack of it, for over there bottoms are pleasant, wriggling before you everywhere, every day. You say you need a bottom... well then, go for it. Have an orgy of the low. I have to return to the U.S., but you may be able to stay in Rio until the carnival. And as religious enthusiasms as a rule don't last long, satiated at last, reconciled with vile matter, at one with the earth, you'll forget those melancholic Gnostic infatuations, you'll find yourself as you would after a summer storm, with a new, blue space around, full of life, and I bet you will want to devote some time again to mathematics. What do you say to it?"

Right now Max can say very little. He is drunk. He finds it hard to move, and next to impossible to think of visiting other countries. Later, perhaps. Lots of AIDS in Brazil, isn't there? Furthermore, he doesn't speak Portuguese. As for mathematics, that door is closed, he is too old. Ah! another thing, before he forgets: he has wanted to know ever since the Tuesday math lecture — he is embarrassed, el Indio won't believe his ignorance. What's the statement of that theorem he called the Minimax?

31

"He's made himself a willow cabin at her gate, and calls upon his soul within the house." From the pizzeria across the street Max watches his mother's windows. Her balcony, the pot with the dwarf palm she took with her, like a bit of fire from the family altar, when the Flores house was sold and she had to move out. The movable Eden around Mother and her dwarf palm. Unlike Adam, however, once expelled, Max can still contemplate the extent of what he's lost, not merely in imagination and nostalgic memory, but, maddeningly, across the street from the pizzeria. Unlike Adam, Max has got nothing to do, no need of procuring bread with the sweat of his brow, and so all his time can be filled with grief. He imagines Mother in the kitchen, listening to the radio news, eating her morning yoghurt. Her face is serious, taut; her eyes quietly enigmatic. The enigma of his expulsion. He could go in, take the elevator to the top: jumping from a high roof, he'd make his mother's radio news. "Max Krocus, a fifty-year-old man born in this city, encoun-

301

tered a sudden and violent death immediately after jumping from a top floor. The motive of the fatal leap is still unclear, but is believed to be the prior expulsion of the deceased from his mother's domicile in the sixth floor of the same building, which occurred some days before. The case is under investigation by the Federal Police, precinct number 10." Suddenly the enigma gives way to open horror. Mother rushes out and runs crazily down the street, like Munch's "Scream," all the way to the tenth precinct. Alas too late: Max is no more. Max, poor Max, the best of sons! Max, her only love! Max, her god!

One morning, bright and warm, two days before Christmas, Max tries to bend the light and peer through the slates of Mrs. Krocus' Venetian blinds, when an ambulance approaches at full siren and stops at the corner. Max leaves his table and stands by the door of his mother's building. When the nurse and the driver come out with an empty stretcher, Max doesn't muster the courage to question them. Of Mother and Max, who will die first? A silent clash of wills, a tug-of-war at opposite ends of a dry umbilical cord. Max is unable to tell which outcome, whose death would be less dreadful.

Tipsy with boredom, he leaves the pizzeria and shuffles the few blocks to the Municipal Library on Carlos Calvo Avenue. A couple of high-school kids and an old man are the only patrons. Max leafs through the dictionaries. Royal Academy, *necrofilia*: Curiosity that certain persons feel to contemplate corpses. The library is dilapidated, with scars and abscesses on the ceiling, but the wainscoted walls lend it a quiet dignity. Here young Borges, back during the roaring twenties, was employed as a library clerk, and his fellow clerks wouldn't believe he was the same man whose name appeared on the cover of a recently acquired book. Perhaps they were right, and they were not the same man, the poet and the clerk. Being unable to read more than short paragraphs, unable to keep his attention locked in onto anything for any length of time, Max reads a short paragraph of the *Refutatio omnium haeresium* of Hippolytus of Rome. Something about the Son, Christ, the Logos and the Serpent being all One, all the same Person. He picks Langlebert's *Elementary Chemistry* and looks at the illustrations: the lead chambers for the industrial production of sulphuric acid, with the two rooms, the hissing pipes spitting SO_2, bring to mind Mother's apartment; the towers of Glover and of Gay-Lussac have something of his mother's forbidding verticality, when she threw him out. The catalogue cards are crusty with the greasy prints of fingers long since silenced and dissolved. A system of cables and pulleys and a box to shuttle books up and down, to and from an invisible attic, as if any attic, any weight could stand above the rotting ceiling. Opening a tome of history, Max reads about Manuel Belgrano, founding father, unsuccessful general and deviser of the blue and white Argentine flag: "His remains were buried in the atrium of the convent of Santo Domingo, by the entrance dedicated to the Virgin of the Rosary. The tomb was closed with a slab of white marble taken from the top of a commode that had belonged to his mother." Tomb and womb, lap and slab. Back in those days people still heard the telling rhymes. The library too seems to have been under a pious slab for many decades. No new books. Not a computer in sight. Just an old Underwood, inkwells, cheweddown penholders, starchy glues. The old books are crumbling into dust.

After another glimpse at lost Eden, Max walks out,

into the sun, sadder than before. Had he stayed with Mother, had he not been expelled, he would have worked every day at this Municipal Library, like Borges. No new books, no journals, no computers. No world-confining data bases. Nothing but the old books, slowly crumbling, and the soft shine of the wood paneling, the cables, the pulleys and the box. A poet needs nothing more. What is he to do? Go back to the North and to his lonely life? Modern, efficient, world-wide information systems, explosive growth, built-in, merciless obsolescence. Knowledge. Power. Knowledge means power. Power means independence, forgetfulness. 97.2% of the population of the U.S. feel they deserve more. More knowledge, more power, more obsolescence, more independence, more forgetfulness. More more. 40.4% of the women in the U.S. declare they've been sexually abused by their father or an uncle. Indeed, such was the case with Sharon. Yet what is he to do? The U.S. is the only refuge in this world for a son who's been expelled by his mother: there is no other place to hide the shame in your soul, once the ground has been removed from under it. Borges' mother never expelled him; she was always nice to her only son, her god, her poet.

The summer sun, devouring, bites fiercely on Max.

"Your fortune for 100 australes (crossed out) 500 australes (crossed out) 1,000 australes (less than a dollar). Tarot. Palmistry. The Stars. Madame Violeta famous psychic." Inside, darkness. Coming from the bright day, Max is blinded. Suddenly, an armlength away from his face, the bare teeth and savage eyes of an animal ready to pounce on him. Max lets out a cry. Someone laughs. He retreats against the wall, remembers his gun, reaches for it, doesn't find it. Idiot. He's left it in the hotel, in his suitcase. He's soaked in sweat. As his eyes get used to the penumbra, an old woman, hideously made up, appears sitting behind a wicker table. Curtains, wicker chairs. The monster which snarled at him turns out to be a cat, crouching on top of a chest.

"Sit down, sit down, don't let Messalina scare you," says Madame Violeta. "You're not going to scratch the gentleman, are you, Messalina? No, of course not. Sit down, sit down, let's see your palms. That's it, both hands. Hmm... lifelines not bad... no immediate danger on that side... Middling fortune, but I've seen worse, believe me... Love, ah, love, that's another problem... Isn't it? Didn't I tell you? Tongues may lie, not hands. What's your name? Ah, Max means maximum, the greatest... Still, unfortunate in love, is that it? Let's find out about it..."

Madame Violeta picks a pack of cards, shuffles it a couple of times. "Cut."

The deuce of coins — it's a Spanish deck, eared and filthy, no Tarot. She slits her eyes and announces, "You've been married twice, I can tell."

Max averts his face to avoid her breath. *Fedor hepaticus.* Her fingers are bony and pale, her nails gnawed to the quick. "Twice, isn't that right? See? Nothing escapes Madame Violeta." The seven of swords. "Wow! Ambition! You're out to conquer!" She has a nasty smile, baring her gums. "You're *very* ambitious, I see. A princess is what you are after. A young and beautiful princess, no less."

Max self-deprecatingly sniggers.

"Nothing wrong with big ambition, mind you," rumbles the hag. "Let's see that third card, the most important one. Ah! The four of cups. It means a woman, a mature woman. What this means to you is, you shouldn't go so much after young princesses; that's not how you're going to conquer love. What you need is an experienced woman to be

305

your guide."

She leans toward him, and Max notices her lipstick is the obnoxious violet seen only once before, on Doris of Retiro Park. The two women, Max is convinced, the part-time whore who introduced him to the glories of twat and the hag who's telling his fortune, are the same person. He puts a 1,000 australes bill on the table and moves away, ready to get up.

"For ten thousand australes I can solve all your love problems," the hag puts her bony hand on Max's forearm. "I'll sell you an ointment prepared by the Gypsies of Pakistan, a secret formula, not available to anyone but me in Buenos Aires. How big's your birdie? May I check it out? No? Timid, uh, at your age. Well, you see, *that's* your problem: Max the greatest ought to be proud to show it. I tell you what: see this jar? You spread the stuff gently on your cornichon, every night before going to bed, and, guaranteed, after a week you'll have a big cucumber, or your money back. Also, twice the staying power, or your money back, no questions asked. There you go, all your love problems solved!"

"No, thanks, Madam," says Max and darts out of the hag's cubicle. He walks aimlessly through the hot, deserted checkerboard. Too bright, too early to go back to his hotel room. "What you need is an experienced woman." The sun, the cruel Christmas sun. "Max the greatest ought to be proud to show it." Yes, he is proud, but he's fainting. He seeks refuge inside a church.

The atrium, dark, confined and cool, smelling of woodwax, brings to mind General Belgrano, the founding Father, buried under the top of the maternal commode. Max feels nauseous. He walks into the deserted nave. Dusky oils representing the Passion. They hold no interest; it is fine and dandy for women to have mystic visions of His wounds, but Max has a different idea. He has never been inside an Argentine church and feels embarrassed; in Europe he visited the Catholic temples as art museums, but for a Jewish boy in Buenos Aires, churches are enemy territory, shameful ground, baser than the seediest porno shop.

There She is, at the place of honor, resplendent, holding Her child. Hail, Mary, holy Mary. Max approaches the altar with lowered eyes, takes a candle, leaves a wad of bills for it, too much for just a candle, and kindles it with trembling hand. Then, timidly, he raises his eyes. Her blue, star-spangled mantle, where sinners seek cover and refuge, hardened sinners whom neither Father nor Son nor Holy Ghost will touch with a ten-foot pole, especially those who have sinned from too much love, out of the sheer monstrosity of their mother-longing. Her tunic, the folds for which medieval draftsmen drew their sweetest curves; Her gracious lap, the gulf to sink one's aching head and heart; Her crown, imperial, magnificent, bejeweled... "Lady, You are so great, so worthy!" Max whispers. He tries to remember St. Bernard's prayer to the Virgin in Dante's *Paradiso*, and suddenly realizes those words also belong to the March of the Peronist Boys. "Perón, Perón, how great you are! My General, how worthy!" Max feels like vomiting. He kneels before the altar and joins his hands in prayer.

"Queen of Heaven, pity me! I've got nowhere to go, nowhere to turn, no guide, no nurse, no comfort!" Her wooden face, cheesy in the candlelight. Her eyes, like those of the Child She is holding on Her arm, seem focused on a point beyond Her kneeling supplicant. "Pity me, help me, save me! A sign, a sign to survive by, a squinch of a smile, the mere flick of a finger, a flutter of Your mantle!" When St. Bernard asked for a sign from a statue of Our Lady, She pressed Her breast and dropped three drops of milk on the lips of Her champion. Why couldn't She bare a tit now, for goodness sake, and... But, come to think of it, who's ever heard of Her helping a Jew? Even though She was no Goi, She hates Yids more than anything. Once, in Regensburg, She made whole the broken leg of a carpenter who had fallen from the top of the old synagogue he was demolishing. How many innocent Jews were tortured with Her sweet name on the lips of their torturers... All those martyrs, his ancestors, the pious and the crooked, the learned and the imbecile, patriarchal beards and smoky matronly wigs, are now, in this one act of idolatry, being betrayed by Max Krocus.

As he averts his eyes in abashment from the majestic image, Max notices the floor tiles and the glazed *azulejos* on the walls: they are exactly like those on the library walls at the old house. Same design, same colors. Everything's the same, except that where the bookcase was, there is the Virgin's altar. "Mary, even though it be sinful, a betrayal... I am all Yours, forever, *siempre, siempre*..." He kisses the *azulejos*, licks the scuffed flagstone and floor tiles. "Take me, female divine, take me in Your arms, worthless as I am, work Your whim upon me, Your will be done upon Your baby!"

Wooden, cheesy, She doesn't smile nor frown. She raises not a finger. She's elsewhere, in some heaven of her own, colder than Schamberg's dolls, more absent than a peep-show actress, deader than the photographs in glossy girly magazines. Max gets up and drops his pants. Proud, yes, he's damn proud to show it, you slut, you fucking whore. Virgin, they call you! Ha, maybe from the front, but, from behind, certainly martyred. Her majesty, her bejewelled crown, her mantle... The azulejos and the smell of candle wax... Above all, the danger that a priest in black cassock might show up and find him cock in hand... All seems calculated to hasten his orgasm. I'll flood you, slut, and you'll ascend to heaven hoisted on my rocket... Isn't that what you always wanted? Fucking Mother of God, Our Lady of the Stinking Cunt... His discharge hits Her on the face, on the breast, on Her Child, and sluices down the folds of Her tunic, a votive offering, like melted wax...

Back in his room at the Hotel Trianon, he lies naked on the hot, sticky bed. "What you need is an experienced woman..." He falls asleep and dreams that he's in Rio, in the midst of an orgiastic crowd, not with el Indio but with Boris. People dance and sing:

Mamá eu quero, mamá eu quero, mamá eu quero mamar... mi dá chupeta, mi dá chupeta para o bebê nâo chorar.

Momma I wanna suckle... Momma gimme your nipple 'cause this baby gonna cry...

Boris blows on his trombone, which in the dream is called by the obsolete name of sackbut, and he puts the sackbut's bell flare against a swaying black butt, and blows, and sparks fly off, and Boris says, "See, Max, this is the way it should be done. See, those sparks are you, Max, they are your soul."

He wakes up. The heat is stifling and he's covered with sweat. Through the open window, the far-away sound of a church bell calls for Christmas-Eve Mass. The iron tongue of midnight, round, precise, expressive of forlornness; the clear, isolated musical note in the cosmic sea of silence, where only the buzz of a mosquito and the whine of a city bus float aimlessly. The distinct and clear sound seems to carry the full weight of his loss, of his expulsion, the whole pain of his being alone. "Momma, momma," he whispers, lying face up on the soaked bed, with each sound of the bell. Why would he leave Buenos Aires, go to Rio or return to the U.S.? The pain would still be there, place makes absolutely no difference. On the other hand, who could guess what griefs may be forgotten in the depths of shimmering flesh, real flesh, not wood... mulatto flesh...

He falls asleep again, a sleep full of dreams. He remembers only the last one before he awakes. The old house in Flores, his parents' bedroom. The oxbow-front dressing table, the semi-oval mirror, the big armoire, the queen-size bed with its fur coverlet. On the wall, above the headboard, the photo picture of Mother, the Bobeh and Uncle Chaim. Max is naked. A woman who looks vaguely like Pancracia and vaguely like Madame Violeta but is really an Inca Queen stands in front of the mirror, naked too, except for a diadem of colorful bird feathers. Raising her arms and her eyes, she fervently prays to the Most High. Her hands are full of filth streaming down her hair and breasts. Max kneels before her and sticks his tongue inside her navel. Suddenly she recoils in terror: "The Señora's comin'! Dontcha hear her?" — "What are you talking about?" says Max, burying his face in her filth, "you're my bride, you're now the Señora, *you* can fire *her*!"

When he awakes, the wind is blowing and the bells have stopped. Outside, somewhere, a metal sheet bangs against a wall. After listening for a while, he realizes it is the street sign, "Hotel Trianon - Transients," being rocked by the storm. He, Max, is that banging sheet of metal, swaying out in the wind like a hanged man. He thought he was getting used to being an outsider, but it hurts worse than before.

Hasn't he suffered enough, hasn't he gone through the darkest night of the soul?

The idea strikes him just as a gust of wind throws the window open and scatters all over the room the sheets of paper he had left on the decrepit chest of drawers. There's a malignant black hole at the center of his being. No light can issue forth, no glimmer from another being can ever get to him and his aloneness, collapsed upon himself by the crushing force of fear. Love is the only possibility of happiness. Love, and the dissolution of fear. Tomorrow he'll go back to his mother.

Rain through the window, cool, cleansing rain drenching his chest, the bed, the whole room. For the first time in the last four days Max breathes easily, and he falls into deep and quiet sleep.

32

He'll wear a tie and a jacket for the first time since his arrival. He'll dress formally, for the occasion requires it: formally begging to be forgiven. Kneeling, if necessary, before Mother. But what if, being dressed formally... Max shudders. What if it turns out he's going to a funeral. Father died while Max was far away: will Mother die without him too? She might die just as he arrives and expire in his arms, cursing him with her last breath, one last time and forever. Life will not be easy after that.

He casts a wistful glance at the room where he has spent the last four days and which he won't see ever again. You end up feeling nostalgia for hell. He checks out of the hotel: ships burned, either Mother will pardon him and take him back, or he will have nowhere to go, nowhere.

But really, that's too dramatic. After a good night sleep Max feels like a new man. It is a splendid day, the night storm has washed away the heaviness, the sun shines jovially through the sprightly air. And really, when he gets

312

to scratch the bottom, he doesn't mind so much his mother dying. It could come as a deliverance, a blessing in disguise, as Fontana said the other day. What Max fears most is his mother's dying curse. She should expire blessing him. Yes, that's it: her last words should be an open mother's blessing, no disguise. Max walks the few blocks to Mother's place and rings the bell. A woman's voice answers in the intercom. Long, heavily circumflexed vowels: that isn't Mother; it sounds like Gloria. "Max!" he shouts at the holey bronze, and the door buzzes and opens. With a heavy heart he loads his suitcase into the elevator and starts the slow ascent. Incongruously, as if getting ready to deliver a public speech, he looks at himself in the mirror, adjusts the necktie and clears his throat. Gloria is waiting for him in the dark hall, before Mrs. Krocus's door. They kiss.

"I tried to contact you, Max, but no one knew where you were."

"Well, here I am."

"That's right, here you are."

"I find it amazing that *you* are here," says Max with a pinched smile.

"A few days ago she was in pretty bad shape," says Gloria; "she called her doctor, and her doctor called me, that's how I came. She was close to death, as the doctor put it, touch and go. I've been here since Friday."

"And how's she now?"

"She's in bed, but according to the doctor right now she's out of immediate danger."

"Let's go in," says Max.

Gloria stops him. She has been standing all the time between Max and the door. "That's just the thing. The doctor said she shouldn't see you under any circumstances. Seeing you might kill her, that's what the doctor said."

Max blanches. "Come on, Gloria, that's preposterous!"

"Preposterous it may be, but that's what the doctor ordered. Apparently you said some terrible things."

"I did?"

"Something about you and Dad having always found her repulsive because she's nothing but shit... That, at least, is what she told me. Max, how could you say something so awful to her?"

"Me? You know what she did to me? Gloria, she kicked me out of this place, just like that, for no reason at all. Thursday morning she got up and told me to leave. I didn't know what to think, I couldn't believe she was serious, I was struck dumb. She was the one who brought up shit, she said I was covered with shit, and that's how all that unfortunate shit business came up."

"Whatever. In any case, if you wanted to kill Mother, you almost succeeded."

"Me wanting to kill Mother? How can you say such a thing?"

"I don't say it, Max; it's the doctor who says it."

"Listen, dear Gloria, I've got to see Mother, do you understand? I've got to see her, doctor or no doctor, because it is my life, and she is my mother, so please, dear Gloria, be nice, be a good girl and get out of my way, because otherwise..."

"Otherwise what? Are you about to punch me, as you used to when we were children? Are you about to make a scene? Creating one awful scandal is not enough for you?"

Another awful scandal is, indeed, what Max is about to create. He has felt for quite some time the urge to punch his sister in the face, and keep punching and punching until that constant source of reproach is stanched for ever, flattened into a silent pulp. A fury's growing inside him, blind, red, all-powerful, when the door to Mrs. Krocus's apartment opens and out comes Uncle Chaim:

"Max! What a coincidence! I was just thinking of you."

"You were?" says Max, dubious.

Uncle Chaim pats Gloria on the cheek. "Well, Gloria dear, be a good girl, keep as gorgeous as you are, and I know you'll take good care of your mother, won't you." They kiss good-bye.

The old gentleman rests his hand on Max's shoulder and says, "We are going out together, you and I."

Back inside the elevator, Max can't avoid feeling like a twelve-year-old. He looks at his uncle: platinum hair, the pure outline of his high forehead, the sharp, aquiline nose, the restless, cynical but beautiful eyes and the skeptical involution of his lips. He hasn't changed much in the twenty years since Max last saw him; Chaim's features are a combination of the best of Mother and of cousin Boris, and he still wears his jacket thrown on the shoulders, à la Marshall Ney. His silk shirt is as dazzlingly white as ever, with its blue monogram, and the open top shows, together with a thick gold chain, that even at eighty his chest is manly and tanned.

"What do you carry in there," says Chaim pointing to Max's suitcase. "The books you've written, or the greenbacks you've been hoarding up in the U.S.?"

This is the moment, the long-awaited moment to open the suitcase and, very quietly, very politely, say: "No, Uncle, I carry here neither books nor money, but something else which might be of interest to you." Then take out the Heftpistole and blow off the old man's brains. "Pay for all

315

you've done to my father! Die, die, son of a whore!" This is the perhaps unique opportunity for Max to carry out his mission and to discharge his duty and his oath. The problem is... Chaim's hand. The obstacle is that hand, his right one, at waist-level holding a button of his jacket. Chaim's hand is sinewy, free of old-man splotches, and, like that time, years ago, when it rested on the Jaguar's stick shift, there's princely elegance in those long, well-manicured fingers and in the gold Patek-Philipe watch peeping from the starched brilliance of the cuff, a sprightliness rehearsed in so many signatures affixed to important documents, so many voluptuous bodies caressed, so many airy, haughty gestures of dismissal. That hand is just too beautiful, too poetic.

"Did you see Mother? How is she?" says Max as they reach the ground floor.

"Your mother? You mean my sister? Oh, fine. Just a little whiny. You know how women are," says Chaim, winking an eye and patting Max on the arm.

"How are they, Uncle?"

"You know, nervous as clucking hens. All alike."

They walk down the hall, Max carrying his suitcase, and Chaim ahead, moving briskly, without a stoop, like a young man. Yet, with his big nose, his pot belly and his dandruff, Onofrio was a prince too in his own way, wasn't he, a bunko prince dethroned by a dark, perfidious palace coup in which he, Max, was the mystified accessory or accomplice. Onofrio must be avenged. His ghost, stuck in the stinking fields of La Matanza, is thirsty for Chaim's blood. The problem is Chaim's miraculous hands, like those of the King of France, of which it used to be proclaimed: "The King touches you, and God cures you." The problem is those poetic hands of his.

316

"But did she say anything about me?" asks Max. "Can she... The doctor apparently said she couldn't... Is she willing to see me? Did she mention anything to you?"

"Do you play golf?" says Chaim. "No? Listen, Max, you should try it. At my *estancia* in Cañuelas I've built a spectacular course. I'll show you. 36 holes. Better, I can assure you, than anything you've seen in North America."

Out in the street, the uniformed chauffeur is waiting, leaning on the door of Chaim's Mercedes: as soon as he sees his boss he doffs his cap and flicks his cigarette into the gutter. The sun shines splendidly.

"If golf's not your thing, we'll play croquet," says Chaim. "Remember how you loved to play croquet in Castelar? How happy we were there! You liked hide-and-seek too. Well, we're a little old for hide-and-seek now, both of us. But we'll get the best fire crackers and sky rockets to celebrate the New Year; we'll eat a great caviar I just bought and drink the best wine in my cellar. You'll see, we'll have almost as good a time as back then, when I was young and you were still a child..."

"Uncle... please, please... either you tell me about Mother, why I can't see her, or I'm going back upstairs, to find out..."

"Find out, find out! What do you expect to find out! How silly, at your age, still trying to find out! It seems she had a tiny infarction, the beginning of a heart attack. Nothing terrible. That's the whole secret."

"But Gloria says that I am not supposed to see her."

"Because apparently the doctor is afraid that seeing you at this point might cause further heart trouble, that's why. You seem to have a strong effect on your mother, Max. On other women too?"

317

"On women, no, not particularly, but on wise-assed old farts I do..." Max sputters somberly.

"Come, come, nephew, don't be a bore. In a week your mother will be fine, and you'll be able to see her. Meanwhile, jump into the car and let's go to Cañuelas. Caffiero (to the chauffeur), grab that suitcase and put it in the trunk."

"Don't!" It comes out more like a bark or a yelp than a human cry. Arms limp, teeth bared, Max stares at his uncle. A flash of himself and Chaim atop a magic carpet, of Father sitting on a cement jail bunk, grabbing the bars. Only a bulk vision lasting no more than a few seconds, and throughout Max is a twelve-year-old, fascinated and cringing.

"Okay, okay," says Chaim. "You're a grown-up boy by now. You can hold on to your suitcase. Hey, I wouldn't want *you* to have a heart attack."

Another flash, of Max and Chaim on the golf links, walking arm in arm, both radiant, beautiful in the twilight... Orphaned Max and sonless Chaim, shedding their lifelong solitudes like useless overcoats, yielding to love... Begone, Satan! But Satan will not be gone. He's there, holding open the car door, a spark on his eye and a smile on his lips.

As Max leans back in the plush seat, just as the car pulls off the curb, a knife grinder turns the corner on his bike, playing the panpipe. Up and down, through the same notes, in the sunshine. Up and down and up again, the shrill, cruel, life-swollen sound. "Let's have some music," says Chaim; "play a record, Caffiero." It's "Sgt. Pepper's Lonely Hearts Club Band," Chaim's favorite.

ACKNOWLEDGMENTS

For help during the composition of this work I thank Jenny Dowling, Michelle Edwards, David Falkner, Bill Katz, Eugene Mirabelli, my son David, and above all Robert W. Greene and Judith Kramer Greene. Thanks to Nancy Hofstadter for the design of the cover.

Instituto de Escritores Latinoamericanos
Latin American Writers Institute

The Latin American Writers Institute is a registered charities organization in New York State, receiving funds from the National Endowment for the Arts (NEA) and the Bronx Council on the Arts (BCA), through the Regional Arts Partnership Program of the Bronx Council on the Arts and the New York State Council on the Arts (NYSCA). LAWI is also funded by the Division for Planning, Development and Community & Continuing Education at Hostos Community College. In the process of receiving 501 (c) (3) status as a not-for-profit organization, LAWI presently welcomes contributions from corporations, foundations, and individuals through the nonprofit Hostos Community College Advisory Council, Inc.

The mission of the Latin American Writers Institute is to promote the work of Latino writers living in the United States. LAWI seeks to recognize and encourage cultural diversity in its membership and in all of its programs.